Praise for The Coalition Rebellion Series

"[*Lord of the Storm* has] so many sparks that it's a wonder the book doesn't set itself on fire while you're reading it."

—*LikesBooks.com*

First two books in the series recognized as

Romantic Times **200 BEST OF ALL TIME!**

Lord of the Storm's **Accolades and Honors:**

Romance Writers of America's RITA Award

Romantic Times Reviewer's Choice Award

Romantic Times Career Achievement Award

National Reader's Choice Award

RRA Book Award

BTC Bookstore Network Award

Skypirate **Accolades and Honors:**

Romantic Times Reviewer's Choice Award

Romantic Times 5-Star review!

Praise and Awards for Justine Dare Davis

Romance Writers of America's RITA

4-time winner, 7-time finalist

Romantic Times Reviewer's Choice Awards

5-time winner, 19-time nominee

Romantic Times Career Achievement Awards

3-time winner, 6-time nominee

Authored 4 books selected for

"*Romantic Times* 200 BEST OF ALL TIME."

Other Justine Davis Books from Bell Bridge Books

The Coalition Rebellion Novels

Book 1: *Lord of the Storm*

Book 2: *Skypirate*

Book 3: *Rebel Prince*

The Kingbird

(A Coalition Rebellion Short Story)

Also by Justine Davis

Wild Hawk

Heart of the Hawk

Fire Hawk

Raider

The Coalition Rebellion: Book 4

by

Justine Davis

Bell Bridge Books

Bell Bridge Books
PO BOX 300921
Memphis, TN 38130
Print ISBN: 978-1-61194-761-8

Bell Bridge Books is an Imprint of BelleBooks, Inc.

We at BelleBooks enjoy hearing from readers.
Visit our websites
BelleBooks.com
BellBridgeBooks.com
ImaJinnBooks.com

10 9 8 7 6 5 4 3 2 1

Cover design: Debra Dixon
Interior design: Hank Smith
Photo/Art credits:
Man (manipulated) © Artofphoto | Dreamstime.com
Landscape (manipulated) © Mega11 | Dreamstime.com

:Lrte:01:

Dedication

This one is for the readers who said the trilogy was not enough. The readers who didn't want to leave this battle behind. It seems we haven't. We'll take the Coalition down yet!

And for the unknown soul who wrote a beautiful soundtrack for a simple, space-based game, and inspired this new adventure. I hope to find you one day and thank you personally.

Chapter 1

THE MAN CALLED the Raider stared down from the mountain lookout at the convoy passing below. The Coalition flags fluttered in the mist. Their symbol was painted on the side of the transport vehicle—the entire galaxy encircled by a grid the Coalition called the connection, but he saw only as a snare. An air rover full of troopers to the front, another to the rear. Armed guards on top, likely more inside.

He knew the big vehicle was empty of cargo now, on the way to the landing zone. But he would have known anyway, by the way the troops acted, loose and a bit sloppy.

But once they had the cargo aboard, that would all change. The Coalition had not overtaken his world by being sloppy when it counted. They'd done it by being fast, efficient, and brutal. In their first attack, they had wiped out half of Zelos with the huge fusion cannon that now loomed over the city. They had followed up by slaughtering a quarter of the entire population of Ziem in the first month. And even on a planet that had had only a million people, that was a hideous number of deaths. Everyone still living in Zelos, or probably on the whole planet, had lost someone.

And the Raider planned to make the Coalition pay for every last grave.

"This is insane, you know."

He didn't look at his second in command, but kept his eyes on the oncoming column.

"Utterly," he agreed.

"We're outnumbered," Brander Kalon pointed out.

"Three to one."

"Those troopers up top have long guns."

"Yes."

"We don't even know what they're picking up."

"There," the Raider said, "I will disagree."

Brander blinked. "You know what the cargo is?"

The Raider slipped a hand into his pocket, felt the folded parchment of the message he'd received this morning. "I do."

He could almost feel Brander's urge to ask how. But the man knew better by now. "Is it worth stealing?" he asked instead.

"Not to us."

Brander frowned. "If it won't even do us any good—"

"But it will do them great harm to lose it."

There was a moment of silence as the convoy trundled on. Then, briskly, Brander said, "I'll need some logistics."

The Raider nodded. "Crates. Three of them. Metal. An arm's-breadth square. And heavier than the cargo itself."

Brander frowned. "Heavier?"

"Shielding. I strongly suggest we don't drop any of them."

He heard Brander's quick intake of breath. "Fuel cells," he breathed.

One corner of the Raider's mouth, the corner beneath the tangle of gnarled scars that twisted the left side of his face, quirked.

"You were never slow, my friend."

"That will make them very irritable, losing the fuel for their power generators."

"They might," the Raider said mildly, "even have to ration usage."

"Then I say to them, 'Welcome to what you've made of our world.'" Brander's tone was bitter, and the Raider knew he was thinking of the hardships the people of Ziem had endured since the arrival of the booted, armored brutes of the Coalition.

He turned on his heel and strode down from the lookout, toward the band of fighters who were gathered at the base. They were known as the Sentinels, taking their name from the mountain that towered over the city of Zelos. The peak topped out above the mist that shrouded their world for three-quarters of the year. The name was a bit grand for the ragtag band, but the Raider measured stature not by looks but by courage, skill, and determination. The Sentinels had all of that, plus the stony toughness of their mountain stronghold.

He wanted no others at his back.

The wind caught the edge of his longcoat, swirled it. The mist was thin today, and he could feel the warmth as the occasional beam of light gleamed on his helmet, that bit of armor carefully crafted to conceal most of his face except the scars. He knew the image he projected, for he did it intentionally. It was against his nature, but he knew the value of symbols, the power of an icon for people to rally to.

"The mist is thin today," he warned them, "so you will have to watch carefully for the signal."

There were nods all around. Each detachment had at least one diviner with them, who was able to see even the slightest trace of glowmist. All Ziemites could see glowmist, the green froth that swirled when mist met heat—slight for a warm-blooded creature, brighter for fire or flare—but it was invisible to those not born here, those without the eyes that had adapted to this world.

The diviners' glowmist vision was the most finely honed. And learning that Ziemites could see the glowmist but outworlders could not had been the key to their unexpected success—and survival—in the year since the rise of the Raider as a symbol to rally around. The Coalition and their minions had yet to understand why they were never able to sneak up on any Ziemite in close quarters.

Of course, this meant that they tended to blast indiscriminately from a distance, with their long guns and that damnable fusion cannon, but the Raider knew enough of them now to realize they likely would have done that anyway. The Coalition did not believe in finesse, only brute force.

"Are we ready?" he asked.

The cheer was loud. He wondered for an instant if it might be audible below, if perhaps some alert Coalition trooper at the tail end of the convoy had heard the sound and wondered what in hades anyone on Ziem had to cheer about.

You will see soon enough. We may have been foolish and naïve when you arrived, but Ziemites learn quickly.

He raised his left hand, which held the traditional curved Ziem saber, a symbol of their history and their world. In his right was the more practical and efficient blaster, a Coalition weapon they'd liberated on one of those annoyance raids.

The cheer went up again.

"Places," he ordered.

They scattered, each to their assigned spot on the mountainside, following paths they'd known since childhood, and ready to strike their first real blow. Beyond ready, the Raider knew, and he could feel the eagerness hammering in his own chest as he returned to the lookout.

Until now, they had been limited to those minor strikes, harrying, harassing, occasionally winning a prize of weapons, even more precious ammunition or supplies, but not much more. But in that time they had learned, trained, and a peaceful people used to a quiet life on their misty world had become warriors. And now they would put what they had learned to the test. Deep in his gut, the Raider knew that if they failed this first test, it might well be the end of any rebellion on Ziem.

Whether that would be for good or ill, he didn't think about. Nor did he think about what he himself would leave behind if he died in this idealistic effort. For all that mattered was that someone had to do something, and he could not live with himself if he did not try. And so he would, and if he died trying, so be it. Better to die free than live cowering in the muck waiting for the Coalition to decide you were of no further use to them.

It seemed forever yet too soon that the convoy, all snap and formation now, again came into view on the pass road. The Raider watched intently as they neared the choke point, that spot where the mountain jutted out and squeezed the road down to a single-lane passage. The first air rover came through, the troopers alert and watchful now, peering in all directions.

Then the transport.

"Now," he ordered Brander.

His second raised his arm and fired the near silent flare down the mountain. It caught, swirled, and lit up the fog into that glowing green mist Ziemites knew well. The Sentinels, ready and waiting for that signal, charged.

The real war for Ziem had begun.

Chapter 2

Two years later . . .

"WHY DO YOU keep it there?"

Drake Davorin paused in his wiping of the taproom tables and glanced over at the dark-haired woman standing before the bar, not with a drink, but simply staring at the painting on the wall behind it.

Because it is your work, and for that reason alone I love it.

He said, "Once the lights come on, it draws the attention of patrons, who buy more brew while they stare at it."

Kye Kalon snorted. He wondered if it was at what he'd said, or at her work being used in such a way. He used to be able to read her more easily, but everything had become more difficult lately. Of his own doing; you couldn't push someone away as he had Kye and not pay a price. But he'd had no choice, not since the death of her father had sent her off to join the Raider. The more time she spent with him here, the bigger the chance she might put the pieces together. So, no matter how it pained him, no matter the baffled pain in her eyes, he couldn't risk it.

But Eos, he missed her. He ached with missing her.

He shifted his gaze to the painting. She'd done it a year before Iolana Davorin had taken that death-plunge off the sheer face of Halfhead, when her beauty had been intact but her ravaged soul and the remnants of visions had burned in her eyes. Kye had captured it all, her skill even at fifteen amazing. It had been her first attempt at a portrait of such size, yet her hand had been steady and her eye true. A prodigy, his mother had once called her.

She had also warned him never to fall in love with her, for loving a person with a passion, as she had loved his father, was hades beyond hades.

The words had come too late. And now he knew the real truth of them. Because loving Kye had ended up bringing him even more pain.

"She was a beautiful woman," Drake said, ignoring the ache in his leg as he walked over to stand as closely behind her as he dared. He couldn't seem to stop himself, even knowing what he was risking. He was better at this pretense now—he'd had more practice at keeping the two facets of his life separate—but Kye was very, very smart. It was why he had to keep her away as much as he could.

That, and that it clawed at him to play the broken, tamed taproom keeper in front of her.

She looked at him. He allowed himself a moment of drinking in those rare, turquoise eyes, so different from his own more usual Ziem blue ones. "You speak of her as if she had no connection to you," she said.

"In the end, she did not." He shrugged, tearing his gaze away from those eyes, for fear of what she might see in his. "Her connection was to Ziem and her people. It was a physical thing to her; she felt what they felt, hurt when they hurt. And her heart and soul ever and always belonged to my father. It was why she could not go on without him."

"So she abandoned you and your sister, and the twins. Yet you keep it here."

And just that easily, she painted the picture of his tangled feelings. He had loved his mother, but hated what she'd done. But he had also loved, respected, and believed in his father and the cause he had died for, so much so that he understood his mother not wanting to go on after losing the likes of him, one of the greatest men ever born on Ziem. How could she have gone back to a normal life?

Not that her life had ever been normal. He doubted a woman such as his mother, with her oft-proven ability to sense coming events in a way that went beyond prescient into something mystical, had ever had a comfortable life with his pragmatic father. And yet, his father had always believed in her uncanny skill, and acted upon it. Had convinced others of her visions, and between them, they had achieved a standing on Ziem unmatched by any other couple. Hardly a normal life.

There's no such thing as a normal life here anymore.

He fought down the bitterness. It was difficult, standing this close to the one woman who made him wonder if all the sacrifice was worth it. He wished his mother had told him what was to come. He might then have saved himself from this particular pain. But her foresight was something she never used for her children, saying she did not wish to influence their futures by foretelling them.

"Perhaps that's why I keep it there," he said aloud. "To remind me of the cost of truly loving someone."

He expected some sharp rejoinder, of the kind she was rarely at a loss for. Nothing came. Instead, a wistful, almost sad expression came over her face.

"Yes," she said softly. "The cost is high. Perhaps too high."

She'd never sounded so sad, so grim before. "Kye—"

A hammering of a fist upon the front door cut off his words. And probably just as well, Drake thought as he hurried over, hiding his limp with an effort. He opened the small slider in the door at eye level. He managed not to wince; Jepson Kerrold.

"We are not yet open," he said, pointing out that the hour was clearly posted about a foot from the man's prominent nose.

"You shall open for me, Davorage."

His voice was imperious as he used the old, insulting combination of

Davorin and average that he thought so clever. Since he, obviously, was much above average. It mattered not that they had once been in school together, that Drake, in fact, had bested him regularly in schoolwork, and always in athletic pursuits. For Jepson Kerrold was of the East Town Kerrolds, as he had never ceased to remind them all, and as such, he was cut from a finer quality cloth. Just ask him.

And now he worked for the biggest traitor on Ziem, with the pretentious title of Liaison to the State. And was even more convinced he had a right to anything he wanted.

Drake heard a sound behind him, glanced back to see his sister Eirlys entering through the back door, carrying a box. He threw up a warning hand and she stopped in her tracks. Thankfully before she would be visible to Kerrold's prying eyes through the slot. Now getting rid of the pest wasn't just a preference, it was essential.

Sometimes he preferred the open evil of Jakel, the administrator's chief enforcer—and torturer—to Kerrold's unctuous mask. Except that Jakel also wanted Eirlys, and the brutal man would be much less polished about it, if only because he had loathed Drake since childhood.

The pounding came again. "Open the door."

"If you insist," Drake said blandly, knowing his adversary well, "but I warn you, we had a party of over-drunk Coalition troops in here until the early hours, and we have yet to finish cleaning up the vomit."

Kerrold, ever fastidious, recoiled. He even stepped back from the door, as if he feared the vile waste would somehow seep out and envelop him.

If only.

"Perhaps if you returned this afternoon," he suggested, putting as much unctuousness as he could into his voice, although it made him want to vomit in truth. "A bottle of our best lingberry would be waiting."

"Your floor had best be unsoiled when I return," Kerrold warned. "And I shall expect that bottle. Without charge," he added, "for my inconvenience."

"Of course," Drake said, thinking even the expensive liquor a small price to pay for the sight of the man's retreating back.

He pushed the slider closed over the door slot. He saw Kye looking at him assessingly. For once not condemningly. Oh, she tried to hide her disappointment in him, but he knew her too well. And it ate at him, in a way few things did anymore.

"Clever," she said, with a flicking glance at Eirlys. She well knew that Kerrold had an eye for his sister, never mind her age.

The approval stabbed deep, telling him how much he had missed it from this fierce, bright flame of a woman. He had to look away before she read the unwanted emotion in his eyes. He could never, ever let her see the longing he felt. Not when she might realize she'd seen that same look in another set of eyes.

Eirlys walked toward him.

"I can deal with him, you know," she said.

"I know, sister mine, but I would prefer not to have to break you out of the cell he would throw you in if you insulted him too harshly."

"He's loathsome."

"Yes."

"And repulsive."

"That as well."

"And weak."

"I will have her, Davorage."

"You will not."

"And how are you going to stop me, taproom keeper?"

The exchange echoed in his head, and he had to force himself to calm. He needed to choose his words very carefully, for ordering his impulsive sister had little effect. He had sacrificed most of what control over her he had to secure the one, most crucial promise, that she not join the Raider.

And in but a few months she will be eighteen and beyond even that control.

He tried not to think about that. Or what he would do when the inevitable happened.

To his surprise—nay, shock—Kye spoke. "He is all of those things, Eirlys. Loathsome, repulsive, and weak. But he wants you. And he has the power of the Coalition behind him."

Drake stared at Kye. He would never have expected to hear such understanding from her. Not since her father had been killed by that same Coalition.

"I will die before I let him put his filthy hands on me," Eirlys declared.

"That," Drake said quietly as he turned back to her, "is exactly what I'm afraid of."

"You underestimate me."

"Never. But what do you think would happen to you when you killed him?"

She appeared gratified that he said when, not if. "Better than the alternative."

"Spoken like one who has never seen the inside of a Coalition jail—"

"They'd never find me. I know the mountains like no one else except the Raider."

He knew this was true; Eirlys had roamed the mountains since childhood, even after the Coalition had conquered Ziem. He studied his sister for a long, silent moment. The ten years between them had never seemed more; he felt old and tired and worn, while she still bubbled with the energy and determination of youth.

He hated this, but he was going to have to mute her obstinacy with some blunt realism.

"You would have to escape, first." At her frown, he clenched his jaw and went on. "Do you really think Kerrold would not call in Coalition troops to hold you? Perhaps even to strip you and hold you down while he raped you?"

She paled; clearly she had not thought of this. On the edge of his vision he saw Kye stir, but she said nothing nor made a move to stop him.

"I warn you he would not hesitate. He has done it before. He likes them young."

"I—"

He went on relentlessly, because he had to. "And even if you succeed in killing him, will you savor your life when they collar you, and you are required to not only service any Coalition member who wants a moment's amusement or pleasure, but to have your brain so twisted by their controls as to believe you *want* it?"

She was even paler now, shocked by his blunt words. He rarely spoke to her so coldly; he loved the bright spirit of her too much. But she must see this was not something to take lightly.

"He has set his sights on you, not just because you are young and beautiful, but because you are Torstan Davorin's daughter. He and the Coalition fear that more than anything, that the people will rally to a Davorin if they are in the least encouraged."

Her head came up then. "Yes. I am a daughter of Davorin."

She said it proudly, fiercely, and his heart sank. She was more on fire than he'd realized, more aware of the power she held on Ziem by virtue of her name alone, and it would take very little to prod her into acting on that power. To offer herself up as that rallying point for the people.

He let the fear that thought engendered into his voice. "They would slaughter everyone, Eirlys. Everyone."

She simply stared at him, silently. He did not like the look in her eyes, because he recognized it, having seen it often in the eyes of others. Perhaps not contempt, but on the verge.

"I only wish," she said, her voice cold, "that my brother was a true son of Davorin."

She turned on her heel and strode out, not even looking back. After a long moment in which he waited for Kye to agree, waited for the flash of pity that from her was so much harder to bear than even his sister's hot anger, Kye turned and followed Eirlys out the back door.

Drake closed his eyes, denied the churning in his gut, fought down the part of him that so wanted to scream the truth at Kye.

He spent the next hour making the already clean floor as unsoiled as Kerrold had demanded.

Chapter 3

"SOMETIMES I hate him."

Kye looked at the girl who sat beside her on the rock overlooking the pond. She wasn't really sure why she had followed her, except perhaps that she hadn't wished to look anymore at Drake. The hollow, agonized expression in his eyes had told her how his sister's strike had stabbed home. And yet since she herself had made the same wish, she had nothing she dared say to him.

"You don't really mean that," she said.

"All right, then I hate who he's become." She had no answer for that. Eirlys gave her a knowing sideways look before adding, "And you do, too, don't you?"

"I admire what he's sacrificed for his family," she said carefully.

"Don't dodge."

She turned to face the girl then. "It is not a dodge. Do you realize that when your mother died and he had the responsibility for three children below the age of ten descend upon him, he was barely a year older than you are now?"

Eirlys blinked. Kye guessed that while she'd known how young he'd been, she hadn't really put it in those terms before, terms of her own age.

"Yes," Kye said. "How would you like to be accountable for a nine-year-old girl and a pair the likes of Nyx and Lux at four, right now?"

"I wouldn't."

"Neither did he. But he did it, because he loves you. He's your brother, and he takes that very seriously."

"I know. He's so protective of me I want to screech to the sky."

"He is very aware you are becoming a beautiful woman."

"That's what he said." Eirlys couldn't have been more glum about it if Kye had said she was starting to look like a blowpig. She smothered a smile at the girl's reaction, but she was grateful she had apparently successfully turned the subject.

"He's afraid Kerrold will attack me," Eirlys said.

Kye took in a quick breath. So much for grateful. She had long suspected that Kerrold wished a daughter of Davorin to be his conquest for very particular reasons, but she did not wish to go into that just now. "Not an unfounded fear," she said. "He has always had an eye for you." *And better him than that torturous muckrat, Jakel. Maybe.*

Again Eirlys gave her a sideways look. "As you always had for Drake."

Not so successful on the subject turn after all. "We are friends."

"But you once wanted more. Don't deny it; I used to spy on you when you were together."

"And you think we did not know this?"

That took her aback, Kye thought. But she knew Eirlys well enough to know when she was fixated on a subject, and true to expectations, she recovered quickly.

"Can you truly say that you do not wish—"

She interrupted before Eirlys could say something Kye had no answer for. "I wish many things. Or did, before I grew up and realized the futility of wishing."

"'Wishing is nothing without action,'" the girl quoted.

Her father's words, Kye thought. Famous words. Words from the speech that had rallied a town, then a region, then an entire planet.

And had brought the fiery wrath of the Coalition down upon them.

"Can you truly say," Eirlys repeated, clearly determined to say the words, "that you do not wish he was more like my father?"

"Your father," Kye said, "spoke out against Coalition tyranny. He was dead within months."

"And we could all be dead tomorrow, if the Coalition decided it. The fusion cannon would see to that. But my father is remembered as a hero still. His name could unite, if only Drake would use it. If only he would stand against them, instead of serving them like a—"

"He does not have that luxury."

She had to stop this. She could not bear anymore. It was truth that she admired and respected Drake for how he had stepped into a parent's role when he had to, but she, too, wished he had stepped into his father's huge footsteps as well. No matter that the two paths were mutually exclusive, for following the one would surely get him killed and thus make the other impossible, not to mention putting those he was supposed to protect at even greater risk. She knew that too well; had she not had to do the same with her helpless father, before that random Coalition bomb had finally put an end to his misery?

But she knew Eirlys was right, the son of Torstan Davorin could rally the people of Ziem like no other, even the Raider. Just the spark of his name would light a fire that even the Coalition would pay a high price to extinguish.

Eirlys stared at her. The bright intelligence and perceptiveness she knew the girl possessed shone in her eyes.

"Are you not saddened by what he has become?"

Kye had no answer for her question. The real answers were too grimly depressing to be faced. For she had once loved Drake Davorin with all the fervor of her young heart. They had been of one mind, similar in all things.

But she was a woman now, and other things were more important to her than a handsome face and a wicked grin. When that Coalition bomb had finally ended her father's torment, proving once and for all that toeing the Coalition line did no good, kept no one safe, her life had been shattered along with the blinders she'd been wearing. She knew then the only recourse was to fight, for expecting the Coalition to leave you alone if you behaved was a fool's notion.

She had expected Drake to see it that way too. That the time had finally come to fight, that the only thing to do was join the Raider. Instead, he had withdrawn, pushing her away as if he feared her newfound commitment to the freedom of Ziem might be catching. He made excuses not to be with her, and no longer smiled as he once had the moment he spotted her anywhere. And so she saw little of him, only when the ache became too much, and then later she regretted it because seeing what he was now, that man too frightened of the Coalition to even speak ill of it, bore no resemblance to the man she'd loved. And so she had accepted the wall now between them.

"Do you still love him? As he is now?" Eirlys's voice was barely above a whisper now.

She could not answer. Despite it all, including the obvious fact that he no longer cared for her in the same way, she still did. How could she not, when she saw so clearly what it was costing him to protect his family, and yet he kept on? If her father were still alive, would she not still be there herself? It tore her inside, twisted her up. It made no sense, but nothing in this world had truly made sense since the day twelve years ago when the first Coalition battleship had slipped into orbit and begun the conquering of Ziem.

And suddenly an image rose in her mind, fierce and undeniable. Drake, young Drake, younger even than Eirlys now. Eleven years ago, sixteen to her own fourteen, he had been the personification of everything her girlish heart longed for. Eleven years ago, when his father had been practically obliterated in front of his eyes, only his head left and placed on that pike as reminder, he had joined the battle with a passion that both thrilled and frightened her. He had picked up the gauntlet dropped by Torstan Davorin, and had charged into the fight like someone possessed. And even at sixteen he had won the admiration of those many times older, surprising them all with his courage and sometimes unusual tactics.

And then his mother had thrown herself from Halfhead and it had all ended for him. Drake Davorin was finally beaten, cowed, and turned to a life so ordinary and inconspicuous that eventually even the Coalition had almost forgotten whose son he was. He was just the servile taproom keeper seen most often in an apron. She'd heard Barcon belittle him often enough to realize they considered him properly broken, and no longer a threat.

And for over a decade now, she'd seen or heard nothing to show they were not right.

Drake Davorin could not more thoroughly appear a coward if he tried.

It ate at her, and, after parting from Eirlys, she felt compelled to do something, anything. And when she later saw a Coalition guard chivvying along two citizens who had dared to exchange more than a passing greeting on the street, leaving his sheltered guardstand momentarily unmanned, she could not resist.

"YOU COULD HAVE been killed."

Kye lifted her chin. "I was not."

"I weary of saying those same five words to you."

Kye gaped at her commander. "You? You of all people, wish to confront me about risking my life?"

If the Raider was taken aback by her boldness, it did not show. But something else did. She knew he had been injured in the last raid, and she could see the pain in his slightly off-balance stance, favoring the leg that had been carved by a laser pistol. It made her ache inside with the worry she always felt for him.

"We are not," he said evenly, "discussing me."

"We should be," she retorted. "For you risk your life all the time."

He held her gaze steadily. "Yes. For a reason, not for the risk itself. I don't want to die, I want to live to fight."

She forgot to breathe for a moment. She hadn't expected him to see that deeply.

"I want to fight," she protested.

"I know this. You could not fight as fiercely as you do, were it not in your blood." There was admiration in his voice, and it made her shiver. As did the way his Ziem blue eyes lingered on her face. The way his gaze made her feel was strange, yet familiar, and the paradox only added to her turmoil.

"Then what are we talking about?"

"I believe it is called a death wish."

She spun away, unable to meet those steady eyes. Eyes that sparked something in her that she'd only felt once before, for Drake. And no amount of telling herself she was a fool and worse, that she should be ashamed that this man stirred her so easily when she knew little about him outside his courage, and his brilliance as a warrior and planner, seemed to quash it.

She stared at the far wall of his quarters, as if there were something more than his ceremonial Ziem saber there.

"I do not wish for death," she finally managed to say.

Not yet, anyway, she silently added. In the end, when the battle was either won or lost, when there would be no fighting left to do, then . . . what would she do with herself? What would she have? Who would she be?

"Feeling you have nothing to live for amounts to the same thing."

She turned back then, as much because of the suddenly gentle tone of his voice as the words.

"I just . . . wonder what will be left. In the end."

"And you have not the courage to face it?"

She drew back, stung. Never had he questioned her courage, only her recklessness.

"I understand, Kye," he said. His voice had softened, into a tone she'd not heard from him before. It made her pulse kick up even as it soothed her roiled emotions. "I once felt the same, that I did not care, that I wished myself dead rather than go on, or face the end of the world I had known."

"You would never give up," she declared.

"Now," he said. "But there was a time when I wished for the decision to be taken out of my hands."

"Do you understand we who live in constant fear of that happening? That you will die?"

"If it happens, it happens. The fight will go on."

"You underestimate your importance."

"You overestimate it."

"I do not. If you die, the fight ends. It will take the heart, the stomach for battle out of everyone."

"They will regain it. A new leader will step up."

She glared at him then. "Only someone willfully blind, or just stupid would believe that. Since I know you are not stupid, it must be willful blindness."

"And you," he said, "have managed to once more steer this from you to me."

For an instant, she thought she saw a hint of amusement in his eyes. He so rarely let anything like that show it nearly took her breath away. A memory, some distant image, sparked in her mind, but it was gone before she could pin it down. She tried to marshal her thoughts.

"Is not the final judge of risk whether or not it succeeds?"

"You're quoting Torstan Davorin again."

"And why not? Is he not the father of this fight?"

His eyes closed for a brief moment. "Yes," he said quietly. "Yes, he is. He is also dead."

"And I am not," she said, thinking she'd won it now. "No one saw me, and we now have a copy of the guard rotations for the next month."

"That is not the point."

"If you did not want me to take the initiative, you should not have made me your third."

"You know I value the ability to think for yourself. Do you really think this is because you didn't clear it with me first?"

"No," she admitted. "You're not that way. But I don't see why you're so wound up about it."

When he looked at her then, it was the steely commander who would brook no further argument. His sentences were short, sharp, and rang with authority. "It is a matter of risk versus gain. In this case, the risk far outweighed the gain. You could have been killed. Or badly wounded, with no help. Or captured. Tortured for the information you hold. Would you wish others to die trying to save you?"

"No," she said, chastened. He rarely spoke to her like this, and it stabbed deeply. "It is of no use, then?"

"I did not say that. Just not worth the risk you took."

She drew herself up straight. She would not cower before him. But she would give him the respect he deserved, having earned it a hundred times over. She bowed her head and spoke quietly. "Yes, sir."

For a moment he was silent, as if he hadn't expected that. But then he said, "And it would be an aggravation to have to find a new third with your skills."

Her gaze shot back to his face. That bedamned helmet hid so much. Too much. And she could read nothing in his eyes at this moment.

But as she left the quarters, the words that echoed in her mind were not his last ones.

I don't want to die; I want to live to fight.

She had not thought of it in exactly that way. But she would, from now on. If she had done so this night—and hadn't been so on edge about Drake—she would not have taken the risk.

And while she had often thought about why he was so able to inspire his Sentinels, she had never dwelt upon the fundamentals of it, the constant weighing of risk against gain, and the cost to him of sending people into situations where they could easily die.

She knew that deep down, he would far rather die himself than send another to their death. But perhaps everyone sensed that, and it was why the Raider was the commander they would all follow into hades, and he would not have to ask.

And yet he did it, because he must.

She had never been more aware of the crushing weight of command than she was in that moment. And her already considerable respect for him grew even stronger.

Almost strong enough to quash the longing she felt. She wanted only to help him carry this load, and instead, she had added to it.

She had learned much in the six months she had been a Sentinel.

But she had much more to learn. And learn it she would. Quickly. For he needed that, and it was the only thing she could give him.

The only thing he would allow her to give him.

Chapter 4

"DO YOU THINK it's true?"

Drake shrugged, not looking at his sister. He was more tired than he'd ever been, his leg was still aching, and he was having trouble hiding it. Despite his relief that she'd apparently gotten over her anger at him, he'd almost dozed off during her recounting of the old legend.

"That was decidedly non-informative."

The very formal words were said in a matching tone he knew was meant to shake him out of whatever mood he was in. Usually she was successful; she was too smart for her own good, and dangerously clever as well. But this time he did not respond.

"Let me ask a different way," Eirlys said. "Is it possible?"

"Which part?" he asked, wearily accepting that they were going to have this discussion, that the time was coming when she could be put off no longer.

"Any of it," she demanded.

He stalled, stoking the fire, adding another log to keep it burning through the night. It was a constant battle now that the Coalition had confiscated most of the dryers for their own use. And rationed the power so strictly they couldn't run them if they had them. The thick mist had turned to rain, and if he didn't keep the fire going, the dampness would permeate everything. And make the pain in his leg even worse. He wished the damn thing would heal faster.

At last he turned to face her. She was watching him steadily, her dark-blue eyes assessing. Her sunny golden hair might have come down from their grandmother, but those eyes looked at him with the same steady regard as their mother's once had. Iolana Davorin had had a gaze that intimidated many a mortal man, and not simply because they feared what she might see with that mystical foresight. It had taken a man of the strength of their father to equal her.

And in the end, when Torstan Davorin died, he had in effect taken her with him, for there had been no heart left in her.

"Well?"

"Do you still believe in the tales of blazers who live above the Edge?" he asked, knowing the answer—his little sister had started scoffing at the classic children's tales of flying, scaled creatures that breathed fire at a much younger age than he himself had.

But then, the world had gone to hades much earlier in her life than his.

"Of course not, but—"

"And now, do you watch for the Spirit of the mountain to come and help us?"

She didn't answer that, which was an answer in itself. So she did hope the tales that had begun to circulate some years ago, of the mysterious healer who also lived above the Edge, were true. He almost rolled his eyes.

He gentled his tone. "You know Trios is a myth, too, do you not? As are the tales of her fighting king? And his son after him?""

"Myths have to start somewhere, don't they? With something?"

He amended his earlier thought. She was too smart for his own good. He tried what usually never failed, hoping to divert her. "Maybe you just like the idea that that prince turned king fell in love with that fighter pilot and made her his queen?"

She snorted then, her typical response to such romantic drivel.

"Still don't believe in love, eh?"

He waited for her response to that, which was usually something along the lines of "Love is for fools and the mentally damaged." She'd never seen real love between two people, not really. She'd been too young to see and understand the undying love that had existed between their parents. Then their father had been assassinated by the Coalition, and their mother had become distant, too wounded by his death to pay them much mind. Until she had broken completely.

But instead of snapping back at him, Eirlys looked at him steadily, and shocked him when she said quietly, "I love you."

He shifted, uneasy about this uncharacteristic display of emotion from his cool, usually brusque sister. "What brings this on? Feeling guilty for losing your temper with me?"

"I'm worried about you," she said in that same tone. "You look so tired all the time, as if you've not slept for an age."

I haven't, he admitted inwardly. And barely resisted hunching over to rub at his leg, where the throb had spread now from knee to hip.

"I'm fine. Don't worry. You won't be responsible for those little horrors just yet."

Eirlys grimaced; their younger siblings were indeed that. If the twins were awake, they were into mischief, or worse. Lux was the one who thought up most of their mayhem, while her brother Nyx was the one who engineered carrying it out. Between them, they were enough to drive anyone mad, and Drake had often thought it would take a force of a dozen to keep them in line, if it could be done at all.

But Eirlys didn't take the bait. At least, not the bait he'd hoped she would.

"'Yet,' you said. You mean I will be."

Damn.

Definitely too smart for his own good. He would do well to remember that.

"I am ten years older than you, so yes, someday, likely," he said, in the most casual tone he could manage.

"If we don't all end up in a Coalition dungeon first."

It prodded him, that grimness from someone so young, who should be thinking of nothing more complex than the animals she loved, who loved her in turn and followed her everywhere.

"I won't let that happen," he said.

She scoffed. "That's what father said. And you saw what happened to him."

Oh, yes, he'd seen. Too well. He had been there that day, when his father had been provoked out of control by yet another Coalition outrage, a regulation essentially outlawing the selling of planium to anyone but them, and at prices barely above the cost of mining the stuff.

The result had been his most passionate speech about the very spine of Ziem's culture and history, as well as its main source of revenue. The only source, in many cases. A speech given not from the dais as the leading member of the council, but from atop the ramparts of the wall the invading Coalition had built around their compound, drawing hundreds before he was through, inspiring them all to a fiery pitch of rebellion.

In the riot that had ensued, his father had been the first to fall, taken out by a blast from the coil gun that arrived to back up the outnumbered and for once losing Coalition troops. It had been like using the fusion cannon to kill a flutterbug, and there had been nothing left to bury after the Coalition had triumphantly grabbed his head and stuck it on a pike in the town square. And all pretense of them being a legitimate purchaser of the precious material was gone forever.

The images of that day that would be forever burned into his memory. The only good thing about it was that he had been the only one of them there to see it. Eirlys had been too young, and the twins barely walking when it had happened. He was the one left with the ugly memory, with the tangled emotions of loving, hating, damning, and admiring his father, all at the same time.

Of course, then their mother had abandoned them too, and by choice.

"You're old enough now to watch over them, Drake. So I must do . . . what I must do. I must go."

He'd never realized when she said that nine years ago, she'd meant forever. That she'd meant she could no longer go on without his father. That she'd meant what love she had for them was not enough to hold her to this life.

Not enough to keep her from throwing herself to her death down the sheer face of Halfhead Scarp.

Leaving him to finish the raising of three children, any one of which would be a handful for an adult, let alone the boy he'd been. The twins a double, inseparable handful.

"But," Eirlys prompted now, scattering the memories, "wouldn't those defeats in that sector explain why the Coalition has so tightened control here? Why would they do that, unless they're afraid?"

"Because it is who they are?" he suggested sourly. "Besides, the why of it doesn't really matter anymore."

"'We slept our comfortable sleep too long, and this is the price.'"

It seemed strange, to hear their father's words quoted in her voice. She had been but six then, but the illicit recordings from that last fiery speech had been widespread in the years immediately after his assassination. Drake suspected she had memorized every word. Probably of every speech, every writing, every impassioned plea their father had made to the people of Ziem, begging them to wake up and see what was happening. She had adored him and at the same time hated him for leaving them.

"Yes," he said, and even he wasn't certain whether he was assenting to the cost or agreeing that they'd not fought hard enough, soon enough.

"And no one in Zelos will fight them." Her tone had turned to a bitter, angry thing, all the more harsh for her youth and the sweet femininity of her face.

"They know they cannot win. Should they fight just for the sake of fighting?"

"And so they roll over like a barkhound in the mud, presenting their throats for the slashing."

That, he thought, hadn't come from their father. His words had been high-minded, elegant, and intellectual. Eirlys's came from deep in her gut, fired with anger and spiced with loathing for her fellow Ziemites. He could not blame her, from her view.

"I'll never give up!"

The anger was still there, but now laced with determination and the sort of dedication he knew her too well to underestimate. Eirlys might be only seventeen, but she had the spirit of a warrior. He would have to keep an even closer eye on her, although with what extra time and energy he knew not.

"There have to be more," she exclaimed. "Others who won't surrender, because it is just not in them. Others who won't give up, who don't welcome the conquering, as some have, as Barcon did."

"He didn't just welcome it," Drake said sourly at the mention of Barcon Ordam, the civilian administrator of all Ziem. "He engineered it."

"And for that he should die."

Her fierceness was impressive, and anyone of any age or gender would be wise to take her seriously, Drake thought. She would make an amazing secret weapon, with that sweet, innocent face that so many never looked past to see the fire in her eyes. And she would dearly love to become that weapon. Yes, more vigilance was going to be necessary.

He smothered a weary sigh. *I am not up to this,* he silently told his departed mother, although he had long ago given up any thoughts of an afterworld where her spirit might dwell. Such ideas were long gone, buried in the rubble left by Coalition destruction.

He chose cold logic.

"The Coalition has coil guns, rail guns, star fighters, and for Eos's sake, the fusion cannon that could wipe out what's left of Zelos in a single shot."

"And look at what the Raider has done anyway, in three short years, with only brilliance and trickery."

And there it was, at last. Her favorite subject.

"The Raider," he said grimly and with utter honesty, "is a fool."

That did it. She leapt to her feet.

"How can you *be* like this? It's bad enough that Brander has become nothing more than a self-indulgent gambler, but how can my own brother be such a . . . a . . ."

"Coward?" he suggested, knowing that was what she was trying not to say.

"But you're not! At least, you weren't. I remember you, when I was barely more than a babe, driving mother to distraction with the risks you took. Jumping off the roof of the meeting house, going through the Racelock Rapids in that homemade boat of yours, nearly blowing up father's office to show him you understood what he'd said about the properties of planium."

He smiled despite himself, remembering that day.

"You put me in a conundrum, my son. How can I be so angry and yet so proud?"

"When they first came, you fought." His sister's voice had gone soft. "And after father was killed, you stepped up to lead, young as you were. The people of Zelos rallied around you, and all of Ziem would have followed you."

"That," he said flatly, "was before our mother left me to be head of the family, with the responsibility to keep you all safe."

She stared at him, and he could almost see her trying to find the balance between the screaming of her emotions and the cold fact of what he'd said.

Welcome to my reality.

"If that's what having children means, giving up everything you believe in, then I shall never do it."

She turned on her heel and fled, up the narrow ladder to the sleeping loft. A moment later, he heard the slam of her door as she closed herself into the small room he'd walled off for her when she'd begun to complain about the utter lack of privacy in their small abode. The twins were still relegated to the open space of the loft; there was no way was he putting anything between those two and his watchful eyes and ears.

In the silence that seemed to echo, at last he was able to turn to his leg. He found the tube of salve. He rubbed it into the aching muscles that were violently protesting keeping up the pretense that nothing was wrong. Eventually it brought the pain down to a level where he thought he could ignore it. If he kept off it the rest of the night, perhaps tomorrow might be better.

And maybe fewer people would be angry at him.

And Trios might really exist, and Darian, the fighting king, might actually have thrown the Coalition off his world, with his son repeating the triumph on his mother's world for good measure.

His mouth tightened as he leaned back in the padded chair that had been his father's, and eased his leg up to rest on the stool before him. The old joke ran through his mind with bitter irony.

What's worse than dying in a Coalition invasion?

Surviving it.

Chapter 5

KYE LOOKED AT the man trudging up the mountain trail beside her. The Sentinel was steep, but the lower paths were fairly wide and smooth. Which was a good thing, down here in the perpetual mist, where a misstep could be fatal. Especially for those who had not run the mountain since childhood as they had.

She heard a low rustle of some creature moving through the ferns. Then from above, the soft call of a graybird that made her think of Eirlys. Funny how the mist carried some sounds so clearly, but muffled others.

She drew in a breath of air filled with the familiar damp and the undertones of her world; the slow decay of the dying leaves and plants, and the fresh, clean scent of the greenery that never faded. Even the mist itself had a scent, to native Ziemites anyway, and she would recognize the cool, refreshing tang anywhere.

"Is he better?" she asked.

"He is as he is," said her cousin, who could be taken as her brother, so alike were they in looks, with dark hair and eyes of that turquoise shade that was rare and admired among the blue eyes of Ziem. And he used them, and his strong build and easy grin and manner, to charm and beguile the unwary. And sometimes even the wary.

"That's helpful," she muttered.

"Even the Raider takes longer than a week to heal from a wound like that."

"He has healed from worse."

"His scars, you mean?"

She nodded. The disfigurement of the gallant fighter's face was part of the legend that had grown up around him. Such grievous wounds would have killed a lesser man. On her first sight of him, she'd been appalled at the wreckage, then admiring that he had survived such a thing.

"If he survived that to fight again . . ."

Brander gave her a sideways glance. "He's not a god, you know. Even though you seem to think so."

She snorted inelegantly as she tossed back the dark, heavy braid she'd fastened off to keep her hair out of her way. "He is a man who fights, which seems rare enough on Ziem to be ranked as such."

"I fight. What god does that make me?" he asked with a grin.

She eyed him with exaggerated speculation. "I don't know. Perhaps you should ask Eirlys."

To her amusement, he flushed, but he shook his head. "That girl hates me almost as much as she hates her brother now."

She grimaced. "And she loves him as much as she hates him, and that makes for a difficult life." *How well I know that, the pain of loving him for doing what he must, and hating that he cannot fight, cannot be what Ziem needs him to be. I can only imagine what his turmoil must be.* "Though not as difficult as his."

"The twins," Brander said dryly, "make for a difficult life under any circumstances."

She allowed him the change of subject. "Those two hellions alone are more trouble than a cluster of buzzers."

"Truly," he agreed. "Although buzzers are more productive, providing honey. The twins merely provide chaos."

She laughed despite her mood. Brander could do that for her, as few could. "They have the right spirit, though. I must grant them that. They would fight, and fiercely, if they could. Even at their age."

"Unlike their brother?"

"I cannot deny he does not." She kicked away a stone that lay in her path. "I hate that he welcomes them, serves them in the taproom, mingles with them, as if they were not the scourge of our world!"

"And so because he accepted the task before him, to be mother and father to his clan, a task some would say is both the most difficult and most important, he has lost your regard?"

Kye winced. "I did not say I don't understand his choice. It is one I had to make myself, to take care of my father. But I cannot see why he doesn't realize it makes no difference. The Coalition will slaughter us no matter what we do. I would rather go down fighting, while he . . . he . . ."

"It would not hurt so much," Brander said softly, "had you not loved him so much."

She stopped in her tracks. A step or two later he also stopped. He turned to look back at her.

"For someone so unmindful," she said with a glare, "sometimes you see too much, my cousin."

"You are better at hiding, now. But then you were not. It was there for anyone to see. Even your blind, thick-headed cousin."

"You are that, you—"

Perhaps for the best, her retort was interrupted by the sound of a squawker calling out from a tree some distance away.

"I'll leave the signal to you," Brander said. "You're much better at it than I."

She turned in the direction of the sound, just as it was repeated. She lifted her head and made the soft, hooting call of the wisebird in answer. She gave the combination of long and short calls that would tell the challenger—

who was no more a black-feathered bird than she was—who was approaching.

The answering call, more of a croak, came back quickly. Three short in rapid succession, the permission to pass. That the guard didn't simply call out to them as himself once they'd given the code was just one of the safeguards the Raider insisted on. And since the Coalition had not yet found them or their stronghold, no one argued with the abundance of caution.

Twice more they went through the challenge and answer, until at last they were at the ruin. They made their way over the crumbling rock, the endless landslide—and warning system—created by the Coalition's own bombs, until they reached the huge boulder that appeared to have been thrown clear of the rest of the rubble.

"This one's yours," Kye whispered, and Brander grinned.

"Fair enough," he said, and put his shoulder to the big rock. By rights, given its size, even Brander shouldn't have been able to budge it. Yet, after a moment of strain, it began to inch sideways, courtesy of the hollowed-out center. He kept his considerable strength at it until enough of the concealed entrance beneath it was revealed for them to slip—or in his case, scrape—through. The approaching guard would push it back in place, sealing them inside. Normally a breath-stealing thing, but the place that had once been the basement of the mining headquarters building that now lay in rubble above them was spacious, the ceiling high, and all of it well ventilated, taking any cramped, trapped feeling out of it. It gave them plenty of room, in a place the Coalition had long ago abandoned as useless, too far from the mines themselves to be worth rebuilding after their own bombing had destroyed it.

Besides, it was hard to crack the whip of slavery from this distance, Kye thought sourly. When the mines had been free, there had been no need to encourage the miners. But the Coalition needed to be closer, to oversee those forced to do their bidding, and so had set up their own headquarters at the very entrance to the main shaft.

"How is he?" Kye asked Mahko, who acted as their healer.

"Resting. I've given the order not to disturb him."

Mahko did that rarely, but when he did, he equaled even Brander, who was second in command, in authority. The rest of the Sentinels never argued the point. In only three years, the Raider had accomplished so much that people began to divide time around him—things that had happened before the Raider or since the Raider. He was already a bigger legend than the Spirit, that fabled healer who supposedly lived above the Edge and who Kye doubted truly existed. To her mind, the tales that had begun to circulate nearly a decade ago were merely wishes, the desperate pleadings of a conquered people.

Only the Raider had ever risen to actually fight. She had yearned to join him immediately, but needed to care for her father, paralyzed by the same Coalition attack that had killed her mother. When he had died six months ago, she was at last free to become a Sentinel. She had used her pent-up rage well, and quickly risen in the ranks to third in command, gaining the trust of those more seasoned than she.

Of course, those ranks weren't exactly vast.

She remembered now how disheartened she'd been by the smallness of their number; she had hoped for more. But when even the son of Ziem's most fiery orator for freedom refused to fight—

She made herself stop thinking of that. Drake had made the choice he'd thought he had to make, and she understood, for she had been where he was. And she had once wholeheartedly agreed with him; living by the Coalition rules had seemed the only way to survive.

But then she had learned in the hardest way that the Coalition didn't play by any rules at all. And yet Drake still wouldn't stand against them.

He wouldn't stand with her. And that had hurt more than anything.

The Raider hadn't been dismayed by the size of their band. He had merely stated that you must fight with the force that you have, and planned accordingly.

As he was probably doing now, despite his injury, Kye thought.

"He will be all right?" she persisted.

"He is the Raider," Mahko answered simply. "If anyone could be after such an injury, it would be him."

Those who were not on guard were gathered around the small fire. It was enough to keep the belowground room warm, thanks to the thermo-reflective qualities of the surrounding stone, yet small enough that there was no smoke to give them away. No radiant heaters out here, nor any other device that would require them to draw on power the Coalition might trace back to them.

She could smell something cooking, rockfowl, she guessed. She saw Pryl sharpening his ever-present blade, the Harkin brothers—two of the few who went by their last names here, since they had no family left under Coalition domination to bear the price of their rebellion—sharing a loaf, and Tuari pressing out a dent in her light armor. She was going to have to repaint that spot, Kye thought. The silver of the planium was showing through, too attention-getting amid the dull black of the rest that could blend into the night and the mist.

Brander, as usual, was already bent over the table to one side, studying the arrayed parts of the Coalition hand weapon they'd captured. They knew little about laser pistols, other than the damage they wreaked. Such as slicing through the Raider's flesh with a beam of humming light.

"Still consumed with that thing?" she asked as she neared the table.

"If I could figure it out, perhaps we could duplicate it."

Although she knew Brander was clever enough to do just that, figure out the complex weapon, it would end there. She didn't bother to point out that they had neither the materials nor the apparatus likely required to produce such a thing. He already knew they didn't. Knew too well; although no one outside the Sentinels was aware of it, he'd been fighting beside the Raider since the first day. In fact, she had once suspected he was the only one who knew the true man behind the mythical name. Brander dodged any talk of it. And said that it was at the Raider's command that no one knew who he really was or where he had come from.

"It is for all of our sakes, Kye. Don't you see? If we do not know who he is, we cannot be forced to tell them. If no one knows, and it's widely known that no one knows, then there is no gain for the Coalition to try and torture it out of us, should we be captured. Or go after the families of those who still have them."

Kye had never thought of it in that way, but once he'd said it, the simple truth of it put paid to all future questioning.

She watched now as Brander picked up what appeared to be the trigger mechanism of the weapon to study it yet again. Kye turned away wearily. The irony of it was biting deep tonight; here they sat, hiding less than a squawker's flight from the thickest layer of planium in all of Ziem, and that prized element was useless to them because, thanks to the Coalition, they now lacked the tools to shape it. She knew the Raider had chosen this place for just that reason. Not because he expected to be able to utilize the precious metal, but because the Coalition also knew it was there—it was, after all, the reason they were here—and would never risk destroying it.

It had its downside, in particular Coalition guards constantly watching over the Ziem miners. But they seemed focused on their task, and like most of the Coalition, decidedly averse to wandering through the Ziem mist they found so odious, and impossible to see through.

That planium made the most powerful weapons the Coalition had was just an added bite to it all.

We're providing them with the means to destroy us.

Torstan Davorin's stark warning had gone unheeded in those early days when the Coalition had seemed no more than the biggest, best customer Ziem would ever have.

First they will disarm us, then enslave us, then slaughter us. This is their history, their method, and their plan.

She'd read that speech so often she sometimes thought she'd been there to hear it herself, although she knew she hadn't. Her parents hadn't believed him, and hadn't even listened themselves.

Less than a year later, Drake's father and her mother were dead, and her own father broken beyond repair.

And everything Torstan Davorin warned about had come to pass. The slaughter wasn't finished yet, but only because they still had need of workers here. When the vein of planium finally ran out, they would probably not just wipe out Ziemites, but Ziem itself.

And nothing this miniscule little band of fighters could do would stop them.

Chapter 6

HER DIVE WAS graceful, as she had ever been, and if one looked only at that, it would be a thing of beauty. Her gown whipping around her slender body, her waist-length hair flowing behind her like a red cape, she looked like an exotic bird who would soar upward at any moment.

It was only when you added the height of the stark face of Halfhead Scarp, and the icy rapids of the Racelock below, that you realized this was no graceful flight but a death plunge. And trapped, held back by others who were watching in horror, a boy watched his mother die before him just as he had watched his father. Watched her body swept away, never to be found. Leaving him behind, to face the ruin of their world ever alone.

Drake awoke in a sweat, sitting up so abruptly his leg shot out a sharp, protesting pain all the way to his hip. He would remember this night, he told himself as he tried to calm his rapid breathing. No more of the palliatives, no soothers for him, no matter how tired he was, no matter how much he might be hurting. He would rather have pain than the nighthaunts such potions brought on.

The finely calibrated sense of time he'd inherited from his father told him it was still a couple of hours before firstlight, and he knew the leg needed the rest. He lay back down, but now his brain was up and running, which meant any chance of true rest was gone. He shifted, trying to ease the strain on muscles still damaged enough to ache at any serious exertion. Like trying to walk without limping, as he had all day yesterday. If this kept up, he was going to have to stage a very public accident to account for it.

He forced himself to focus on the day's work to come. He had gotten as far as planning a reorganization of the casks in the storeroom when he heard the whispering from above. He could almost see their impish faces, eyes so like their mother's, as was their hair. He had never told the twins he could hear them from down here. He preferred them to think he just somehow knew whenever they were plotting something, as their mother once had. It gave him a small edge, and he needed every bit he could get with those two.

He waited, knowing that as they got more excited about whatever they were planning, their voices would rise just enough. And if he was lucky, he'd be able to pick out a word or sentence that would give it away, and if it were something risky or too troublesome, he would head it off before it got started.

This time, it seemed nothing worse than sneaking into Enish Eck's barn to determine if he truly had a green two-headed snake in there, so he decided to let it go. Enish Eck was a gruff old man, but he wasn't a danger, and if he caught them, he would likely only scare them with threats and bluster. Which wouldn't necessarily be a bad thing. They needed the juice scared out of them now and then. In fact, he might just see if he could make sure Eck did discover the little miscreants.

He tried not to think of how the Coalition had destroyed most of their communications apparatus, and what was left intact had been seized; his leg would have appreciated the days when he would have only had to go to the linkup and connect to warn the man to keep an eye on his mutant snake, if it indeed existed.

And if it does, I hope it isn't venomous.

He turned onto his side, gauging his condition. The last remnants of the palliative were still in his system; he could feel them trying to lure him back to sleep. He considered fighting it, remembering the nighthaunt he'd had, but realized he needed the rest if he hoped to be able to function, and let it take him.

This time, the dreams were filled with images of two-headed snakes and a barely penitent set of twins, morphing into the mischievous duo lying swollen and dead from the snake who, with two heads, had been able to strike them both simultaneously. Dying together, as they would wish.

It wasn't much of an improvement.

When he awoke for good, the twins were, in fact, gone. And his leg, thankfully, seemed much better. He contemplated going after them, decided it wasn't worth betraying that he could hear them for something so paltry. Better to save it for the days when they decided to do something much worse. Like blow up the Coalition command post, which he had little doubt they would try eventually.

You'd be proud of them, Father. And of Eirlys.

What his father would think of him, he had no idea. The thought of a Davorin tending a taproom would no doubt make him cringe. But it was the job that put food on the table for them, and even his parents had had to make adjustments after the invasion.

With a smothered sigh, he rose and dressed, then headed for the taproom to prepare for the day's business.

"HE'LL BE ALL RIGHT," Eirlys assured the child, "but you must keep that injured paw still for at least two days. Can you do that?"

The little boy nodded fiercely, holding his tiny pet hedgebeast close to his chest. Luckily the small, prickly creature ate mostly leaves and stems of plants too tough for more tender palates. Pets were a luxury in this conquered world; most people barely had food for themselves, let alone enough to feed animal mouths.

At least the Davorins usually ate well, she thought as she put her small aid kit back to rights. Thanks to the tips Drake gathered at the taproom, and the hunts he made in any spare hours.

Both thoughts made her frown. The tips came mostly from Coalition troops, which turned her stomach. And the meat Drake brought home from his odd-hour expeditions up the mountain only reminded her that he, the best hunter in all of Zelos, who knew the planet like no other and could be one of the Raider's best fighters, was instead a lowly taproom keeper.

She knew it wasn't fair. If it wasn't for Drake and his outsized sense of duty, she and the twins would have ended up homeless and starving, as so many others were. Instead, they had a solid roof, a warm fire against the damp, and enough food to eat. More than many.

But those who were in such a dire state were often those who refused to buckle, to give in to the Coalition yoke. Those who would never dream of serving them as Drake did.

Most of those resisters had vanished now, either taken and likely killed by the Coalition patrols, or off to fight with the Raider. Where she wished she could be. Where she guessed even Kye was, now that her father was dead.

Where she would be the day she reached adult status, whether Drake liked it or not, Eirlys vowed to herself. She had promised him she would wait until then, but in one more year, she was done with this. She would rather risk an early death fighting this plague that had enveloped their cool, misty planet than live for decades under Coalition boots.

"Eirlys?"

She turned at the soft query. "Rula," she acknowledged with a smile, but it faded when she saw the woman's expression.

"What is it?"

"I'm sorry, but it's her again."

Eirlys steeled her expression. She hadn't yet told the woman that her precious milker was on her last legs. She knew that in the shattered economy of Zelos, the animal was their main source of income. Her milk they both drank and traded was a large part of their sustenance. But she had no cure for the disease that was invading the animal's body. She had managed to slow it, but she could not stop it. Someone with more knowledge might have been able to, but the only remaining animal healer in the entire city had been killed by one of the random bombardments the Coalition engaged in periodically, apparently for no other reason than to keep them beaten. Eirlys did her best, but eventually the rampaging cells would kill the beast.

But not today, she vowed as she trudged after Rula.

We progressed too far. We left behind the creatures and our knowledge of them, abandoned traditions, and the principles of men like her father. We had the wealth of the mines and the possessions it purchased, we were free to indulge in any whim, honorable or not. We decided we needed no defense but our remoteness, and disbanded what army we had and instead built hologram parlors, and an elaborate council building for grand speeches.

We thought it would go on forever.

And then the Coalition had come. They were lulled, deluded, lured . . . and then bombed into meek submission. Beaten, cowed, and rounded up like a herd of milkers. Those who went to their knees and vowed allegiance to their new masters were spared, as long as they did not ever put a foot out of line. Those who resisted were slaughtered outright.

And resistance to the Coalition, they quickly learned, consisted of anything a Coalition official didn't like. Rula's mate had merely tried to intervene with a Coalition soldier who, unfamiliar with milkers, decided that the best tactic to deal with the stubborn beast was to beat it. Both he and the milker had ended up a smoking pile of rubble and flesh, blasted by the soldier's hand weapon.

She shook her head, trying to clear it of that vivid, ugly memory. She'd been only seven at the time, but she'd been bare yards away, and it was etched into her mind as if with a laser pistol. And the smell . . . by hades, she would never forget the smell, cooked meat, milker and human combined.

After a few minutes, she and Rula were clear of the town square. Were clear of the people walking in the head-down, solitary manner that had become usual. For no gatherings were allowed—a gathering being any two or more pausing for even a greeting—for fear rebellion was being plotted. Even she was prey to it, keeping a couple of paces behind the sturdy figure before her, making it clear they were not plotting together, merely headed in the same direction.

To Eirlys the Coalition crackdown only solidified the possibility that something had made them very nervous. Which in turn made her hope the latest tales were true, that in that distant place across the galaxy, the son of a fighting king and the daughter of a notorious skypirate had proven themselves worthy of their lineage, and once more the Coalition had been beaten.

Which would mean it was still possible. They were not invincible.

She tried not to think about the fact that, according to the stories, the fighting king had seen to it that the Triotians and the Arellians had been much better armed and prepared than Ziem had ever been. Tried not to—

"Is it true?"

Rula's whisper brought her out of her reverie, and she realized the woman had slowed until they were close enough for her to hear. She quashed her immediate lurch of fear, hating herself for even feeling it.

"What?" she asked with a quick glance around; all seemed clear, no Coalition troops in view, no vehicles hovered. In sight, anyway.

"The Raider. Was he really killed?"

Eirlys jerked back at the words. "No!"

It broke from her involuntarily, so horrible was the very idea.

"Thank Eos," Rula breathed softly.

Eirlys didn't explain, wasn't sure she could, that her response hadn't been one of knowledge, but one of fear. She had no way of knowing, in fact had not even heard this latest rumor.

"What did you hear?"

"That he and his band blew up the guard overlook, but that he was killed in the process."

"And where did you hear this?"

"From Kerrold."

She let out a silent sigh of relief. Jepson Kerrold was living proof of the old warning, mind your source. "And why would you trust the word of Kerrold?"

The older woman shrugged. "He was boasting about it." She gave Eirlys a sideways look. "In your own taproom."

"It's not mine," she answered automatically. "That is my brother's domain."

"Such a shock," Rula said sympathetically, "to see him serving them, as if they hadn't murdered your father and been responsible for your mother taking her own life."

"My brother's decisions are his own," she snapped, stung by the reminder.

"Forgive me," Rula said quickly, her tone apologetic. "I know it irks you more than anyone."

"Irks," Eirlys muttered, "is not the word for it."

"In truth, he has little choice. He must look out for you, and the twins." The motherly woman put a hand on her arm. "When you have children, you will understand."

"That," she said flatly, "will never happen."

The more she thought about what she'd said to Drake, the more certain she was. This was no world, no universe to bring offspring into. Not while the Coalition ruled. They had already taken anyone young enough to be brainwashed, and newborns were confiscated as if they were some kind of illegal property. Any child born today would be shaped and formed and told what to think by the Coalition, and they would never know anything different.

And, in the meantime, they look for reasons to kill those of us who remember a life before. Someday, there will be none of us left, and the Coalition way will be the only way anyone knows to live.

She had wondered aloud one day long ago why they hadn't just killed everyone. To her surprise, it had been a grim-faced Drake who had explained that the Coalition knew nothing of mining planium, of handling it in its raw, unstable state, and so kept those who did alive, and the others to, in turn, keep the miners alive. Better to enslave the locals to do your bidding than have to commit too many of your own number to do it.

"We're not a sought-after posting," he'd said. "They don't like the cold and the damp, they can barely function in the mist and their mining equipment not at all, and we're too far off the main track. No chance to get noticed, or promoted. Even Ossuary is closer to Coalition Command than we are."

She'd been surprised at his concise summation. Although nowhere near as surprised as when, shortly after mother's suicide, Drake seemed to have forgotten everything their father had ever said or thought, everything he had ever taught them, and turned to accepting their new masters with a servility that had stunned everyone in a son of Torstan Davorin.

He'd taken over the taproom with every evidence of eagerness when old Daff had passed. And, just as quickly, he'd made it clear the Coalition was welcome there. They were wary at first, since no one else in Zelos appreciated their presence, and especially since he was the son of the man who had been their fiercest opposition. But Drake had publicly explained he thought his father wrong-headed, and that he was trying to make up for his foolishness by showing his loyalty. Words that had made Eirlys ill, her stomach churning like the maelstrom of the Racelock, until she'd had to run out for air before she deposited her firstmeal all over the floor.

It was true they lived better than many, but Eirlys for one thought the price far too high. She still loved her brother, and always would. He'd been a rock for them all in a time of unbelievable grief. And he'd been loving, kind, and generous when it was there to give.

Yes, she loved him.

But she didn't like him very much anymore.

Chapter 7

THE MIST SPILLED down the ravines and gullies in a silent, damp flood. Yet the tall man with the odd gait moved up the mountain path with certainty; he was born of Ziem and had the mist vision. Besides, Grimbald Thrace knew exactly where he was going, and every inch of the path that would take him there. Had he not traveled it countless times since they'd taken refuge here?

He crossed the border, that tree line they called the Edge, beyond which legend had it nothing but myth could live. Barren, empty, it was a landscape nearly as cold as the air around it. Here there was no fresh aroma of green trees, only the faint scent of damp on unforgiving stone. But he was inured to it, and barely shivered as he continued on. Not many dared to go past that point, even those who claimed they were not superstitious, who insisted they did not believe in the folk stories of demonish winged creatures with scales who spit fire, and other murderous beasts harbored by the mountain that rose above all others.

Not even to meet the woman they called the Spirit would they venture beyond the Edge; only the most desperate even tried. Not even the Coalition had dared the heights of the Sentinel.

Grim took care with his balance; his leg had healed well but slightly bent, and the difference in it had put a roll into his stride, so he had had to adapt. He still had the leg however, and it pained him little. And for that he would be eternally grateful to the woman who had healed him, and for the magic of the mountain that had so enhanced all her abilities, both healing and visionary.

He would serve her to the end of his days, and be thankful for the chance.

He reached the entrance to the cave. Or rather, the spot where he knew the entrance to be; what he saw was a wall of rock as barren and solid as the rest of the edifice of this mountain.

Still unable, even after all this time, to simply walk into that wall, he closed his eyes and took three quick steps forward. When he opened them again, he was in the cave. The chill had vanished, replaced by the unexpected warmth the mountain itself provided from vents deep inside.

She had warned him, in the beginning, that the vents that heated this place were signs that the mountain still lived, and that one day it would prove that to all by exploding in a massive blast that could wipe out half of Zelos. But that, she had added with a smile, would not happen until millennia after they had both turned to dust, and so he had decided not to care.

He rounded the outcropping of rock that jutted out into the cave, masking the deepest interior, and serving also to contain the heat from the vents, keeping it warm enough that he could shed his heavy coat.

"Sit, Grim, it is ready."

He could smell the enticing aroma of food. "You knew I was returning?"

"Of course." She said it easily, and with a smile. "Eat, and then you can tell me what you've learned."

He eased himself down to the seat she had indicated. The Spirit was indeed a healer of miraculous power and wide repute, but she was a woman of many other skills as well, including the weaving and needlework that had produced the cushions filled with feathers left over from the fowl of many meals.

She was also a woman of great beauty. He knew she did not think so, that she thought the scars and the years had changed that, but he did not. She was still young, by Ziem standards, and she was still the same graceful, lithe creature he'd served since his youth. It did not matter that she was changed, or that in some minds she was but a legend. He knew the woman behind those mist-inspired tales.

He did not know the truth of what power she had, the source of her visions, or how she healed even those who seemed beyond help. Indeed, he did not know if the latter was anything more than simply the power to inspire others to rise above what they thought were their own limits, but he did know it worked.

Had it not worked on him?

"You are supposed to be eating, Grim."

Her voice, sounding almost amused, roused him out of the memories.

"I am sorry, my lady."

She gave a sigh of mock exasperation. "I am never going to break you of calling me that, am I?"

"No," he said honestly.

She laughed, and it was a beautiful, musical sound. "Where were you, just now?"

"Remembering how you tended me, when I was hurt."

"A favor you have returned, in much greater measure."

He shrugged, not liking to remember that day when he had found her, broken nearly beyond repair. Or the long days after, when he'd fought to bring her back from the brink of death.

"What I knew of healing I learned from you, so in truth, you healed yourself."

She laughed again. "Such an intricate pattern of logic you have, Grim. But you must admit you taught me all I know of fighting. And fine, strengthening therapy it was."

He merely nodded, and took a bite of the tasty rockfowl she had prepared. She waited kindly until he had sated most of his hunger before asking,

"What news have you from Zelos?"

"It is much the same. Ordam is himself, as is Kerrold. The governor is still a glutton and cares little for details. Jakel still roves the streets in search of anyone to torment, and he still loathes the Davorins." He paused for a moment before going on. "The Davorins themselves remain the same, except those twins are becoming notorious. Not always in a bad way, mind you; they recently set fire to Ordam's cloak. As he was giving a fine speech in the square."

She laughed, and it was a delighted sound he heard too seldom from her.

"He spoke yet again of the Coalition, and how it is for our own good. That they will take care of us; all we must do is swear allegiance and be useful."

An expression of utter loathing crossed her face. "And surrender our freedom. Become a prisoner to Coalition will."

"Someone called out from the crowd then. 'What will you do when they realize you are useless, Ordam?'"

The laugh returned, and she looked much cheered. "It is good to hear they have not all given in."

"I believe," he said, "it was Eirlys Davorin."

She went very still. "She risks much."

He nodded. "She is very brave. And, I am afraid, very angry."

It was a moment before she nodded at him to continue.

"There are rumors there will be a new Coalition post commander soon, but there are always rumors." He took a sip of the ale she also managed to brew, just for him since she never partook, before adding, "And they are all, as ever, in an uproar over the Raider."

Her face changed then, going from interested to intent. "So he continues?"

"To drive them mad? Yes."

She smiled then, nodding. "But he is well?"

He hesitated before saying, "It is reported he was injured some days ago." She went very still. He thought perhaps she was not even breathing as she awaited his next words. "The Coalition tried to say he had been killed, but I have reliable people saying it is not true."

Her voice was taut as she asked, "They have seen him?"

"No one can admit to that, of course," he said. "It would cost them dearly. But yes, I believe so."

Her delicate brow furrowed deeply. "How badly was he hurt?"

"That I do not know."

"Have there been any raids since?"

"No."

"So it could be that he was injured badly enough to take him out of the battle."

"Or not. He has never worked on any kind of regular schedule," Grimbald pointed out. "Perhaps he is just waiting for the next good opportunity."

"Perhaps," she said, looking troubled. "And I have a message to be delivered that might be just that."

But her expression didn't clear. And he knew what was coming.

"I must know, Grim. Not just for myself, but the very future of Ziem depends on him."

He sighed. He'd expected this. "Yes, my lady. If you will allow me a night's rest, I will return to my search for news, and check for any messages left you by supplicants or those grateful to you."

He studied her for a long moment, wondering if he dared.

"Speak what you will, Grim."

"Will you ever return yourself, my lady?"

"You know why I have stayed away, Grim. I had much to learn, much power to absorb from our mountain. And painful as it was, for Ziem and the ones I love, certain events had to happen without me. I've shared that vision with you."

"I know. But you have held yourself apart for so long, even from—"

He stopped when she waved a hand. "No." But then, for the first time, she added two more, very telling words. "Not yet."

Someday, then, he thought. He would have to be content with that.

Chapter 8

"THERE HE IS, our favorite tapper!"

The booming voice rang out in the manner of a man who thought volume and joviality was the way to get people to notice him. The volume was real, and heads turned up and down the street where Drake had been unloading a delivery. But the joviality was patently false, and Drake was certain everyone who had turned to look at Jakel knew it. The big man's expression didn't hint at his brutal nature, but the truth was in his strange eyes, small, oddly colored, almost pink, and nearly hidden beneath his heavy brow. And they lit with a depraved gleam whenever he was able to torment someone who didn't dare defy him.

You didn't get to be Barcon Ordam's enforcer and chief torturer with jolliness.

And as for Ordam, the less said or thought about the man who had betrayed his world, who had handed Ziem to the Coalition in exchange for ruling it, the better. At least Jakel had ever been honest; he had openly hated Drake since childhood, although the Davorin name had been protection as much as target. But now the man took great pleasure in tormenting him, when Drake had no choice but to take it.

And the man paid far too much attention to Eirlys.

Drake settled the final keg into place, taking the moment to school his expression to an equally false joviality, then turned to face Jakel. It was a measure of his own success, he supposed, that the man hadn't cut him in half with that laser pistol of his for taking that extra moment.

"Thank you, Agent Jakel," he said, putting all he could manage of cowed gratitude into his voice. "That cask was your favorite brew, so I didn't want to lose it."

"Good!" Jakel's booming laugh echoed off the wall of the taproom. "Then you won't mind opening up early for a thirsty man, will you now."

It wasn't a question, and Drake knew there was no option to say no, despite the fact that he wasn't due to open for an hour yet. He said nothing about the propensity of indulging in intoxicants before the sun had even lightened the mist. Jakel was hardly the only one who so indulged; this time of year, the mountains and mist held the daylight back until nearly midday, and it was dreary enough to drive many not born to Ziem to the relief of strong drink.

Their scientists—before the Coalition had destroyed the labs and exe-

cuted them—had nearly isolated the factor in their makeup that allowed the
natives to better tolerate the steady gloom, possibly linking it to the factor that
almost universally gave them eyes in varying shades of blue. And eyes that
could see through the mist, and could see the glowmist.

And it was something they were born with. Jakel, whose eyes were an
odd, reddish shade, besides being narrow and constantly darting about, did
not have it. It was suspected he was at least part Carelian; he had the eyes and
claws for it. His parents had arrived from parts unknown, and seemed un-
willing to talk about it. They had died decades ago—at his hands, most suspected—and with them any pretense of him being controlled.

But Drake would no more comment on that than on the early need for
drink. Saying such things to this man would likely land him in the torture
room, on the stretcher getting every joint ripped apart, if not killed outright
here and now.

Or worse, he'd end up collared, his mind enslaved just as his body would
be, subject to the whim of whoever held the controller. The pure evil of that
Coalition device never failed to appall him. He suppressed the shiver that
went through him at the idea and all it entailed. To him, this more than anything spoke of the unbelievability of the tales of King Darian; surely no one
could survive such a thing with their mind intact.

"If you don't mind a bit of damp, you are, of course, welcome inside," he
said carefully. "No power yet, so I've not been able to turn on what dryers we
have."

The spectrally thin man, who looked as if he'd been pulled to his abnor-
mal height on his own stretcher, frowned. "Why have you no power?"

"It is not turned on for us until second moonset." Drake shrugged as if it
had always been thus. As if Zelos hadn't once been the town that never slept,
roiling with light and energy throughout the misty, dark nights of Ziem. Until
the Coalition had changed all that, trying to control the population with their
own climate. And, for the most part, Drake thought sourly, succeeding.

"Well," Jakel boomed out again as he clapped him on the back, "we'll
have to see about that."

The blow masked as a friendly gesture was hard enough that he was put
off balance. His injured leg strained to hold. He had to hold. Rumors the
Raider had been injured were echoing on the mist. If there was anyone on
Ziem he had to fool, it was this man. His life would likely depend on it.

He used the stagger to turn on the heel of his undamaged leg and con-
vert the motion into an apparently eager dive to open the side door to the
taproom. As he did, he grinned up at the man like a mindless fool. Drake was
a tall man himself, and not used to needing to peer upward. A good reminder,
he told himself, of how others might feel around him.

Jakel bought it. After all, did not people all over town, all over the planet
in fact, know of his power and hasten to do his bidding?

"Your usual, sir? Or would you prefer something else? I have a small supply of a very fine Clarion effervescent that might better your day."

"And what," Jakel asked coolly, "is wrong with my day?"

Damnation. He'd put a foot wrong there. "Having to sit in my damp tap-room, of course. My apologies again, sir."

As if a power unit that had made an odd sound had settled back into a steady hum, Jakel chortled. "Yes, yes, bring me that brew."

The joviality had returned, and this time, there was a touch of genuineness to it.

Because he genuinely enjoys watching you bow and cower.

Drake tried not to visibly clench his jaw, at least, not until he had escaped to the back room where he poured off a glass of the expensive, bubbly drink. He took an extra three seconds to steady himself. He hadn't been mentally prepared to deal with Jakel this morning. He'd never known why the man seemed to hate him for simply existing, and always had. It seemed more than just because his name was Davorin, more personal, but he'd never done anything to earn it. Not that Jakel needed reasons for his brutality.

The other Coalition servants that came in at various times were bad enough, but this man grated him like no one else. Except Ordam himself; any time the traitor of Ziem lowered himself to appear here, Drake feared he would throw it all away and slice him down where he stood.

That would be ever so wise, Davorin. Sacrifice everything for the momentary pleasure of gutting the man who had sold his own world into this slavery.

The mere thought of that pleasure made him almost wish it would happen.

Almost.

He sucked in a breath, forcing himself to calm, making himself remember the truth of what he had to do. Which was go back out there and act like a man who knew where his bread came from, and who was appropriately anxious about the man who could take it from him. Eirlys could likely survive on her own, as long as she stayed away from Jakel; his little sister wasn't so little anymore, and she had that frightening intelligence to draw upon. But he had the twins to think about. He shuddered at the very idea of what would happen to those two troublemakers were he not around, not to keep them in line, for that was impossible, but to at least get them out of the worst of their scrapes.

And so he picked up the glass and hurried back to present it with an obsequious flourish before all the bubbles died away.

That night Drake lay exhausted, yet again unable to sleep, when it began and the whispers drifted down from above.

"We should do it."

"Of course we should. But we must think of the best way."

"And how to keep Drake from finding out."

"Sometimes I almost believe he has the foresight. Or can read thoughts. How else could he have found out about the cycler?"

Drake nearly smiled at that. How often had he thought the same thing of his mother, that she not only had the foresight, she could read his thoughts? She almost always had known when he was hatching mischief.

"Are you still on that?" The volume was increasing in direct ratio to the enthusiasm of the two. "Must you figure out *everything?* Besides, it was a good thing he did. Old Heksin probably would have killed us for taking it if Drake hadn't talked him out of it."

"Aw, we only wanted to ride it a little. And Heksin's all bluff."

"His scyther didn't look like a bluff."

"Maybe."

Whatever they were up to, or going to be up to, it was clearly still just in the planning stage, so Drake let out a sigh and rolled over as the twins fell silent. But it was a weary sigh. It had been a difficult week. On the other hand, a plan of his own had occurred just this evening, as he'd served the three Coalition officers who'd stopped in for a last round before heading back to Legion Command, where they would have to be more circumspect in their partaking than here on remote Ziem.

"I heard Paledan drew the black rock this time," one of them had said with a laugh.

"I'm not sure about that," the man across from him had said. "Why would they send a hero the likes of him *here?*"

"I heard he was wounded, and is still recuperating. But he'll hate being post commander here," another had rejoined. "Not a chaser parlor to be had in this back of beyond hades hole."

"But he's bringing a relief troop, so the men'll be happy. They've been guarding the base of that damned mountain for an age now."

They ignored Drake, as they always did. He'd been a fixture long enough now to become no more human to them than the table they sat at. Word had quickly spread that they were not treated with disdain here, and eventually visits from several officers had unofficially put the Coalition seal of approval on the place, and by extension him. Worth the slavering, even if it did turn his stomach.

"Do you really think they got him? The Raider?"

"I hope so. Legion Command was not happy."

"If it's true, you'd think Governor Sorkost would hang his body in the square."

"I heard they cut him to pieces. Maybe there's nothing left to hang."

The laughter that rang out then set his teeth on edge. He fought yet again not to let it show.

Instead, he refilled their glasses with an obsequious smile. For that was his lot, the path he had chosen.

A servant of the Coalition.

years to me."

"He serves and bends to the Coalition, yet you defend him?" one of the men asked.

"I defend my friends," Kye said, eying him levelly. "Him just as I would you, should the need arise."

"There was talk," Mara said, still watching Kye, "that you once were more than friends."

"We were children. It would have come to nothing anyway."

"She's got her sights set elsewhere now," one of the men, Slake, she thought, said with a leer that was more teasing than cruel.

"Better you than I," Mara said with a barely suppressed shiver. "I admire, respect, and follow the Raider, but . . ."

Kye knew she meant the scars, understood that few could look past them. She herself was not repelled by them, only distressed at what he had gone through. She could not remember the exact moment they had become inconsequential to her. She just knew that one day they did not matter anymore, that she dwelt more on the roughness in his voice, indicating his vocal chords had likely been injured in the blast that had scarred his face. She liked the sound, as she liked the way he moved with a grace and power that belied the damage done to his body.

And his courage, intelligence, and audaciousness outweighed all else, to her mind.

"All I have to say is, it's about time we struck again," Slake muttered.

"He has his reasons," Kye retorted. "Foremost being he doesn't want to cause so much trouble that the Coalition feels compelled to call in aid from Legion Command to crush us."

"It is wise," Mara agreed. "They could wipe out Zelos with the cannon, or all the people of Ziem with a single pass from a cruiser, if they were provoked enough."

"But what good does this do?" Slake demanded. "Small raids, tiny victories. It does nothing to drive them out."

As if we have any hope of that.

"If you would prefer to lie down for them, you can always go to work for Drake in his taproom," Mara snapped at the whiner.

Again Kye winced inwardly, but she would not defend him this time. She had made her point, and she agreed with the sentiment too much to fight it again. And then the Raider was there, standing in the doorway to his quarters.

"I have gotten word that the trail guards changed this morning," he said, his half-ruined voice scratchy but clearly audible. A low buzz instantly went up among them. "They will not have had time to learn this ground, and will be at further disadvantage in the dark and mist."

Smiles were starting to break out around the room. Kye joined them; to those who did know the mountain, there were many ways down to the valley below. And the Raider knew this mountain as few did. Her pulse picked up as she waited, knowing a mission was coming.

Brander, arms crossed, long body at an angle with his shoulder propped against the wall, lifted a brow. "And where, my leader, are we going?"

Only Brander spoke to him this way in front of the others. Only Brander would dare.

The Raider paused long enough that the room went utterly silent. The silver helmet shone in the flickering light. And then, with a slow smile that seemed reckless, a smile marred only slightly by the twisting of his scarred flesh, he answered. "I think it's time we liberate some transport. Anyone here know how to fly an air rover?"

The roar that went up echoed off the walls and rough ceiling of the great room. Hoots and yells of excitement punctuated the solid wall of sound. She herself was grinning widely. It never failed to amaze her how perfect the Raider's sense of timing was; every time his fighters got restless, every time the hopelessness of their task began to overwhelm them, he came up with something that put the fire of the fight back into them.

As he put the fire of many things into her.

Chapter 10

"YOU'RE SURE THIS thing's going to work?"

"I'm sure. As long as I'm close enough." Brander gave the Raider a sideways look. "I'm more worried about the diversion. If we get Eirlys's pet ringtail hurt or worse, she'll send us both to hades."

"You have no faith in her training?"

Brander snorted. "She could train a blazer to toast bread. As soon as he hears the signal, that rascal will start such a racket even Sorkost would get off his ass to investigate. I'm more worried about him getting clear."

"The sense of self-preservation is strong in most creatures."

Except you. "I hope it's strong and deep in this one, then. I don't want to have to explain how we let him get trampled by a cluster of Coalition guards."

"More likely he'll bite one or two of them before departing. He is peevish with anyone except Eirlys."

I know the feeling.

A sudden memory of the child who had tagged after him in those halcyon days before the Coalition had arrived on Ziem, always trying to badger him into helping her with one creature or another, flashed through his mind. He let it stay a moment, to remind himself how young she was.

"Let's just hope he gets back to her unscathed," he muttered, although he knew the creature followed Eirlys everywhere on her expansive ramblings—she sought out her animals, and they flocked to her, even the wild ones—and likely he could find his way home from anywhere.

"I'm afraid that," the Raider said, "is up to his reflexes and your accuracy with that device."

Brander grimaced. He was about to make some retort when he realized where they were. As he thought it, the Raider raised his arm and gave the signal for operational silence. Not that they had been making much noise anyway, but as of now, as they passed the marker the Raider had chosen—the rubble of what had once been a prosperous inn at the edge of the flats—there would be no word spoken.

Words were not necessary. As always, they had rehearsed this countless times. Each of the ten Sentinels specifically chosen by the Raider for this foray knew his part. Or hers, he amended, thinking of Mara, who had surprisingly turned out to be the most qualified of them all for this particular undertaking. She had handled an air rover extensively on a trip to Clarion the year before the Coalition had set its sights on Ziem.

They crept silently down the last slope in the utter darkness. Their black clothing and dull-finish armor made them practically invisible. Except for the Raider's silver helm, which seemed to gather and reflect what light there was. It was, Brander knew, intentional; the man wanted it to stand out, be noticed. It was not out of ego, but an understanding of the power of the legend he'd built.

And the fact that it would draw Coalition attention to him, and away from his fighters. Brander didn't like it, thought it too risky, but that was old ground, an old argument.

Each of them knew their path intimately; they could all see the glowmist caused by those moving ahead of them. There was no stumbling or hesitation. Brander doubted they were even thinking of what it would mean if they succeeded this night; they were thinking only of what was to be done next.

When everyone was in position, Brander looked at the man who led them. He saw the movement of the silver helmet as the Raider nodded, the silent motion an order. Brander grabbed the large bag he'd been carrying on his back. If he hadn't been trekking up and down The Sentinel carrying weapons countless times in the last three years, he wouldn't have been able to do it; this ringtail came up to his knee and was heavier than he looked. All that thick fur, maybe.

Brander felt the creature inside the bag stir at the movement. In the dark folds of heavy cloth the ringtail had been calm, quiet; it was their nature to go docile and still when confined in darkness. And this particular beast was familiar with him, and thus allowed his touch with only mild protest. But once let out of the bag he would be angry, and fiercely determined not to go back into it. And an angry ringtail made a sound like no other.

He crept down the slope, taking care not to disturb any rock or branch that might betray his passage. He made his way to the shelter of a large boulder surrounded by thick brush, where he could hide yet see the hulking shape of the transport annex building. He watched just long enough to see that the four guards were keeping to the schedule Pryl had observed and tracked. There were advantages to having such a regimented and closely controlled enemy.

He waited until the two sets of two guards were close to crossing paths at each front corner of the building. Then he unfastened the bag.

The ringtail poked its head out. It looked up at Brander warily. He shook the bag. The creature hissed at him, baring not unimpressive fangs. It scrambled free, fluffing up the long, striped tail that gave rise to its name. Brander held on to it, glad for his heavy gloves in case the animal decided to bury those fangs in him. It hissed again.

Here we go. Brander gave a low, distinctive, up-and-down whistle.

The ringtail let out a piercing screech. It set Brander's teeth on edge even though he'd heard it countless times. And with the way it echoed off the walls of the building, it probably sounded even stranger out there. The guards froze, then whirled, peering into the darkness. He doubted any of them had ever encountered one of the shy animals before. Since the whole plan hinged on that, he had to hope he was right. Especially since he'd been the one to convince the Raider it would work.

He hunkered back in the shelter of the boulder, using the hand that wasn't holding the ringtail to free his latest invention from the sling over his shoulder. He gave the low whistle again, and again the ringtail screeched, even louder this time. And longer; the sound seemed to rebound again and again, until it sounded like there had to be a pack of them surrounding the building.

He watched as the guards gathered near the front door. He could not hear them from this distance, but their body language told him there was an intense discussion going on. Guessing they were arguing over who and how many of them would go investigate, he gave another low whistle, this time three times in succession.

The ringtail howled this time, rising, falling, ending in that grating screech that sounded disturbingly unnatural. Even here, holding the creature in the shelter of the rock, it seemed eerie and uncanny. Eirlys's pet was en-joying himself now, and the howls came again, and again, until the four men were staring into the brush in attitudes of utter trepidation.

Brander saw one of them lift something to his eyes, guessed it was a night spotter. He crouched down behind the boulder, taking care that no part of his—or the ringtail's—body was perceptible to the night lenses. When he was set, he took out the small, highly polished reflector he carried and angled it to watch. The mist wasn't heavy tonight, but there was enough glowmist to show him their positions.

And then three of the four began to move. Spread out but in a single line, they started toward his position. The ringtail began to get nervous, but Brander held on to him; if he let go and one of the guards spotted him, the animal's chances of escape—and of getting back to Eirlys—were almost nil, and Brander did not want that on his already overloaded conscience. He'd already lied to her, saying he wanted the animal for a joke. He could just im-agine the way Eirlys would look at him if the ringtail were injured, and the image haunted him even though it hadn't happened. Yet.

He stroked the animal's fur as he'd seen her do, and it settled a little. But the men were still coming. He glanced to the south but could see nothing. He had to trust that the Raider was there. He would take out the remaining guard—probably the leader, knowing the Coalition officer propensity for ordering others into danger—leaving him only these to deal with.

He whistled once more, even lower now that the targets were almost within range. The ringtail let out his howl again, making Brander's ears ring with it. He watched the men approach, beginning the count in his head.

Closer, closer, closer . . . one more howl . . . that's it, boy . . . almost there . . .

He released the ringtail.

"Home," he whispered, nudging it in the opposite direction from the men who were two steps from where he needed them. He caught only a glimpse of the striped tail as the animal darted into the underbrush and headed for home and Eirlys. For a split second, he envied the creature that, but then it was time. He turned back, lifted the weapon at his side, waited one more breathless moment. The three men were a bare ten feet from the underbrush now. And, as he'd hoped, the nearer they'd come to where that eerie howl had come from, the closer they'd drawn together, instinctively seeking the protection of numbers.

They made the last step. Into his mental strike zone. He fired.

There was a loud pop that made the three men freeze. The projectile from the gun arced upward. The casing that held it compressed fell away, and there was a whoosh of air as the insert unfurled. The three men looked up. In the same instant, Brander heard the Raider fire, and with his peripheral vision saw the fourth guard go down. But he kept his gaze on his three, and before they could react, they were swamped in heavy coils of rope and net, tangled, helpless, unable to even raise the weapons they already had in hand.

"Now!" came the shouted order from the Raider, and the Sentinels stormed out of the shadows.

Brander, being closer, beat them all to the doors of the transportation annex building, and cut away the lock with shears made of their own planium. Then the others were there, moving with speed and precision as the Raider had planned. The best of them had taken seven minutes to get out from under the web of rope and mesh made sticky with crawler vine sap. They had the new rovers uncovered and fired up in three, giving Pryl the time he would need to cover their tracks and get to safety.

Mara moved the first rover smoothly out through the wide doors. Galeth drove the second, not quite as steadily, but without hitting anything. Then Maxon dinged one door slightly, not inflicting any serious damage, but making Pryl, who was already working to erase any trace, dodge back for a moment. And then Brander followed with the one he'd fired up. Once the first four were clear, the Raider roared out in the last, ordering them with a sweeping wave of his arm to head up the mountain. Then he lingered, dangerously too long, Brander thought when he turned back to look from the shelter of the trees. But the Raider had a message to leave, and he would also not leave Pryl alone on foot, not this close to the command post.

The seconds ticked down, and Brander caught himself holding his breath. Then, as he watched, Pryl ran for the Raider's rover. As soon as he was aboard, the Raider spun the nimble craft on its axis and purposefully angled it slightly as he hit the throttle. The blast of its passage wiped even Pryl's footprints from the loose dirt. And then they were clear. Without a single precious shot fired except the Raider's to take out the last guard, they were clear.

With five brand-new, fully armed and charged Coalition air rovers.

Chapter 11

"WHAT DO YOU mean, five air rovers?"

Barcon Ordam suppressed a tremor of fear as Governor Sorkost rose from behind his huge desk, looted from the Zelos city museum. The man might be old, portly, and soft, but he was still the voice—and the power—of the Coalition on Ziem, and thus to be feared.

"I . . . sir . . ."

"You cannot be saying five brand-new air rovers, barely off the transport ship, are *gone?*"

"I'm afraid so, sir."

The governor leaned forward, his knobbed, heavily veined hands propping up his considerable weight. Barcon tried not to look at the left one, where two fingers were missing. Rumor had it they'd been lost in the first invasion of Trios decades ago, on the other side of the galaxy, when Gradle Sorkost had been in the merciless General Corling's command. Some even said the old Trios king himself had taken the fingers off, before he'd been captured and executed.

Others, less admiring, speculated Sorkost had chewed them off in his haste to gobble up a tasty dinner.

The only thing that mattered to Ordam was that Sorkost had the power, the only civilian power on Ziem greater than his own.

"How," Sorkost ground out, "did this happen?"

He'd practiced this, wanting to present a calm, impersonal report, hoping his tone and delivery would divorce him from the facts, at least in Sorkost's mind. But he couldn't control the timorous undertone in his voice as he began.

"They came in at night. Overpowered and contained the guards with some primitive rope device we've never seen before. No one heard anything except screeching animals of some kind. They left no trace. Not even a footprint. No one knows how many of them there were."

"So they merely floated in and stole *five* air rovers, and no one saw *anything?*"

Barcon resisted the urge to loosen the collar that suddenly seemed too tight. Still, he chose his words carefully, to avoid any semblance of connection or responsibility. "One guard was hit from a distance. The others were attacked from behind."

Sorkost's already narrow gaze tightened even more as his jaw clenched.

His voice came out in a hiss that lingered on the "s."

"It was that skalworm raider, wasn't it?"

"That is not certain," Barcon said. "One man thought he saw that silver helmet, but he is unsure. But it is . . . logical to assume so. No one else dares."

"So much for your idea to spread the word that he was dead, you fool. It probably provoked him to this."

Barcon cringed inwardly. He tried desperately to think of a way to extricate himself from this. The Coalition had a tendency to blame whoever was handiest when things went wrong, and right now, he was in the direct line of fire.

There was a knock on the door, and Barcon cringed again, wondering who had the temerity to interrupt the governor at a moment like this. The lowly trooper who entered at Sorkost's angry shout scuttled in, saluted, dropped something on the governor's desk, mumbled something about it being found at the scene, and then escaped before he was even acknowledged. Something Barcon was certain he would pay for dearly later. But he understood; better a certain punishment later than possible death at the hands of the enraged governor now.

Sorkost stared down at the card on his desk. Barcon swallowed against the sudden, horrified tightness in his throat; he didn't have to see it to know it was the calling card of that damnable renegade. He knew it bore the image of the famous curved Ziem saber, and those two ominous words: Without Warning. Which this raid had certainly been.

The Raider.

Again.

Damn the bastard.

The governor slowly turned around.

"Tell me, Barcon Ordam," he said, too calmly now, "how did they get to the transport annex in the first place? Do we not have the mountain trails guarded?"

Barcon took a breath. This, at least, could not be laid at his door. "A new troop has rotated in. It is assumed that is how they got past, because the new men did not know all the paths."

"Were they not shown, trained?" Sorkost demanded.

"Of course, but only on maps, when they arrived yesterday. And they are not yet used to the mist."

Sorkost went very still. Too still. "Are you saying this change of force took place only yesterday?"

Barcon stopped himself from gaping. Barely. Did the man not know the movements of his own forces? "Yes, sir."

"And on *that very night* that damnable marauder attempts—nay, *succeeds* in this raid?"

"Sir?"

"Are you blind as well as stupid? Do you think this a coincidence?"

Barcon had in fact not thought of it at all, but he was not about to admit that to the governor. Especially not when his rage was becoming both palpable and towering. "I did wonder," he began.

"We have a traitor in our midst. Someone betrayed us to this mutilated blackguard, and I will have his head."

Barcon's mind raced, not something he was adept at even under normal circumstances. He preferred plenty of time and planning and calculating exactly how much he could get away with. The approach had served him well. After all, had he not handed Ziem over to them, intact and with the mines still functional? And when they and their equipment had been unable to counter the mist of Ziem, had he not pointed out the most vulnerable of the native miners, who could be forced to work for them?

They owed him. And he would not allow himself to be blamed for this. "And his entrails, governor, I'm certain," he said, his tone as obsequious as he thought Sorkost would tolerate.

"Get me Frall!" the governor shouted.

Relief that Sorkost was apparently going to channel his rage elsewhere flooded Barcon. And then he remembered, and apprehension filled him anew. If the proper target of his fury was not available, he knew too well Sorkost was likely to vent it on the nearest target. Which was equally likely to be him.

"Frall isn't here. A new post commander came in with the new guards."

"Then get me him, whoever in hades it is!"

"Immediately, sir!" Barcon turned on his heel. He wished more than anything to run, and in fact did the last few steps to the door. He didn't draw another breath until he was safely outside and the door was closed behind him.

He ordered the guard—despite the fact that there had been little trace of rebellion other than that hideously scarred raider in years, Sorkost maintained the pretense that he needed guarding—to get the new post commander here instantly. He sent another messenger for Jepson Kerrold, his liaison in matters of state. He would have him handle this from here on. For having come from one of the most elite families on Ziem—at one time, anyway—the man was rather useless, too terrified of even the lowliest Coalition official to do much good. But Barcon had no hesitation about sending him into the breach for just that reason; if a Coalition official became irritated enough with Kerrold to cut off his head, it would be no great loss to him. No, if he needed something actually done, he used Kerrold as a distraction and called in Jakel, the agent who saw to his dirtier work with a brutal efficiency.

Orders given, Ordam retreated to his own office, a suite of rooms looking out over the town square. The office that had once belonged to Torstan Davorin, a fact that gave him no small amount of glee, and was the reason he'd chosen it of all the ones available to him.

This was where the true power was. The power he wanted, anyway. Power over the people of Zelos, and by extension all of Ziem. And he had achieved it. He had shown all those who had belittled him over the years, those who had laughed at his awkwardness, his way of speaking, the way his ears sat upon his head. He had shown all those who had preferred the likes of the Davorins, especially that craven Drake, who in the end hadn't had the nerve to stand up to anyone.

He'd always suspected there was a coward hiding behind that dashing, handsome exterior, and it was one of the greatest satisfactions of his success that the entire planet knew it now. Especially the women, who had once fluttered at the man, whispering over his pure Ziem eyes, thick black hair, and even, disgustingly, publicly slavering over his taut, strong body. While they looked past he himself with dismissive or even derisive glances.

It was not his fault his eyes were so pale, barely blue at all. Or that he was thin, and his ears stuck out a bit. At least he was not a slimehog like Sorkost, concerned only with the delights of the flesh.

It would all come out right in the end. He knew that. What he had done, and continued to do, was the best thing for Ziem. It was not his fault they could not yet see that, that they were much better off with the presence and support of the Coalition.

But someday they would see it. This would pass and he would maintain the position he had worked so hard to attain. Eventually even the Raider would fall; the odds would see to that. The man was reckless, and by now likely blinded by his successes, small though they were. He would one day— hopefully soon—take that risk too far and come to a messy end. Barcon simply had to be patient.

And he had learned long ago how to be patient.

Chapter 12

THEY WERE LIKE children with new toys, the Raider thought, watching them touch and poke at the air rovers. It gave him no small amount of satisfaction. His band had little enough to fight with; these vehicles would make a mountain's worth of difference. They might only carry a half-squad, but they were quick and powerful, and brand new, with fully charged power cells that would last a year at least. They would have to have a charging source then, but time enough to work that out. He—or more likely Brander—would think of something.

Besides, they would serve a more important purpose soon.

Brander left the excited group and strolled over to him. "This has done them good."

"Yes."

"Worth the risk."

"Yes."

"So what's next?"

He gave his second a sideways look. "Did you not say this should hold everyone for a while?"

Brander grinned. "I didn't mean me."

His mouth quirked. "Of course not."

"I know you have something brewing."

"Do you?"

"I can see it. Practically feel it. Your brain is running in the highest gear, my friend. Has been for a while now. You have something even bigger in mind."

He turned, gestured to Brander to follow him. They stepped into his quarters. It was a chilly day on Ziem, and he could feel the cold from the tunnel, his back way in and out, known only to a few.

He turned his head to look at the man who had stood beside him since before the day he had begun this misadventure. Over and above his knack for clever inventions and unusual tactics, he was uncommonly brave and there was no man the Raider would rather have at his side in a fight.

"I do."

"But you're not going to tell me what this plan is."

"Yet."

Brander studied him for a moment, then nodded. "All right, my exalted commander." He added an exaggerated bow. "Do as you must."

"If you continue with that blathering, you'll find I must pummel you into oblivion."

"Now that would be an interesting contest," a woman's voice said.

Kye had quietly slipped up behind them. Quietly enough that he hadn't been aware until she was almost within a double arm's reach. Kye had become that good. She had become everything he'd known she could be, even as it pained him to watch her change.

"And would you oversee it for us?" Brander asked her with a grin.

"No. It would be embarrassing for me to have to rule against my own cousin for cheating."

Brander put on an exaggeratedly aghast expression. "I'm hurt, cousin. How can you accuse me of such?"

"Perhaps because you cheated in a game of seek when I was but five?" she asked, her tone sweet. Too sweet.

Brander winced. But there was a twinkle in his sideways glance at the Raider. "Be thankful, my friend, that you do not have a cousin with the memory of a leathertrunk."

"I shall consider that fair warning," he said, wondering if that had been Brander's intent. If so it was needless; he already knew Kye remembered well. Everything. It was why he had to hold himself apart from her, whatever guise he was in.

How much he wished it could be otherwise was something he didn't dare think about.

He spoke before he could lose himself down that alley. "I am glad you are here," he said to her. "I have need of your artistic skill."

"Going to have her do a mighty portrait of you?" Brander teased.

"Better than a portrait of an insufferable creature such as yourself," she retorted.

"Children, children," the Raider scolded, hiding a smile. They were like siblings, these two, and sometimes as difficult to keep in line. "I have need of a map."

"A map? You know this countryside like no other except perhaps Eirlys Davorin. If you need aid, perhaps you should call her in." Kye eyed him levelly. "She would come in an instant."

"She is too young."

"Not for long. And she has promised her brother only to wait until she is of age." She lifted one brow. "And it could not hurt to have a Davorin alongside you."

He trusted to the helmet and the scars that masked the left side of his face to hide any change in his expression. And said only, "This map needs to be large enough for . . . a briefing."

She went very still. "A mission briefing?"

"Yes." She did not, he noted, ask what mission. He knew she was clever enough to realize that if it required preparation this formal, it was something big. "It needs to cover from Halfhead and the Brothers to Highridge, and from The Sentinel to the mouth of the Racelock."

Kye frowned slightly. "That's a huge area. And you know mapping is not one of my greater skills."

"There are images to be used. Brander got that flyover working."

Her expression cleared. "Aerial pictures?"

He nodded. "We do not have the paper to print and join them, so I need you to use them as a guide and transfer the necessary details."

"That I can work with," she said.

And if he knew her—and he did—it would be as near perfect as could be done by hand. Again, the ache that she was using her talent for such purposes rose in him. He fought it down, as he always fought down his other reactions to her lovely, vibrant presence. In either guise he wore. Drake Davorin might want her desperately, but the Raider—and the rebellion—needed her. So it had to be Drake who pushed her away. It had to be.

"On what?" she asked.

He shoved aside his roiled emotions. "Whatever you can find that is big enough to be seen across the gathering room."

She nodded, clearly already thinking. "I will see what I can find," she said, and left the room.

He turned to Brander, who had been uncharacteristically quiet.

"Have them get those rovers under cover. You know they're searching like sniffhounds. And have them keep them separate, not all in one place."

Brander nodded, all light-heartedness vanished now. When need be, his second could project incredible command presence. Perhaps because he was so droll most of the time; when he was serious, everyone knew it was time to take notice.

Alone now, the Raider faced the fact that soon he would be regularly alone in his quarters with the one person he needed to keep at a distance. The one person he had to keep separate from. The one person who made him want to jettison everything and grab for some tiny bit of a normal life.

But he was who he was, the Coalition was who they were, and a normal life was nothing more than a fool's dream.

He was grateful when he was interrupted by a knock on the door.

Galeth, the eldest Harkin brother, came in and handed him a folded page, then stood at attention before him. It still disconcerted him a bit, yet he understood the need for it. Command wasn't only for battles, it must be in-grained so that there was no questioning when instant decision and response meant getting out alive.

"Where did this come from?"

"It was in the hive, sir."

He looked the man up and down. There were no visible telltale marks or welts. "No stingers returned?"

Galeth smiled at that. "No, sir. I think Brander's repellant solution worked."

He smiled. "Get yourself something to eat."

Galeth nodded gratefully. Making the comm rounds was a long day. The various message drops were scattered not just all over the mountain, but up the canyon, on the flats, and in town as well.

When he was again alone, he smothered a sigh of frustration. To be reduced to such means was beyond slow and irritating, it was infuriating. To think a people who had once but to activate their wristlet to speak to anyone now had to leave words committed to paper, paper that was in constantly shorter supply thanks to Coalition crackdowns for precisely this reason, stirred up the fury that was never far from bursting to life in him.

He knew it was what they intended by never rebuilding any sort of system other than one for their own use; it was that much harder to conspire against them if you couldn't communicate easily. And it was effective; each day of checking the drops was a day the runner was out of the fight, and yet they must be checked daily. Even so, information was often received too late to act upon, and a prized target was missed because of the delay.

It was not that they could not reproduce the technology; he knew Brander could put together a system easily, given the time and materials. The problem was reproducing a system the Coalition could not spy upon or jam. And that was beyond their capabilities at the moment. So they made do with things like the hive, their most successful drop. They'd had to change many of the others, the tree hollow, the rock wall, but never the hive. Kye's idea of adhering several dead stingers to the outside, in a manner that made them appear alive, had been genius. For who of sane mind would dare to stick their hand into what appeared to be an active stinger nest?

But then, the woman was insanely clever.

And a brilliant fighter.

And brave to the point of foolishness.

An old pain jabbed at him at the thought of the danger she put herself in. She should be safe at home, pursuing the talent she'd been born with and the work she'd been born for: creation. Creation of things of such beauty they took human breath away.

Instead, she pursued destruction. Often risking her very life to rain it down on the Coalition.

That it was most often at his own order made it a thousandfold worse.

Shoving that worry aside, he unfolded the page Galeth had pulled out of the hive. He knew immediately who it was from; the graceful signature accented with a drawing of a feather told him. The being that most thought was only fable, the unknown creature he himself never spoke of except to agree she was but a legend, to avoid drawing undue attention, or the suspicion he had finally cracked and lost his mind.

The Spirit.

When the first note had come years ago, he had scoffed and tossed it. He had thought it the work of a prankster, or perhaps even a Coalition spy, attempting to set them up for a trap.

But later, when he was in a more reflective mood, he had remembered the note and its claim. And when the opportunity arose unexpectedly, he set out himself to see if there was any truth in it.

It had been all true. From his hiding place above the Coalition compound, he had watched as they unloaded cases of rich food and kegs of brew, things his own people had not seen nor tasted in years. Had he believed the information in the note, they could have waylaid the shipment before it was delivered. The big cargo ships could only land on the flats, which meant transport from the landing zone through the high valley. And he and his band could take anything less than a full battalion in that narrow valley. They had. He had learned early on to use the Coalition need for uniformity, precision, and unthinking obedience against them.

The next time a note signed with the feather had come, he had again watched and found the information to be both valid and valuable. And again, until the string of accuracy became too clear to deny. And the next day another message had come, saying only, "Trust me."

So while he still didn't believe this was truly the legendary Spirit, rather assumed it was someone using the myth for their own reasons, the next time he took a small squad with him. And had managed to liberate three cases of fuel cells, leaving the Coalition scrambling for power for nearly a month. Although they could not use them, the thought of the Coalition existing in the same darkness they had brought upon Ziem had been beyond sweet.

The next result of one of the notes was a cache of fresh crops shipped in from some other world the Coalition held and looted, that had fed them for days. He had even allowed those of the band with families to take some home with them, with the instruction that, were they discovered, they must lay the blame at his feet. The Coalition was already after his head, so he would lose nothing. And build the Raider's reputation in the process, not because he wished it, but because it would help rally the people.

And that had been another bit of advice that had come from the one calling him or herself the Spirit. Along with the suggestion of a calling card, to be left at the site of each successful foray. Eventually he had seen the sense of it. The people—and the Coalition—needed to know not all had buckled. And while having the occupying troops on high alert at all times had both good and bad sides, he could see that the wear and tear was worth the danger. And besides, being always on edge could lead to mistakes. And they could capitalize on mistakes.

This was, after all, a war. The Coalition might not think it so; they might consider Ziem well and truly conquered, but as long as even one man stood, they were wrong.

And so he had turned even then to the one person he knew could do it. He had sent Brander to Kye, to ask her to draw something that could represent the rebels, something both stark and taunting, to be left for the Coalition to find. Then still trapped in Zelos with her paralyzed father, she had seized upon the small idea with relish, and what she had presented them with mere hours later was a triumph. The bold sweep of the traditional Ziem saber with the words she had pulled from his statement of their mission, "Without Warning," had encapsulated what he'd wanted it to say. And that symbol had been left clearly visible after every successful raid, until not just the Coalition but everyone was buzzing with it. Were it not for the fact that it would betray them—some lived here in the mountain ruins, but many more led double lives, responding to his call but otherwise staying with their families—he thought many of his force would have it permanently etched on their skin.

And now, three years after they began, they were established, practiced, and effective. Including Kye, who made his life both easier—her staunch support and sheer nerve were irreplaceable—and harder. Every time he saw those rare, turquoise eyes fastened on him, he had to remind himself there was no place in this life or this time for the kind of things she made him think.

He shook himself out of the reverie. He rarely had time for dwelling on the past, and supposed it a sign of his weariness that he had done so now. He brought his attention back to the note he held. It was short, with the feather taking up as much space as the words.

You have become much more than a mere nuisance to them, and an inspiration beyond price to your people. Well done.

He swallowed against the sudden tightness of his throat. He wondered at how he could feel pride at words from someone he did not even know. And yet he did.

He had never set out to be a legend. Had wanted it even less. But he had come to realize that it would take a legend to keep this fight going. And so he had accepted that burden along with the others.

Do not think too small. You have power and momentum now; use it.

That had been the Spirit's advice as well, and had spurred him to make the rover raid. And their success buoyed him. He knew he might not see victory in his lifetime, especially as their forays became bigger, bolder. He had accepted that.

His job, as he saw it, was to make sure the battle continued after he fell.

"YOU'RE CERTAIN IT was him?" Major Caze Paledan, the new commander of outpost Ziem, asked.

He hadn't even unpacked yet, and he was already in the midst of an apparent crisis. Things appeared worse here than he had been led to believe. The reports he'd read in transit had been short on details and long on excuses. And his briefing had been sketchy, filled more with speculation and rumor and exaggeration than could be credited. They were building the man into a legend, for surely no one on such a backwater planet could be so fearsome.

Or so he had thought.

"Yes, sir," the young trooper said. "I saw the silver helmet, and those scars are as nasty as everyone says." He swallowed visibly. "And they found that calling card he always leaves, didn't they?"

"Yes," Paledan answered. It was in his pocket right now. That image of a Ziem saber, like the ones crossed on his office wall, and the slogan, "Without Warning."

This had certainly been without warning.

But it had been openly claimed afterward.

So total secrecy was not the Raider's goal. The opposite in fact. And it had been exquisitely planned, timed, and carried out.

So was he a tactical genius who wanted everyone to know it?

Paledan pondered this as he made his way back to his quarters to finish his unpacking. And he couldn't reconcile what his instincts were telling him with the image of a man who wanted notoriety. The use of a simple device Sorkost called primitive, but which had clearly been very effective. And the fact that the men caught in that sticky, heavy net had not been slaughtered outright as they helplessly struggled. He would have killed them when he had the chance, while they were helpless, as per Coalition policy. Any chance to lessen the numbers of your opponent should be taken.

And yet the Raider had not done it. He had used no more force than was necessary to accomplish his goal.

Was he soft? His heart not in this battle?

That did not fit, either. Only someone completely dedicated would have kept going this long. And a half-hearted leader could not keep this ragged band together, could not inspire them to raids like this, so audacious in the face of Coalition might that it was difficult to believe.

And yet Paledan sensed no ego here, for there had been opportunity enough to take the steps that would assure the man even more fame, and he had not done so.

So not glory-seeking, and a true leader.

Which left him only with the option that what his instincts were telling him was true, despite the fact that he had only just arrived. He had learned to trust his instincts. He'd honed them in too many fights to count and across the entire sector.

The Raider did not let himself be seen, that silver helmet gleaming amid the black, matte armor of his band, the scars clearly visible, and the calling card left to both announce and taunt, because he wanted fame and glory.

He did it to keep the attention on himself. Not because of ego, but because if the focus was on him, then no one was looking for the others. They barely noticed the others.

A true leader. The most dangerous kind of opponent.

Admiration sparked in him.

He smiled inwardly. It had been a long time since he had had such a truly formidable adversary. It was simple to outnumber your opponent, or out-think those who had never fought for anything in their lives and shrank at the very idea, like the few Ziemites he had met thus far.

It was an entirely different matter to deal with someone like this. Who-ever this man was, whoever he had been before, he was a warrior now. Even though this remote, mist-shrouded planet had apparently never seen war, it had spawned a fighter worthy of the appellation.

And worthy of his own skills.

He had no doubt what the end would be. The Raider might be a great thinker, brilliant leader, and courageous fighter, but Paledan was better. He'd been proving that since he'd put on a Coalition uniform.

He laughed at himself, for having all the ego the Raider apparently lacked. He allowed himself that, for he also had the wisdom to understand that no man was infallible, and to appreciate that his enemy was clever, quick, and fearless.

It would take no less of a warrior than himself to take this one down. And take him down he would.

And in the process, he would enjoy the fight. No true warrior passed up the chance to sharpen his skills on a worthy opponent. He would test this raider's mettle before he ended it.

This backwater planet was turning into quite the interesting assignment.

Chapter 13

"WHAT IS THIS?"

Kye grinned. Whatever it was, he thought, she was excited about it. That alone warmed him, even as it made him wary.

Also excited was the boy with her, although he wasn't grinning quite so widely as he stole sideways glances, as if he expected to be slapped down by the Raider at any moment.

"Dek," he said, and saw a shift in the young man—barely more than a child, and one of the newest arrivals—as he called him by name, "what have you two come up with?"

Encouraged, as he'd intended, the boy held up a paint-stained shape. "This."

"Picture it," Kye said excitedly, "showing up on every still-standing wall in Zelos. Imagine the town waking up after longnight, and seeing this every-where. Better, imagine the bedamned Coalition waking up to find this image painted on their own walls!"

The Raider stared at what she held, trying to see it as she did. Finally, he shook his head; all he could see was a vague shape cut out of a piece of what had been the thin metal siding of one of the crates they'd liberated in the last raid. He'd doubted the contents would be of any use, but Kye had eagerly seized the supply of paint.

"You have the artist's eye, not me. You will have to explain."

Her grin widened. "We'll do better. We'll show you."

She looked around. Nodded at Dek, who gathered up what they'd brought in and walked to the far, back wall.

"A smoother wall would be better, but this will do," she said.

Dek held up the thin sheet of metal, placing it flat against the wall. Kye grabbed up the other items she had brought in. He recognized one of the cans of paint, and what was apparently a nozzle of some sort. She deftly at-tached the device to the can, then turned to the wall. In mere seconds she was done and the boy was carefully lifting the metal sheet away.

He stood there for a moment, staring. And more than a little amazed at what she'd done in just a few lines and shapes. For there on the wall was the Raider. In a stylized form, but unmistakable. She'd even managed, by some clever outlining, to give the impression of the helmet and the scars. And with the rippling dark shape of his coat billowing behind him as he strode forward, toward the viewer, even he could see the power in the image.

"Give me three teams of two, and we can blanket the city. If we can spare more, hit the outskirts, and it'll be on every fence, every cottage wall, even a few trees. You saw how quick it was to do. And how silent. We know how the mist flows through Zelos on longnight; we can follow it, use it. They'll never know until daylight, when it will be too late; everyone will have seen it."

He could not argue with one facet of her impassioned plea. And her energy, her drive was contagious. Even Dek was grinning at him now.

"You see, sir? That we do it under their noses is almost as good as what it is."

"Exactly," Kye agreed.

For a moment, all he could think about was the risk she would be taking. And that he thought of her risk before he thought of those who would accompany her warned him he'd once more let his guard down too far.

"I see the value," he began, keeping his gaze on the image, not daring to look at her face when he already knew, despite his efforts, that his voice had softened for her.

"Of course. Think what it will do for the morale of the people of Zelos. If only because they will see the Coalition flummoxed."

"And angry," he warned.

"But they will find no one who knows anything, for we won't be seen."

"I see the value," he said again, well aware that the power of the Raider went far beyond the actual man, and building the legend was nearly as important as the raids themselves. "but ordering six people—"

"Eight," Dek corrected, with a glance at Kye. "I mean, we're going, right?"

"Absolutely," she said with a grin. "It was your idea, after all."

The boy grinned back. Kye turned back to the Raider. "And you won't have to order anyone."

He raised a brow at her beneath the helmet.

"We already have double that in volunteers."

Clearly, he wasn't the only one who saw the value, even if it was only in blatant defiance. And they would have cover, he thought. On longnight, that protracted night of the Ziem year, the mist grew deeper, thicker, more concealing, until your hand would vanish in front of you before you fully extended your arm. Only those with the vision for the glowmist would be able to stay together, see each other or anything else moving.

"All right," he finally said, "but with the warning that should something more crucial arise—"

"Of course," Kye said. "This is merely spirit-lifting. A chance at, say, a cargo of rail guns would take precedence."

"I don't underestimate the power of lifting the spirits of Ziem," he said softly, looking at her at last. The smile she gave him then warmed him far beyond what was wise to allow. She was affecting him too much. He was afraid one day he might hesitate to give a necessary order, because it would put her at risk. Or someone else would die because he was trying to keep her safe. He could not let that happen. This fight was bigger than all of them. But he was having to remind himself of that more and more.

"Let's get started," Dek said, excitement clear in his young voice. "We've got to make more of these stencils by tomorrow night."

"With you," Kye said, sounding nearly as excited—and almost as young—as the boy had.

"The Spirit is with us," the boy exclaimed as he ran out.

In the doorway, Kye turned back to look at him. "Oh, I forgot. Fair warning. We had to test it a few times until I got it right."

He drew back slightly. "And?"

"You're sort of all over the walls out there," she said gesturing toward the main room.

He didn't know whether to laugh or groan, and ended up simply closing his eyes and giving a rueful shake of his head. When he looked again, she and the boy were gone.

"IT'S QUITE DELIGHTFUL down in Zelos these days," Brander observed with a grin. "All those dramatic posters of the Raider painted everywhere."

The subject of those dramatic silhouettes didn't turn as he answered. "I'm still not certain it was worth the risk."

"If you'd seen the Coalition racing around like maddened brollets trying to paint over them all, and then running out of paint because we stole it and used it to make the very things they're trying to wipe out, you'd think differently, my friend."

The Raider did turn then. "I never said it wasn't a good idea."

"And," Brander added, "you won't have any skin left if you keep that up."

Brander slouched in the makeshift chair in the corner of the Raider's private quarters, watching him as he stood before the fire, sleeves rolled up and head bare, as he did only in this room. One hand was at his face, worrying at the mass of scar tissue, the part of his disguise Brander knew he disliked most, but also agreed was the most crucial.

"It itches," the man muttered, but he stopped.

"Better than hurting," Brander said. "Speaking of which, how's the wound?"

"Fine. Healed. For the most part. Did I not prove that?"

"You moved well enough on the raid," Brander agreed. "But do not forget I saw you after, when you could barely stand after the strain. Jakel's laser pistol is brutal."

He heard the long breath the man let out. "It was as well I did not have to run in our escape."

Brander grinned. "Riding is much better," he agreed.

He got a rare smile in return.

"I'm just thankful that blessed ringtail made it safely home to Eirlys."

"Your idea worked well."

Pleased, Brander said, "The flock will be happy with this success for some time. Time enough for you to get some rest."

"I—"

"I know. You would prefer to hit them again, now, while they're still reeling and cursing your name."

"Yes. It would double the blow."

"And make them doubly angry. Perhaps enough to start purging again."

That hit home. Brander knew neither of them would ever forget the horror of people being pulled off the streets and out of their homes, to be slaughtered in front of them all. As both warning and demonstration of the Coalition's intent and ruthlessness, it had been beyond effective. Not many had the steel to resist them after that.

Until the rise of the Raider.

He made a suggestion. "They know we have those air rovers now; they have to be wondering when and how we will use them."

The Raider studied him for a moment. "You mean it might pay to let them steep in it for a while?"

Brander nodded. "They'll be strung up, at high alert. And even the Coalition can only maintain that for so long. They'll get tired, sloppy."

"It is a good point."

"You yourself have said you do not wish to force them to call in aid from Legion Command, to crush Ziem totally. "

"Yes."

He didn't sound convinced. Brander understood; his blood was up, they'd succeeded on this raid beyond anyone's hopes, and he wanted to strike a maiming, if not killing blow.

"You have also said unpredictability is a large part of our success."

"I talk too much," he muttered, and Brander knew he'd won.

"Rest. You need sleep, and you've sure as hades earned it. Time enough to strike again when they have relaxed."

"The weapons that were in the rovers—"

"There is no way they can find them. They are safely cached, in the places you ordered." A grin flashed across his face. "Well, except for those," he added, gesturing toward the table against the far wall, where lay a brand-new blaster that looked as if it had never been fired, a laser pistol even bigger than the one that had caused the injury that had taken the man out of action for so long, and the other two long guns Brander himself had separated out of the haul.

Only three of them knew the prized weapons well enough to use them, and now they would have the chance to hone those skills with new ones rather than the battered relics they'd been using. He had been grinning when he'd grabbed his own. His commander had said nothing about the extra one, which suggested to Brander that he knew what it was intended for. Even now, he was staring at it, his brow furrowed.

"You know she must have it," Brander said quietly. "She is the best shot of us all."

"I know."

How could he not, given she had outshot them all in testing, including that unbelievable dead center hit from the west wall to the bell tower, at an impossible angle and distance. After that, and her reckless but stunning success in sending an entire caravan of Coalition mining carts over the side on the steep road to the mines, no one had questioned her swift rise in the ranks to become the Raider's number three. They all knew that after the death of her father she had the fire in her blood, and the faith of the Raider, and they accepted her wholeheartedly.

"She would not stand for you curbing her because she is female."

"Nor would I do it. She is a fighter, and it would kill her spirit to be told she cannot." His mouth quirked. "And she would not stop even if I ordered it."

"I think she would do anything for you. Except that."

Brander didn't draw back from the sideways look that got him. "You're the smartest man I know," he said simply. "You cannot be unaware of her feelings for you. Even if she's not quite clear on which of you she loves."

"I lay no claim to any knowledge at all of the female brain. Besides, it matters not. There is no time for such. Not in the midst of this war."

If he knew nothing else, Brander knew when to cut his losses. "I think the Coalition doesn't quite consider this a war."

"Yet."

It came with a grin, and Brander knew he was still jubilant over the success of the raid. Five brand-new air rovers was a triumph. A good moment to make his proposal.

"I've been thinking. If it's true that the new post commander is a fan of chaser, perhaps I should set up a regular game."

He watched as the Raider considered his words. The man knew he was the best chaser player in the city and beyond. It wasn't that he never lost, but more that he could always judge when the other players had an unbeatable hand. In the long run, which was what he played for, he always came out ahead. And he rarely made anyone angry at him, for he took care not to have blatant runs of good luck that might lead to charges of cheating.

"That," the Raider said after a moment, "sounds like a double problem. You cannot afford to lose too much, but with the Coalition, you cannot afford to win too much, either."

"It would be a fine line," he agreed. He pulled a single Romerian withal out of his pocket, held the golden coin up to gleam in the firelight. "But if I play it right, the real payoff would not be in withals."

The man's gaze narrowed, pulling the mask of scars tighter. "You mean information."

Brander nodded. "Who knows what I might pick up? Just as we learned about the changing of the guard."

"At the risk of putting your face before them enough that the chance of you being recognized in a fight goes up considerably."

Brander's gaze flicked to the scarred half of the Raider's face. He knew it was his protection, that the mass of scars not only made him look more bloodcurdling, but also served as distraction. No one noticed much else about him before they instinctively looked away from the ruin of his face.

But he said nothing of it. Instead, he merely shrugged. "Me, a wastrel gambler, running with the Raider? It would never occur to them."

"Not just running. His second in command, closest friend, and good right hand."

The words warmed him, but he kept his own light. "They're too busy looking for you to worry about me. Besides, I—"

He broke off as a tapping came on the door. In the pauses between the knocks was the same combination of lengths that identified them on the way up the mountain. Kye.

Brander saw a look of resignation coupled with acceptance in the Raider's eyes. Brander rose, glancing again at the table that held the other two long guns, then at his commander.

"Good luck," he said with a flashing grin. His answer was a pained grimace Brander had never seen prior to a Coalition battle. He waited until his friend and leader picked up the battered metal helmet and put it on, masking most of his face except the scars. Heard him cough slightly, as if roughening his voice was a physical thing. Then he went to the door and pulled it open. Gave the woman waiting there a wink as he shifted the long gun on its sling over his shoulder. Her sharp gaze followed the movement, and he saw it linger for a moment on the coveted weapon.

"Good luck," Brander repeated.

"Wish it to him. I don't need it."

"Already did. More, because he will need it, my fiery cousin."

She gave him a disgusted look. He laughed, and edged past her back into the great room.

He would give much to be the proverbial zipbug on the wall for this one.

"SO IT IS TRUE," Kye said as soon as the door closed behind her cousin and the weapon he'd had in his hands. "There were long guns in the rovers."

The Raider finished settling the helmet in place on his head, adjusting it to hide the half of his face that he apparently thought even worse, or perhaps just more in need of protection than the visible half. Then he turned.

"A few, yes," he said.

His voice was its usual raspy, rough thing. She still found it not unpleasing. But then, she admired him so greatly she had to admit that could color her perception.

She focused on his eyes, that classic Ziem blue in contrast to her own turquoise shade. Some said her color was more prized for being rarer, but she thought with the black rim around an iris the color of a sun-season sky, his were much more striking. She was long past being distracted by the scars that twisted across his face. He looked weary, she thought. And yet energized at the same time, as if the vigor of the successful raid on the transportation annex still carried him.

She shoved her worry about him into the barred cage where she made it live, alongside the other feelings she had for him that would, given the slightest encouragement, blossom into something even more foolish. She could not allow that encouragement. There was too much at stake to let her personal feelings interfere.

And in that moment it struck her that this was very like the decision Drake had had to make. His family responsibility outweighed all else, and so he had had to close the door on anything else, including his feelings for her.

For a moment, she wobbled, her stomach knotting, her heart aching with the pain of wanting something so very much, and knowing she could never, never have it.

"Kye."

The Raider said it quietly, with a new softness in his voice, and the warmth it sent spiraling through her nearly was her undoing. Her gaze shot to his face, his eyes, and for an instant, she saw an echoing warmth, before it vanished from the cool blue of his eyes.

She struggled to regain her composure. "Where are the rest of the long guns?" she asked.

"They are cached, along with the rest of the arms. For now."

"Yet Brander has one." She folded her arms across her chest. "And you as well, I presume."

"Yes," he said mildly.

She'd expected this battle, and was ready. She had few qualms about facing down this legend among men, but she had meant to stay calm, present her case coolly, irrefutable item by irrefutable item. But that softening of his voice, that flash of heat in his eyes, had thrown her completely. She ruined her plan quickly, words pouring from her like the Racelock at the narrowest part of the gorge.

"That makes no sense. I'm the best shot of all of us. I had the long gun when we only had the one. And I used it well, until it was fried by that rail gun burst."

"Brander is a fair shot himself," he said mildly.

"As are you. That's not the point. The point is that I'm better than both of you."

"I see you've lost none of your confidence."

"And why would I? I didn't miss with that old piece of—" She stopped, knowing she was heading the wrong direction. She tried again for calm, but this mattered so much it was difficult. "It is only logical that a long gun be in the hands of the one who can make the best use of it."

"Indeed."

Her brows lowered. "So?"

When he spoke it was gently, and she could have sworn she saw a flicker of . . . something in those vivid blue eyes. Laughter? Teasing? From the Raider? On top of that bit of heat she had seen in his eyes?

"Had you looked before you launched, you would have seen there are yet two on the table there. Mine . . . and yours."

Her head snapped around. She stared at the two weapons. Felt color stealing her neck and into her cheeks. It took some nerve, but she turned back to face the man she admired above all others.

"I am sorry. I was prepared for a battle when there was none."

"I would have you save that fervor for the enemy. But do not mistake me, Kye. Would I rather that you stayed safe at home, or at least here in camp? Of course."

"I could not!"

"Being a carrier of the long gun means dangerous, solitary missions. Often on your own, apart from any backing or aid."

"Haven't I done that for months? I cannot sit safely back while others fight."

"I know that to do so would suffocate you."

"Would that others would be so clear-sighted," she muttered, but she gave him a smile that held everything of her regard, and her thankfulness that he did not coddle her.

For the first time, he looked sad. "You are an artist, Kye. I would give anything for you to be able to become what you were born to become. It pains me to see your artist's eye turned to such work."

"There is no place for art in this world the Coalition has created."

"I know."

She thought she had never heard more pain and sorrow than in those two words.

But it was the Raider, the warrior, who spoke then. "It is a wise commander who knows the skills of his troops and uses them. No matter what I would prefer, I would be a fool not to use your sharp eye and steady hand."

He could not have said anything that pleased her more. Except, perhaps, that he wanted her safe because he loved her. But he was the Raider, and those words would never come.

And she would be the fool if she thought otherwise.

Chapter 14

DRAKE STARED DOWN at the ripped tunic in his hands. He fought for calm, but there was no mistaking that the stains near the top were blood. Not a huge splotch, so it didn't bring on panic, but still . . .

He tilted his head, looking up toward the loft. Silence. Which was suspicious in itself.

"Nyx! Lux! Both of you. Down here. Now."

He heard a whispered oath no child should be speaking. He'd address that later.

Two sets of footsteps—very slow footsteps—echoed down the stairs. He stood with his arms folded as the two scamps came to a halt before him. They stood, as always, side by side, touching, as if neither of them felt complete without contact with the other. They were staring down at the floor, avoiding looking at him. And yet he felt relieved to see there were no wounds obviously needing a healer's attention, despite the blood on the garment he held.

It was like looking at two versions of the same picture, alike yet different. Nyx, thin, almost gangly with his most recent growth spurt, which put him nearly to Drake's shoulder. And also made the bloody tunic his. Lux, still smaller but no less of a threat because of it; her power was in the head beneath that hair so like her mother's, red with spirited fire.

It struck him in that moment that soon Lux would change, that the transition from girl to woman would begin. Perhaps it already had, and he'd been too distracted—or oblivious—to realize it.

His stomach knotted. He'd done a horrible job with Eirlys, not understanding at all what was happening until it was too late. Had it not been for Kye, who had walked this motherless path before Eirlys, and her generosity in providing a refuge for the young woman struggling to adapt to the changes that were overtaking her, he knew his little sister would not be even half the woman she was well on her way to becoming.

He didn't want to think where he himself would have been without Kye. It was bad enough to realize where he was now, and that he would be without her forever, having long ago lost her love and respect. And the only way to regain it was to do something he could not do. It did not matter what he wanted. Nor did it matter how much it hurt to want what he could not have.

"What's wrong?" Lux demanded.

He only then realized she had at last lifted her head to look at him. Fear glowed in her eyes, more than just fear of whatever misdeed he'd caught them in this time. She was, he realized, afraid he had bad news. And that they knew enough to fear that at their young age made his stomach knot even more.

He took in a breath to steady himself. Held up the stained tunic. "Explanation, please."

The two exchanged glances. If the situation had been more serious, he might have separated them for their stories, for they always backed each other up when together. Whoever spoke first, that was the version that stood, for neither of them would ever contradict the other. At least, not in his presence.

"It's a tunic," Lux said, her overly sweet tone telling him she knew perfectly well that wasn't the right answer, and also making him wonder if all females were born with the knack for that tone that any male would be wise to recognize as warning.

He issued a warning of his own. "Do not. Explain the blood."

"Blood?" they chorused innocently.

"Do you wish to shed more?" he countered, his voice as ominous as he could make it.

"We didn't shed that," Nyx said. Lux groaned as he indirectly answered the question.

"Who did? And why were you close enough that they bled on you?"

Again the exchange of glances. If they ever progressed to the point of actually communicating without speaking, which he wouldn't put past them, he would never keep up with them.

Finally, Lux shrugged, as if giving in. Nyx, as usual followed her lead. "It is Vank Kerrold's blood," he offered.

Drake blinked. "Jepson's nephew?"

Lux rolled her eyes skyward as he stated the obvious. The boy, a couple of years older than the twins, was a mirror image of his insufferable uncle. Except he was worse in the way only a teenaged bully could be.

"And how," he said carefully, "did Vank Kerrold's blood get on your clothing?"

Nyx sighed. "I punched him."

It was all Drake could do to quash the grin that threatened. Dear Eos, was he supposed to punish the boy for doing to Vank Kerrold what he himself had done to his uncle at almost the same age? Especially when more than likely he deserved it, and more?

"Why?" he asked.

Nyx went silent. He lowered his gaze to the floor and kept it there.

"Nyx?" he prodded.

When the boy stayed silent, Lux finally spoke up.

"He called you a coward—"

"So I called his uncle a traitor," Nyx finished.

"He swung—" They were in the familiar rhythm now.

"She tripped him—"

"And he punched him."

Succinct, he thought, even as his stomach knotted all over again. Would that some adults could report a situation with the same brevity and conciseness.

"You don't need to defend me," he said to the boy, his voice harsh.

Nyx's chin came up. "You won't."

"And besides, his uncle *is* a traitor," Lux said vehemently.

"Yes," Drake agreed, fighting for calm. "But should you take that out on him? Unless you want others to blame you for . . . my being your brother?"

Eos, he hated this. Nyx only shrugged, and lowered his gaze again. But Lux continued to stare at him.

"Sometimes," she said finally, "I just don't understand you."

"Sometimes, little one, neither do I." He sighed. "Just try not to draw any more blood, please?"

Realizing they were getting off easily, they turned as one and dashed toward the back door.

"Wait."

They skidded to a stop but didn't turn back.

"If I hear that word out of either of you again, the next blood you see will be from working your fingers to the bone scrubbing the taproom floor."

The glances they exchanged then were of pure horror, and he thought that might just keep them in line for at least an afternoon.

Unless something too tempting to resist cropped up.

Chapter 15

PALEDAN HID HIS distaste at the obvious preening of Barcon Ordam, who bustled into his office as if he were taking time out of his very busy schedule to meet with the new commander. He knew the type well; they had their uses, but that didn't mean he enjoyed dealing with them.

He cut off the florid welcome the man was spewing. "Tell me of Davorin."

Ordam grimaced. "He is to this day the biggest thorn in my side. The people, the ordinary people who refuse to forget, bemoan that there is no one to rise to take his place. They think him the greatest orator in Ziem history, and yet I have given many brilliant speeches myself. He is more than ten years dead and still they cling like lost children to his memory."

Paledan waited as Ordam droned on, thinking that if there was anything to bemoan on Ziem besides the miserable mist, it would be that this was the man they were forced to work with. A certain amount of cooperation from the locals made things easier in these places where portions of the infrastructure needed to be kept intact. In the case of Ziem, the mines must keep functioning, and thanks to their bedamned mist that wreaked havoc with Coalition equipment, that required the miners be left alive. Planium was tricky stuff, dangerous in its raw form, and no one knew its quirks better than those who had mined it for generations. The material was an essential resource, and for now it required Ziemites to mine it. Their own people were learning the mining, and their scientists were working on adapting equipment, but it would take time.

Ordam knew who the miners were, and who among them might be problems. He also knew about much of the population of Zelos, and, according to the logs, many potential troublemakers had been weeded out in the first passes, based on his guidance.

If the governor were anyone besides Sorkost, who required such sycophants to function, they would have rid themselves of him once they no longer needed him. Obviously he was of no help with the one remaining problem, the Raider, and keeping a traitor around, even if he was one who had aided you, had never seemed wise to him.

"I meant," Paledan said when Ordam's whine finally ebbed, "the taproom keeper, not his father."

"Drake?" The man sounded genuinely startled. "There is nothing to say. He's a pitiful, cowardly wreck."

There was so much satisfaction in Ordam's tone, it spiked Paledan's curiosity. "Ziem histories show he was not always."

"Oh, yes," Ordam said, dismissing his world's history with a fluttering wave of his hand. "He was as stubborn as his father in the beginning, fighting the inevitable, unable to see the benefit of the coming of the Coalition. And even after his father was removed, he continued, giving those same ridiculous speeches about freedom and self-determination." Ordam gave an inelegant snort that reminded Paledan of nothing less than a Carelian blowpig. "But what a surprise to his loyal followers when it turned out he was just a mother's pet. When she threw herself from Halfhead to her death, she might as well have taken him with her. Overnight, he became who you see today, broken, meek, and docile."

Again the satisfaction, Paledan thought, although that part of the tale did surprise him. While shocking, it didn't seem enough to dampen the fire of the man he'd read about. "You must have known him before we arrived."

"Of course. One could hardly help but know of the vaunted Drake Davorin." The satisfaction shifted to remembered disgust. His lip actually curled with it. "It was nauseating, the accolades poured upon him. Beloved by all, especially foolish females, best climber and hunter on Ziem, leader at the institute in both academics and athletics, being groomed to fill his father's shoes at the Council." And then the satisfaction snapped back. "But he is not his father, could not be further from him in fact."

"And yet it seems to me there is more to him than what appears on the surface now."

"You're wrong," the man said sharply. Then, as if remembering whom he was speaking to, he hastily added in a conciliatory tone, "You just haven't been here long enough, Major. You will soon see Drake Davorin is nothing more than a coward. He will cause you no trouble."

"I think you and I might have very different ideas of what constitutes trouble," he murmured to himself after the man had gone.

He turned his gaze to his viewscreen, where an image of Torstan Davorin glowed. Once he had weeded out the Coalition rhetoric, he thought he had the bones of the man's story. He had indeed been the flashpoint for what resistance there had been, and it had been unexpectedly strong. Which was to the man's credit, despite the Coalition spin that it was merely the logistics of this rugged planet and its perpetual mist that had made this conquering take two full years. Paledan was adept at both reading between the lines and combining official reports with battle reports and arriving at something near the truth, which was that Torstan Davorin had inspired his woefully unprepared people to hold on for much longer than the Coalition had ever anticipated.

And his son had seemed well suited to continue that battle, indeed, had picked up his father's ceremonial saber while it was still wet with blood, and had rallied the stunned fighters into nearly taking the Coalition gun that had arrived to quell the disturbance. And the younger Davorin had fought on, even after the main resistance had ended.

And then he had stopped. Abruptly. Had given up, retreated, become the cowed, beaten taproom keeper who was whispered about and called coward in all quarters. Paledan was somewhat surprised Sorkost had let him live, until he realized the daily presence of the defeated warrior, the sight of him as a lowly tapper submissively serving the Coalition, was worth much more than a death that might have turned him into the same kind of martyr as his father had become.

He knew this had not sprung from any wisdom of Sorkost, but rather simply a perverse enjoyment the man took in grinding people beneath his boots.

But nowhere in all the voluminous Coalition records and reports could he find any clue that told him why. Why Davorin had suddenly given up, why he had turned his back on his father's legacy, laid down his sword, and changed into a very different sort of man practically overnight. It had to be more than the mother's suicide. Wouldn't that have inspired him to even further resistance? That the Coalition had taken both his parents from him?

It had been Paledan's experience that there was always a reason when a man changed so radically. And when it was the man who had once so rallied opposition to the Coalition, it was not in his nature to give up until he had an answer he was satisfied with.

And so his questions about the quiet, inhibited taproom keeper remained.

THE LINGERING intoxication of the successful air rover raid, plus a bit of brew the Raider had okayed, was still carrying them. When Kye arrived at the ruin, she was greeted cheerfully with grins and back slaps. And one slap on her backside from Maxon, because he was slightly inebriated. She smiled at him, but not before she'd put him on the ground on his own backside. She also accrued several approving comments on her stenciled artwork, still scattered about the city, and the beautiful irony that the Coalition was having trouble wiping it out because they were short of paint.

"We're not," she said blithely, earning another round of raucous, cheering laughter, and calls that the Spirit had surely been with her. She might have to broach the possibility of another round, she thought. Perhaps with a new design.

But first, she had something else to do. Something it had taken her far too long to work up to. But now that she had, she would let nothing divert her.

When she entered the Raider's quarters, Brander was with him, and they were laughing. It took her aback; she did not think she had ever heard him laugh in the six months she had been with him.

But when he saw her, he went still, and half turned away, settling that blessed helmet. It would sting, if she let it, but she could not. She had worked up her courage on the trek up the mountain in the darkness, and she would not let it fail now.

"And we could all be dead tomorrow, if the Coalition decided it."

Eirlys's words had rung in her head and the image of that huge cannon, looming over the city, had haunted her every step of the way. And by the time she got here, she was convinced the worst fate of all would be to die without ever having told him how she felt. And she would never have a better time than now, when all had gone so well. She had to know if she was alone in this, because if she was, she needed to start building some kind of wall around her heart.

Maybe Brander could teach her about that. He seemed to do it well enough.

"Could you give us a moment, please?" she asked her cousin.

Brander's gaze shot to the Raider, who, after a moment's hesitation as unlike him as the laugh, nodded. Only then did Brander leave them. It was another moment before he turned to face her, one brow lifted in query, barely visible below the rim of the helmet.

And then she did not know how to start.

"Do you never remove it?" she asked, eying the ever-present silver covering.

"You would not like it if I did."

"Wrong. I would not care."

His mouth twisted. Bitterly? She couldn't tell, given how little she could see of his face.

"Oh," he said, "you would."

"I would be saddened at your injury, and the pain you must have endured. Angry that it happened. And even regretful that I did not know you before. But nothing could change how I feel now."

There. It was out. She met his gaze, held it, daring him to deny he understood what she meant.

"Kye," he began, and stopped.

"We could all die tomorrow," she said, "and I must know. Even if it is to learn how big a fool I am."

"It does not matter. It can't matter."

"It matters to me."

For the first time, the Raider lowered his eyes. "We cannot."

Kye lifted her chin. "Nor can we pretend this does not exist."

"I know."

Kye sighed. "Then what would you have me do?"

"What would I have? What you will not do. Stay safe."

"And leave you to fight this war for me?"

He looked up then. She stared at him for a long, silent moment. She had only his eyes, dark-rimmed blue ice, to judge by. But she saw a knowledge there, understanding.

"You know what I feel," she whispered.

"I know," he repeated. Then, as if it were against his will, he added, "I know it exactly."

Because he felt the same way? Her heart gave a tiny leap in her chest.

"It cannot be. For so many reasons."

"Name them," she demanded.

"Kye—"

"Name them," she repeated, "for that is the only way I can abide it, if I have it in my head, in your voice."

He closed his eyes for a moment, leaving her only the scars, the helmet, for her to focus on. When they snapped open again, it only emphasized the power of them, of his steady, unwavering gaze. And when he spoke, it was sharp, rapid-fire, like bursts from a blaster.

"In this kind of war, you can't care. I've told your cousin I consider myself already dead. It is not a death wish," he said even as she began to object, "because I think of each day I am still here to fight as a gift. But caring means you can no longer do what's necessary. Especially if it means using one you care about as a tool or a weapon. And caring gives your enemy the most powerful weapon that exists."

She was wincing inwardly as if each word were a blow. Not because they were harsh, uncompromising, but because they were true.

"What most powerful weapon?" It was all she could manage.

"A lever."

A lever they could use against him. And she had no illusions that the Coalition wouldn't do exactly that, were they to discover the Raider had a vulnerability. No, she could deny none of it. And yet she clung desperately. "And if this battle ended tomorrow?"

"It will not."

"But if it did," she insisted.

"Ifs, and wishes," he said softly, "are for children in a sane world. You are not a child, nor is our world sane."

So he would not give her even that much.

She turned on her heel and left without a word. And set about walling off her heart.

Chapter 16

DRAKE WATCHED AS the new post commander stood in the doorway of the taproom. The man scanned the crowd, and he saw his gaze snag on each Coalition member in the busy room. Not long enough to be noticed, unless you were looking for it as Drake was, just enough to register their presence.

His assessment of Paledan was by needs swift; it wouldn't do to draw attention by staring at the new Coalition boss. But he felt he'd learned much in that quick look; with some men, you knew instinctively what they were made of. And this man, tall with close-cropped hair, lean but muscled, and with an unreadable expression, was made of stern stuff. He was alert, watchful, and even though he appeared relaxed, Drake sensed he was ready for anything.

"Hurry it up with that brew," one of those called out from the table where Brander was holding his game.

Tonight was a night he could use some help in here. Every seat was taken, the bar was shoulder to shoulder, and he'd been running full bore for two hours now. But this was exactly the kind of night he did not want Eirlys in here, even without Jakel, so he was on his own. And he once more acknowledged the irony of his position, that anyone who would be willing to work for sympathizer Drake Davorin wasn't somebody he wanted to hire.

He pumped out the brew, having to do it by hand since under Coalition rationing they were running on the minimum tier of power for another few minutes yet. Then he hastened over to the back table with two foaming mugs, dodging the occasionally reeling drunk, a tricky task in the dim light. He set the full strength one in front of the man who'd yelled, who now scooped it up and took a huge gulp. The other mug—indistinguishable and yet intentionally less potent—he put in front of Brander. For an instant, as he set the mug down, his back was to the rest of the room, and he saw Brander's eyes flick toward the doorway. He gave the barest nod to indicate he'd seen the major come in.

"Busy night," Brander said, lifting the mug. Then, casually, he added, "I wonder why?"

His answer was a huge burp from the man guzzling the brew, followed by a crude laugh.

"Answer, or opinion?" Brander asked dryly.

Don't antagonize him.

But so well established was Brander's reputation as a careless wastrel that the man only laughed again.

"Haven't you heard? We're celebrating the departure of our not so beloved commandant."

Since the man wasn't looking at him, Drake risked a glance toward the doorway. The new man had stepped inside, slowly, clearly in no hurry. And, Drake guessed, taking in every corner of the room, and every occupant in it, Coalition or not.

"What if the new one is worse?" Brander asked, in a tone that said it meant nothing to him.

The man downed another gulp of brew. Then he leaned in and said in a low voice, "Haven't you heard? We're getting Paledan. The man's a bedamned hero."

"Well, that would be a change," Brander said.

The Coalition man snorted with laughter. Slapped down his mug, slopping brew over the rim. Drake pulled the bar rag from his apron pocket and set about dutifully wiping up the mess. The man ignored him. He was only the tapper, after all.

"Frall was a fool. Thought awards for being a desk minder were worth the same as those won in battle."

Brander laughed, and the half-drunk trooper grinned. He played them very, very well, Drake thought as Brander picked up the dice scattered across the table and seemed intent merely on getting them back into the toss cup as he asked, "I gather your new leader is different?"

"Paledan's got more medals then any major in the Coalition. And honestly earned ones at that. Turned down the honorary garbage. And promotions as well. No desk chain for him."

"Did that make them angry?" Drake dared to ask. "Is that why such a hero ended up posted here?"

He saw the man's brow furrow as if he were trying to figure out the question. Or as if some part of his brew-numbed mind realized that there was a subtle insult to himself in there; after all, he was posted here. Drake busied himself with the last of the spillover, as if whether the man answered or not mattered little.

Finally, the trooper shrugged. "Rumor has it he was wounded on Darvis, and will only be here until he's fully operational again."

Drake considered that silently. The man certainly didn't move as if he were injured. However it was, with effort, possible to hide such things.

And then the man leaned forward again, to whisper, "But some of us think he's here to take out that damned raider."

Brander never missed a beat but rattled the cup with the dice thoroughly, as if all that mattered was getting them thoroughly mixed.

"Your toss, I believe?" he said, holding out the cup.

"And let me top off that brew for you," Drake said, "after that spill. No charge, of course."

That was one good thing about a full room tonight, he thought as he followed through on the words. He could afford the little extras that kept the men like that trooper coming back.

When Drake at last settled behind the bar again, the major had yet to take a seat, although more than one Coalition member offered their own to their new commander. The man was now standing near, but not at the bar. Even as he looked, he saw the man notice the mirror behind the bottles, and turn to face it. Drake had the feeling it was the only reason the man would ever turn his back on a crowded room; he was using it just as Drake did. It was ostensibly there to highlight the reds, ambers, clear sparkle, and rich browns of the various brews, but for Drake, it served the purpose of allowing him to observe the entire room surreptitiously.

The lights came on as the Coalition allowed them the three hours of normal power. There was the typical moment of silence as everyone reacted, then the low drone of taproom chatter resumed. Drake was never sure the lights were an improvement on nights like this, but it made his job easier.

He switched out the wet rag for a dry one, then reached to turn on the pumpers on the brewtaps. As he did, he noticed the new man's focus had shifted.

He was staring at the painting, now lit by the spotlight above it.

Most men did stare, when they first saw it. It was, after all, a beautiful portrait of a beautiful woman. They were taken by her slender, almost delicate figure, the gleam of the white silk as it flowed over her body, the pure Ziem blue of her eyes, and perhaps most of all, the vivid red of the mane of hair that tumbled down her back in a fiery fall. There was an otherworldly feel to the image, and to those who knew who she was, it added another layer of sadness to her story.

But most who came into the taproom these days had no idea they were looking at the wife of Ziem's greatest hero, the woman who had inspired the orator, who in turn had stirred a world to rebellion. They saw only the beautiful woman she had been, and assumed that was the reason for the portrait's presence.

"Who?"

Drake froze. He wasn't certain the word had been directed at him, it had been spoken so quietly. And the man had never even glanced at him. But this was the new commander of the Coalition forces on Ziem, and it would not do to anger him so soon.

"Sir?" he asked, politely.

Paledan glanced at him. "The woman."

He shrugged, but underneath he was very aware this could be treacherous. "She is long dead, forgotten. But it is a lovely painting, is it not?"

"Dead?" The man's gaze shifted back to the painting. Odd, Drake thought, he sounded genuinely saddened, unlike most who simply paid lip service to the news and went on about their drinking.

"Yes. A suicide."

Paledan's head snapped around. "That woman," he said, sounding disbelieving, "killed herself?"

Interesting, Drake thought. "Leaving four children behind to fend for themselves."

The man's gaze narrowed. And for a moment, Drake had the feeling Paledan knew exactly who she was. If so, the man truly did his studying, to know this so soon after his arrival.

"And the artist?"

It was all Drake could do to keep his expression even. No one ever asked that question. That this man had was a many-faceted warning.

"Some local student at the time, I believe," he said carefully, keeping his hands busy with glassware.

"No mere student produced that."

"A very gifted one?" he suggested.

"A prodigy, nothing less, if that is true."

That, I cannot argue with. And he wondered what this new Coalition commander would say if he knew that prodigy, that brilliant artist who should be famous across the sector, who should be painting beautiful portraits and glorious landscapes, was instead running with that notorious brigand. And was behind those mysterious, evocative, and spirit-lifting images of the Raider that had appeared all over the city and countryside on longnight.

Worse, he wondered what this new commander would do if he knew. Because it was already very clear Major Caze Paledan was a much different breed than old Parthon Frall.

"DID I SAY I WAS always glad to see new blood in a game?"

Brander's words were sour as he stared across the table at the man who sat opposite him.

"Problem?" the man said mildly.

"Just my run of abysmal luck." Brander hoped he sounded suitably irritated, but not really angry. He was neither, because things were proceeding according to plan.

Well, except for the fact that he very begrudgingly liked the guy. Or the way he played, at least. It had taken three games for him to even begin to get the man's measure, and that was unusual enough to pique his interest above and beyond the task at hand.

As for the man himself, every warning bell in Brander's gut had gone off at his first sight of the new commander of the Legion Post. No strutting, puffing bird, this one. Tall, broad, Coalition Major Caze Paledan had the stride, the grace, the demeanor, and the steady gaze of a fighter. And those eyes, a bright shade of green, gave away nothing yet seemed to see everything.

No, this was no payback appointment, or family partiality. And yet, no real fighter would want to be posted here, with little chance to use his skills. Was the speculation he had been wounded true, and was he here only until he was healed enough to return to full-strength Coalition conquering? There was no sign of an injury, but Brander guessed he was also the type who would conceal such a thing if possible. No sign of weakness to make him vulnerable would be allowed, if he was reading the man right.

"It must be your luck," Paledan agreed, his voice still bland. "Your skills seem well enough."

"Do they?"

A smile flitted around the corners of his mouth. "I've heard you're the best player in Zelos."

He'd been here less than three days and he'd heard this? Brander checked off three more things on his mental list; the man clued-up quickly, did his study, and perhaps most important, had not gone searching for easier prey.

"People who lose," Brander said, "often look for reasons that may or may not be there."

Paledan laughed. The full, hearty laugh of one genuinely amused.

And one utterly confident in his abilities.

Frall had been a fool, a graceless bumbler with little intelligence and less nerve. It had been almost easy to get things past him, or convince him that no one in Zelos would dare join the Raider.

Paledan was no kind of fool. And Brander knew instinctively he would be the worst kind of enemy.

He grimaced inwardly. He glanced over at the bar, where Drake was cleaning up, preparing to close. He looked, as he often had lately, exhausted.

He looked back across the table to see Paledan watching him intently.

"Problem?"

Brander resisted the urge to look away; of all opponents across a game table, this one must never think he had anything to hide except a good hand.

"Near closing time," he said blandly.

"Perhaps another time we can continue," Paledan said just as blandly.

"I wouldn't miss it."

He watched the man go with the certainty that life in Zelos, and probably all of Ziem, would completely change once more. Caze Paledan was the kind of man who had that effect.

He gathered up the dice. The Raider would adapt, he knew. But he wondered if their days had just become numbered. Because Caze Paledan was also the kind of man who got things done. Coalition things. And Brander knew ending the Raider had to be very high on that list.

Chapter 17

THE RAIDER CROUCHED in the shadow of the wall, watching the vehicle approach. He signaled the others with a sharp gesture, and both of them spread out and took their own cover. He'd told them all of the goal; he didn't want these men to unknowingly die for a load of communicators that they couldn't use for fear of the Coalition overhearing. Destroying them to keep the Coalition from having them was a valid objective, and if they were successful, that would be well and good and he'd leave the card to claim the victory. If not, they would simply melt into the mist and leave them wondering.

The ponderous cargo mover was slow, slow enough that waiting was a chore. He had tasked the other two Sentinels with keeping any citizens who might be in the area safely clear, although it was unlikely many would be out for a stroll here, at the back of the Coalition compound. But it was more likely here than at the well-guarded front gate, so he issued the order.

He allowed himself a brief smile at the large patch of scraped paint on the side of the big transport. He'd seen many of them today, and knew the scrapes were where they had tried to eradicate any sign of Kye's stenciled silhouettes.

As he watched the huge vehicle, the Raider found himself thinking of the sheer massiveness of the Coalition and the smile faded. It was something he didn't allow himself to contemplate often. He could not afford to care about the size of them overall; he only cared about eradicating them from Ziem. And he knew he walked a line finer than the hair of a hedgebeast between keeping the occupying force too busy to focus on murdering more Ziemites, and annoying them so much they decided they would find a way to do without the miners and rained their full wrath upon them all.

They had been so isolated here on Ziem that they had known little of the behemoth that had taken over the far side of the galaxy in the past half-century. But once the Coalition had learned of their immense reserves of planium, they had suddenly moved to the top of the list for Coalition attention.

We were not even ill-prepared for it. We were completely unprepared. Unprepared, unsuspecting, untrained, and unqualified to resist.

The Coalition must have laughed at how easy it had been. They had a near-unlimited supply of something they needed tons of, and had gained it with barely a token resistance. Torstan Davorin had seen it coming from the beginning, but by the time people had begun to listen, it had already been too late. His father had managed to keep the resistance going for two full years, but in the end, it had claimed his life and many others.

He diverted his thoughts with the ease of long practice. He noticed that the mist had, as he'd hoped, begun to settle as the sun began to drop behind the Sentinel. A few more minutes, and the top of the compound wall would be obscured to anyone without the vision. Surprise hinged on that happening before the cargo mover arrived at this gate.

It was, perhaps, a reckless stunt. As Kye had told him with no small amount of energy.

"Let someone else do it; the danger is too great."

"The very reason I will not."

"It is what you would tell me"

"Yes. But not what the Raider must do."

"You need to stay safe."

"Staying safe is not how you build a legend."

"And you wish to be a legend?"

"It's not what I wish. I never wanted this, deciding for others. But it's what Ziem needs."

What Ziem needs. And to hades with what he needed, which was a dark-haired, turquoise-eyed woman with the eye of an artist—or a sharpshooter—and an unconquerable spirit.

A woman he could not have.

He gave a short shake of his head to clear it of all thought except what came next. The mist had settled enough. It would happen.

In the moment the lumbering vehicle reached the turn in the road that led toward the gate, the moment when the trees would obscure the line of sight from there to here, he leapt. He caught the top of the wall with his fingers and levered his way up to where he could swing one foot up to catch the top as well. He visualized the thin red line Brander's spray had revealed. The perimeter sensor stretched between the upright columns of the wall. He knew it would be a close thing to slide under it without triggering the warning signal, especially wearing the two weapons he carried.

He flattened himself atop the wall. Inched to the other side, holding his breath, fearing even the rise of his chest would break the beam and set off the warning claxon. For an instant, he thought he had, but the silence remained unbroken except for the sound of the approaching transport.

The Coalition penchant for thick, solid walls was going to hurt them here, he thought, for it would give him room to stand without breaking the beam once he was atop the barrier. He was hidden in the mist, but he could hear the cargo transport as it neared the gate.

He saw the front of the vehicle gradually take shape through the gray. Then the top of the cargo compartment. It came closer. The gates slid open, he guessed triggered by a control within the vehicle since there were no guards at this delivery gate that received only routine shipments.

The cab of the vehicle passed through the gate. The body was so wide it barely cleared the side posts of the gate. It inched forward carefully. A quarter through. Now a half.

He stood. Unslung the first weapon, his long gun. Put it to his shoulder. Aimed at the roof of the cargo compartment. Fired. Immediately slung the long gun back over his shoulder. At this range, the cartridge, trailing a line of green glowmist with its heat, put a foot-round hole in the roof. As he'd hoped, the driver either heard the sound, or perhaps felt the hit.

The vehicle stopped. A stationary target. He grabbed the much heavier, blockier, second weapon. He would have only one chance at this. But he trusted his eye, his skill, and his knowledge of the refractive ways of Ziem mist. He fired.

The shell went through the hole without even touching the edge.

He threw himself flat on the top of the wall. Setting off the alarm meant nothing now. The claxon blared, and the lights along the top of the wall came on in a flare of brilliant light.

The shell exploded. Brander had packed it well, and it destroyed the cargo compartment completely. It sent up a swirling, furious cloud of flame and smoke that brightened the sky even more than the lights. To them, the roiling cloud of glowmist was as bright as a beacon. He felt the heat from here, grimaced as it got a bit too hot for comfort. The driver staggered out of the transport. He heard shouts from across the compound as the Coalition troops scrambled to head for the breach.

The instant the flames receded enough he stood. Aware he was silhouetted by the flames and the lights, he gauged how long he had before they would be within range to take him. He bent and fastened a placard to the column that was blackened now.

Without warning indeed.

He straightened. Timing was of the essence now. He looked over his shoulder, saw that Galeth was already at the road, urging a man out of the way.

When he knew he could wait no longer, he threw up an arm in signal. His coat swirled, accentuating the movement. In the instant the air rover came into view, a shot whistled past his ear, and he knew it would be only a second, maybe two, before they had him sighted in. Galeth pushed the rover to a speed that was reckless given he was headed straight for the smoking pyre of the transport. The nimble little flyer shot through the smoke and was there, slowing but not stopping below his position.

He jumped.

By dint of long practice, he landed perfectly in the cockpit. Galeth hit the controls and the rover leapt to full speed. Shots were coming in a constant barrage now, but most flew uselessly over their heads thanks to the smoke. A couple struck the rover, but not for nothing had Brander been working on its armor; they barely dented it. And in between the reports he heard a peal of raucous, joyous laughter as the man Galeth had ushered away watched.

"The Raider!" the man shouted in glee.

He looked back, saw the troopers trapped behind the ruined hulk, unable to pursue until they got to their own rovers. And even then, they would never catch them; Brander had worked some of his magic on this one, and added a nice bit to the top speed and to its altitude capability.

Still, they took the pre-planned evasive route, leading any possible followers far away from their eventual destination. Only when they were certain there was no one anywhere close did they return the rover to its hide and make their way to the ruin on foot.

Brander was already there, waiting. And his own squad of Sentinels were lively enough that the Raider guessed even before his second spoke.

"Mission accomplished," he said. "We got it."

He turned and threw a heavy cover off a large weapon, clearly encased in planium, with a distinctive base and complicated-looking mechanics.

A Coalition rail gun.

Brander was grinning. The men around him were grinning.

"Nice diversion, sir!" one of them called out.

He let them celebrate; it was an occasion worthy of it. And when the word came in the morning that news of the Raider's daring act had spread everywhere among the people, he even allowed himself a smile.

The legend, the hope Ziem needed was building.

Chapter 18

"A RAIL GUN?"

The incredulous query made the man sitting across from Major Caze Paledan shift uneasily on the hard wooden chair, for at least the third time in as many minutes. It seemed Ordam was even more nervous than the last time he'd been here. Perhaps the mere discussion of the Raider struck fear into him. He seemed the type.

"Who is this raider?" he demanded.

"It was not him," Ordam said hastily. "He was in town—"

"Blowing up a cargo transport," Paledan snapped.

"Er . . . yes."

"A diversion, you fool. Who is he?"

"Some say," Ordam began hesitantly, "it is the ghost of Torstan Davorin."

Paledan barely managed not to snort his disgust of such theories. "And you believe this?"

"Of course not. I only say that is what some believe. That, or that it's Davorin himself, that he somehow is not dead."

"I have seen the recordings of the day he died," Paledan said dryly. There was absolutely no doubt that, save his head, the man had been reduced to fragments of bone and tissue no bigger than his own thumb. He'd seen firsthand what a rail gun did to a human body, and the survival rate was zero.

"And I saw his head," Ordam said.

"Then we have dispensed with that irrationality," Paledan said. "So who is this raider in fact?"

"No one knows."

He lifted a brow at the man. "No one?"

"It is . . . common knowledge," Ordam added hastily.

"So it is common knowledge that no one knows?"

If the man saw the absurdity, it didn't show. Paledan didn't bother himself about it; men who never looked beyond the surface failed on their own, one way or another.

"Yes," Ordam said. "But it wouldn't matter if they did. They would protect him," he added with clear disgust. "And they condemn me. Fools."

For hating the man who handed them over to an invader?

Paledan had few illusions about the Coalition. He knew too much, had seen too much. For that matter, he had done too much to hold on to any illusions, acknowledging it was necessary for the long-term goal of keeping the machinery oiled and moving. He had achieved his own position because he was not subject to emotions; he was harshly efficient, excellent at reading people and predicting their actions, and unmoved by the plight of those foolish enough to believe anything the size of the Coalition could be benevolent.

And he had little sympathy for those who buckled so easily, who wouldn't fight for themselves or their world. In the case of Ziem, he suspected they had naively assumed their distant location and damp, misty climate would protect them. Not that the blasted mist wasn't an obstacle, but when weighed against the lure of a huge supply of planium, it was a mere irritation. And, as usual, there had been some people willing to trade their world's sovereignty for individual reward, who welcomed the coming of the dominant—soon to be only—power in the galaxy, as long as they benefitted from it. In that, people were sadly consistent.

"And where does he strike from?"

"The mountains."

Given that Zelos was surrounded by mountains, that was almost as helpful as saying "Ziem."

"Just how hard have you tried to discover who this man is?"

"Very hard," Ordam retorted instantly. "No one wishes that pestilence gone more than I. But the results are unvarying. No one knows who he really is, where he came from, not even his own followers. By his command."

Now that was interesting.

"His own command?"

"It is said he orders it, so that no one can be forced to betray him."

He leaned back in his chair, studying the man before him. "Ziem's total population is a quarter that of any other planet the Coalition has reached. Two-thirds of those live here in Zelos. And you're saying no one recognizes this man?"

"Have you not heard? The man is hideously scarred."

"I have heard."

And if the scars are all you see, if you notice nothing else about him, not his height, his build, his way of moving, his mannerisms, then you are even bigger fools than I thought.

Ordam glanced quickly around as if he feared a hidden watcher, then whispered, "They say he wears that helmet not to protect from injury but to hide something even worse than the scars that are visible. Some say there is no flesh left on his skull beneath it."

Paledan didn't bother to ask who "they" were. He'd encountered enough of the types who simply had to have a horror story to pass around, for the momentary importance it gave them. In their own minds, anyway.

"This is all you know?"

"It's all I want to know," Ordam said with a shudder that was visible.

And I'm sure you are very good at limiting your knowledge to what you want to know.

He dismissed the man with a wave of his hand. Ordam stood, hastily, but then hesitated.

"Something else?" Paledan asked, not bothering to disguise his distaste for the man.

There was another moment of hesitation before Ordam asked, "Does this mean you intend to do something about him? I only ask because . . . Frall never did."

Paledan's gaze narrowed sharply; he might not think much of the bumbler himself, but he would not tolerate such disrespect for an officer from a man he thought even less of.

"Are you referring to Coalition Major Frall?" he asked, his tone icy.

"I . . . of course. I'm sorry."

"We're finished," Paledan said flatly.

"Yes, sir." Ordam nearly tripped over his own feet in his hurry to leave.

When the man had gone, Paledan leaned back in his chair, steepling his fingers before him. He thought about the orders Legion Command had given him. Or rather, the result the Coalition expected; how he got there was left up to him. Which was both a mark of his own reputation, and the Coalition habit of deniability; what they hadn't specifically ordered, they could not be held accountable for. Not that they cared what they were blamed for; the more horror stories that circulated, the more fear existed, which suited their purposes.

Besides, when everyone was following the same handbook, orders didn't need to be spelled out. He didn't need to be told all Ziemites except for the planium miners were expendable; that was a given.

But he also knew that wiping out the rest of the population, including their families, could tip the miners into a refusal to work. When men lost everything they loved, they seemed to no longer care about life or death. He did not possess or quite understand such emotions, but he knew they existed. He knew as well that the lack made him an oddity, but it also meant that by not being prey to emotions, he was better able to see the necessary path through them.

He leaned forward and keyed the comm system.

"Brakely."

"Sir?" his aide answered almost instantly. Marl Brakely had once been a rising star, expected to go as far as his famous uncle, who had made his reputation as the much-honored commander of the *Brightstar*, a premiere Coalition battleship. Commander Brayton Brakely had survived, barely, the misfortune of having had two traitors serving together on his crew. That they did not turn traitor until long after they had left the *Brightstar* did not alleviate, in the Coalition mind, the fact that they were the two most infamous and grievous traitors the Coalition had ever known: Califa Claxton and Shaylah Graymist.

Commander Brakely's heroic career and stellar history had saved him then, but it had not saved him from Coalition rage after the second defeat on

Arellia just a few months ago. The Coalition had taken out its anger on the man who had been in charge during the battle that had ended with Coalition forces unable to even approach for fear of being blasted to bits all over again by the unexpectedly fierce resistance of a people they had thought easily defeatable.

Something those who thought the same of Ziem might be wise to remember.

Brakely's nephew had been condemned to the same fate, having first committed the sin of being a cadet at Claxton's much vaunted academy at the time of her betrayal, and now being related to his disgraced uncle. Such was Coalition thinking. He saw the sense of it; if you knew your entire extended family would pay for your sins, you were more likely to think thrice before betraying your masters.

But, by the other side of the token, saving someone from that fate earned you a kind of loyalty it was hard to gain any other way. So plucking the younger Brakely out of the death line had been a calculated move that had paid off well. When he had offered him the position as his aide, the look in the man's eyes told him he had assessed him accurately. And the man had served him loyally ever since. Now there were few he trusted more.

Although there was no one he trusted completely.

He glanced at the document open on his viewscreen. Claxton's classic *Aerial Combat Tactics*. Although he was not a pilot, the treatise had always been in his collection for the simple reason that, in the end, surprisingly for an air fighter, Claxton had agreed with him. Or rather, the other way around, given that he'd been all of fifteen when he'd first read it. She'd stated that while great strides could be made by air in any battle, it could not be finished without troops on the ground.

Of course, agreeing with a notorious traitor was never a good thing to advertise.

Of Graymist and Claxton, Claxton had been the harder for him to believe; he'd studied all her writings on tactics and strategy and thought her a genius. He'd regretted that her academy had been closed before he'd been old enough to attend; he'd been looking forward to it for years. But it had been bombed to rubble after her defection to the Triotian forces. A defection the Coalition had tried to cover up, but she was too well known, and the whole Triotian fiasco too big to hide for long. Someone had fallen down on the job; someone should have noticed what was going on with Claxton a lot sooner.

And he'd be damned to hades if he would fall into that trap. If he was ever beaten, it would not be because he failed to track potential threats.

"Gather everything you can find on this raider," he said over the comm link. "I want it all, fact or legend, any rumor you can pick up, including hearsay and speculation."

"I've already begun, Major."

And that, Paledan thought, was the mark of a good aide, anticipating what his commander would want. "Excellent," he said.

"Do you want what I have so far?"

He considered that. "No. I want to see it all at once. But make it your first priority, Brakely."

"Yes, sir."

And in the meantime, he would change into civilian clothes and take a walk through the streets of Zelos before the night curfew. Not many knew what he looked like yet, and he might be able to pick up something of interest himself.

Chapter 19

THE MIST HAD vanished.

The sky glowed clear and blue, and the white light of the center star blazed over Ziem and burned off the near-constant fog. Some claimed they could even see the second star, tiny and distant, behind the center star. With a sigh, Drake thought of the time when a day like this would have sent many scurrying to the observation center to take a look through the big scope. But the center was controlled by the Coalition now, and no one wished to draw that much attention to themselves. Especially given the suspicious nature of the Coalition scientists that ran it; they were unable to accept innate curiosity in those they thought beneath them in intelligence, and thus attributed any interest to subversive reasons.

As if looking at the center star would help somehow.

He shrugged off the feeling of futility that had overtaken him last night. It was stronger now than it had ever been, yet with less reason. They had a rail gun now, which was no small feat. Yet it still seemed small, if he let himself think about the galactic might of the Coalition. If he let this feeling grow, take hold, he would not be able to rouse himself to any kind of action, including getting out of his bed in the morning.

How did you do it, Father? How did you keep going, in the face of insurmountable odds and the viciousness of the Coalition tyrants?

As always, no answer came to him. And so he did the only thing he could do at the moment, and set about his daily work. Donning the apron that had become his regular attire here, he focused on wiping down the bar, sweeping the floor yet again, and setting the chairs at every table neatly on the floor. As if each task was the only thing of import in his life. As if each thing required every ounce of his concentration. For right now, the only thing that mattered was keeping his mind from straying to things that had no answer except pain.

When he reached the table in the corner, where Brander held his games of chaser, he paused. He'd seen the new post commander come in again last night. He'd heard the whispers among the patrons first, then turned to look. The air of command about the man was unmistakable. It wasn't just his breadth of shoulder or steady gaze, it was something more intangible but very real, a sort of presence that spoke of confidence and the skill to back it up.

And after the man had gone—with, according to the buzz, a sizeable chunk of Brander's coin—he saw in his friend's expression a combination of grim contemplation and respect. Not a good combination for the people of Zelos.

Brander would go up the mountain, where they could discuss his assessment in detail, later. The mountain where his sister was likely roaming at this moment.

And, that quickly, he was back to that nagging concern, keeping Eirlys alive and safe. She might be nearing adulthood, but she was still and would ever be his little sister. Her safety was his responsibility, as was that of the twins. It was a difficult load to carry, but there was no one else. This was not the life he had wanted, expected, or would have chosen, but it was the life he had. He must balance it as best he could.

For a brief moment, he allowed himself to think of a time ahead, when Nyx and Lux would also reach, Eos willing, adulthood. Then, perhaps, he could turn to his own life. If there was anything left of it. He shook his head sharply. He'd already lost Kye in one form; did not dare let her in in his other guise. Better to assume there would be nothing if and when this was over, than to hold out hope and have it shattered.

He would always feel a responsibility toward all three of his siblings, especially the twins, but even they would be off to make their own way eventually. Hopefully wiser and more cautious than they were now.

And he grimaced at the thought of how much trouble those two could get into were he not here to disentangle them. It was a sobering thought.

It suddenly all seemed too much. He threw the wipe rag down on the chaser table, turned, and walked out the back door. The normally dark alley behind the taproom was flooded with golden light. The noises from the street, mostly troopers shouting orders, seemed distant, even without the mist to muffle them. He closed his eyes and tilted his head back, letting the warm rays wash over him. But after a moment, he opened them again and looked around. The alley itself was not improved by the brightness; there were things piled here and there that were probably best when hidden by the usual mist. And the aroma that was rising, of discarded leavings that had no doubt attracted muckrats and other charming scavengers, and the signs of a flock of squawkers that nested in the various abandoned buildings, could also do with the cooling effect of the mist. Gone were the days when Zelos had been spotless, when no one would have thought of leaving a trail of garbage behind them.

He himself preferred the mist anyway, the foggy coolness, although he didn't mind this occasional visit by the light. This one was unseasonal, given they were still in the early rebirth months, but it would fade soon enough, perhaps until it returned in the sun-season and stayed for several weeks.

A noise drew his attention. A scrabbling sort of sound in the alcove of the back door of the old weapons shop, long ago closed by the Coalition, across the way. He saw only a large, male figure, but something about the way he was moving warned him, in the instant before a tiny, terrified scream hit his ears.

A child. He reacted instantly. Instinctively. He moved, as quickly as he could and still maintain stealth. The dark figure—a hulking man in a Coalition uniform of guard rank—didn't turn, didn't seem to be aware of his approach. He was intent on his prey, a small girl not even as old as Lux, who was struggling wildly against his crushing grip.

He had no weapon. The man had at least half again his body weight on him.

You fight with what you have.

Drake freed the ties on his apron. Pulled it off in the last few steps. In the moment he got within reach, the man jerked away the hand that had been covering the girl's mouth. Drake heard a sharp curse. The girl screamed. Louder now.

"Bite me, will you?" the man growled out.

Good girl.

The man lifted his hand for a blow. Drake took the last two steps. Lifted the heavy cloth of the apron. In a split second, he had it over the man's head, over his face, with the ties wrapped around his neck holding it in place. Now sightless, attacked from behind, the man roared. His hands flailed toward the blaster at his belt. Drake pulled the ties tighter. Then grabbed the blaster from its sheath. The temptation to use it, to blast this child assaulter to tiny pieces, was strong. Only the likely aftermath stopped him. He tossed it aside.

He dodged the man's blows, wild and blind, easily. Pulled back even harder. Forced the man to stagger back. His shouts were mere strangled gasps now. The brute stumbled over the rough stones of the alley. Went down hard. His huge, bald head hit the stone. He went limp.

Drake whirled. The girl, a tiny thing with huge eyes, stared at him. Tears streamed down her face.

"It's all right. You're safe now."

She scrambled to her feet. She was wearing a worn tunic that had seen many better days even before this lout had torn it. She looked at him warily. He took a step back, held up his hands to indicate he meant her no harm.

She darted away, toward the entrance to the alley. He stayed where he was, reasonably sure by the way she was moving that she wasn't badly hurt. He'd gotten there in time.

When she got to the alley opening, she turned back to look at him again. He thought of Lux, and his stomach turned at the thought of her in such a brute's hands.

"Thank you," the girl whispered, so softly he almost couldn't hear it.

He nodded. And then she was gone, out into the street that was beginning to fill with people going about what business the Coalition allowed them.

Quickly, he knelt by the Coalition soldier. He freed his apron, revealing a face that was vaguely familiar. Someone who had likely been in the taproom before, he decided. He thought quickly. Grabbed up the blaster, wiped it with the apron and slid it back into the sheath, as if he had never touched it. Then he put the apron back on as he ran back to the back door of the taproom. He opened it and stood just inside, leaving it open just enough to press his ear to the gap.

After a moment or two, he heard a scraping sound, of something moving across the stone. A second later, he heard string of curses that started out low and grew in volume and foulness until it was a yell of obscenity aimed at everyone in the vicinity and their mothers.

Drake waited until it had lessened to intermittent indictments of various creatures, including a suggestion for a goat that he thought was physically impossible. Then he steeled himself, put on his most worried expression, and shuffled out into the alley.

"Oh!" he exclaimed, as if he'd just seen the big man who was leaning against the opposite wall. "Oh, sir, are you all right?"

The man blinked, as if his vision wasn't quite right yet. But after a moment he seemed to focus. And to recognize Drake. So he'd been right about him being a taproom customer.

"You're the tapper."

"Yes," he said, trying to sound worried as well as look it. It wasn't hard, given the suspicion in the man's narrow eyes. He thought about rubbing his hands together anxiously, but if he judged by the look of him—and the smell—such subtleties would be lost on this man. "I heard some noise out here, and I got nervous. Do you need help, sir?"

The fawning words and tone worked a minor miracle. The suspicion vanished. And it didn't seem to occur to the man to question why he'd come out at all, if he was so nervous. "I was attacked."

Drake widened his eyes. "Right here? In my alley? That's . . . disgraceful!"

"It is," the man boomed out, confidence regained. "And I'll hunt them down, you can be sure of that."

"Them, sir?"

"At least two of them. Maybe three. But I fought them off."

Right.

Mostly out of curiosity over what the man would say, Drake asked, "Were you looking for something back here, sir?"

The expression on his brutish face became guarded. "I was merely taking a shortcut."

"Of course," Drake said with a nod. Never mind that this alley in fact was the longer way around to anything else on the street.

"You should take better care to clear this alley of rubbish." Back in full Coalition mode, Drake thought.

"Quite, sir. Would you like to come inside? A nice glass of brew to set you to rights? No charge, of course. I would be honored."

Puffing up now, the trooper looked down his nose at him. As if the offer of a free drink were only his due.

"Perhaps a quick one," he said. "I'm on duty later."

Perhaps you should rethink having a brew at all, then. Or molesting helpless children.

"Of course," he said aloud as he gestured the man toward the door. "But today it will be light much later, if the mist stays gone."

The man snorted. "This foul, benighted place is enough to drive a man mad. That mist is a demonish thing, I tell you."

Drake held the door for him with the most respectful air he could summon up. And he poured a larger glass than he'd planned, one that surprised even the greedy trooper.

He busied himself washing the rest of the glasses while he kept an eye on the man in the strip of mirror that ran along the back wall. The man gulped down the brew, taking it in faster than Drake would have thought possible, even for a man his size. When he finished, he slammed the empty glass down on the bar, and wiped his foamy lip with his sleeve. Drake turned and picked up the glass.

"Another? Surely you have time?"

"You're a good man, Davorin. Despite your name."

Drake let a wince show. It wasn't difficult; the comparisons to his father always caused a jab of pain, even ones like this. But his father had become a martyr, and that was a path he did not want to follow.

The trooper laughed. He looked Drake up and down, then reached out and flicked at the edge of the apron. "Nobody'd take you for your father, and that's certain."

"I'm thankful for that," Drake said, meaning it.

He downed the second brew, not quite as quickly. As the man strode out the door, the front door this time, Drake noticed the slightest of wobbles in his step.

He finished the glasses, wiped his hands on that blessed apron, allowing himself a smile as he remembered the trooper's scorn for the very thing that had taken him down out in the alley.

He turned to measuring what was left in the various bottles and flagons on the shelf.

And hoped that the little girl had gotten safely home.

Chapter 20

"SO THIS IS WHAT we are reduced to? The terrorizing of children?"

"They are Davorins!"

Caze Paledan turned to look at the governor. He'd wondered once, while reading an historical account of the Triotian Wars, what had become of the man, but it was of so little import to him he'd never thought of him again. He'd been much more interested in the account of the battles. He was adept at reading between the lines, and enough of a tactician to see what had been left out or twisted. The end result had been a reluctant but definite admiration for the king who had managed to defeat the forces of the Coalition with courage, a ragtag force, and sheer bluff.

And who had apparently passed the same courage and cleverness down to his son, as the second invasion of Arellia had shown.

And he'd smiled inwardly when he read the scathing opinion the chronicler had let creep into what was supposed to be a dry, historical recounting. The writer obviously disapproved mightily of the king's choice of a disreputable, notorious skypirate as his defense minister. The skypirate who had spawned the woman who, together with the prince, a Triotian orphan rescued by that same skypirate, and a homegrown hero, would repel the Coalition a second time, permanently ending for all intents and purposes the Coalition domination of the region.

He had smiled because as a very young cadet being transported on a Coalition cruiser to the training facility on Alpha 2, he'd had an encounter with that same skypirate. And the results were something he'd been sworn never to admit to; no flight captain would ever willingly admit he'd been bested by the likes of the infamous Dax Silverbrake. Which had perhaps led to the badly flawed assessment in that chronicle.

But now he had a much less worthy opponent to deal with. A man he found to be the worst kind of bureaucrat, one who was in it for what prestige and power it would gain him. "So," he said coolly, "it is a name you are afraid of?"

"Afraid? Of a name? How dare you?"

He met Sorkost's glare levelly. "The eldest Davorin is by all appearances cowed, beaten. The next is but a girl. And these two barely reach to my elbow. Since there is nothing to fear there, what is left but their name?"

"You only say that because you did not know Torstan Davorin."

That much was true; he had been nowhere near Ziem when the riots sparked by Davorin's fiery speeches had turned into outright rebellion. But when he had been given the assignment to quell the last of the troubles here on this mist-shrouded planet, he had done his studying. He had spent most of the trip here secluded in his quarters, reading and watching not just the accounts of the conquering, but the history of Ziem itself. He had always thought that in order to keep order, one must understand those you were trying to control.

And he had immediately seen the problem with Ziem. It was a planet with a relatively small land mass amid expansive seas that gave it the climate so loathed by the troops stationed here. And an also relatively small native population, a large portion of which was centered in the city of Zelos. The rest was scattered along the main road from the shrouded lowlands to the upper flats, the only place crops of any use could be grown. And the more scattered, the harder they were to control. Especially when those in the outer sections were notoriously independent and resistant.

"No," he agreed, "I did not know him."

And he regretted that; after reading and watching recordings of several of the man's fiery speeches, he would have liked to have met him. He could appreciate a fine orator, even when what they were speaking was treason, at least to the Coalition.

"If you had, you would see the threat in his name surviving," Sorkost said, seeming calmer now.

"And this," Paledan said thoughtfully, "would perhaps explain why you monitor Drake Davorin as if he were a greensnake you are not quite sure you've beheaded?"

"He is beaten," Sorkost said. "But that does not mean others might not try to rally to him, force him to follow his father's path of treason and sedition."

"And what is it you are afraid these . . . children heard? What is it you were discussing out in the open?"

The governor shifted uncomfortably. "Nothing of import, but that is not the point."

"If there was nothing for them to overhear, then what is?"

"The point is they're Davorins and—"

A knock on the door, followed by the door swinging open without waiting for an invitation, interrupted whatever Sorkost had been about to declare.

Speaking of treason, Paledan thought as he watched the man who hurried in. He had no respect for Barcon Ordam. His actions may have made the conquering of this resource-rich world much easier for the Coalition, but Paledan had always preferred an honest fight to the hidden intrigues and manipulations men like Sorkost and Ordam dealt in.

He also knew that someone who would betray his own would betray them just as quickly.

"Governor, I hear—" Ordam stopped suddenly when he noticed who else was in the room, and Paledan had the pleasure of seeing fear spark in the man's narrow eyes. He enjoyed this one being afraid of him. He sat on the edge of Sorkost's desk with arms folded across his chest, saying nothing, and making no move to leave. Technically, the governor could order him out, but Sorkost had no more nerve than Ordam, and Paledan was confident the man wouldn't even try.

He did not.

"What is it, Barcon?"

"I . . ." Another glance at him. Paledan stared steadily. Nervously, the man turned back to the governor. "I understand you have the Davorin twins?"

"Yes. They were caught spying on a private meeting."

"A private meeting?"

Paledan nearly laughed aloud, not only at the absurdity of the charge, but at the sound of Ordam's voice, which had taken on a note of umbrage. As if any meeting from which he was excluded was an affront.

"Between Jakel and I," Sorkost said, just the mention of the enforcer's name an implicit threat. Paledan had yet to meet the man, but he'd heard enough already to know what sort he was. He had also heard that, while he ostensibly worked for Ordam, he could be bought.

"I see." The nervousness in Ordam's voice increased.

"What has it to do with you?" the governor demanded.

Ordam swallowed visibly. "Have you decided what you will do with them?"

Paledan had had enough. He uncrossed his arms and stood. Two heads swiveled as both men looked at him with visible unease.

"That is my province," he said flatly, brooking no dissembling.

"But I—"

"It is why the governor requested my presence."

"I just thought—"

"You question Coalition authority in the dispensation of spies?" he asked with a brow raised at Ordam, but the governor in his peripheral vision. Both of them blanched slightly.

"Of course not," Ordam said hastily. Sorkost merely grimaced, then waved his hands as if washing them of the entire question.

"Then I will be about my duty," he said, and left them there.

He walked down the hall toward where two men stood outside a door. They snapped to attention the instant they spotted him, and saluted formally when he stopped before them. He barely managed not to grimace at the sight. Two fully armed guards for a pair of thirteen-year-olds? Sorkost was a bigger coward than he had even thought.

He said nothing, only nodded toward the door. One of the men quickly unlocked it and pulled it open for him.

In the corner of the room two children huddled together. They looked up when he stepped in, the boy's expression defiant, the girl's quietly mutinous. Whatever else they were, these two were not broken. He felt one corner of his mouth twitch and suppressed the urge to smile.

He could see the resemblance, in the upturned noses, the red of their hair, the stubborn chins, and the glint in their matching, Ziem-blue eyes. He could also see marks upon them: a red mark on the boy's left cheek that would soon be a bruise, and a similar mark on the girl's right wrist, as if she'd been grabbed and yanked.

He turned on his heel. Stepped back outside and spoke to the guards.

"Bring them to me. And," he added, his brows lowered at them both, "they had best arrive in no worse shape than they are now."

The man who had unlocked the door merely nodded, but Paledan saw the other man glance toward the governor's office. He gave the man a closer look, saw the distaste that flickered in his eyes for an instant. He eased his voice, knowing for certain now what he had guessed before; it was not these men responsible for the bruises on those children.

"Quickly," he said, but not sharply.

"Sir," the man with the key began, "the governor—"

"I have dealt with him. Bring them. I want them in my office."

He thought he saw the other man smother a smile before he stepped in to gather up the prisoners.

He had only been back a few minutes when the tap on the door came. He took just long enough to shut down his comm system—he wanted no listeners to this—blanking out the viewscreen that was displaying an annoying number of messages that had come in during his brief absence, and shelving the maps and technical sheets he'd been studying. When he called out "Enter," the man who had betrayed his feelings about Sorkost opened the door.

"They are here, sir."

He glanced about the room once more; it would not do to underestimate this pair and prove Sorkost right. But there was nothing still visible they could learn anything from, so he nodded at the guard.

The two shuffled in. He heard the clank of metal, realized the two had been chained. He strode over to them. They looked at him warily, but did not cower. Which was more than he could say for half the contingent here, he thought wryly. He looked at the cuffs that held their small wrists linked together.

"Truly?" he said, looking up at the guard.

"Governor's orders, sir."

He reached down and took the boy's hand. He resisted.

"Don't," he said quietly, and lifted that hand. His fingers encircled it easily. He turned it in the metal cuff until he could put his own thumb over the boy's and press down. He took the cuff in his other hand and tugged. With a minimum of effort, it slid off the slender wrist and over his hand. All the while he watched the boy's face. There was no sign of surprise.

He had known he could free himself. A glance at the girl's face told him she had known, too.

Moments later, they were free of the chains and he ordered the guard out. The man hesitated.

"I think I can hold my own should they decide to attack," Paledan said.

Flushing, the guard nodded and backed out the door. And Paledan turned his attention to his two spymasters.

This should make my day more interesting.

Chapter 21

THE CHILDREN WERE looking around the office with wary curiosity. Paledan saw the boy's eyes widen at the arrangement of crossed swords on the wall behind the desk.

"Ziem sabers, I believe?" he said.

"They're on your wall," the boy said. "Don't you know?"

This time he nearly lost the battle not to smile. He was not lacking in nerve, this Davorin.

"Contention valid," he agreed.

"Take one away," the girl said sweetly, "and write 'Without Warning' on the wall, and you'll have your very own calling card from the Raider."

Again, he battled the urge to smile. He'd found little enough besides the occasional game of chaser to amuse him here, so he was enjoying this.

"You admire this raider of yours."

"Every true Ziemite does," the boy said staunchly. "We will join him as soon as we are of age."

"If," the girl added pointedly, "he hasn't destroyed you all by then."

This time, he couldn't beat back the smile. So neither of them were short in the courage department. He found that surprising in ones so young. And, from what he'd heard, their sister was the same. Which made him wonder, if Davorins indeed bred true and these had such spirit left, what had happened to really break their elder brother?

"Why did you not try an escape on the way here, when you found you could slip the chains?"

The girl rolled her eyes at him. "Um . . . blasters?"

"Even we can't outrun those," the boy explained as if he were unable to figure it out himself.

He felt a sudden jab of sympathy for the man responsible for these two.

"Names," he ordered firmly.

"Nyx," said the girl.

"And Lux," said the boy.

He studied them both, saw that glint in their eyes again.

"Perhaps I should have been more specific. Which name goes with who?"

Surprise flickered across both faces. And he caught a note of grudging respect in the girl's voice when she said, "Opposite."

"Ah." He gestured toward the two chairs that sat before his desk. Hard, wooden chairs, for he did not like to encourage anyone to stay too long. "Sit."

They obeyed without further comment.

"Explain to me what really happened," he said when they were seated.

The boy, Nyx, blinked, clearly surprised. "Since when does the Coalition care about the truth of anything?"

"Don't trust him," Lux declared.

"I trusted you when I unchained you," he said to the girl. "Left myself at your mercy."

"We're just children," Lux protested.

"And that," he said, "leads many to underestimate you, I'm sure."

The two exchanged a glance that told him how accurate he'd been.

He found himself in a difficult and unaccustomed position. He liked these two little scamps. Yet he did not assume that because they were children, they could not have been spying. Who better?

"Tell me," he ordered again, "what happened."

The boy started. "We weren't spying, no matter what that old slimehog says."

He supposed he should correct this maligning of a Coalition governor, but couldn't quite bring himself to do it. It was, after all, something he'd thought himself. And besides, he was finally getting answers.

"We weren't," the girl confirmed.

"We were there—"

"First."

"It's our tree—"

"And we were just sitting up there—"

"Like always, when they—"

"Happened to stop there."

"And Jakel—"

"Is evil—"

"So we don't mess with him. He'll—"

"Slice your throat as soon as—"

"Look at you."

"So we stayed quiet up—"

"In the tree. But—"

"Jakel saw us."

It was like trying to track two individual stingers through a swarm of them. He almost laughed aloud. He'd never been around twins before. And now he envied their keeper even less.

"And did you hear anything of interest?" he asked when they appeared to have paused long enough for him to get a word in.

"Nothing."

"No, nothing."

Too insistent. "So, something," he said dryly.

"We learned the governor is an even bigger blowpig than we thought," Lux said.

"And Jakel a rabid barkhound," Nyx put in.

Since he could disagree with neither assessment, Paledan said nothing. And while he doubted the governor had been truthful in saying he'd discussed nothing of import with the brutal enforcer, he had little choice but to take the man at his word. And let the results be on Sorkost's head.

He turned just enough to activate the comm system. His aide answered instantly. "Have a guard bring me the taproom keeper," he ordered. "Tell him who we have here."

He sensed the twins going very still the moment he spoke.

"Under arrest, sir?" Brakely asked.

"Not yet," he answered.

He in fact had nothing to arrest Davorin for, at the moment, but he thought it might capture the attention of these two little demons if they thought their brother was in jeopardy. And it apparently had. They stayed quiet.

"Nothing more to say?" he asked mildly.

The boy grimaced. "Drake'll say enough when he gets here."

And I will be very interested to hear it.

DEAR EOS, WHAT had they done now?

Drake didn't try to hide the worry that had flooded him upon the arrival of the Coalition trooper with orders from Post Commander Paledan to present himself immediately in the matter of Nyx and Lux Davorin. He would be expected to worry, would he not?

"What has happened?" he asked, more to give himself time to assess the possibilities than with any thought the man would actually tell him anything. He was proven correct in short order.

"Just hasten. The commander is not one to keep waiting, if you know what is good for you. And them."

He had to work on the assumption that this was only about something the twins had done. And that the trooper's implied threat meant that at least they were still alive. Given that, the best thing all around would be for the new commander to be presented with what he expected to see: the quiet, ineffectual taproom keeper. He stopped what he'd been about to do—pull off the stained apron he wore. Instead, he left it on and moved quickly from behind the bar, as if he were in a hurry to accede to the trooper's demand. Satisfied, the man turned on his booted heel and no less than marched out the door, assured that the lowly tapper would of course follow on his heels.

Which he did.

He had never been inside the compound in daylight. He knew the ground it stood on well; it had once been the courtyard of the council building where his father's office was, before the Coalition had arrived and thrown up this large complex practically overnight. They had used the building itself as one wall of the compound. Never let it be said they weren't efficient.

Drake looked around, wiping his hands on the apron as he did, as if he had a twitchy sort of feeling inside. Which he did, for several reasons. He let his gaze dart around as if he were nervous, but the trooper didn't seem to be bothered; in fact, he barely glanced at him as they reached the headquarters building that had been the council building itself. Nor did he pay him much mind as they walked down the wide hallway, even when he glanced through the few open doorways they passed along the way.

When they stepped into the office at the end of the hall, he looked around quickly. The walls were bare of ornament save for a crossed pair of traditional Ziem swords on one wall. The rest of the space was taken up by, surprisingly, old-style paper charts, maps, and a few books that he hadn't seen the like of since his father's collection of the old tomes had been confiscated and burned after his death. The requisite viewscreen, holographic station, and other gear was present, but to one side, as if there only under protest.

And nowhere were the twins. Drake's pulse kicked up at the thought that he'd been wrong, that they were already dead. He clamped down on the burgeoning apprehension and faced the man behind the desk that he guessed was large for use, not show.

He didn't know what the office of the prior commander, Frall, had looked like, but he somehow doubted it was as stark and severe as this.

But then, Commander Frall had been nowhere near the man Paledan was, and Drake didn't need the man's history to know that. He needed only to look at him across the expanse of that desk, watch as he stood. The office needed no ornament, because the man who now owned it needed none. The aura of power and command was enough.

He put on his best imitation of a man who had been through this many times before. Since it was nothing less than true, he hoped it would work to trivialize whatever they'd done.

"What," he said with an audible sigh, "have those two hedgebeasts been up to now?"

"Spying," Paledan said.

Drake's heart jammed in his throat. A sudden fear that he couldn't get them out of this one shot through him.

"At least," Paledan continued, "according to Governor Sorkost."

Something in the way he said it, some faint undertone he couldn't—or didn't—quite mask, made Drake risk saying, "They are children. I'm afraid they don't quite respect the governor's office."

"Or the man in it?" Paledan suggested.

"They are children," he said again. Then, carefully, "I don't believe they yet realize there can be a difference between respecting the office and the one who holds it."

Paledan walked slowly around the desk, leaned a hip on the edge of it, and crossed his arms over his chest. "You surprise me, tapper."

With a sinking feeling he'd gone too far, Drake masked his misgivings and said only, "I do?"

"I was given to believe you barely above a muckrat in intelligence, and below a skalworm in courage."

"I lay no claim to great amounts of either. Sir."

"And yet you have raised two imps that have an overabundance of both."

"It is their nature," he said. "They take after our parents, I'm afraid."

"Hmm."

Drake said nothing more as the man studied him for a long moment. He wasn't sure what he would do—what he could do—if Paledan had indeed killed the twins, or had them killed.

"You do not ask for details," Paledan observed.

Drake steadied himself inwardly. "I have learned it is wiser to wait to be told what the Coalition is willing to tell."

"And one should always follow the wiser course, is that not true?"

"That," Drake said, "I cannot argue with. Sir."

He could have sworn the man's mouth quirked slightly, as if suppressing amusement. "Then allow me to point out that your wisest course now is to keep those two out of the way of the governor for the foreseeable future."

Drake sucked in a breath. "Then . . . they are alive?"

Paledan frowned. "You thought otherwise?"

"The governor is . . . of uncertain temper at times."

"Odd," Paledan said, "I've found him of a steady and certain temper— bad—most times."

Drake didn't dare let himself smile, but it was an effort.

"I do not intentionally slaughter children, Davorin. Not even those with the name of an infamous rebel."

"I am . . . thankful for that, commander."

He used the title purposely, for the first time. He saw it register. After a moment, Paledan nodded. He leaned over and spoke into the communicator on the desk.

"Bring them in." Then he looked back at Drake. "I wish you luck with those two. I fear you will need it."

"I fear I've already run through my allotment with them," Drake said.

The man did smile then. And Drake had the oddest feeling it was with a sort of relief that the twins were not his to deal with.

A relief he could completely understand.

Chapter 22

SHE IS LONG DEAD, forgotten. . . . A suicide.

Paledan looked again at the painting as he took another drink of his brew, Davorin's calm, unemotional words echoing in his head. Only now they were followed by Ordam's derisive rant about Davorin himself.

". . . just a mother's pet. When she hurled herself from Halfhead to her death, she might as well have taken him with her."

Was it possible? Could that ethereal beauty in that painting truly be Iolana Davorin, widow of Torstan? The woman whose grief had driven her to throw herself off a cliff to her death? Mother of the man who stood just a few feet away, placidly wiping a spill off the bar?

And if it was, how could her son speak of her so coolly, with such detachment, especially if her death had so beaten him down? How could he live with this portrait before him, day after day?

Leaving four young children behind to fend for themselves.

Or rather, leaving her oldest son the responsibility of the younger three. Including those two mischief makers he had already encountered. Perhaps that was the explanation for the detachment. Surely any boy of that young age would resent having that kind of responsibility thrust upon him.

And yet it appeared he had lived up to it, to some extent anyway. His family ate, and had a solid roof. And he worked hard in this place to see to that. And was wise enough to see that a careful neutrality, if not outright servility, was the best way to assure keeping what he had.

He took another sip of the brew that was surprisingly good for this remote place. He glanced again at the man behind the bar.

It was a wise man who accepted facts and adjusted accordingly, as Davorin had. Far better than continuing to fight an impossible battle, and perhaps losing the very thing you were fighting to save in the process.

He had come to know a lot of different sorts of people in the Coalition's romp across the galaxy. And a lot about each sort. Those who resisted, those who did not. Those who resented, and those who welcomed. Those who openly fought, and those who gave in. Those who talked, and those who led.

And a few who were combinations of two or more. Those were the ones that were the most dangerous, the ones that could lead to trouble larger than a few skirmishes here and there.

And that thought led him back to the man who had greatly occupied his mind of late. This raider, known only by that name, spoken by people as if it were a royal title, was more than just a thorn—he was a genuine wound. One that might hemorrhage if they were not careful.

There were different ways of dealing with such men. The success of any of those ways depending on knowing as much as possible about them. And Paledan had the feeling he still had much to learn about this one.

And so I will.

He drained the last of his brew, tossed a coin on the bar, and left without waiting for his change.

"YOU LOVE HIM, don't you?"

Kye snapped out of her haze abruptly at the question. Ever since she and Eirlys had stopped here again at their favorite place beside the pond, her brain seemed to have slipped its tether and gone wandering.

"What?" she asked, stalling.

"The Raider. You love him."

Images of that useless discussion raced through her head. She quashed them, and gave the answer the Raider would have. "Don't be foolish. There is no time or place for such in our world now."

Eirlys laughed, and that laugh sounded much older than her tender years. "As if even the Coalition could change the nature of humans. Have you not heard that war only intensifies such things?"

"Your brother is right," Kye said dryly. "You are too clever for your own good."

Eirlys looked away so quickly that Kye knew she was hiding something, something she feared would show in her eyes. No doubt the same as always; her disappointment in Drake. Or perhaps her distaste and disillusionment had descended into something worse, perhaps downright disgust. Kye would hate to think that was true, yet she would understand if it were. And for once, she couldn't even bestir herself to try and defend the man she had loved so dearly.

It was not that she did not see the immensity of the burden left him by his mother's suicide, and the courage and determination with which he undertook to carry it. It was that she missed the other side of him—the dashing, courageous, utterly planium-nerved cool side of him. The man who had dared things no other did, who had rallied a devastated city, and then an entire planet to him.

But that man was long gone, buried as surely as if he had died along with his parents. What remained only looked like Drake Davorin, and handsome as he was, she had no pleasure in looking at him any longer, not when all she could see was the servility, the bowing, the humiliation and mocking heaped on his head without rejoinder. And no matter how well she understood why he'd had to do it, how she lamented what it was costing him to do it, it still hurt. Especially when she disagreed that it would save them in the long run.

"If there is anyone to blame for what my brother has had to become,"

Eirlys said, "perhaps it is my mother."

Kye was so startled by what she'd said she barely noticed that the girl seemed to have followed along with her own thoughts with an eerie accuracy. "Your mother to blame?"

No one ever spoke ill of Iolana Davorin. Only sadness and loss were acknowledged. She had been their visionary, and the widow of their greatest man, and all of Ziem understood how it could be that she could not go on after his loss.

"It was she who abandoned us, was it not? She who left Drake to care for us? You said that yourself."

"I never said that," Kye said, protesting automatically. This was near heresy in Zelos. "I said only that Drake was very young to have all that responsibility dropped upon him."

"But he had it dropped upon him because she could not carry it any longer. Or would not. She loved us, but not enough to stay."

"Eirlys—"

"I know what you will say. She loved my father too much to go on without him."

"Yes."

"I," Eirlys declared firmly, "do not ever want to love anyone like that."

And yet it is what I wish more than anything, but cannot have. "I see," she said, her tone carefully neutral.

"The price is too high. If you lose them, it is like the heart being ripped out of you."

Kye thought of a man in a carved-out quarters on the mountain, his ruined face something that made people look away, and helped strike fear into those he fought. Thought of feelings denied, longings buried deep.

"You do love him, don't you?" Eirlys repeated softly.

"Many people love the Raider for what he's doing."

"Yes. But that's not what I mean and well you know it. You are in love with him. I can see it in your face."

Kye turned to look at her young friend. "And if I were? Would you tell me I was a fool? Ask who could love a man with such scars?"

Eirlys drew herself up straight. "Never. For not only do I know you are not so small-brained as to let that matter, I know you are wise enough to see beyond that exterior damage to the man within. The man brave enough and steadfast enough to stand against the entire Coalition if need be. The man who would die for his people and his planet, if it is asked of him."

"But would be bedamned sure to take as many of the Coalition with him as he possibly could," Kye added.

Eirlys smiled, widely. "Yes. And that."

For a long moment, Kye just looked at the girl before her. She was, as her brother often said, frighteningly clever. And fierce, even as she dealt with her beloved creatures with the gentleness of a true healer. Kye knew Eirlys had come to look upon her as a sort of older sister, especially after the loss of her mother. She had had no other older female to turn to.

And it was with that thought in mind that Kye answered her original question, as honestly and openly as she had ever answered it to anyone.

"Yes. I love him. I think I was half in love with him before I ever met him. But that was the idea of him, I think, the idea of a man who stood, who fought, who refused to be cowed no matter the odds, no matter the likelihood that he would bring about his own death. I had made him, in my mind, into something beyond reality. I believed in the legend of the Raider, and had forgotten one essential thing."

"What?" Eirlys asked, looking at her raptly.

"That he is, in the end, only human. A man with a life to lose, and who has come very close to doing so more than once. More than any of us."

When Eirlys smiled at her then, it was a different kind of smile, an oddly adult one. "I am glad that you see that. Many who think of him only as the legend do not."

"I know. And that makes me even more afraid for him, for I think some of them believe him immortal."

Eirlys frowned at that. "Meaning?"

"They might not take the care they could or should, if they think he cannot die."

The girl went pale. "I had not thought of that."

I do. Every day.

And it made her wonder if Eirlys was right. Perhaps the price was too high.

Chapter 23

CAZE PALEDAN looked once more over the report Brakely had compiled. It was accompanied by a few odd-shaped bits and pieces of paper that he had managed to acquire. One was a handwritten report of a raid conducted three years ago, and was the earliest mention his aide had been able to find of the rebel who would later become known simply as the Raider. The paper it was on was ripped raggedly at the top, but Brakely's note indicated it had been fastened to a post in the town square, where it had been read by several people before being discovered and torn down by a trooper.

Those several people had been enough to insure that by nightfall, all of Zelos had known of the exploit. And that was only the first.

He scanned the collected data on the viewscreen, the rough sketch that had become the first wanted poster, the list of possible suspects, and how each of them had been eliminated one way or another. He read again the list of raids, one long column of those they knew were the Raider's work, and a second of those that could have been, before he started leaving the now in-famous calling card. There was one of those cards in the batch of papers as well; Brakely was nothing if not thorough.

Then came a collection of the rumors and speculation about the brigand and his identity. He saw the rumors about what had caused the scars, and what lay beneath the concealing helmet. Saw the speculation about who the man actually was, from the ghost of Ziem hero Torstan Davorin to some mysterious stranger come down from above the Edge. The collection in-cluded the attribution of incidents that, as far as Brakely could find, had never even happened.

And that, Paledan thought, was when a legend was truly born.

He read Brakely's conclusion again.

All I am reasonably certain of about the Raider is that he is a man of the mountain, born and bred Ziem. The people appear to care about nothing more than that he is one of them, and he will lead them. It seems that is all they need to know.

He leaned back in his chair. Thought again of his own tour through Zelos. Of the voices, whispering yet ringing with pride in this son of Ziem who had risen to fight when all others had long ago surrendered. Of the rumors he himself had heard, rumors of supernatural powers and invulnerability. He believed in neither, but to him that only made the Raider even more remarkable.

He called up the images of the other report. Dozens of images, captured with Coalition thoroughness, of a dark, slashing figure that was merely a silhouette, and yet quite obviously the Raider. Images stenciled in their own stolen paint, on every surface that didn't move and a few that did—including the side of a Coalition cargo truck.

He smiled slightly, although it was broader on the inside, at the memory of Governor Sorkost's outrage. He'd watched the large blood vessel on the man's forehead bulge and pulse, wondering if it would burst right there and then. He'd had to hide his own amusement even as he wondered aloud if there was any aspect of waging asymmetric warfare the Raider did not have command of. This only served to anger Sorkost further, and while he did not dare to take it out on the post commander, Paledan did not envy the man's aides when he left. If one or more of them was found dead after having delivered one more piece of bad news, he would not be surprised.

"Were you not sent here to rid us of this nuisance?" Sorkost had yelled.

Paledan thought the Raider had moved far beyond the category of mere nuisance, but he kept that observation to himself. "I was sent here," he said evenly, "to resolve the problems you have not. But I will do it in my own time."

Sorkost ignored the insinuation. "But I want rid of him now."

And you sound like a petulant child. "I'm afraid Legion Command cares only about my record of success in this, not your desires. Unless, of course, you'd rather go after the Raider yourself, personally. I'll be happy to make that request to General Fidez for you. Of course, once he has the full history, he might wonder why you have not succeeded in eliminating him before now."

Sorkost had blanched, and that had been the end of the discussion. As Paledan had known it would be. He had always lived by the axiom that to know your enemy was to know how best to defeat him. And in his mind, that applied to enemies within as well as outside.

And for a while, he sat there pondering the irony that of the two, it was not this bloated Governor of the Coalition he admired, but the Raider.

"YOU HAVE NOT asked."

Kye looked up from the table that held her paints, pens, the bowl of sand she used to dry them quickly, and the large piece of canvas she had liberated from a pile of them near the cargo shipment entrance to the Coalition compound. She had to treat it with a base to keep the paint from being absorbed and vanishing, but what was left of the spray they'd used for the silhouettes had worked well.

The Raider stood across from her, staring down at the work in progress, his arms folded across his chest. Light glinted off the metal of the helmet. She had known he would not be looking at her when he spoke. She would have felt it. Any time she felt that tiny shiver at the back of her neck, that tickle of awareness that made her shiver, she would turn and catch his gaze darting away.

He was so bold, so unflinching with everything else, this avoidance was striking. She wanted to believe it was for the same reason she was so often caught watching him a little too intently, even though if it was, it still made no difference. He'd made it clear there was no place for this—for them—in this war.

She steadied herself and her voice before answering.

"You will tell me when it is time for me to know," she said, although curiosity about the need and plan for this map was twisting her into knots.

He raised his head. She couldn't be sure because of the helmet—did he truly never take the blessed thing off?—but she thought he raised a brow at her. "You are unusually patient."

"And you are an unusual commander," she countered.

"Odd, I will grant you."

"No. Unusual." Since these were the only compliments he would allow her to give him, she would do so. "You see your force as individuals. Let them think for themselves. You learn each of their skills, and use them. Allow them to use them."

"If you're referring to the long gun, there was never a question you would have one."

"My point proven."

"I only regret that your true skill is used in this way," he said, gesturing to the map.

She had only begun. And it was going to take a very long time. The detail he wanted was extraordinary, and some of it she could not derive from the images projected on the wall by the small flyover craft that had obtained them.

"I will need aid with some of these locations," she said as she pushed her small sketchbook, always with her, out of the way of the next section she was going to work on. "I know you do not wish the girl Eirlys to come here, but have I your leave to speak with her?"

"You are close."

She wasn't certain if it was a question or an observation. "Yes. As sisters."

He looked away then, toward the image projected on the wall.

"As such," she went on when he didn't speak, "it would not look amiss if we spend time together. And she knows this region like no other."

After a moment, he nodded. "You must take care. It would not do for anyone to overhear. For her sake, yours, and ours."

"Of course." Did he think she was a fool? She reined in the surge of temper, knowing it was born of her feelings for him, and her wish that he never see her as less than capable. "I will phrase it so that she has no idea why I am asking. Or even that I am asking. She loves our home, and it is no trick to get her to speak of her favorite places."

She thought she saw him smile then, an unusually soft smile for him. It put her in mind of something, but before she could finalize the thought, there was a rap on the door. Brander's signal, she thought. The Raider called out for his second to enter.

"I still think we should move one of the rovers beyond Highridge. Just in case," he said without preamble.

Kye frowned. On the other side of Highridge were the badlands, their escape route of last resort.

"You would have me run?" the Raider asked.

"I would have you live."

"And leave the rest to their fates?"

Kye watched as the two men stared at each other. In his own way, her cousin was as stubborn as the Raider. He just preferred to do as he wished and worry about the details—such as permission—later.

"Sometimes, my friend," Brander said quietly, "you underestimate your meaning to this band of reprobates. Without you, the rebellion is over."

"I don't believe that."

"Believe it," Kye said softly. "You are the heart and soul and conscience of Ziem. You must live." *For me as well as them.* She daren't say it, but she knew it was true. If he was killed, there would be nothing left for her. "Whether you like it or no."

It was clear from the narrowing of his gaze as he looked at her that he did not like it. "Some would say a martyr would serve as well."

"We have had enough of those," Brander snapped.

Kye was a little taken aback. Even for Brander, with the freedom his friendship with the Raider gave him, that tone had been sharp. As if there were more to the words than the simple truth of them.

She watched the two men as silence spun out in the room. She wished she didn't feel compelled to speak, but the tension was too high and they would gain nothing by fighting among themselves.

"He is right. The Davorins are martyrs enough for this war."

"That they are," Brander said, looking at the Raider steadily. And Kye still could not put a name to the edge in his voice.

"All right," the Raider said at last, but added, "for now."

That he gave in was, she supposed, a sign of the respect and liking he had for her cousin. Which she understood. Infuriating as he sometimes was to her, Brander was a good man and true, and a fighter worthy of both.

Brander knew when to quit, for he merely nodded. And, as if he were glad to see the end of the subject, even temporarily, he turned to look at the table. The heavy canvas she was using draped over the edges of the table.

"So large?" Brander asked.

"I have need of every detail." He glanced at Kye. For an instant, she thought she saw one corner of his mouth quirk. But as always, in that blasted helmet it was hard to tell. "She will be weary of me before it is done."

Never. "I shall endeavor not to show it," she said instead, and this time the quirk upward was unmistakable.

"I presume you have a plan for it?" Brander asked.

"It is a beginning," he answered. "There are many pieces to gather yet."

Brander left it at that as he leaned over to inspect what she'd done so far. His hand brushed her sketch book, nearly sending it to the floor. In an instantaneous reaction, he caught it; her cousin's reflexes were very, very quick.

"You are good, Kye," he said as he looked at the small corner she had finished.

"Your flyover," she said, looking at her cousin.

"Do not short yourself," the Raider said. "You have great talent."

His words warmed her greatly. She had come to prefer compliments on her skill with the long gun or her stealth, but this still meant a great deal to her. Once a compliment on her artistic skill would have meant everything, but there was no room for that in their world any longer.

But a compliment on anything from this man warmed her more than anything else could. Except that which she could not have.

Brander's hands moved, one tapping her sketchbook against the other. She looked at him. Their gazes locked. The usual glint of mischief was gone from his eyes, and all she saw there was understanding. Then he made a quick motion with one hand, and Kye thought she saw a sheet of the paper from her sketchbook slide out and disappear into his pocket. Then he set it down on the table, and turned to the Raider.

"Unless you have something else for me, I'll be off. I have a game of chaser with Major Paledan waiting."

Kye grimaced. "That man makes me nervous."

"Things have changed since he arrived," Brander admitted.

"Then perhaps you should rethink this game," she suggested.

He shrugged. "Do we quit because the Coalition happens to send a competent man?"

She sighed. "No."

"Just be wary," the Raider said. "He is not a man you want as an enemy. And I'm told he's very good."

"Which is why I am convincing him I'm nothing but a harmless wastrel. Besides, it's better than playing with that slimehog Jakel."

"He is still coming around?" the Raider asked, rather sharply.

"Only when Eirlys is there. Another reason for me to be there, too."

Brander threw his commander a salute and was gone.

"How is it," she asked as she picked up her sketchbook, "that you hear of everything, even from up here?"

He didn't look at her, but after a moment he said, "I have many sources."

She didn't doubt that, but Paledan had only been here a few days. Or perhaps the new post commander's reputation was such that it spread quickly. That did not bode well for—

She stopped suddenly as she came to a torn edge of paper in her book.

She looked at the drawing before it—a quick sketch of Nyx and Lux, which was all they would sit still for—and the one after it, a detailed study of the mountain which might, she realized now, come in handy for the map.

But more important just now was the page that was missing.

"Eirlys," she said, almost to herself.

"What?"

She looked up at the Raider. He was definitely looking at her now. "Sorry. It was a page he took."

"Brander took a page from your book?"

She nodded. "A portrait of Eirlys Davorin."

He went very still. "Why?"

"In truth?"

"Preferably." There was an odd note in his voice she couldn't pin down.

"He cares for her."

"He has known her all her life."

So he knew that, too, she thought. She wasn't surprised. She guessed there were few secrets between the two men.

"It is more than that. He cares for her as a man cares for a woman."

She couldn't hear what he said under his breath, but she guessed it was a particularly tasty oath. She understood; the Raider knew such things were beyond foolish in times like these.

"Do not worry," she said hastily. "He believes her too young for him."

"As she is," he muttered.

Kye was not so certain of that. Eirlys might be not yet of adult age, but she was very smart and had, as they all had, grown older faster in the years since the Coalition had stomped Ziem under their heavy bootheels.

But his reaction told her more than she had wanted to know. He thought Brander a fool for such feelings.

And he would no doubt think her even more of one. And that she could not bear. She must accept the fact that he would never let any softer feelings emerge. Not for her, not for anyone. She understood it. She acknowledged it.

She hated it.

Chapter 24

BRANDER STARED down at the paper the Raider had handed him. Then looked up at the man who was only now taking off the silver helmet.

"This is how you found out?"

He nodded silently.

Brander looked again at the signature of the note detailing the shipment of the communicators. "The Spirit?" he said with a laugh. "Somebody's been listening to too many tales from above the Edge."

"Perhaps."

Something in the Raider's voice made Brander's gaze snap back to his face. Without the helmet, he could see more of his expression, despite the scars. And what he saw puzzled him. "Next thing I know, you'll be telling me you believe in her."

"I do not know if she is the miraculous being some say: a healer whose powers are near magical. Or that she knows all, sees all. Or that she is even the true subject of the lore." His mouth quirked. "I do not even know with certainty that she is a she. What I do know is that the information is accurate. It has proven to be time and again."

Brander looked down at the note again. "But how could any one person know all that she has told?"

"How the knowledge is come by, I do not know either."

He turned the page over, noted the folds, and the slight stain on the back side. "This came from the hive?"

"Yes. But others have been found in the other drops."

"The number," he began, tapping at the figure in the lower corner.

"It is a simple count. So we would know if we had missed a message."

Brander blinked. "You've gotten nearly forty of these?"

The Raider nodded. "They began shortly after we set up the drops. At first they were just . . . approval. Encouragement. Then the information began."

"And you trusted it? That easily?" Brander asked in disbelief.

The Raider gave a wry laugh. "Hardly. I assumed it was a trap. But I investigated the first few, just watching. They were accurate, down to the time and place. The fuel cell raid was the first time I acted upon a message."

Brander remembered the raid on the caravan headed to the landing zone that had deprived the Coalition of badly needed fuel cells and turned the outpost into chaos for weeks. It had been their biggest success at that point.

"And after that?"

"If it was possible, I slated the mission. I'd say nearly half of our successes have been based on information from the Spirit. Whoever that might be in reality."

Brander shook his head in amazement. Only the Raider himself knew the full extent of the net of spies he'd built. He had eyes everywhere; even those unable or afraid to join them saw things, heard things, and if this was the only way they had to fight, they would do it. But none of the reports he'd seen had ever been as complete and concise as this one.

"Are they always like this? With exactly what's needed in so few words?"

"Yes."

"Well, whoever it is, they're bedamned good."

"Yes."

Brander studied him for a moment. "The drops have been in use almost since the beginning. Why have you decided to tell me now?"

"I wasn't keeping it from you for any—"

Brander cut him off with a shake of his head. "I didn't mean why haven't you told me. I long ago accepted that you have your reasons for whatever you do. I meant . . . why now?"

He saw him draw in a deep breath. "We have had some success."

Brander grinned. "Indeed we have. You are driving them mad. One man, with less than a hundred fighters, and you harry them as if you had a force equal to their own."

"The more successful we are, the angrier the Coalition gets."

"And it's wonderful to behold. They—"

He broke off suddenly as the implication hit him. It was followed quickly by realization. "You're telling me this," he said slowly, "in case they kill you."

The Raider's non-answer was answer enough.

Although the risk was always there, for all of them—you didn't go up against the full might of the Coalition with minimal antiquated and patched weapons and equipment without knowing you had no chance of winning and a grimly good chance of getting killed—Brander hadn't really contemplated the extent of the consequences should those planium-brained tyrants ever succeed in taking out the only man who had ever rallied Ziemites to fight back. This rebellion would die a quick and undistinguished death if that happened.

And yet he knew better than to suggest the Raider keep himself safe, or tell him he was more important alive than leading an attack. For never would the man stand down and send others into danger in his place. He had not built the fearsome reputation of the Raider by hunkering down in safety.

So instead, Brander looked again at the message in his hand. "Perhaps," he said thoughtfully, "we should use this."

The Raider looked at him questioningly. He shrugged.

"I mean, think of it . . . two legends, the Raider and the Spirit, working together to save Ziem. People would gorge on it. It would give them hope, perhaps even inspire some to join the fight."

Above the scarred face, the Raider's eyes looked thoughtful. "You might have an idea there."

Brander nodded. "You know I do. You know I can read people at the chaser table, and what we're doing here is just a bigger gamble."

The Raider made a sound that could almost be a laugh, a rare enough occurrence to make Brander smile.

"I'll have people thinking we'll have the Coalition driven out by next sun-season."

"Careful," the Raider said, "or we'll have our own rebellion when that doesn't happen."

"Okay," Brander said easily, knowing he'd won, "the one after that, then."

That night, in the taproom, Brander chose his target carefully. Carag Dreese himself wasn't the sort who spread rumors, but he was pledged to Alcana, the biggest tale-teller in all of Zelos. And he told her everything.

He lingered in the corner of the room, hidden in the shadows, until Carag made his way up to the bar. Before the man could order—Drake was busy with two Coalition officers at the end of the bar—Brander slid in beside him, two drinks in his hand. One happened to be the man's favored sun ale, made from a combination of grains and flowers that grew only in Ziem's sun-season.

"It seems I've been forsaken," he said with a heavy sigh. "The lady clearly isn't going to show up."

Carag glanced at him, then grinned.

"Another conquest?"

"Not tonight, obviously. Here, you might as well have this," he said, sliding the mug of brew at him.

The man's face lit. "Why, thank you."

"Someone might as well enjoy it." Brander turned to face the man, leaning on the bar with one elbow. "I envy you, having a good woman to go home to every night."

Carag snorted. "There's good and then there's good." He took a gulp of the brew as he gave Brander a sly glance. "Example, the Davorin girl."

"Eirlys is but a child." He gave a carefully disinterested wave.

"She is hardly that," Carag said. "And lovely into the bargain. She'll soon have all the unpledged men in Zelos at her feet. And probably a few who are pledged."

That was a situation Brander didn't care to contemplate. In part because he feared it was nothing less than the truth.

"That," he said, "is Drake's problem."

Carag snorted, and foam from the brew frothed down his chin. He wiped at it with his sleeve, glanced around, spotted Drake still at the far end, and went on. "As if he'd stand up to anyone. Why, if Sorkost himself came to claim her, he'd probably hold the door for the skalworm."

Brander said nothing, and after a moment, Carag shrugged. "Apologies. I know he is your friend. And it is true he has much to deal with already. Those twins alone . . ." He shook his head as he spoke of those two imps. Then he glanced around again, as if to see who was within hearing before adding, "No, it takes the likes of the Raider to stand up to those thuggers."

And there was his opening.

"Speaking of the Raider, I heard the craziest story today," Brander said.

"Oh?"

"I heard the Raider is working in concert with the Spirit. That she's been providing him with information, gathered however she gathers it."

"The Spirit?" Carag scoffed. "Everyone knows she's just a tale told to children."

"That's what I told the man, but he was certain she is real. He said he had seen her himself, heard her true story."

"Which is?"

"That she lives quietly above the Edge, practicing her healing arts. That she has healed many, some even on the point of death. That her skills are unmatched."

"We've all heard those tales. That only the most desperate would risk the dangerous trek up the mountain for her skills, but those who survived returned with miraculous stories of her healing. Stories all. No first-hand accounts."

Brander nodded. "But *this* man said that after she had saved his son, he'd seen her sending a message to the Raider. She told him they were working together to try and rid Ziem of this pestilence. And that people she has helped tell her things, things she passes along to the Raider."

Carag looked oddly and unexpectedly wistful. "Now that's a tale worthy of telling, the Raider and the Spirit working together to save us."

Brander nodded. And when Carag had finished his gifted brew and taken his leave, he knew the story was started.

It would be interesting to see how long it took for it to get back to him, and what form it would be in when it did.

"LOOKING AT YOU, it's hard to believe heroics are in the Davorin blood."

Drake kept stirring the stew, not even turning at his sister's jibe. It was pointless, and he wished she would stop. "If you think constantly worrying at it is going to change it, perhaps you should go find a bone to chew on, like Eck's barkhound."

"I am just reminding you that, as much as you try to forget or ignore it, it is there. Our father, his father, and his father's father."

"Not in me."

"Then I suppose it's up to me to keep the honor of our name."

He spun around then. "If you are thinking of brolleting up the mountain to join the rebellion, forget it."

"*I*," she said pointedly, "am not a helpless brollet."

Her implication was unmistakable, that if this room held one of the easily frightened creatures whose only defense was to quickly run away, it was him. But right now, there was something more important to deal with.

"I have your word, Eirlys, and you will hold to it."

Her head came up, and her eyes, darker than his own but still a clear, Ziem blue, narrowed. "You will make me?"

She said it as challenge, as dare, and it was only with an effort that he didn't rise to the bait. "I will not have to. You do not give a promise lightly."

For a moment, she looked flummoxed, he supposed because he had in essence complimented her while she was attempting to spit him for roasting.

"You truly are content . . . like this?" she asked, stark disbelief echoing in her voice.

"I never said I was content."

"Then why don't you do something?"

He whirled on her then, unable to hold back. "What would you have me do? Kill them at the door? Openly charge their gates? Climb the walls and give a speech, like our father? All of these actions end the same way, me dead and you alone to take care of yourself and the twins."

"But to welcome our oppressors, cater to them!"

"I have my reasons."

"What reason could possibly—"

He held up a hand to stop her. "Please. We have been through this before. Countless times."

"And you—"

This time it was a hammering on the door that cut her off.

"'Tis Rest Day," she muttered. "Can they not leave us alone even then?"

When she crossed the room and yanked the door open, Drake's heart sank to see the very man he'd just referred to, Enish Eck, standing there, glowering.

The twins. It had to be.

"What did they do now?" Eirlys clearly had the same thought.

"If you don't control those two demons, I will lock them in my cellar until they're of age," the older man declared in a rage.

"Don't tempt me," Drake muttered.

"You'll do no such thing," Eirlys said to Eck. "You're too good a man."

Eck blinked, then stared, as if he'd never seen Eirlys before when in fact he'd known them her entire childhood.

"Now," she said, taking his arm and drawing him inside, "come in. We have a lovely brollet stew almost ready; you must join us while you tell us what those two pests did this time. With some brew, of course."

Was she actually patting his arm? Drake wondered. And when had his little sister turned into a diplomat?

He was so surprised he barely followed Eck's tale of a broken window, some type of incendiary device, and a fire that he began by saying nearly burned his house down but ended, by the time Eirlys poured him a second glass of brew, with a confession that it had barely singed his back door.

When the man had gone, after accepting her promise that the twins would personally see to repairing any damage, Eirlys closed the door and added, "And serves them right that we've fed him their share of dinner."

"And then some," Drake said; Eck was not a light eater when given the chance at free food. But he would consider the price cheap enough, considering. "So tell me, my sister, when did you become so . . . tactful?" *With others, if not with me.*

She shrugged. "I knew the brew would mellow him. He gets little enough chance to partake anymore."

She's grown up, truly. The thought did not cheer him, for it meant she was closer to the day when she was free of her promise. And he knew what would happen when that day came. And that had ramifications he was too weary to think about just now.

But he said only, "I thought I'd not seen him in for some time."

She turned then, meeting his gaze. "You've not seen him, and many others, because they do not care to enter a taproom full of Coalition scum."

And, that quickly, she was back at it.

"And how else do you think we eat as we do, not having to scrounge Coalition garbage heaps for food?"

"I think," she said, "I would rather go hungry."

"Then do so," he snapped. He couldn't stop himself. He was worn too thin, and she'd pressed too hard.

Eirlys turned on her heel and slammed out the same door Eck had used. All he could think of was what a far cry she was now from the girl who had once trailed worshipfully at his heels, who thought her big brother painted the sky.

Drake sank back down into his chair. He put his elbows on the table and cradled his head in his hands.

It took him a long, silent few minutes to chide himself out of his weariness, labeling it self-pity he had no time for. Then he stood, and went back to work. Moments later, he was putting a crate of new glassware—amazing how the storage doors were opened when the Coalition were the ones facing drinking out of chipped glasses or stained wooden cups—on the bar. Only then did he look at his left hand, which had been telling him ever since he'd picked up the wooden box that he'd managed to acquire a sizeable splinter.

He frowned as he plucked at it. It was jagged, and buried deep, and his flesh clung to it stubbornly. In the string of aches, pains, and injuries he'd experienced, it was a mere pinprick, but it was nevertheless annoying.

But not annoying enough to keep him from hearing the faintest of steps from behind him.

He barely managed to stay as he was, feigning ignorance. The taproom keeper, after all, had no reason to be so aware, or to react as anything other than a cowed, broken servant. Only when even the most oblivious of men would have realized someone was there did he turn around, letting out a gasp of shock and cowering back.

He was trapped, pinned against the bar by a man in a Coalition uniform. His gaze shot to the man's face. Caze Paledan.

And the man held a gleaming, razor-sharp blade. Pointed at him.

His prediction to Eirlys about his end might come true after all, and quickly.

Chapter 25

"NASTY," PALEDAN said, gesturing with the point of the blade at Drake's finger.

Drake started to say it was nothing, then caught himself. "It's very painful," he said, with a visible wince.

"Here. Use this."

The major reversed the blade in his hand with a quick motion, offering Drake the handle. Drake hesitated. Not because it wouldn't work, but because he was afraid of what he might do with that well-honed blade in his hand and a Coalition officer within stabbing distance.

As if the tapper could ever work up such nerve.

He realized two things then; first, that this was likely a test of just that. The man had probably heard he was broken, submissive. But given who Drake's father had been, Paledan had probably wanted to test him out himself.

And secondly, and of primary importance . . . Paledan had no fear for himself. It was the self-assurance of a man who knew he could take on any man and win. Even if the tapper showed an unexpected spark of defiance, he had confidence he could put him down like an infected barkhound. Easily.

Drake took the dagger gingerly. He poked it at the thick sliver of wood. The spot quickly began to bleed, and he winced blatantly. But he got a large chunk of the splinter out, and quickly decided that was enough. The rest would work its way out eventually.

"Thank you, sir," he said, handing the blade back in the same way it had been handed to him. Using a clean bar cloth to press against the small wound, he looked at the man who had so nearly snuck up upon him. "You left the other night without your change. I have it waiting for you."

"I didn't wish for change." The man lifted a brow. "Are you always so scrupulous?"

"I've seen men killed for less," he said neutrally. *By other men in your uniform.* "What can I get you, Major?"

"I understand you have clingfruit nectar available."

Drake didn't react, but inwardly, he was surprised. The juice of the native clingfruit was not frequently requested here where more potent brews were the usual fare. Clingfruit nectar had no effect except the soothing of an irritated throat.

"Of course," he said. "I hope you're not ill?"

"Not yet," the man said dryly. "But I have a meeting with Jepson Kerrold shortly. I must assume nothing but talk will be the order of the day."

Drake couldn't stop the smallest quirk of his mouth before he turned to grasp the bottle with the drawing of the pinkish-orange fruit on it.

"You have met him, then?" Drake said neutrally as he filled a glass and held it out.

"Not yet. But I have heard enough to guess he is the sort of blowhard aspirant to glory I have dealt with in many places." He took a sip of the nectar, seemed surprised at the taste, and took another. Then he looked at Drake levelly. "And you, tapper. Do you have an opinion of your representative?"

"A man in my position cannot afford opinions, sir."

Paledan grimaced. "But if you did," he persisted.

"If I did," Drake said carefully, "I would say you are well prepared."

There was a fraught split second of silence. And then Paledan gave a hearty laugh. "And you are the soul of diplomacy, delivering agreement without saying so, and leavened with a compliment."

Drake caught himself smiling. And was startled to realize it was genuine. Something he never would have expected in the presence of a Coalition major. Paledan downed the last of the juice, insisted on paying for it despite Drake's demurral, and nodded as he turned to go.

Drake's smile vanished as the door opened before the man got there, and Kye stepped inside. Paledan looked her up and down, as any man with a beating heart would. And as any man would be, he was appreciative.

Kye, on the other hand, merely lifted her chin and strode past him without a word. Again to Drake's surprise, the man merely smiled, and continued on his way. Most of the Coalition would have paused no matter what their agenda for the day, to remind the woman who was in charge. Had that Coalition man been Frall, the old commander, Drake shuddered to think what that cool disapproval would have earned her. He watched assessingly as the man exited, still trying to get the measure of this new commander who would in essence rule over Zelos and Ziem much more personally than Barcon and the governor.

He knew better than to express concern about the way Kye had treated the man. She would not welcome it from him. Not anymore. But he couldn't completely quash it. "Why didn't you just slap him?" he asked, keeping his tone mild.

"He said nothing to be slapped for. In fact, he said nothing."

She took a seat at the bar and watched as he tore a strip off the bar cloth with the small bloodstain before he set it aside. He wrapped the strip around the spot on his finger the knife had slit, then took up a fresh cloth to wash the nectar glass. She seemed to be studying him rather intently, and he wasn't sure why. He knew he probably wouldn't like the reason, however, so he did not ask.

"You slapped Kerrold for looking at you like that," he said instead.

"Kerrold makes my skin creep."

"And a Coalition major does not?"

She glanced toward the door he'd exited. "He seems . . . different."

He'd thought the same thing himself, but did not like hearing it from her. "What do you mean?"

"He is . . . impressive."

He really didn't like that.

"Impressive?"

She shrugged as she turned back. "In the way a powerful predator is impressive. He seems a man to be taken seriously."

No, he didn't like this at all. "As you once had an infatuation with Jepson Kerrold, I'm not sure how seriously you should be taken."

She scowled. It wrinkled her nose in that way that had always made him smile inwardly. "I was a child. He was fancy. What did I know?"

"Truth," he admitted.

She let out a breath that was almost a sigh. It was unlike her enough that he stilled his hands and waited.

"But you are right. My judgment of men was dreadful then, and still is now. Perhaps it will be always."

It was not said in the way she had when she was aiming it at him, but there was still a ring of heartfelt ruefulness in her voice, and Drake hated that he was at fault for at least part of that. Perhaps all of it, if he counted what he'd done to her in both guises.

"Someday," he began, then stopped.

"Someday what?"

"Nothing. Just stay clear of Paledan, will you?"

"He is a Coalition major, no matter how impressive. Of course I will."

And he had to be satisfied with that.

BRANDER'S KNOCK sounded on the door. The Raider looked up from the message signed with the Spirit's feather and called out for him to enter.

"It's true," he said without preamble. "The Spirit was right again. I had it from Cuplin and Weel that the miners have been accompanied the entire week by Coalition workers and new equipment. It's probable they're the ones who arrived on that transport last week."

The Raider let out an oath under his breath.

"Do you think they've come up with a way to get their equipment to work in the mist?"

"It seems the logical conclusion."

"So they may not need our people anymore."

"Yes." The Raider's jaw tightened. "And we know what the Coalition does with things they no longer need."

"What will we do?" Brander asked.

He had been thinking of this while Brander had been off confirming the intelligence. He outlined the only plan that had come to him.

"It would work, I think," Brander said slowly.

"Yes."

"But how to pull it off? Explosives are out, if it must seem natural."

"Yes."

"Some of the old miners, from the days before the borers, might have ideas." Brander frowned. "If there are any left alive."

"Put out the word. See who remains, and would be willing to venture suggestions."

Brander nodded.

By the next day, the rumors, likely sparked by Brander's inquiries, were rampant. But unlike most hearsay, they were very consistent. Because there was only one logical explanation—the Coalition had new tools and if they worked with their own people, they planned to do away with the Ziem miners. And once that was done, they would have no need of any Ziemite at all. They would wipe them all out, with no more thought than a blazer would give his prey.

And the Spirit had somehow known well beforehand. He did not know how she gained her information, only that it was unfailingly accurate.

He holed up in his quarters, pondering methods and logistics, all the while aware he knew too little of mining to be sure what might work.

Two days later, Brander brought him a visitor.

"Samac Rahan," he said.

The Raider recognized the name of one of their pioneer miners, who decades ago had been instrumental in finding the vast reserves of planium the north mountains held.

"You won't like it," Brander added, "but I think he has the answer."

He nodded, and Brander stepped back to usher a man into his quarters. He left and closed the door, leading the Raider to think he already knew the man's plan, and would wait only to hear if it was to be implemented.

He saw the age of the man, and instinctively got to his feet in respect. They had spoken of the old miners, and Samac certainly had the look. Even paler than the normal Ziemite, a good foot shorter than he himself but broad-chested and well-muscled. Even at a clearly advanced age, he looked strong, as those who had mined with hand tools had had to be, in the days before the arrival of the powerful borers that dug through the hard, unyielding rock of the north mountains. And yet there was something else about him, a slight off-tone of his skin, the slight shuffle in his step that spoke of more than just age.

"It is an honor," Samac said, bowing his head.

The Raider shook his head. "It is I who am honored, elder. Will you sit?"

Surprise, then gratification flickered across the old man's face. "I thought there was no place in the Coalition world for the old ways any longer."

"I am not in the Coalition world."

A broad smile creased his face, and the Raider saw a flash of the man he must have been in his youth: alive, vital, strong, and powerful.

"You give me hope for Ziem, young man."

"Do not surrender that hope. Now what is it you have?"

"An idea," Samac said. "A plan, even."

He laid it out then, in a meticulous, logical manner that told the Raider he had thought it through carefully. When he had finished, it was all the Raider could do not to immediately shake his head in negation. "I cannot ask you to do this."

"You didn't ask. Sir."

"Samac," the Raider said gently, "there is no way to assure your escape."

The old man lifted his head, looked at him with eyes that were clear and bright despite his many years. "I know."

He took in a deep breath. "You have already given your life to Ziem. You have designed and dug her mines, the system which brought us wealth, and fought bravely when the Coalition arrived to steal all we had built."

"And now I am dying."

The Raider drew back. The man, for his age, looked healthy enough.

"It is true," Samac insisted. "The town healer warned me, before he was killed. And I feel the pressure of the growth, increasing every day. It will soon cripple me, leave me helpless. I do not choose to go out that way."

"Samac," he began, not wanting this sacrifice. And hating the fact that once, it would not have been a death sentence; once, the man could have been healed, before the Coalition had destroyed every medical facility on Ziem, and the healers and scientists along with them. No one outside Coalition protection was to have care, yet another way to force people to welcome their bootheels.

"Let me do this. For my world."

"It might be pointless. It could well be we will lose anyway, in the end."

"But we can make the Coalition fight for every gain, make it as costly for them as we can."

"It would only delay them."

"And how often have I heard that you have fought a delaying action and then turned the time gained into a victory?"

"I do not deny that it would be valuable. I quibble only at the cost."

"I have no one left, sir. They've taken everyone I loved and everything I had. My death is inevitable, and soon. Let it mean something."

"Samac," he began, but the man shook his head.

"Let me put those years, this knowledge I have of the mines, to use one last time. I will know how to do it, and the exact moment to make the final move."

The Raider studied the man before him for a long, silent moment. Saw the determination in his eyes, his weathered face. "Are you able?"

"For this, I will be."

The Raider waited a long, solemn moment. Reached out and laid a hand on the old man's arm. Samac stood up straighter, prouder.

"Then prepare."

The Ziem blue eyes lit. "Yes, sir."

"I will send word when it is time to begin."

"Thank you," Samac said, his voice steady, resolved, unwavering.

He stood, walked toward the door with a much steadier gait than when he had come in. The Raider walked beside him as escort, with a respect that had grown a thousandfold since the man had arrived. He would never, ever get used to this. Sending people to certain death. That Samac had volunteered, that he was merely avoiding a more painful future to come, made it no easier, just painful in a different way.

The old nightmare vision of his mother, plunging off Halfhead to her death to avoid her own painful future played vividly in his head. But she had not been old, only a few years older than he was now, given she had been but sixteen when he was born. And yet she had surrendered to her grief, her four children not enough to tie her to this life in the face of her pain.

He buried the old, useless ache deep, and reached to open the door for Samac. But stopped when the old man spoke. "Since it will not matter," he said, looking up at his scarred face, "will you tell me?"

"Tell you . . . ?"

"Who you are."

He hesitated only a moment. This man was willing to die, intentionally, to sacrifice himself to buy Ziem more time.

He leaned over and whispered into the old miner's ear. The smile flashed again, wider, brighter. Happiness glowed in his eyes. He looked like anything but a man who had just volunteered to die. And to the Raider's surprise, the old man engulfed him in a hug worthy of a mountain bear.

Brander was waiting outside, along with Kye.

"See him safely home," he said.

Brander nodded.

"Then return." He looked at Samac and smiled. "There are more rumors to spread."

IT WAS AN EFFORT for Brander not to laugh when Nard Rejel sidled up to him at the chaser table just as he was getting up to leave, and whispered in his ear.

"Have you heard? The Raider and the Spirit have joined forces. They'll drive the Coalition out for sure!"

"That would be a formidable combination," he admitted, as if reluctantly.

The optics man pushed his own lenses back on his nose, then rubbed his hands together almost gleefully. "Maybe those thuggers will find Ziemites have some bite after all."

Brander decided it could not hurt to plant the idea, and said, as if it had just occurred to him, "If this rallies more to the Raider, things could change."

"Exactly. Thinking of going myself, if only I knew where they were."

Now that was something he should have thought of before. "I've heard," he said slowly, stalling as his mind raced, "that you can leave a message in the crack of the smallest bell in the tower, and he'll get it."

He figured that would be safe enough; he knew the location was scheduled to be rotated off the message drop list in a couple of days anyway, so it wouldn't do any harm for Nard to know.

"I think I'll do that," Nard said, now rubbing at his bewhiskered chin.

Brander wasn't sure the man would, thought it likely that good sense would overtake him before he got it done. But that didn't really matter. What mattered was that it had worked. The story was circulating. One more brick in the formidable Raider legend.

And now it was time to start the next rumor on its way. He looked around until he saw his quarry. Pryl had a nephew in the mines. Besides being the canniest woodsman and tracker around, he was also one of the Sentinels who risked the double life of fighting and staying here in Zelos.

He walked over to the table the man was sitting at, carefully chosen to allow virtually anyone in the taproom to overhear. But most especially the two Coalition troopers who sat at the table to Pryl's back.

"You look more peevish than usual," he said as he pulled out a chair, speaking just loudly enough that he could be heard by all, yet not so loud it appeared he was shouting. He carefully sat so that he could see both Pryl and the troopers.

"You'd feel that way too," Pryl said, his voice at the same level, "if you had a nephew in the mines when there's going to be a cave-in any moment now."

Brander sensed by the drop in the surrounding chatter that they'd been heard by much of the room. But most importantly, they'd been heard by the troopers.

"I've heard they've been having trouble."

"It's those Coalition meddlers," Pryl said, his tone excessively sour. "They don't know the first thing about planium mining, and they're going to bring a collapse down on them all. Then only the Spirit can help them."

Brander saw the troopers stiffen.

He gave a barely perceptible nod to Pryl, to signal him to continue. "Only good thing is, now that they're there, there will be as many of them taken out as us."

He could almost read the dilemma on the troopers' faces; take out the insolent Pryl, or scurry back to headquarters to tell what they'd heard. They could, of course, split up to do both, but he doubted either of them had the courage to face down Pryl alone, never mind the fact that they couldn't be sure the crowded taproom didn't hold more than one rebellion sympathizer. He knew in fact it held several. Intentionally.

After a moment, the two scrambled to their feet and headed for the door.

He and Pryl lifted their mugs in a mutual toast.

When he finished and walked over to the bar, Drake appeared to ask if he wanted a refill. He shook his head.

"Late," he said.

Drake nodded. "Near closing time."

Brander nodded in turn. "I'm done. I'll be off."

"Good night."

"Mmm."

He left his friend there washing the mug he'd handed over. And wondered what it must feel like to be the lone hope of a world and yet have just about everyone in your town consider you coward. True, they thought he himself a wastrel, but that was truth enough.

He did not envy the path—the paths—Drake had chosen to walk.

Chapter 26

"SIR?"

Brakely's voice from the doorway cut through his thoughts. Paledan was both surprised and irritated, he'd given orders not to be disturbed while he went over the reports on losses to the Raider. But his irritation ebbed quickly; Brakely knew better than to interrupt him for anything minor, so this had to be something more.

"What?" he asked without looking up.

"There's been an incident. At the mine."

Paledan's head came up slowly. "An incident?"

"A major cave-in. Two of the guards were killed, along with a handful of our trainees. Several injured. And the new equipment is buried."

"Accident or intent?" Could the Raider have somehow engineered even this?

"They think accident, sir. The leader of the detachment agrees, since one of their own—a leader of the miners, in fact—was also killed."

Paledan considered this. According to his study, Ziemites put a ridiculously high value on one individual life, so perhaps this was truly an accident. "Get me the details, and the identities of the dead."

"Yes, sir."

"And a report on the condition of the mine."

"Yes, sir. They already say it will take weeks to clear it, and I'm told it will not be safe to even start again until the rock has settled."

"For now, pull our men out. Our contingent is not so large I can risk more without replacements. But tell the miners I want it cleared and work underway again before I leave for legion command."

"Yes, sir." Brakely hesitated, but then added, "The miners are shaken. The man who was killed was the most knowledgeable among them."

Paledan weighed what he was certain would be Legion Command's demands against the need to keep the miners if not happy, at least not mutinous. Many of his superiors, he knew, would scoff at such a thought; the people of conquered worlds were to be used, and if not useful, they were expendable. There had, recently, been mutterings about simply wiping them out and taking over, eliminating the need for the native population. He had in fact been sent here with the authority, should it be needed, to use the fusion cannon on the city, but not before they had people trained to take over.

And even the most vociferous agreed this was a special case; while they were proficient with extracting other resources, planium mining was not a skill the Coalition could boast of, and they needed these men of Ziem not only to work, but work well. That was what made Ziem different than most Coalition conquests; they needed the population to work the mines and service the miners.

Fortunately that population was relatively small, and thus controllable.

But once they had enough people trained to take over, they would no longer be necessary.

He decided.

"Give them three days' leave. A day to tend to the injured, a day to mourn their leader, and a day to prepare to return. Order the troops to show respect for the loss. The miners must feel valued, or production will drop."

"Yes, sir," Brakely said, and backed out the door.

KYE WALKED SLOWLY back to her rooms from Drake's taproom, taking the circuitous route she usually did, just in case. She didn't think she was being followed, and there was no reason for anyone to, but she wished to keep her hiding place secret as much as she could. Eirlys knew where it was, and Drake, but no other. She savored the peace she found there, and sometimes thought it was the only thing that kept her going.

But now she was only giving the route half her attention. The rest was consumed with something else. With something she had seen when she'd first entered the taproom. True, Paledan was impressive enough to suck up all the attention in any room, but she hadn't missed the way Drake had been watching him as he left. The expression he'd worn, as if he were . . . calculating something. It was more than niggling at her, it was nagging, and she wasn't sure why. It seemed both strange to see on Drake's face, and yet at the same time familiar. Which made no sense at all.

When she arrived home, it was nearly dark, but instead of eating and resting as she had planned, she found herself pacing. She was so restless, she finally did something she hadn't done in a long time. She pulled out her sketch pad for a reason other than maps and planning.

She had not sketched something not related to the rebellion in a long time. She had purposefully quashed that part of her. In fact, the portrait of Eirlys, staring into the distance, her hair in a loose, thick braid with wisps blowing about her lovely face, the portrait done nearly a year ago and that Brander had stolen, was the last thing of pure art she'd done.

Until now.

Until tonight, in a darkness lessened only by the glow of the lantern at her elbow, when she pulled out her book and a stub of charcoal and began.

It was the long spell of working on the map that had her unsettled.

"What is it?" she had been asked countless times. "What are you working on?"

"A map," was always her simple reply. "A very large map."

A very large map, in their minds, meant a very large plan. That alone quieted them, such was their faith in their leader.

And their faith was nothing as compared to hers. She would, freely and willingly if necessary, die for the man they called the Raider. She admired him, respected him, and gloried in the simple fact that here was a man who would stand, who would fight back and not be moved.

She also loved him.

She had given up trying to deny it to herself. It didn't matter anyway. For it was unlikely that both of them would survive this conflict, and she would not, could not muddy the waters. He needed clear thinking, and she could not distract him with thoughts of things that could not be.

So now she sat in her room, the small sanctuary in the back of what was left of her parents' old home. The front section had been turned to rubble by a Coalition strike, at last putting an end to her father's helpless pain. She stayed here partly as reminder of what the Coalition had taken from her, partly for the quiet refuge it offered.

From the front it appeared uninhabitable, but in fact the back three rooms, which included the kitchen, a washroom, and what had been a storage room, were fairly intact. She had left the front uncleared. Not only as a shrine to her father's death there, but there was some measure of safety in the Coalition thinking they had already destroyed this target, and she was far enough distant from the center of Zelos for them not to find the location attractive enough to clear out and rebuild.

So now she sat unmolested in the storage room she had converted to a living space, as comfortable as it could be under the circumstances. The light from the lantern was masked by the sheet of metal she had salvaged from a wreck and placed over the one window. It was her father's extending chair she sat in, the only furnishing that had survived relatively unscathed. It now served her as both seat and bed, and it was large enough that she had had to have Drake's help to move it out of the wreckage and back here.

Drake.

Her mind skittered away again, as it always did these days. Eirlys had suggested, when she had first seen the ruin, that she move in with them behind the taproom. At the time, it had been merely a stubborn refusal to abandon her home that made her turn the girl down, but it was soon after she was glad she had. For there was no way she would have been able to hold her tongue as Drake descended into the pit of meek capitulation where he now lived.

And yet that expression she'd caught this afternoon still hovered.

Shoving the thought aside, she turned to the task she'd realized she must do now, or it might never get done. She could be killed at any time, with this need unmet. Or worse, the Raider could be, and she would have to do it knowing he was gone forever, and it would likely drive her to follow him.

Which losing him might do anyway.

She shifted in the chair, angling so that the lantern light fell on a new page. She had few left, and there was no way to justify spending precious coin on such an extravagance when even food to keep living another week was so dear. But she had two, enough for this. And she needed to do this. She wasn't even sure of all the reasons why, but she knew there was no denying it any longer.

Her hand trembled slightly as she moved the chalk to the top of the page. Whether because it had been so long, or that she was afraid to do this she was not certain. She began anyway, because she had to.

She began with his eyes. She needed no time to stop and recall. She knew them as well as she knew her own. The color rimmed with dark, surrounded by thick, black lashes, they were the icy blue eyes of Ziem. Typical of many—some said it was the mist that caused them—but in this man they were both intimidating and beautiful. And in the ruin of his face, they were the purest representation of the man within.

She let her heart, her subconscious, guide her hand, and found herself drawing the remaining undamaged parts. Although she had no intention of ignoring the scars, she went to that small part of his strong jaw line that was untouched, and then his mouth. That mouth, that she had too often found herself studying as if it were something she would later have to recreate. Perhaps some part of her had always known this day would come.

The way her hand was moving, swiftly, sure and true, with no need of the tiny bit of expunger she had left, told her that part of her she had smothered for so long was alive and well. It came pouring out of her, this need, as if every quashed bit of feeling she had for this man was rushing out through her fingers and a tiny stub of chalk.

Even the scars came easily, and she knew somehow she was capturing every curved ridge of flesh that twisted his face exactly as they were. Then she began the helmet, with the added sweep that covered the right side of his face, and realized she knew it almost as well, every curve, every dent, every battle scar, as well as the etched design she had long ago recognized as the work of Fortis, one of Ziem's most famous sons, a planium worker of no small genius. He had been lost in the first attack on Zelos, and their world was much the poorer for it.

When she finished, she stared down at the portrait for a long time. Without self-pride she knew that it was some of her best work. She would have to leave it here, for it would not do for him to ever by chance see it. Not when her heart, and everything she felt for him practically cried out from every line. Nor could she risk it falling into enemy hands; it would tell them no more than they already knew about the Raider, but it was better than any image they had and she truly would die were he ever taken with help from her hand.

It was good, yes. And yet her hand, and that part deep within her that drove this inexplicable talent, were restless still, as if she were not truly finished.

When it finally came to her, what was yet undone, she resisted. She did not want to do this, had a down-deep certainty she would regret it. And yet she recognized the compulsion, and knew it would eat at her endlessly until she complied.

She turned the page, to her last sheet of untouched drawing paper. For a moment she didn't even breathe. But then she lifted the chalk, calling up old lessons learned long ago, when Ziem's teachers had included artists as well as scientists, lessons about faces and asymmetry. She knew how to do this. She had done it before, in a classroom, and she could do it now.

The question was, should she?

The question is, do I have any choice?

She knew she did not.

She began again with his eyes. Then the line of his jaw, extending it to the other side, and how she guessed it must have looked before the flames that had disfigured him. Although how anyone could look at him, even scarred, and consider him disfigured was beyond her. She went on, duplicating what she knew of his uninjured face on the damaged side, with slight alterations she knew were typical from one side of a person's face to the other. She worked quickly enough that she knew that this, too, had been bubbling just beneath the surface.

Perhaps when she was finished she would ask Brander if this is what he had looked like, although she did not actually know if her cousin had known him before the injury. How strange, that she knew so little, yet felt so much. . . .

She focused on sections, going back and forth, filling in what she knew— the eyes, the dark hair, the strong jaw, corded neck—with what she was guessing at, the areas hidden by the helmet on one side and the mass of scar tissue on the other. She did not let herself think of what the helmet masked, what awful thing it covered if the mass of scars he let be seen were better. She quashed the whispers she'd heard, horrified tales of bare skull and sinew. None of it mattered now.

It was odd to be focused on the pieces and not the whole man as she drew. When she laid down the last stroke, a final shading of the taut cord of his neck, she closed her eyes. Her chalk was down to a nub she could barely hold, and she set it on the crate beside her that served as a table. She sat for a long moment, afraid to look at what she had done. Only the knowledge that the oil that powered her lamp would run out soon, and she would be hard-pressed to get more, forced her to it.

She drew in a deep breath, opened her eyes, and at last looked down to the sketchbook on her lap. Really looked at the whole for the first time.

Her breath shot out in a rush. She felt a swirl in her head, as if she were dizzy. She blinked, hard. Shook her head.

"No," she whispered.

But there was no denying what she'd done.

She'd drawn the Raider. She'd extrapolated from what she knew to what she couldn't see. And she knew she'd drawn it correctly. Knew she had drawn the man as he had been, before the mass of scars had deformed and twisted his face.

There was only one problem.

The image she was staring at was unmistakably Drake Davorin.

Chapter 27

ALL OF ZELOS heard the crash; the Raider heard opportunity for salvage at the expense of the Coalition. In the cellar ruin, the Sentinels rushed to follow rapid-fire orders, taking no time to speculate if it had been freighter or combat vessel that had gone down. When the Raider had come out of his quarters, he was already in his armor, helmet and gloves in place, ready to go as they still scrambled to suit up.

When one of the Harkins marveled at the quick string of assignments handed out, his brother said simply, "It's why he's the Raider and we follow him."

He pretended not to hear, although the words bolstered him.

Within minutes, they were on their way, three of the captured air rovers fully loaded. Brander had the one from the cave at the falls with a crew to patrol the likely approach from the Coalition post. Kye, who had just arrived moments ago, he sent to fly another to the ridgeline above, with her long gun; his orders had been to be ready to flip on the autopilot and use the airborne vehicle as a shooting platform if necessary. She had hesitated, looking at him oddly for a moment, and he'd thought she was going to question her assignment. But then she had nodded, rather sharply, and headed out to pick up the rover from the nearby forest hideout.

The Raider himself piloted the one headed for the crash itself, now marked by a rising spiral of smoke that would soon be noticed in town. He slowed once the wreck was in sight. The smell was stronger here, an ugly mix of smoke and freshly turned dirt, softened only slightly by the mist. Immediately any thought of salvaging the ship itself vanished; it was far beyond any repair they could manage with what they had.

It appeared no one could have survived it, but he'd learned early on—and the hard way, gaining the scar that slashed across his rib cage—to never assume.

"Clear in the valley, sir!"

Galeth's call indicated Brander had fired the flasher to indicate there was no sign of the Coalition incoming yet. The rebels' ability to see in the mist and knowledge of the terrain had given them the advantage, but not for long. The Raider had no doubts the Coalition would be here soon. Very soon.

"Cover in position," Galeth's brother said as he handed over the scope, indicating Kye was in place above. He quashed the inward shiver at that thought of her out in the open, in danger. She would not welcome his worry, and he could not let it distract him. But he could not seem to stop it, either. Every time he had to send her out it ate at him. The best he could do was avoid admitting to himself why.

He eased the rover forward. Used the battered scope to inspect. Class four freighter. Minimal armaments. Crew of three. No sign of any of them. Not a footprint outside the wrecked vessel, or even an open hatch. Yet there was no sign of fire, either. Which could bode well for recovery of cargo, or ill if it was a trap.

"I think they bought it on impact, sir," Galeth said.

He studied the front of the craft, which had crumpled to barely an arm span's depth as the freighter had cratered into the rocky slope.

"Agreed," he said, collapsing the scope. "But we will spread out and approach as if they are alive and waiting to fire."

The men obeyed, keeping enough distance between each other that a single blast could not take more than one of them out. They approached warily, carefully. They stopped at the Raider's command. Pryl looked back, and he nodded. The man edged forward alone.

He hated this part. Hated ordering people to do dangerous things that he would gladly do himself, were he free to do so. It had taken him a long time, and a few lectures from Brander, and by letter from the Spirit, to make him admit he couldn't take every risk himself.

Pryl crept up to the wreckage, his blade as always at the ready. "Three bodies," he called back. "No sign of anyone else aboard."

The Raider gave the signal, and his squad advanced on the ruined ship. The men began to go through the cargo bay, which, while damaged, looked as if it would hold long enough for them to get what could be carried. Including, he thought with grim pleasure, the crate of new blasters he could see from here. He wasn't sure how they'd transport the heavy thing, but he'd think of something.

He went forward toward the control deck, stepping past the bodies Galeth and his brother had pulled out and laid in a neat line. More than they would do for us, the Raider thought as he edged forward as far as he could go.

It seemed pointless—the controls were smashed, even the throttle broken off by the force of the crash. He took a step back, thinking he would join the others in selecting what cargo that was portable that they could best use.

A tiny, blinking light caught the edge of his vision as he turned. He leaned over. Reached out and pushed back a large chunk of metal—planium, he noted with some irony—to reveal the navigation system. He doubted it was functional—it likely hadn't been even before the crash, or they'd be safely landed on the flats by now—but maybe . . .

He reached out, trying to remember what he'd once read in stolen schematics and plans. He tapped three buttons with no response. Tried a different order. The cracked screen flickered to life, although the menu it displayed had several blank spots. But the one he'd been looking for was there, and he tapped it.

A log popped into view. It showed the arrival and departures of the ship for the last month. He tapped for the next page, hardly daring to hope.

It was there. A schedule for the next month, including the destinations. Ziem was there twice. Once with a cargo labeled as needing refrigeration. Food, he guessed.

And one more. His breath jammed up in his throat.

He spun around.

"Hold!" he ordered sharply.

The men pulling cargo from the bent racks froze. Galeth turned to look at him.

"Return it all."

As one they all drew back, staring. "What?" Galeth asked.

"Return it all. Exactly as you found it. Including the crew."

Teal stared. "The bodies?"

"Yes."

"The blasters?" Galeth said rather faintly.

"Don't take even one. Of anything. That's crucial. Move quickly!" He turned to Pryl, who was staring at him equally bewildered. "Go outside. Erase any trace of our presence. And stand by to obliterate our trail back to the rover. Now!"

He knew he was testing the obedience of these men to the limit. But the power of the Raider held, and they began to follow his orders. He spun on his heel and leapt from the ship, pulling the flasher gun from his belt. He fired the red signal for pulling back. Brander would linger, he knew, until they themselves were clear, and if he knew Kye, she would do the same, which made it even more imperative that they on the ground get clear rapidly.

They finished quickly. He left only Pryl, the best woodsman among them, to watch with the scope from a perch in a large mistbreaker tree.

He only breathed freely again when they were back in the shelter of the forest and he saw Kye and Brander's rovers riding their wake. They got to the ruin, returned the rovers to their hiding places, and at his order assumed the highest alert status.

"What was that about?" Brander asked as soon as they were in his quarters. Kye followed her cousin inside but simply waited, as if she knew he had a reason and she was only waiting to hear it.

"Bigger fish," he answered shortly.

Brander's expression changed. "How much bigger?"

"A lot."

His friend's mouth tightened, and then he nodded. "All right. I'll go see if I can settle the troops."

He almost reached to free himself of the helmet before he caught himself. He turned to look at Kye, still just inside the door Brander had closed behind him. She stood with her arms crossed, her face expressionless. Which in itself was a warning.

"Such is the power of the Raider," she said, "that his fighters will walk away from invaluable supplies and weapons on his order, without question."

He wasn't sure if she was criticizing his decision, or merely making an observation.

"It will be worth it," he said.

"I don't doubt that for an instant."

Something about her voice, some undertone he'd not heard before, and the way she used that name as if speaking about him, not to him, was unsettling. And he sensed she was wound up about something. He doubted it was the just-aborted mission, for Kye was ever cool on a raid.

No, he thought something else was working on her. And when she went on, he was sure of it.

"The Raider is rarely, if ever, wrong."

"I am," he said, looking at her quizzically, "right here."

Before she could respond to that, there was a knock on the door. Almost grateful—and surprised at himself for it—he called out permission to enter. The door opened.

Pryl. The relief at seeing the older man hit him. "No trouble? You're all right?"

"Of course," Pryl scoffed. "As if they'd see me unless I wanted them to."

His mouth quirked upward, and he nodded. "As you've proven, time and again. They arrived?"

Pryl nodded. "Less than five minutes after you cleared. Watched for another twenty. No sign at all they knew anyone had already been there. Didn't even look around outside. Tunnel vision, them skalworms."

"Good work. Thank you."

The man turned to go, then looked back. "We'll eventually find out what made you go peculiar, right?"

"You will."

The man nodded and closed the door behind him.

"So the Raider lets an old man question him."

He smothered a sigh. Whatever this was, he was going to have to deal with it. That it was Kye only made it harder. Because only Kye made him regret, made him wish, made him yearn.

"An old man who knows more about these woods than the Raider ever will." If she could talk about the legend as if he weren't before her, then so could he. "An old man who has fought with the Raider from the beginning. An old man who was beside Torstan when he defied the Coalition Council and refused to submit. The Raider would let him do a lot more than merely question."

"You speak as if the Raider were someone else."

"As did you."

She studied him intently for a moment. In an odd way, it reminded him of the new recruits upon seeing him for the first time. It took an effort that surprised him to hold her gaze. Usually he took what small pleasure he allowed himself from watching her, the way she moved, the sound of her voice, the way her rare smiles were as bright as a flasher. He always knew he dared not dwell upon it, or he might quail at doing what he had to do, which sometimes—too often—included ordering her into danger. For she would always go.

Such is the power of the Raider. . . .

It was not his power. It was hers. Her courage was endless, her nerve never failed her. And so of them all, save Brander, she was ever in the most peril.

"Shall I tell you what I think happened out there?"

"Can I stop you?" he asked wryly.

"You are the Raider. Your orders are followed."

At least she was no longer speaking of him as if he weren't in the room. He didn't give that order to stop. And she continued, ticking items off on her fingers.

"It was a freighter," she said, "with a regular schedule. Gareth says you went up front, then started snapping orders at them. You saw something. Something that changed your plan, on the fly. You wanted all evidence we were ever there erased. Which says you wanted the Coalition to think the wreck had been undiscovered before they arrived. And that in turn says that whatever you saw, you didn't want them to know you saw it. And the only reason I can think of for that is that you thought if they knew, they would react. Change something. Do something . . . or not do something."

He was thankful for the scars that masked what his expression would likely be without them as she worked her way through the exact process he'd gone through.

"And so," she continued, "I'm guessing you saw something. Something even more important, of more value to us. And you didn't want them changing their plans, now that you knew."

For a long moment he said nothing. He would not admit to what she'd deduced, so if the worst happened, she would have the ability to honestly deny she knew. But finally, softly, he gave her the salute she deserved.

"When I made you third in command, I chose wisely."

He saw the faintest bit of color hit her cheeks. She rarely showed such emotion, at least not here, so he had that at least, knowing his words had pleased her. And what a sad, tiny bit of recompense that was, for this woman who, were he able to allow it, could be the center of his life.

She didn't thank him, but only nodded, as if the truth of his words was self-evident. As it was, to anyone who had watched her work or been with her under fire. Then she turned away, and walked over to the canvas spread out over the table against the wall. "I have finished the southwest quadrant. What do you wish next?"

A whole string of wishes piled up behind his lips, none of which had anything to do with maps. He battled the urge, the need, realizing yet again that each time it grew more difficult. And telling himself he had no choice, that there was no way what he was feeling, wanting, could mesh with what he had to do, was getting less effective every time he was alone with her.

He tugged off his gloves with more force than was necessary as he crossed the room toward the table. He shoved them into a pocket as he leaned over the map that was already nothing less than a work of art. Not in her usual sense, that of the amazing portraits and landscapes she had done before, but in preciseness and efficiency for their purposes.

He reached out and tapped an opposite corner of the blank section of the canvas.

"Here. The northwest quadrant."

She didn't speak. She was staring at his hand. Too late, he curled back the finger with the small, telltale bandage.

And then she straightened, turned to face him.

"All right," she said, then added, pointedly, "Drake."

Chapter 28

HE RECOVERED SO quickly that had she not seen that instant when he'd tried to hide the cut from the splinter, Kye might have doubted herself.

But she had seen it, and she knew that she'd been right.

"What?" he said, with the perfect puzzled look on his face.

"You heard me."

"I did. But I don't know what you mean by it."

The Drake she'd known had not been such a smooth liar. But the Drake she'd known was indeed gone, but not in the way she'd thought. He hadn't been replaced by the broken man who had made her wonder at herself because she still cared for him.

He'd been replaced by a man who'd led an incredible, impossible double life for years. Who had carried it off so well that no one suspected, that everyone believed that somehow Drake Davorin had become the antithesis of his fiery father and bold, enchanting mother, while the Raider had risen out of nowhere, with no one knowing his true origins, to lead the fighters of Ziem with the best traits of them both.

She stared at him. "You're really going to hold to it?"

"I need this map. The biggest operation we've ever mounted depends on it."

"And if I were to say I won't do it until you tell me the truth?"

For a moment he met her gaze. "You will not. This battle means as much to you as it does to me."

The accuracy of his words took some of the fire out of her. And now that she stared at his eyes, knowing, it seemed impossible that she hadn't guessed long before. For while the color, that clear, sky-blue was typical on mist-shrouded Ziem, that dark rim around the iris was rarer. Yet what had seemed merely striking in Drake was overwhelming in the Raider, and she wondered how the same eyes could seem so different. But then she realized it was because the two roles were so different, and the new Drake, the one that made her heart ache, rarely met anyone's gaze anymore.

"Which role is the hardest to play?" she asked softly.

Something flashed in those eyes, again only for an instant. But she knew she'd seen it.

"The map," he repeated.

She drew in a deep breath, let it out slowly. "All right," she finally said. "For now," she added, warning him this was far from over.

"You know how soon I need it."

"You will have it."

And then I will have my answers.

DRAKE LOCKED THE door of the taproom after a long day, with another long night to follow. The raid tonight was to be on the supply depot, and he hoped to liberate enough food to keep them going another month, and with luck, enough to spread among the people of Zelos. While one of their great advantages was that they were not tied to supply lines in the way the Coalition was, knowing the territory and hunting, supplementing their stores with liberated Coalition supplies, meant his men were stronger, more fit than they could ever be with the sparse rations.

And he was focusing on that because it kept him from thinking about Kye. And all the ramifications of her discovery. At least she was safely up in the ruin, working on the map. The streets of Zelos were frothing with Coalition troops, up in arms and still angry over the loss of the rovers, the destruction of the cargo transport, the theft of the rail gun, and the crash of the freighter which they were blaming on the Raider as well, despite absolutely no evidence.

Most of all, he suspected, they were angry about looking like incompetent fools. Which made them all the more dangerous.

He was several steps into the room before he realized his sister was already there. Eirlys had a cloth spread out on the bar, and was tending to one of her birds. One of the gentle, cooing graybirds that had always seemed to him too soft for this world as it now was.

He wasn't about to complain about the bird on the bar, given what her pet ringtail had helped them accomplish. As he got closer he saw the she was fussing with one of the bird's legs.

"Is it hurt?" he asked, stopping where the bird began to get nervous at his approach.

"She's fine," Eirlys said without looking up. "I'm just trying . . . there. Got it."

"Got what?" he asked, risking another step as she soothed the bird with those wondrous hands.

She lifted the bird. He saw something attached to the creature's leg. A small tube that looked like the pour spouts on the bottles along the back wall, except it was capped at both ends.

"What is that?"

She gave him a brief glance. "The solution to a problem, I hope."

"What problem?"

"A Sentinel problem." She said it briefly, without further explanation. Because of course, it could be of no interest to her cowardly brother.

"Eirlys—"

"Don't get in a stir. I haven't sought out the Raider to join. It was just something I overheard two troopers saying."

He went still. "Overheard?"

She gave him an exasperated glance. "I'm not skulking about like the twins, spying. I was simply passing as they were speaking of how crucial it was to keep the Sentinels unable to easily communicate."

He couldn't deny that. It was, in fact, one of the biggest problems.

"So why the bird?"

"I've been training her."

His brow furrowed. He looked at the bird, wondering what hidden talent it had that his clever sister was luring to the surface. "To?"

"Fly a round trip."

"I thought you'd given that up."

"Only took a break, because I couldn't figure out how to get her to fly both ways. I could release her on the mountain and she would fly back here, but only the one way."

"But now?"

"Why all the interest?"

"I'm curious." *And wondering what you're up to that would help the Sentinels.*

She looked at him then. "Last month I started feeding her at two locations, at regular times. Here, and the old bell tower. The twins waited for her there, and kept a log. I waited here and did the same."

"And?"

A look of triumph flashed in her eyes. "It worked. She went like an arrow, straight and true. Both ways. So now she's going farther."

"How far?"

"To the old mine headquarters building."

He stiffened. Searched her face for any sign she knew what she was saying. He spoke carefully. "You know it's not safe for you to go up there."

"And I haven't. Brander took her."

A memory slammed into his mind.

"What are you doing?"

"Feeding the birds."

"I can see that. Why?"

"They make a good early warning system."

He'd thought—as he was sure he'd been intended to—that Brander meant having a flock around indeed was a help, startling and taking to wing when anything or anyone approached. Leave it to Brander to tell the truth, but leave out the most crucial part.

"You will not let me fight in the way I want to, so I must do what I can in other ways," she said.

And suddenly the tiny metal tube made sense.

"Messages," he said.

"Yes. She can make the trip in twelve minutes."

He blinked. "What?"

"We clocked it."

Now that he thought about it, he believed it. What made the trek so slow for people was that the last third of it was so steep. Which was part of what kept them safe. Without an air rover, it took almost two hours on a good day. And there weren't a lot of good days on the mountain this time of year.

The possibilities of such rapid communication, which should have been a joke in a world where once talking to someone thousands of miles distant, even on another planet, had been a matter of merely pushing a few buttons on a screen, tumbled through his head. They could get word to people to stay clear of raids. In turn, get word of useful targets before it was too late to act. They could have known about that last shipment of dryers and heaters in time to hit it. They, or Zelos, couldn't use them for fear of discovery, but they could keep the Coalition from using them. And the more miserable they were, the better.

"—seen him?"

He snapped out of his thoughts. "What?"

She didn't roll her eyes at his inattention, but he knew her well enough to know it was an effort. "Have you seen Brander today?"

"I . . . no. Not today." Technically it was true. They'd ended their planning session before today, barely. She looked concerned, so he added, "I believe he'll be in tonight, though. He said something about seeking another game."

"With the new commander?"

Drake shrugged, not wanting to admit he knew that was exactly Brander's plan. He stepped behind the bar, where he could both check supplies for the day ahead, and watch his sister.

"I wish he would not," Eirlys said with a downward twitch of her mouth. "That man makes me very nervous."

He picked up a clean bar rag. "More than others of the Coalition?"

"Yes."

"Why?" He had his own thoughts about Caze Paledan, but was curious about hers. He had not told her of the twins' encounter with the man, knowing she would worry more than she already did. It was enough that one of them was a wreck about those two.

"He's . . . different. Sorkost is but a glutton, Frall was a bumbling fool, and most of the troops either buffoons or foolishly young. All they needed for this remote outpost where we crumbled at their first incursion."

"That is who ends up posted to the likes of Ziem," he agreed.

"And yet they send Paledan. He is harder. Tougher."

He could not argue with her assessment, in fact was a little surprised it was so accurate.

"So he seems, yes."

"Makes you wonder why, does it not?"

And there she spiked it, he thought. It did make him wonder why. He picked up a glass that was already clean and began to wipe it down. "Any ideas?" he asked, thinking he'd spent too little time of late tracking the workings of his clever sister's brain.

"Only two. Either it is for him, if as rumor has it he was injured or in need of down time, or . . ."

She hesitated as if she were doubtful of going on. Because she didn't want to say it, or didn't want to say it to him?

"Or?" he prodded.

She let out a long breath. "Or the Raider has gotten to them, and they've sent Paledan to deal with him."

It was a concise, and, he feared, accurate assessment. He was beginning to realize his little sister had few illusions left about what their world had become. Perhaps he was doing her no favors, trying to shelter her from the worst of it. And she was too sharp, too determined to keep out of the fight for much longer. But giving in would only cast him deeper into the dilemma Kye had put him in already.

But in his heart, he knew that sooner rather than later he was going to be in the position he dreaded twice over; sending a woman he loved into danger.

The Raider could not afford such luxuries as caring.

Drake Davorin could not seem to help himself.

The pull from both sides threatened to rip him apart. At this moment, it was a physical thing, sending the weakness of fear to his knees, so that he had to steady himself with a hand on the bar. He tried desperately to pull himself together; he had much yet to do tonight, and he could not afford to falter.

"Drake? Are you all right?"

He looked up into his sister's worried face. "I—"

His voice broke.

"You look absolutely gray. Have you some injury you've not told me about?"

"No."

"Then you are ill."

"No. I'm not." He set down the glass he'd been holding before it shattered under his grip. He pulled himself together. "I just don't like the idea that there may be fighting in the streets of Zelos again."

And that was true, no matter which mask he wore.

Chapter 29

EIRLYS WATCHED HER brother sleep. The internal churning of every emotion she possessed would not allow her to sleep herself. Not after what she'd learned this night.

It had not been honest, she supposed, what she'd done. But the way Drake had looked yesterday had terrified her. For all her disgust at his cowering before the Coalition, she knew they would be lost without him. She had begun last night with some vague idea that he was ill and hiding trips to a healer she didn't know about. But now she knew, and it took everything in her not to shake him awake and scream at him.

Instead, since she now knew how precious that sleep was, she simply watched.

She had never imagined she could feel so conflicted, her anger and joy at what he'd done warring within her, with neither ascendant. In fact they seemed to trade off, anger that he had not trusted her, that he had felt her a child in need of sheltering and protection from the truth was then supplanted by sheer elation that he was in fact the man she had once thought him and so wished him to be again. And then she would veer back into anger again.

And all of it was spiced heavily with an irritation aimed inward, at herself, for being so blind. Of all people, should not she, his sister, have guessed long ago?

She stared down at the final proof in her hand. All the suspicions she'd quashed over the past couple of years, ever since she'd grown old enough to notice the inconsistencies, the dodging, the answers that were not really answers, haunted her in this moment.

She hadn't just been fooled, she'd been a fool. She should have known. She should have realized no one, especially no Davorin, could change as much as quickly as Drake had seemed to.

He stirred restlessly, muttered something she could not understand. But his brow was furrowed, even in sleep. He muttered again, and this time she could make out one, short word.

No.

It began to creep in then, the other realization, the one she'd had no room for. All this time Drake had insisted she stay home, stay safe, while he—

"No!"

He jolted upright. His expression was fierce, his jaw set. Sweat had beaded up on his brow. He blinked. Realized she was there.

That quickly he shifted, went from the intense, forceful man she'd glimpsed just now to quiet, meek Drake. But there was still an edge in his voice when he spoke to her. "What are you doing here?"

"I believe I live here. For now," she added.

"You know what I mean. What are you doing . . . hovering?"

"You are usually up by now."

"I told you I had to go to—"

"Stop," she said, waving a hand as if to brush off words she knew were a lie.

His gaze narrowed. She studied him for a moment, this man who had done so much to make her love him and hate him. It seemed so obvious now, but he had fooled her for a very long time. That he had fooled others just as completely somehow did not ease her.

"And," she added, her voice as cold as she could make it given the feelings roiling in her chest, "stop lying to me."

"I don't—"

"Stop!"

It burst from her, and she saw his gaze flick upward, toward the sleeping loft where the twins would be.

"They are not here," she said flatly. "I sent them to overnight with Rula."

His eyebrows rose. "And how much did that cost us?"

She didn't rise to the joke. But still, she hesitated. She knew this would change everything. Forever. But it had to change, did it not? Her own reluctance surprised her. But if she was to be the woman she wished to be, the adult she wanted him to see her as, she must behave like one. She was no longer some child, able to pretend that ignoring reality would somehow change it.

"I can see why you would want to be free of them," he said, in the usual jocular way he talked of the two imps who sucked up much of their lives. "But why now?"

She took in a deep breath to steady herself. The plunge would be irrevocable. From this moment on, her relationship with her brother would never be the same.

But the way it was now was intolerable.

"So I could follow you last night." She said it softly, quietly, even though they were alone.

He went pale. And in that moment, she knew, deep in her soul, how much this man who had practically raised her in fact loved her. The very thought of what she had done had terrified him, he who had faced worse. So very much worse.

"I know, Drake. Finally, I know. And I should have seen it long ago."

"Eirlys—"

"I should have *known*."

"I don't know what you think you know, but—"

"Stop. Lying. Just *stop.* "

He said nothing. He threw back the worn blanket, swung his legs over the side of the cot he slept on and sat there. So he could avoid facing her?

"Is the Raider too afraid to look a girl in the eye?"

He winced as if she'd struck him. She guessed that until she put it into words that he'd yet hoped she was speaking of something else.

"I followed you, until you disappeared into the ruin. The sentries are very good, by the way. Twice they almost spotted me."

She saw a shiver go through him. But still he did not speak, so she went on.

"And then I came back and searched the house."

She reached into her tunic pocket and pulled out the evidence he could not deny. The synthetic mask, the rippled slab carefully formed and colored to appear as twisted, deformed, scarred human flesh. She tossed it on the bed.

"Did you think you were the only one who knew of that hiding place in the wall? That your very curious little sister hadn't searched this place top to bottom the day we moved in?"

He rested his elbows on his knees, dropped his head into his hands.

"You're lucky the twins didn't find it."

He looked slumped, exhausted in a way she'd never seen. She gentled her tone.

"I understand," she said softly. "Truly, I do understand why you had to keep it from others. What they do not know they cannot tell. Your life depended upon this secret. But me? You felt you had to lie to me?"

For a long moment, there was more silence. But at last he said, low and harsh, "It was for your own good."

She'd never heard that voice from him. Even at his meekest the taproom keeper had never sounded so . . . broken. Still, it was an effort to keep her voice level as the anger rose within her.

"Good? What was good about thinking my beloved brother a coward? What was good about hating the man I once loved and admired above all others? What was good about hearing people laugh and mock the Davorin name? *My* name?"

He snapped upright. And for the first time, he looked at her face-on. And it was the old Drake she was looking at, the Drake who had been full of fire and fight. And yet there was a coldness, almost bitterness in his expression, and it echoed in his voice. "Would you like to trade? Because I would. I would gladly trade you that for living in constant terror that you would be taken. That you would be tortured by those who would think you might know the Raider's identity because you were the Davorin left with spirit."

She had never thought of such a thing, had assumed it was his own life he was protecting. Yet it was clear he had thought of it, and often, the fear of it, the exhaustion of it, was there in his eyes, his face as he went on.

"Or that they would come after you simply because you were that one

Davorin who openly stands against them, and thus you must be connected to the rebellion. Or that you would break your word and join the fight."

She had come near enough to that that she had to mask a wince.

"And the twins, you know they learn everything from you eventually. Do you really think they could keep such a secret? You know they would burst with it; they are but children."

She had not thought of that, either. But Drake had. She should not be surprised by that, either, she realized. Had he not always thought of everything?

"So you let me think the worst of you."

"Against all that, your disappointment and disgust, even when you lashed me with it, didn't count for much."

And she had. She thought now of all the times she'd called him coward or worse. And he had borne it, not defending himself, never fighting back. When all along, he had in truth been the one man fighting back more than any of them.

When he spoke again, the fire was gone, and his voice was tight. "I cannot lose the rest of my family, Eirlys. I could not bear it."

The enormity of what he'd done, what he'd accomplished these last three years, stretched out before her. And she knew somehow this was a turning point for her. She could react as a child herself, continue to be hurt that he had excluded her from this knowledge that would have meant so much to her. Or she could look at it as the adult she so wanted to be, and realize why he had done what he'd done. And that it was, indeed, for the best for all of them.

Like a child, she had thought mainly of herself when their parents had died. Yes, she had clung to Drake, as the only constant in an upended world, but her pain had been hers alone, and, at nine years old, she had spared little thought for the fact that he, too, was mired in grief.

And yet he had taken care of them. He had stepped into shoes he had never wished to fill, and she realized now how much of his own pain he must have had to set aside to do so.

It was time—past time—for her to grow up in more than just days lived.

"I should have known," she whispered. "All the evidence was there, but I was too angry . . . I was a fool. I should have realized long ago that no one, especially no Davorin, could change as much as quickly as you seemed to."

She rose and went to sit beside him on the cot. When he went so very still, she put an arm around his shoulders. Felt the broadness of them. And wondered yet again that she had not seen her brother's strength and determination in the Raider.

"You are," she said solemnly, "the best brother—and the best father—I could ever have had."

She felt a shiver go through him. That alone nearly broke her. She fought down tears, but realized there was no need. In fact, her tears were probably the only thing that might heal them.

She reached up to cup his face and turn it toward her. Let him see the droplets streaming down her cheeks.

"I am sorry, Drake. The way I treated you, even were your deception the truth, was unforgiveable. You took over a job you never wanted and were hardly equipped for, and you did it well."

"Those who deal with the twins might differ," he said, but she read the emotion in his eyes.

"The twins," she said, "are a law unto themselves. But that they have not yet destroyed half the town and themselves is a tribute to you."

She saw a spark of something warmer, stronger in his expression. She went on, needing now more than anything to get this said. "I have been acting as a child, and a spoiled child at that. And if it is worth anything to you, I knew that before this night. Every time I said those nasty, cruel things to you, I swore to myself that it would not happen again. But like a child, I spoke first, thought after."

"It means more than you can imagine."

He said it quietly, his head lowered once more. And she thought that it was going to be a long time before she realized the true extent of what this double life had cost him. Other Sentinels led double lives, living in Zelos with their families, hiding their connection to the Raider, but Drake was the prize the Coalition would most like to take. And he was the one who put himself constantly in front of them in the taproom, risking his very life every day.

"Brander," she began. "Is he . . . ?"

He shook his head. "Every Sentinel is under orders not to speak of who is or is not with us. I cannot hold myself to a lesser standard."

A sudden thought struck her. "But Kye knows?"

He snapped upright. "What?"

"Does she?"

"Why would she?"

"Perhaps because she's very smart? Or because she has been regularly in the presence of both of your . . . guises?" She eyed him levelly. "Or perhaps because she loves you?"

He made a choking sort of sound, again something she had never heard from him. She regretted that, but not having said it.

"She loves the Raider," she said, "because he is the Drake she loved before. So she is nothing but consistent."

His gaze snapped back to her. Clearly, he had not thought of it in that way.

"Kye is as true as the western star," she said softly. "You of all people should know this. Whichever face you wear."

He let out an audible breath. "There is no room for such in this war."

"Feelings are stubborn things. You may quash them, but they will rise."

"Wisdom, Eirlys?" His mouth twisted. "Are you not the one who just said she acted as a child?"

"I am also the one who has decided it is far past the time to grow up in my thinking as well as my years."

He looked at her rather oddly, almost distantly, as if he were seeing the child she had been rather than the woman she was. And, for the first time, she truly saw the weariness in his face, and thought of the incredible load he had carried since their mother's death, but especially these past three years. How had he managed it all, both playing harmless, broken taproom keeper and being the Raider? Had he slept more than this couple of hours any night in those years?

She stood up abruptly. "Go back to sleep."

He blinked. "What?"

"Go back to sleep. I will open the taproom, and run it today."

"But you hate it."

"More childish thinking, to hate the thing that keeps us housed and fed. This too, will change."

"You cannot change too much. You must still treat me . . . as you have been."

She shook her head. "I cannot."

"You must. Others will notice if you don't. And wonder. And some of those might be with the Coalition."

She saw his point. "I don't like the idea of . . . being like I was."

"Believe me," he said dryly, "I much prefer the way you look at me now. But it cannot be."

Her mouth tightened, but after a moment, she nodded, for she knew he was right. "Rest. If anyone asks, I shall say that you're ill. Frail thing that you are."

"Eirlys—"

"Just do it." She gave him a wry smile. "I have much to make up to you for. Let me begin with this."

Chapter 30

"YOU TWO AGAIN."

Caze Paledan grasped a twin with each hand. He'd caught them during his morning exercise circuit, up in a tree that grew next to the outer wall. From that tree, he noticed, they would have a clear view into the Coalition compound.

"We weren't doing anything!" the boy declared.

"I suppose you claim this tree as yours as well?"

"Of course," the girl said. "This is Ziem. We are Ziem."

He wasn't sure if her tone was meant to instruct or insult. And had the thought that when she was older, this pretty child would be a formidable woman. She was formidable enough now.

He pushed them, rather gently, considering, up against the stones of the compound barrier. He took a step back, so he could see them both.

"And what was it you hoped to see, spying over the wall?"

"We weren't spying, we—" the boy, Nyx, began.

"Were just looking," the girl finished.

"For?"

The two exchanged a glance. Lux started this time.

"We wanted to see—"

"If it was true you had—"

"A leathertrunk in there."

He drew back. "You expected to see a beast from Zenox, here?"

"Not expected—"

"Hoped."

"Have you not heard," he asked, "that they are . . . of uncertain temper?"

"Why we were up on the wall," Lux explained.

"Else we would have been on the ground looking for it," Nyx contributed with every evidence of unconcern.

For a moment, he almost laughed at the chaos that would have brought on, these two found strolling about inside the Coalition walls. But he also knew what would likely have happened.

"And you would likely be dead by now," he said severely.

"They would kill children for exploring?" Lux asked with an aghast tone in her voice that Paledan thought was a bit exaggerated.

"My troops are on edge, and they would likely blast first and identify after." *If there was enough left of these little ones.*

"They're afraid of the Raider," Nyx declared.

His brows lowered. His voice was harsh when he said, "Take care, boy. It would take only saying that to the wrong person and you would end as barely a spot in the dirt."

Nyx paled slightly. But the girl was studying him intently.

"And you are not the wrong person?" she asked.

Formidable might not be a strong enough word, he thought. "I am not yet reduced to silencing children with a blaster."

Lux's gaze shifted to his hip, where that weapon was sheathed. "Do you always wear it?"

"And what business is that of yours?" he asked, genuinely curious to hear the answer.

"Because the old fat man never did," the boy said.

It took more of an effort to stifle his laugh this time, at his decidedly apt description of Major Frall. After a moment he said, "If you do not have a weapon, you cannot be called upon to use it."

An understanding beyond her years dawned in the girl's eyes.

"I knew he was a coward," Nyx said, showing he, too, had not missed the subtext. Both of them were very clever. "And he *was* afraid of the Raider."

He suspected that was true. In fact, he suspected the boy's first declaration was also true. This marauder had them all not just on edge but apprehensive. He was very, very effective. And he was unpredictable, striking at odd times and in odd places, so there was no way to prepare. When he did strike, it was pure precision, in and out quickly, using what was obviously an intimate knowledge of the region to his great advantage. And any predictions they had tried to make on where he would strike next had all been wrong. And thus all possible targets must be guarded, and there was not the manpower to do so.

That one man and a small force had brought the Coalition to this was ridiculous.

And, he admitted grudgingly, admirable.

That some would say such a thought was nearly seditious did not bother him. He admired a good fighting man who clearly inspired great loyalty and had a brilliant tactical mind, no matter where or how he came across him.

But that did not mean he would not hunt him to the death if he had to.

And he was already realizing it would very likely come to that.

"YOU DID WHAT?" Drake asked.

Lux rolled her eyes, since she had just carefully explained.

"Stop that," Drake ordered. "I understood what you said, I am just having trouble believing you could be stupid enough to climb the wall around the Coalition compound in broad daylight!"

Brander smothered a smile as he watched. Never was he more thankful that it had not been he saddled with these two than in these moments. Which came all too often.

"He does have a point," Nyx said, looking at his sister.

For an instant, Lux was silent as she met her twin's gaze. Since Drake had often bemoaned the fact that her brain ran at ten times normal speed, Brander awaited with interest what the girl would say next.

"I suppose," she said thoughtfully. Then she looked back at Drake. "We're sorry. You're right. We'll avoid daylight from now on."

Brander couldn't help himself, he laughed out loud.

"You shut up," Drake snapped at him before turning back to the twins. "Don't you even *think* about sneaking out at night."

"Oh, we won't think," Nyx said.

"We'll just do," Lux added sweetly.

Brander wasn't sure what was digging at Drake more, the fear of them roaming about after dark, or that it had been his own words that had seemingly inspired them. And this on top of Eirlys having learned his secret. . . .

He tried not to think about it, that her life could now depend on her never doing anything that might even hint that she knew.

"You will not," Drake said to the pair before him. "And I'll have your word on it, both of you."

Again, a look was exchanged between them. This did not bode well for Drake, Brander thought, again having to smother a smile.

"Maybe," Nyx said.

"If you won't punish us too much for exploring in the day," Lux put in.

"And maybe cover for us a little if some trooper gets mad at us," Nyx added.

"How about if I just promise to bury what's left of you when they kill you?" Drake said flatly.

The twins looked shaken for a moment, and Brander had the sudden thought that perhaps they had believed their brother incapable of countering their mischief with his own. He could have told them differently. Had not he and Drake gotten into their own brand of trouble often enough, when they'd been the twins' age?

But then Lux set her chin stubbornly, which spurred Nyx to do the same, and Brander knew it was over.

Drake sighed. "No more climbing the wall. No more skulking around the Coalition compound. And for Eos's sake, no more taunting the Coalition commander! This is the second time you've come to his attention. A third could be fatal."

"We didn't taunt him," Nyx said. "It was—"

"A conversation—"

"That's all."

Drake rolled his eyes this time, and the resemblance to Lux made Brander let loose a smile this time.

"And you stay home at night," Drake finished with emphasis.

Lux looked thoughtful again. "Define 'night'," she said.

Drake set his own jaw then. And when he spoke, his voice was deadly calm. It was as close as Brander had ever seen him come to being the Raider in manner and tone inside these walls.

"If I say for you night is high noon, or around the clock, that's what it is. Don't make me do that."

The duo abruptly surrendered, apparently realized they had pushed their luck to the limit. Or perhaps a bit beyond, he thought, as he saw Lux swallow as she lowered her gaze from her big brother's face.

"Yes, Drake," she said meekly, and Nyx echoed her.

"Upstairs. And stay there until your sister gets home. Then you will help her with preparing dinner, or anything else you can help her with."

When the door closed behind them, Drake gave a slow, weary shake of his head.

"Better you," Brander said. "I would have locked them up for good by now."

"Don't think I haven't considered it," Drake said dryly.

"I don't understand him," Brander said. "Paledan, I mean."

"Nor do I. But I think it would not be wise for either of us to underestimate him."

He left it at that. Any more discussion, even here in the storage room of the taproom, would be a breach of one of Drake's most inviolate rules. Brander knew he lived with the constant worry that somehow his secret would be discovered, and he couldn't say the fear wasn't valid. The wrong word, or even a name, said in the hearing of the wrong person, could lead to disaster.

Once the twins were gone, Drake moved a large cask and reached into a cubbyhole hidden beneath. He took out something wrapped in a cloth, pulled it free, and set it on top of the cask.

Brander stared. "And just how did you get your hands on this?"

"It fell at my feet, actually," Drake said. "But I need you to get it out of here. The last thing I need is the twins seeing it."

"Or one of the Coalition?" Brander suggested dryly.

"That as well."

Brander stared down at the weapon. He'd never seen the likes of it before, and already his mind was breaking it down into components he recognized and those he did not. With his conscious mind distracted, his subconscious suddenly shouted an answer to his first question. His gaze shot back to Drake.

"The accident this morning," he said slowly. "The aircab that hit a tree."

Drake shrugged. "Our overlords are still not used to our conditions. And they can't see two feet in our mist."

"You were noticed, helping them out of the wreckage."

Drake looked at him then, his face expressionless. "And I can imagine what names were used."

"Nothing you haven't heard before," Brander said. Drake had chosen his path, and there was no use debating it at this point. And that most of the population of Zelos thought him a coward and a near-traitor, some even saying he was worse than Barcon simply because he was a Davorin who had let them down, was something he knew Drake knew. "And I suppose this just fell into your hands?"

"In a manner of speaking. Now will you get it out of here? I have to open in less than an hour."

Brander shrugged, then picked up the weapon. It was heavier than it appeared, which gave him another facet to file away. "It will be interesting to see what it does."

Drake didn't look surprised. "Just don't try it out in town, please?"

Brander grinned. "Me?"

Drake ignored that. "And when you take it apart, try to remember how to put it back together?"

Brander let out a snort. "As if I would not. See you later?"

"Yes. It's Eirlys's turn."

Poor girl, Brander thought. Her nights watching the twins spared little time for anything else. So he set off up the mountain, choosing his route at random, his excuse of hunting for a fat, juicy brollet at the ready. But he safely skirted the trail guards, and set off around the base of The Sentinel.

When he was far enough—he hoped—from Zelos and any Coalition guards or patrols, he took out the new weapon. It took him a couple of tries to find the safeguard and release it, at which point a small light glowed green at the back end of the barrel. He looked around for a target. Settling on a large boulder some twenty feet away, he fired.

The boulder vanished.

Brander gaped. The big rock had simply turned to tiny pebbles and dust. And the only sound he heard was the faint sliding of the remnants down the slope. No blast, no report, just . . . silence.

"Damnation," he breathed, still staring in disbelief. He shifted his gaze to the weapon in his hand. Saw the light on the back of the barrel, now glowing yellow. As he looked, it changed back to green. Ready again?

Okay, that was a rock. Let's see what you do against something organic.

He shifted his aim to a small tree not far from where the boulder had been. And fired.

The tree vanished completely. He thought he might have seen a ripple, like the mirages he'd read about, and then it was gone. Not even a leaf was left to drift down to the dirt. He moved forward, slowly, warily. In the spot where the tree had been was a slight depression, as if the ground beneath the surface had collapsed somehow.

The roots, he realized. Not just the tree but its roots were gone, and the ground had settled into the void they'd left. Was that the ripple he'd seen, the destruction flowing downward through the tree?

And what in hades would this thing do to a living creature or person?

He sat on the destroyed boulder's neighboring rock, pondering, until one of the ubiquitous, ever-adaptable but not too bright brollets he'd ostensibly been hunting wandered into the clearing. He hesitated, but knew it had to happen. He didn't like killing for no reason, but there was definitely reason enough now.

Forgive me, Eirlys.

He fired.

The brollet didn't make a sound, or even jump. It was just gone. And again, the weapon was utterly silent.

The possibilities of such silent slaughter were endless, varied, and terrifying. If the Coalition had these in mass production, this entire battle was going to change.

And Brander had little doubt who would be on the losing side.

Chapter 31

MORE CAREFUL THAN ever to avoid being followed, Brander made his way to the ruin. There were only a few of the Sentinels in the gathering room, and he merely nodded as he went straight to the Raider's quarters, although the man was not there. He wanted the privacy. He commandeered two lanterns and placed them on a table, then went to get his box of tools and parts and other bits of various things that he had accumulated.

He barely remembered the days when, as a boy, he'd had shiny new kits to assemble, or models to build. Now that aspect of his mind was occupied trying to make scattered and sometimes battered fragments into a functioning whole. Or, in rare cases such as this one, taking apart something new and unknown and trying to figure out how it worked, with an eye to replicating it somehow.

That they had absolutely no equipment with which to do that was something he didn't let stop him. Because they never knew what they might get hold of next.

He had the weapon mostly disassembled and was lost in studying the various pieces intently, a glimmering of how it worked beginning to form, when a voice jolted him out of his concentration.

"You're getting too comfortable in here," the Raider said.

Brander turned, scowled at the scarred, helmeted figure who had stepped into the room through the hidden tunnel entrance.

"You think I did not hear you coming?" He had, in fact, although he only realized it now. He just hadn't reacted, still focused on his puzzle. He *had* become too comfortable here.

"Just because the Coalition has not yet realized we are here does not mean they never will."

"Contention valid," Brander said, conceding the obvious.

The Raider's gaze shifted to the table. "Progress?"

"I'm getting the idea of how it works." He straightened, turned to face his leader and friend. "Were there more of these?"

"I do not think so. It was boxed, by itself, and I think it was being carried by the highest rank aboard. There were no other boxes like it. Perhaps it is a prototype."

Brander frowned. "Do you not think they will deduce who took it?"

The Raider shrugged. "There were many there, and some were grabbing other things that spilled out after the crash."

Brander's mouth quirked. "But only you grabbed the box that happened to contain this?"

"I told you. It fell at my feet. The box broke open. The men in the aircab were dazed, and too concerned about themselves to notice. And it was addressed to Paledan." He studied Brander for a moment. "I gather it is functional?"

Brander let out an oath he didn't often use. He saw it register, and the Raider frowned.

"This," Brander said, all trace of amusement or banter gone, "changes everything."

He explained his test firings, the rock, the tree, the brollet, and what had happened. How he had later tried various combinations of things, and how it only destroyed what it hit, leaving something next to it, even touching it, unharmed. Most of all, the silence with which it had all happened, and the absence of debris or residue afterward.

"It's fairly short range, but it obliterates the target. Completely. You could take out an entire patrol one at a time, and if they were spread out enough, they would never know what hit them."

"Silent?"

"Utterly. Not even a whisper except for the debris settling on the boulder and the tree."

"And the brollet?"

"Gone as if it had never existed. Not even a tuft of fur left." He grimaced. "Eirlys would be angry with me."

"Eirlys," the Raider said, "loves her creatures, but she understands the cost of war."

Brander saw the furrow of his brow, knew he was thinking of the danger his little sister was now in, knowing his secret. He tried not to think of it himself.

"Just the same, I'll keep this from her if you don't mind." He shook his head. "Just think of it. Not even a body left behind to betray your presence with this . . . obliterator." He pointed to the largest piece of the weapon he'd taken apart. "I believe this is the energy coil. I can see how it's powered, but I have no idea what it produces to have that effect. But the housing, the sights, the grip," he added wryly, "are all, of course, planium."

"We've indeed given them the weapons to destroy us," the Raider said.

"And probably destroy a great many other places," Brander agreed, feeling as grim as he'd ever felt. And as close to wondering if they should just give it up, and resign themselves to living under the Coalition yoke forever.

Or at least until the planium ran out. The Coalition would likely abandon Ziem at that point, as no longer useful. The only remaining question was, would they just leave, and leave whoever had survived until that point alive, or would they blow the planet to bits?

He didn't realize what his expression must be until the Raider spoke. "Do not wander there, my friend."

"It is hard not to."

"It is harder," the Raider said grimly, "to live under their boots. Believe me on this."

Brander studied him for a moment, thinking of the impossibility of this man masquerading as the beaten, cowed, crushed Drake Davorin. For, despite the helmet and the mask, that was the true disguise.

"You walk the hardest path of any of us," he said softly. "Doubled."

"It's nothing, compared to the sufferings of the people of Ziem."

"It, and you, are everything to the people of Ziem." Brander cut off the denial he knew was coming. "And because of that, no one would begrudge you any joy to be found amid all this grimness."

Brander saw his gaze narrow sharply. "What exactly is that intended to mean?"

"Only a wish that you, of all people, take something for yourself amid all this. Especially," he added, "when it would also mean joy for someone else important to me."

He saw the flicker in the Raider's eyes. In a lesser man, he would have labeled it yearning, but the Raider was not a lesser man, and he quashed it quickly.

"There is no—"

"—place for that in war. Yes, so you've said. And yet . . ."

The Raider let out a sigh Brander knew he never would in front of anyone else. Except perhaps the very person they were discussing without acknowledging it.

The Raider was staring down at the pieces of the weapon when he said grimly, "A joy likely to be so brief and come to a painful end is not something to wish on anyone."

"She long ago decided it would be worth any cost."

The Raider's head snapped around and he found himself under icy scrutiny.

"She is my cousin," Brander said with a shrug, unintimidated by the stare that cowed many. "She tells me things." A brief smile flitted across his face. "Often without meaning to."

The Raider still said nothing. Brander watched him for a moment before going on. "She suspects, you know."

To his surprise, the Raider winced. And Brander belatedly realized he'd never seen the man betray so much as in these few minutes. And that worried him. No one man could be expected to carry what he carried, on both fronts, forever.

Even this warrior who had never wanted to be one had limits, and Brander was afraid he might have finally reached them.

HE KNEW BRANDER was worried. If he was honest, he also knew it was not without reason.

"You cannot go on endlessly, my friend," Brander said. "Even the Raider needs respite."

Brander didn't know the half of how weary he was, but there was still only one answer. "There is no time for that."

"You must take time," his friend warned, "or your body will see to it. Strong as you are, you can only push so hard."

"I'm fine."

"Of course. And it won't be a problem if your body decides it's had enough in the middle of whatever this big operation you're planning is?"

"I am fine," he repeated with emphasis.

But his second would not be dissuaded. "Look, the way Kye's been working, you'll have your map within the next day or two. Surely you can rest until then."

He let out a compressed breath. "You want me to rest while she works into the dawn hours?"

And who ordered her to?

"She's tougher than either of us would like to admit," Brander said.

"She is tough enough," he agreed, knowing it was true even as it warred with the urge to keep her safe, protected.

"Yes," Brander said, his tone suddenly very pointed. "She is tough enough for just about anything."

The Raider's jaw tightened instinctively, but he knew the words were nothing less than the truth. He looked at the man who had stood by him through it all, from childhood through the devastation of his father's assassination, his mother's suicide, and all the wearying years since. And when he turned to go, he stopped him. "Brander."

His second turned back. He owed him this honesty, he thought. This, and much more.

"She doesn't suspect."

"But she—"

"She knows."

Brander stared at him. Then he let out a long, low whistle. "You told her?"

He stopped the words with a shake of his head. "Not yet. But she . . . guessed. I've stalled her. For the moment."

"It won't last," Brander warned him.

"I know."

"You can trust her with this. She can keep a secret." His mouth quirked upward. "I know this firsthand."

"I do not want her to have to. It is bad enough that Eirlys knows."

"I wish you luck then. You will need it, my friend."

"I know."

He headed for the door, then turned back again. "She *is* tough enough."
The Raider let out a compressed breath.
And said for a third time, "I know."

Chapter 32

SHE WOKE UP IN the Raider's bed.

Kye froze in place, afraid to move. Afraid to even open her eyes, although she sensed she was alone there.

She risked just a peek. She had her back to the room, her gaze registering only the rough unevenness of the cave wall. She closed her eyes again, trying to think. Whatever sleep she'd gotten hadn't been enough, and the dull ache behind her forehead declared the fact.

The last thing she remembered was finishing the map. She'd been pushing hard after he'd told her to merely sketch the southwest quadrant and focus on the rest. When he had told her he needed it by week's end, she'd blinked, swallowed, and dove in. She'd lived in the ruin for that week, leaving only for an occasional break to give muscles weary of bending over the table something else to do. She'd eaten with the Sentinels who made their home here, those who had been recognized and posted as wanted by the Coalition, and to their credit, they did not pester her with questions she couldn't answer.

She'd also slept in the main quarters. Apparently, until now.

She did a silent, swift inventory of her body, feeling nothing other than a lessening of exhaustion. But she couldn't remember anything besides working on that blessed map.

Yet here she was.

If he took me to his bed and I cannot remember it . . .

If he took me and I cannot remember it . . .

She had no words for the feeling that flooded her then.

"Welcome back."

She jerked upright. Some of the weary fog cleared and she realized then she was still fully dressed. Felt a fool for even thinking that, of all men, the Raider might have weakened.

The Raider.

Drake.

"I was becoming concerned. You pushed yourself too hard."

She turned at last to face him. He was sitting in one of the rough-hewn chairs from the table, but he had moved it next to the bed. It looked for all the world as if he'd been there, watching her sleep. And he wore the oddest expression, one she couldn't quite pin down.

"How did I get here?"

His mouth quirked. "I put you there, after I came in and found you face down on your own map."

"You mean your map." The words were merely a defense against the sensations rippling through her at the thought that he had picked her up and carried her to his bed, and she had slept through it.

And she could tell she was still groggy, because her brain was having to remind her this was Drake. So completely did he become the Raider that even without the helmet, her first instinct was to think of him as such.

Without the helmet.

Finally, she was jolted completely awake. And realized belatedly that sometime, while she'd slept, he'd given in. And all the anger she'd felt when he'd denied what to her was now obvious drained away. He was letting her see him without half of his disguise. He even sat now with the unmarred half of his face visible to her, making her wonder how she had gone so long without realizing. And his voice. His voice was no longer that rough, damaged-sounding thing. It was Drake's.

He had, without saying a word, admitted she was right, given her the truth.

Drake Davorin was the Raider.

Drake Davorin could not more thoroughly appear a coward if he tried.

Her own thought came back to her in a rush, making her wonder if on some level she had realized the truth, that indeed he was trying.

But no longer with her.

She would give much to know why he'd changed his mind. What thought process had he gone through, while she lay here sleeping, in his bed? What had brought him to the point of admitting she was right, of letting her see behind the masquerade to what she already knew was true?

She wanted badly to ask, but was afraid to disrupt what suddenly seemed to be a very intimate moment. And wary of that expression. Seeing that one side of his face made it so much easier, although she still couldn't categorize this one.

She supposed it was too much of a risk when he was here to remove whatever kind of mask the scars were. And even now, without the helmet to further distract, they looked utterly real. The artist in her was fascinated.

"The scars. How?"

He blinked, as if of all the questions she could have asked, he hadn't expected that one. But then he smiled. Her breath nearly stopped.

"You, actually. Indirectly, anyway."

It was her turn to blink. "Me?"

"The toy blazers you made for the twins."

She frowned. That had been over three years ago, for their ninth birthday.

Her breath caught anew. Three years ago. Shortly before the rise of the Raider. But what did her admittedly fantastical renderings of the mythical, fire-breathing and scaled creatures have to do with anything?

And then the memory blasted into her mind, Drake, asking how she'd made them, and about the materials, in a detail that had surprised her.

"Flexion," she breathed. "They're made of flexion."

He nodded. "You said the amount of fluid determined the consistency. Too much and they were too soft to stand on their own, too little and they were brittle. It took some experimenting to get the texture and flexibility right, and then the design, but . . ."

She stared at the twisted mass, marveling now that she knew, at how perfectly they resembled what they were supposed to be.

"A mold?" she guessed.

"Yes." His mouth quirked again. "I didn't know how long they would last, so I wanted more than one. And I didn't want them to be changing, not that anybody ever looks that closely. They're usually repelled at the sight."

"Which is exactly what you counted on," she said.

He shrugged. "It's the nature of people."

"Whatever made you think of it?"

He grinned then. And even with the mask in place it was potent, powerful thing. "Nyx. What he said when you gave his to him, and he was so excited."

She remembered the boy squealing with delight and thanking her profusely, enough that it had been worth all the effort to get them just right, but that was all. "What?"

"He said, 'A blazer could melt your face off.'"

Her gaze shot back to the side of his face, to the mask. And despite herself, she laughed. Laughed at the ingenuity, the sheer brilliance of it.

As if her laughter had been some sort of signal, he said in an entirely different, solemn tone, "I'm sorry, Kye." It took her a second to make the jump, to realize what he was apologizing for. "It was the only way."

She'd worked through all this in the hours she'd sat in the unrelieved darkness of her haven, contemplating in her mind the drawings that had led her to the truth. She'd knew why he'd done it, had even seen the sense of it. It stung that he hadn't trusted her, but she understood. So she brushed away his words with a wave of her hand and a shake of her head.

"You're not angry?" He looked puzzled.

"Only at myself. For taking so long to realize."

His mouth twisted ruefully. "You took less time than I'd hoped." Her gaze narrowed. "You have an artist's eye," he said. "I knew it would happen."

She considered that. And jumped right to the core of it, for her. "Then why didn't you just tell me?"

He sighed. "For your own good."

"What I don't know, I can't be forced to tell?"

"Yes."

"You didn't trust me to be able to hold your secret?"

His feet hit the floor then, and he left the chair in a barely controlled surge of motion. "I wouldn't trust anyone to hold out under Coalition torture. Including myself."

He turned on his heel, strode halfway across the room, then stopped, with his back to her.

"Besides," he said harshly, "they have methods, drugs, the collars . . . they would learn what you knew, and leave only an empty shell behind. I could not bear that."

The emotion that had crept into his voice at the end sent a shiver through her. "Then why admit it now? Why not keep denying it?"

He turned back then. He seemed to be fighting his own words. And she saw in his face that same expression she hadn't been able to pin down.

"Relief," he finally said, putting the name to it. "The relief of no longer lying to the one person I least wanted to lie to."

Her lips parted for air that was suddenly harder to get as she stood up herself. For relief was what she herself was filling up with. Not just that she knew the truth, but that the reason behind her tangled feelings, her inability to let go of Drake while at the same time admitting she loved the Raider was finally clear. She had not been able to separate the two because they were one and the same.

"You—"

"And selfishness," he added.

She scoffed. "You? You are more selfless than any man I've ever known."

"Not selfless enough—or strong enough—to be able to swallow the way you looked at me when you . . . didn't know. I could live with it from Eirlys, but not you."

Remorse flooded her. Her hand shot to her mouth, for fear she would cry out. It left her voice a strangled whisper. "Eos, I was so awful to you."

He shook his head. "No more than I deserved, given what you knew."

She had to blink away the sudden moisture in her eyes, as if her regret had taken a physical form. "How do you stand it?" she asked, still in that choked whisper.

"I knew how it would be before I ever started. I worked hard to make it that way. Eirlys's anger told me it was effective. And I counted every slur, every disgusted look, as a sign of success." He let out a long, compressed breath. "Except with you. When you would look at me with such disappointment and despair, I . . ."

His voice trailed away, and he gave a weary shake of his head. She tried not to think of all the times she'd done exactly as he described, all the times she'd railed at him for being a coward or worse, and all the time he was the Raider, risking his life, his very soul, to do exactly what she'd berated him for not doing. In that moment, she hated herself, and struggled to think of something else, anything else. And it struck her that his odd hunting habits had clearly been as much excuse for his coming and going as they were for actual food supply.

It was then that another thought hit her.

"Eirlys. She knows now."

He let out a breath. "Just a few days ago."

"That's why she—" She broke off when she realized she'd been about to say his sister had quit disparaging him, and had no longer wanted her agreement in that. He looked away, as if he somehow knew what she hadn't said. "How did she figure it out?" she asked hastily.

He grimaced. "She sent away the twins on her night with them and followed me. And then she found the set of these—" he gestured at the scars "—that I keep at home, just in case. I should have realized she'd know my hiding place."

"Your sister is very smart."

"Too smart, on occasion."

"Who else knows?" she asked.

He met her gaze then. "Brander. He's always known. The Raider was practically his idea."

"I guessed that."

"And he helped with the mask, came up with the adhesive that holds it in place." He grimaced. "My skin did not appreciate his early efforts, but now it leaves no sign if I remove it properly."

She remembered suddenly that time when he claimed to have run afoul of a fire plant, causing the fierce reddening of his face.

"He is ever clever that way. Who else?"

"No one."

She blinked. "No one? Not even Pryl, or the Harkins? Mahko?"

He shook his head. "They may suspect, but know, from me? Only Brander, and my sister. And you."

And that suddenly what had seemed a slight became instead an honor. But she needed one more thing from him. The admission she had thought never, ever to receive.

"Why did you say telling me was selfish?"

He didn't even pretend to misunderstand. And it was the Raider who answered her. "Because it was. In the midst of chaos and destruction, with the evil of the Coalition surrounding us, when my mind and heart should be on nothing except the fight, I was taking something for myself. Taking the one thing that would make it all easier, but only for me."

"Not just for you," she whispered.

He shook his head. "Don't you see the burden I've put on you? For this can only work if no one knows. And it must work. Eirlys, and the twins, if the Coalition ever found out, they would—"

He stopped words that were clearly too painful to even speak. And she couldn't help herself. Despite how un-warrior like it was, despite that they were in the heart of the rebellion, she ran to him. She threw her arms around him, as she had once done with Drake without thought. She felt his split-second of hesitation, but then his arms came around her and pulled her even closer. She felt as much as heard his shuddering breath and knew without doubt that he had missed this, longed for it, as much as she had.

"They will not find out," she promised fervently.

"You can act no differently," he warned. "You must treat . . . the tap-room keeper as you always have."

"Horribly, you mean," she said, remorse surging again.

"And publicly," he said. "Although not so much that they suspect you're one of us."

She said nothing, remembering how he'd warned her that coming and going, as those who kept part of their lives still in Zelos did, was doubly dangerous.

"You must stay safe, Kye. If anything happened to you—"

"Now you know how I have felt all this time," she whispered against his chest.

And at last, that particular torture was over.

Chapter 33

HIS ARMS TIGHTENED around her. Kye heard the hammering of his heart beneath her ear.

"You cannot change either," she said when she could speak past the knot in her throat.

"What?"

She pulled back, looked up at him. "You cannot treat me any differently. I am still a warrior, and I won't be treated as less."

"Kye—"

"Your word, Drake."

"Do not use that name. Even here."

"Fine," she agreed, but she was not deterred. "I must have your word. I am still your third in command, and I will take what missions I'm suited for, as always."

"Or?" he said, his voice tight at her ultimatum.

"Or we do not take the next step."

He went impossibly still. His arms were still around her, and hers around him, but they were as frozen as the winter snow above the Edge.

"The . . . next step?" he finally said.

Uncertainly suddenly bubbled up inside her. "Or perhaps you do not want it? Do not want . . . me?"

She heard him suck in a breath, hard and fast. "Dear Eos, Kye, how could you ever think that?"

"Then why have you not—"

"It was not right," he said flatly. "To take that step when you did not know. Besides, I knew it was the Raider you wanted. Not . . . me."

She took a step back. He let her go. "Would you like to know what has driven me mad?"

"I'm not sure."

"It was the fact that although I loved the Raider, I still loved Drake Davorin. Despite it all, I still loved him, and I could not resolve the conflict, even in my mind." She heard him suck in a breath. "When I was with the Raider, I felt disloyal to Drake. When with him, I could not understand how I still cared when a man such as the Raider walked Ziem. I felt torn in two, every day."

"I thought you hated me."

"Never. I hated what you'd become." She gave him a wry smile. "What I thought you'd become. A part you played all too well, I might add."

"The Raider is just as much a façade," he said, and it sounded like a warning.

"The trappings, yes. But the man behind the creation? No, he is true and real and brave, and the heart of this fight."

"And you loved him . . . in spite of this." He gestured at the scars.

"Do they reach your heart, your soul?" she asked. "For it is that I love."

"Kye—"

"I will wait longer, if I must—" she thought of whatever strategy he was building with her map, thought of the size of it, the likely danger "—though it pains me when every day could be the last for one or both of us."

"I—"

"And there must be no regrets, either way."

"I wouldn't—"

"I understand your hesitation. Truly. So I will have no hinting, no hedging, you must say it straight out. If you want this, want me, or no, you must say so. I must know that much, at least."

He didn't say anything. He merely stood there, looking at her. She thought she saw the faintest trace of amusement, tickling at the corners of his mouth. That mouth she wanted to kiss more than she had wanted anything that she could remember.

"Well?" she demanded.

"I was waiting to see if you'd finished this time," he said mildly. She'd been right about the amusement, and her cheeks heated.

"If it did not matter so much—"

"I know." It was he who interrupted her this time, but gently. "You are not a chatterer. Thank Eos."

This time she waited, watching him, her heart hammering, her emotions knotted as if the rest of her life depended on his answer. For it did. Silence spun out for a moment that seemed an eon long to her.

But then, finally, he spoke, in a voice she'd never heard from him before. "I've wanted you since that day I caught Petro with you."

That startled her. "What?"

"When I came around that corner and saw him trying to kiss you, I nearly put him on the ground. If he had not run, I think . . . no, I could not think for my mind screaming, 'She's mine!'"

Her pulse leapt just at hearing him say that. And then so many things were tumbling through her mind she could barely sort them out. She hadn't been blameless that day, and she had chosen badly. At sixteen, she had been in despair that she'd had so little luck with getting the two-years-older Drake to notice her, she had wondered if any boy ever would. Even under the Coalition's ever-tightening grip, it was the sort of thing a girl wanted to know. Especially when she was infatuated.

But she hadn't been merely infatuated. The nine years since had proven that. Her love had never wavered.

"I . . . never knew."

"Brander," he said simply. "He is my best friend, and he was very protective of you. He was quite clear on what he would do to the next one he caught trying anything."

"And that . . . kept you away?"

"Only because of our friendship, and the Coalition chaos. And then . . ."

"Your mother."

"Yes. My life was no longer my own."

"And then . . . the Raider."

"Yes. After that, I had no right. I could not ask anyone to share what my life had become."

"I would have," she said, reaching up to touch his face. "Without hesitation."

"I know that now. But you would have been another lever for them to use on me, if they ever found out who I was."

"But a lever who could fight back," she pointed out.

Something changed in his gaze then, his eyes narrowed, and a suddenly palpable heat seemed to radiate from him. "Yes. Fight with as much courage and daring and honor as any of the Sentinels, and more cleverly than most. It tore me to pieces to send you on those dangerous missions, yet I was filled with such admiration and respect when you returned successful that it only fed what already hid inside me." He took a deep, shuddering breath and then said, "I love you, Kye."

And there it was, the balm to her soul, the dream she'd held for nearly a decade in her trembling hands at last.

"And I you," she whispered. "Since I was fifteen and saw you try so hard to rescue that injured hedgebeast for Eirlys."

He looked surprised. He'd probably long forgotten that memory, but it had never left her. She realized that some would find this backward, that she admired the gentleness in him, and he the fight in her, but they each already knew the other had more than enough of both. The Raider a little too much of the fight, perhaps. But then, he thought that of her, as well.

He moved then, almost tentatively, unlike his usual confidence. It was that as much as anything that told her he was about to kiss her. And that knowledge alone had her ready before his lips even came down on hers, so that that first touch was all she needed to go up in flames.

She had once wondered if, when it happened, it would somehow be less than she had always imagined. It was not. It was more. So much more.

They went up like one of Brander's flares, roiling, hot, churning. His mouth was hot, hard, and she wanted him to devour her even as she tasted her fill. When his tongue swept over her lips, she nearly cried out at the sweet, jolting shock it sent through her. She tasted him back, and the shudder she felt go through him only heightened her own sensations.

She had never allowed herself to think much beyond this moment, but suddenly all she knew, and everything she'd heard or imagined about this act between two people, blasted through her mind. And she wanted him in every one of those ways, and a few more they might have to invent.

When he broke the kiss, she felt bereft, and her fingers clutched at his arms. Was he going to stop, now? Her world fairly reeled at the thought.

"Not here," he said, his voice oddly thick.

She glanced at his bed, puzzled. While narrow, it was enough, wasn't it? True, she knew little of it other than the basics hastily explained by her mother and what she remembered from once walking in on her parents as a child, or with animals when the mist thinned as sun-season approached. Not that opportunities for her hadn't arisen, but she had wanted no one but Drake since she was a child, and then the Coalition had arrived on Ziem and normal life and hopes vanished.

"I must work here, focus, and I would ever be thinking of us," he said, and she understood.

"Home?" she asked, still uncertain.

He grimaced. "The twins. They hear everything."

She knew her confusion must show. "But we'll be quiet—"

He lowered his head then, until his lips were at her ear. "No," he whispered, "we won't."

Her breath caught. At the images his words evoked, a new kind of heat rippled through her, a kind she'd never felt before, that careened around inside her until it seemed to pool somewhere low and deep. Her entire body clenched at the thought of what sounds she might draw from him, and he from her.

"Mine, then?" she suggested, marveling a little at how that that new heat seemed to settle into a hollow ache she somehow knew only one thing, only one man could fill.

"I cannot be that far away just now," he said, sounding as if he would like nothing more than to have that privacy. He turned, grabbed up the heavy blanket from his bed, then faced her again. "This is not what you deserve, fine linens and an elegant bed—"

"It is not the setting I care about, but the man in it. And," she added, "waiting no longer."

She heard him say something under his breath; she wasn't sure what except that it was heartfelt. And, she realized, his voice had taken on a rough, husky note similar to what he'd put on as the Raider. Only then did she realized she'd missed it, that gravelly sound. Only now it held an undertone that sent a shiver through her, an undertone she'd never heard from him before. And she realized she wasn't the only one who had unleashed long held-back feelings.

And then he took her arm and led her to the back of his quarters, toward the screen that blocked the view of the back corner. She realized now this was where he donned the guise of the Raider, out of view. But she hadn't realized until now it also masked the entrance to the tunnel, the passage in from the wooded side of The Sentinel. A few knew he had some second way in that brought him directly to his quarters—she thought he'd chosen that room for his quarters just for that reason—but few knew exactly what it was or where it came out.

She'd grown used to the need for primitive torch lights here, to save what power they had for charging weapons, yet moving down the narrow passage carved into the mountain itself with only the dancing light of the flame to show the way seemed more elemental at this moment. Perhaps because she was feeling that way.

When he stopped, and fastened the torch in a holder on the wall, she realized they were in, not a room, but a small alcove cut out of one side of the tunnel. There were a few weapons and other supplies here that she stared at for a moment. Her tactical mind had been buried by the avalanche of need she had at last unleashed, and the rush of sensation he had sent sweeping over her, so it took her a moment to realize this was a fallback position, with enough here to fight with, or bring down the tunnel if he had to.

"Tell me, Raider," she said softly, "do you ever tire of thinking ten steps ahead of anyone else?"

He turned to her then. "Yes."

She ached at the simple answer, one word that said so very much. She reached up and cupped his cheek, her fingertips on his skin around the scars. "Then just for now, do not."

"Yes," he repeated. "I want to think only of each moment, savor it, taste it, drown in it . . ."

His words, spoken again in that voice she'd never heard before this night, made her knees tremble. He kissed her again, and the flame from the torch seemed to flare, or else it was her body providing more heat than she would have thought possible.

And then they were somehow down on the floor of the alcove, the thick blanket beneath them as cushion, and she wasn't sure at all how it had happened. Nor did she care; she cared only that he was with her, and that she at last could touch him as she had been aching to do for so, so long.

They shed clothing quickly, the urgency of limited time hovering over them. As, in fact, it always did, in more ways than just this moment. There was nothing of shyness in her for this, for she wanted to learn every inch of him, and for her that meant offering the same to him.

It was both familiar and strange. Familiar, because she knew Drake, knew him with an artist's eye, knew the way he moved, the way his hair grew in a wave over his brow, the shape of his hands and the length of his fingers, all the things that should have made her realize long before she had. Strange because he was also the Raider, with the genuine scars he'd acquired in the fight, a new, wire-strung tension that fairly shivered through the body that was leaner, tauter than she had ever realized, and a driven spirit that had made him the leader his father could never have been.

He was a finely tuned warrior.

And then he touched her, his hands sliding over her skin, leaving trails of fiery sensation in their wake. And she could think of nothing else but the feel of him, drank in the sight of him as if he were to be the last thing she ever saw. And if that were true, it would be enough.

She felt as if her body were singing, as joyfully as one of his sister's birds. Every nerve seemed to be interconnected, and when he touched her skin, tasted her mouth, she felt it everywhere. And then he lowered his head to her bared breast, teased the peak with his tongue, and she cried out in shock and amazement at the sensation that blasted through her.

"But we'll be quiet."

"No, we won't."

And suddenly she wanted nothing more than to wring such a sound from him as well, and her hands began to move. She traced the long, lean lines of him, the powerful muscle, the places here and there that marked him as that warrior. She lingered there, to show him that scars, real or fake, meant less than nothing to her. It was that spirit, the essence of the man, she loved, and made love to now.

He suckled her, teaching her for the first time there was a direct connection between that nipple and the deep, hidden place inside her. It was aching now, desperate for something, and she couldn't stop herself from moaning as she twisted beneath his touch. She slid her hands over him, wanting, needing, and it didn't matter that she didn't know exactly what.

She heard a gasp break from him as her fingers brushed the silken skin of his distended shaft. Yes. Yes, this was what she wanted to hear from him, and her fingers curled around him, stroked him.

"Kye."

It broke from him as if against his will, wrenching, guttural. And it heightened every sensation that was already driving her to madness. She squeezed gently, rubbed, her fingers memorizing the length and breadth of him. A little shiver went through her at the thought of what was to come—it didn't seem possible.

And then his fingers were there, stroking near the entrance to that hollow, aching place. She vaguely registered surprise that his fingers slid easily, that she was slick, wet.

Ready. It hit her then, that her body had readied itself for this, that it didn't matter what she did or didn't know, her body knew that it was this man it had been waiting for.

She stroked him again, and he went rigid in her arms.

"You're certain?" His breath was hot, stirring against her ear. "For in ten seconds there may be no turning back."

"I've been waiting," she said, "for ten years."

He traced the curve of her ear with his tongue, sending a new kind of shiver through her. She could not be still as he moved down her body, wanted to scream at him to hurry, could he not see that she was going to die if he did not ease this ache? And then he was there, his erect flesh sliding into her with startling ease. Too soon, he stopped, and she shifted beneath him, wordlessly begging for more.

"I don't want to hurt you," he ground out, his voice a tight, tense thing.

She'd nearly forgotten that, and cared nothing. A bit of pain seemed little enough to pay for the easing of this impossible need. She slid her hands down to this hips, used his own body as leverage to lift herself sharply upward.

A sharp groan broke from him as the barrier within her gave. The pain was sharp, tearing, but quick. He hesitated even then, until she whispered, "Please."

He drove forward. Her breath left her in a rush at the sensation of being stretched, filled. It felt so right that she cried out again. And then he was moving, his every stroke pushing, driving, until she was clutching at him desperately. She hovered on the edge of something, some wondrous thing that she somehow knew would make everything, simply everything vividly clear, why she was here, in this place and time, in this moment. Why she was alive.

He drove hard and deep, and growled out an oath she rarely heard from him, as if it were too much to hold back.

And then he said her name, in a cry that sounded as desperate as she felt. The sound of it was like a new, unexpected kind of caress, and sent her soaring over the edge in an explosion that she thought would consume them both, and she didn't care. Cared about nothing but having him at last, and having lived long enough to experience this.

"WE'LL BE MISSED," she whispered.

He let out a long breath, as close to a sigh as the Raider would allow. For he knew she was right, and these stolen moments were ticking away too quickly.

"Yes."

"Do you care? If they know?"

"Only in that it might hurt those who are separated from those they love, some forever."

"I would have expected no less," she said softly.

She snuggled up against him. He had pulled a layer of the blanket over them, for this passage never truly got warm. But between them, they had generated enough heat to sear him to the core.

He had known, in those rare moments when his guard was down enough to allow the thoughts to creep in, that mating with Kye would be something beyond anything he'd ever experienced.

He hadn't known it would change him, would shift not just his thoughts but his very core. That he would become a different man, simply because now he knew he'd been missing a part of himself that only she could give him.

He knew he had made his life more difficult, that he had added yet another layer of strain and worry. But what he had gained so surpassed all that that it was barely worth thinking about. He would be afraid for her, yes, but this joy that she was finally and ever his overwhelmed even that.

Her hand slipped downward over his chest, to the raised scar that ran along his ribs. That was a souvenir of the first raid, before Brander had fashioned the lightweight, flexible armor they used now. He had no doubts now that she had meant what she'd said, that the scars, be they genuine or assumed, did not repel her. Had she not caressed every one of them, both with her fingers and later her mouth?

A shudder went through him at the memory.

"Mmm," she murmured, and slid her hand lower.

He sucked in a breath, his belly tightening in response as his body surged to readiness with a swiftness that made the next breath near to impossible. Her fingers curled around him, her thumb creeping up to rub over the swollen tip, and what air he had left shot out of him in a gasp.

"It does not seem possible that we fit," she whispered.

He could tell her a thing or two about how well they fit, what it felt like to be buried in her tight, welcoming flesh, but he lacked the air to do it.

Her hand slid lower yet, cupping him, and his hips jerked involuntarily, pressing himself into her palm. "Kye." It came out through clenched teeth.

"Yes."

It was both acknowledgment and answer and assent in one, and he surrendered all efforts at control. Soon enough, he would have to don the garb and the weight of command once more, but for now, in this moment, he would steal one more time the glorious wonder they had found.

Chapter 34

"ABOUT TIME."

Kye knew he had to have heard the mutters as they walked into the outer quarters, but he didn't speak. She was only certain he'd heard Pryl by the catch in his breathing before he walked on. She ignored it and walked over to the table to pour a mug of the morning brew she'd smelled the moment they'd come in. They'd agreed as they lay in the alcove that they would not flaunt this change in their relationship, especially in front of the other Sentinels. Too many had suffered great loss, and others were separated from their families and alone. He had told her what Brander had said, that no one would begrudge him, but she agreed with him that it would not be fitting to parade it.

She'd also told him she had to return home; she'd spent so much time here working on the map that she was afraid of what she might find. He would stay, to put her work into use, to map out whatever great plan he had that required such detail. He would not tell her yet, said only that there were still pieces missing, but now she was content to wait.

She made it safely; in fact, the streets seemed quite deserted tonight. And it took a great deal of effort for her to stay vigilant, when her mind kept wanting to steal back to those precious hours with Drake, when they'd discovered the incredible power of finally giving in to desires that they had suppressed for so long. The memory of touching him, of feeling him touch her, of uniting as one and setting off an explosion of heat and sensation, would stay with her forever.

A check of her little home showed nothing disturbed, and she relaxed a little. She set down her pack and pulled out the jug of lamp oil she'd managed to get hold of. She fueled up the lantern, then lit it. She barely thought anymore of the days when a mere voice command would have lit the entire house if she wished it. The power was only turned on to this sector for a couple of hours in the evening, so people could cook and bathe, and then it went dark again. But she never took advantage of that time, for she did not want there to be any sign that someone was living in this ruin. So she used this lantern, bathed in cold water, and counted it as her way of enduring what the Sentinels endured.

Then she reached back into the pack and pulled out her sketch book. In the quiet of midnight, she'd shown the two drawings to Drake, and explained how just doing the second one had led her to the truth. He'd seemed taken aback at her portrait of the Raider.

"He does not seem as fearsome as I thought."

She'd smiled and caressed his bare cheek. "He is fearsome enough, to those who need to see him as such," she said. "But this was drawn with love."

It was later, when they lay once more sated in each other's arms, that he had reluctantly said, "These cannot be kept, Kye. It is too clear, you are too adept."

She hadn't thought of that, but knew he was right. They could not risk anyone seeing these two portraits side by side by anyone else.

So now she took one long, last look at the drawings that had changed everything. Then she picked up the lantern and made her way to the ruined front of the building. And there, in the rubble, she burnt them both to ash.

THE SCRABBLING noise awakened her. Kye rolled out of the chair she had fallen asleep in, grabbing for her blaster as she went. She pinpointed the sound as coming from the back, near the metal plate she'd put over the single window that remained here in the back portion of what had once been her family's home.

She crouched behind the heavy chair, her blaster braced on the arm and aimed toward the direction of the tiny sounds. More came, and she heard the sound of pebbles skittering across the pile of bombed-out rubble.

And then she heard the whisper of voices. Low, at a certain pitch . . . and familiar.

She stood up, sliding the blaster back into the holster and shoving the whole out of sight behind the pillow in the chair.

"You two make less noise when you're not trying to be quiet, you know," she called out.

The whispering abruptly stopped. She walked over and slid the metal plate slightly away from the window opening. And then she heard a tumble of smaller debris as two figures scrambled down the pile and tumbled into the room. They rolled, then stood, resolving into Nyx and Lux.

She put all she could muster of sternness into her expression as she put her hands on her hips and looked down at them. "What are you two doing out at this hour? And alone? And why here? And how did you know about here in the first place?"

The twins exchanged a look. Then Lux spoke, naturally choosing the easiest question to answer first. "We've known about this place for a long time. We followed Eirlys once when she came here."

She didn't miss that they'd dodged the what and why questions.

"And I don't recall inviting you over tonight," she said, her tone still severe. *And I almost wasn't here, because of your brother.*

"We know," Nyx said. "But we want to give you something."

"Well, not you, exactly," Lux put in.

"It's for the Raider," Nyx said.

That startled her. Warily, she eyed the duo who led Drake such an exhausting dance. And once more she realized how amazing it was, that he had kept any control of them at all, on top of Eirlys, and let alone doing it all while maintaining a double—and very dangerous, more dangerous than any of them—life.

I would have collapsed long ago under the strain.

"The Raider," she said slowly. "And what makes you think I have anything to do with the Raider?"

Lux rolled her eyes. Those Ziem-blue eyes, identical to her twin's, but darker than Drake's clear, sky blue. "Please. We know you know people who are with him."

She felt a rush of relief; at least they didn't seem to think she was as well. Still, she thought it safest not to speak, to wait them out. She folded her arms across her chest, and silently looked at them.

"We'd give it to our sister," Lux began.

Nyx then. "But Drake would be really mad—"

"If we sent her to see the Raider—"

"And he's already mad at us for—"

"Something else," Lux interrupted before he could confess to some other transgression.

"So you brought it to me?" Kye asked.

Nyx nodded. "He'd get mad about that, too—"

"Since he worries about you but—"

"You're of age and so—"

"He can't really reprimand you—"

"The way he does us."

She nearly laughed at that, remembering the times the Raider had done just that when she'd taken some risk he thought too extreme. She had realized, finally, that that was another of the things about the Raider that had reminded her of Drake. And again she grimaced inwardly at her own slowness in grasping the truth. But Lux's admission that Drake worried about her, and always had, took most of the sting out of it.

"So here," Lux said, pulling a small card out of her pocket and holding it out. Kye took it, saw that it was a pass card, of the kind used to enter Coalition facilities.

"And just how did you come by this?"

"It almost fell out of a guard's pocket," Nyx said quickly. Too quickly.

"Almost?"

"I might have helped it a little," he admitted. But he was grinning as he said it.

Kye tapped the card against her fingers. "I . . . appreciate your initiative, but I'm afraid without the password that goes with it, it's not much use."

Lux rolled her eyes. Again. "Of course not. That's why we only took it *after* we had the password."

Kye blinked. "What?"

"We overheard the big oaf complaining about having to change his password," Nyx explained, more patient than his sister. "That's what gave us the idea to grab his card."

"It's 'sporky'," Lux said, then sniffed in disdain. "Probably after his pet skalworm."

She stared at them as possibilities raced through her mind. "I don't suppose," she said slowly, "you have any idea where this . . . oaf's guard post is?"

Both twins grinned widely. "Barkhound's office," they chorused, using their derisive nickname for Barcon Ordam.

Well, now.

"But he'll notice," Lux warned.

"By tomorrow—"

"When he goes to use it again—"

"At six—"

"He was complaining about that, too."

She tapped the card on her fingers again. "You know," she said casually, "I might just know someone who might know how to get this to the Raider."

"The whole point?" Lux suggested.

Kye laughed then. "You need to work on your diplomacy, little one."

She was still chuckling inwardly when, the card tucked safely into her shirt, she made her way up the trail. She'd sent the twins home with a promise that she would report back on a successful delivery, and after extracting a blood oath that they would not speak of it to anyone, even their sister, who she knew was the one at home for them tonight.

She didn't bother asking them not to tell Drake; she knew they wouldn't for fear of getting in more trouble. Not that it mattered, since she herself would be telling him momentarily. He was going to be hard-pressed not to clamp down even tighter on the pair, and to pretend he didn't know what he knew.

She reminded herself that once she got there, he was no longer Drake, and she must not even think of him as such for fear the name would slip out. Even in their closest moments alone, she had to hold back. And that was when it hurt the most, when she wanted to cry out his name, to declare him hers, yet she could not.

For she was stealing him just as they were stealing those moments.

Chapter 35

KYE WAS NEARLY at the ruin when another question occurred to her. And it was the first thing she asked when she got into his quarters, after going through the motions of requesting entry, as everyone had to do. A standing order she understood a lot better now, given he needed to be sure his disguise was always in place. And an order she still complied with; until they had decided what to do, she kept to the routine. And when she was in front of him in his quarters, she asked her question.

"So where did Eirlys think you were, those times when you left the twins to her?"

He didn't seem startled by the question. Perhaps he'd gotten used to them, for she'd had a lot once she'd gotten over the initial shock. And once she'd realized he would, for the most part, answer them for her.

But he did look slightly uncomfortable.

"Where?" she repeated, truly curious now.

He grimaced. "I believe she thought I was visiting Sanguine."

Kye's brows shot upward. For the neighborhood of Sanguine was known for only one thing: paid companionship. Mating for hire, to put it more bluntly.

"And why," she asked, "would she think that?"

He gave her a sideways look. "I have, in fact."

Something made her hold back the words that leapt to her lips at that. She knew him, and knew there had to be more to this. She thought for a moment. And then smiled.

"I would guess," she said slowly, "that the women of Sanguine sometimes hear some interesting things."

The smile he gave her in return was payment enough for her forbearance. "Yes, they do. And they care about Ziem, more than some others I could name."

"Barkhound comes to mind."

"Indeed."

"So Eirlys thought . . ."

"Yes. It seemed the only likely thing she would believe, so I let her believe it." The grimace again. "Besides, she thought the women of Sanguine were the only ones who'd have a coward like me anyway."

"And wouldn't they just be pleasantly surprised?" she asked archly.

He looked so startled even the mask couldn't hide it. And she remembered when he had offered to remove the mask when they were alone, so she would not have to look at or touch such a disfigured man.

I love you in all your forms. Have I not proven that?

Her answer had driven him a little bit wild, and when they'd withdrawn to the alcove, he'd let go of all boundaries, and driven her so wild in turn it had been all she could do not to scream with the bursting pleasure of it. Only the knowledge that there were many of the Sentinels close by had halted it. So instead, she had turned the suppressed cries into physical release, clawing at him, writhing beneath him, digging her fingers into the solid, powerful muscles of his back and shoulders until he drove deep one last time and she heard his own barely-stifled exclamation. And afterward she kissed away the blood from his lip, where he had bitten it to keep from shouting her name.

"Dear Eos, do not look at me like that, Kye. Or I will take you right here on this table."

His voice was breathless, his jaw tight. And the shudder his words and the image they painted sent through her was fierce. And visible; she did nothing to try and hide it. He groaned, took a step toward her. She reached for him.

Then he stopped. Swore under his breath.

"Pryl will be here in a few minutes."

"Then I will hold that thought close. And clear the table."

He groaned, and she saw his fists clench. It pleased her to know he felt the need as strongly as she did. It quickened her breath, and the rise and fall of her breasts, the friction of the fabric of her tunic against nipples aching for his touch, his mouth, nearly made her echo his groan.

But the thought of her tunic reminded her of what was in its hidden pocket.

"I did come for a reason," she said.

"Is not driving me out of my mind reason enough?" he asked, his voice harsh.

"Yes," she admitted. "Although I believe it's only fair to point out that thoughts of you drove me mad first."

She heard him swear again, and his jaw tightened as he turned his eyes upward as if looking for help. It may have taken him a while to let down the Raider's barriers, but once he did, he did it wholeheartedly. And she smiled inwardly as she pulled out the card.

"I brought you this," she said.

He gave a last shake of his head and then took it, his brow furrowing as he recognized it. "A Coalition pass card?"

"With the password."

"How did you come by this?"

"That's for later. The best part is who owns it."

"Oh?"

At his raised brow she grinned. "The sentry at Barcon's office."

His eyes widened. His gaze shifted back to the card.

"Well, now," he said, and only in that moment did she realize where she herself had picked up the phrase. *Well, now*. . . . She'd thought the exact same thing upon getting this information.

"Yes," she agreed, still grinning.

"You know it's not likely he has anything of use to the Sentinels in there."

"And who cares?"

He raised a brow at her again.

"He has things he has no right to. Things he's taken from the people of Ziem. Things he's purloined from the dead, for Eos's sake. Would it not be worth it for the sheer pleasure of taking whatever the pretentious blowpig does have?"

She saw his mouth quirk. Saw him fight it. But then the grin broke out. Even beneath the mask of scars it was potent. To her, at least.

"Indeed it would."

They laughed together, and she thought in that moment her heart had never been so full.

"There is one problem," she said reluctantly.

"I assumed there would be."

"We've only got until six in the morning. That's when the owner will likely discover it missing."

"Time enough," he said mildly, not at all rattled. And for a moment, she allowed herself to marvel anew at the man Drake had become. "And now," he said in the same mild tone, "the rest of the tale of how you acquired this?"

She sighed, knowing there was no way to put it off any longer. "I got it from the twins."

He went still, and she hastily explained what they'd told her. When she'd finished, he closed his eyes and let out a compressed breath. "They'll be the death of me, those two," he muttered.

And for an instant, the world seemed normal to her, and Drake no different than any adult responsible for two imps who could not stay out of trouble.

But then all the other, much more likely things that would be the death of him came flooding back, and the moment evaporated.

He tapped the card against his fingers, much as she had. And then he walked to the door and pulled it open.

"Teal!"

The younger Harkin brother was there quickly. "Sir?"

"We need a diversion," he said. "In town. West side of the compound. Can you come up with something in the next couple of hours?"

A wide grin split the man's face. This was his favorite thing to do, since it usually involved blowing something up. "Aye, sir. I can manage that."

As the man hustled off, he turned to the table and pulled something out from under the canvas of the map. He held it out to her. She took it automatically, before she realized what it was. When she did, she stared at it, then at him.

"I came across it among Samac Rahan's things. I do not think he would have minded."

Her gaze dropped to the book of drawing paper. It was nearly full, only a few sheets missing. In the Coalition world, this was a treasure worth more than coin. At least, to her, since it was harder to get.

"It seemed only fair, since I made you burn your last two," he said.

She looked up at him again, fighting the emotions that welled up inside her. That he knew this, that he understood what it would mean to her, meant more than she could possibly explain. She wanted to throw herself at him, hug him fiercely, but as usual, there were other demands that came first.

"Thank you," she said, barely managing the husky words through her tight throat.

He smiled, a personal, intimate sort of smile, as if he'd heard everything she hadn't said.

"It will help with something I was thinking about," she said.

"What?"

"I was thinking to design a commemoration of some sort. For those who have sacrificed, as he did. Something we could put up somewhere, so none of us ever forget who we've lost."

"A wall of honor," he said softly, voicing perfectly what she'd been trying to express.

"Yes. Yes, exactly that."

"It is a good idea, a wonderful thought, Kye." His smile warmed her in yet another new way. "Perhaps even something more, if you could. Something for those they leave behind, to have and hold."

"A medal of some sort?" She liked the idea.

"If you could draw it, Brander could devise it."

"Yes. Of course. We could call it the Rahan," she suggested.

His gaze went warmer still. He reached out, cupped her cheek. "And this is why I love my tough, hardened warrior."

It was a long moment before she could force herself back to the matter at hand.

"I'd better get started back down, if I'm to be in place before Teal wreaks whatever havoc he comes up with."

She saw the shadow flit across his face, as it always did whenever she did anything with the slightest risk. But he kept to his word once more and said nothing, did not hesitate, or worse, forbid her what was her right. "Yes."

"A second set of hands and eyes might be worthwhile," she said as she considered the building she was about to breach.

"Yes."

"Who should I take?"

"Me."

She blinked. "No," she said, finding herself in the odd position of being the one to forbid. "This is too small, merely an annoyance raid, to strike at Barcon."

"It is personal," he agreed. "A chance to hit the man who handed our world over to the Coalition. And who is directly responsible for the deaths of my parents. No one else would be as invested in this as I am."

She hadn't thought of it quite that way. And as much as she hated the idea of the Raider risking himself on such a small foray, she could not argue his reasons.

"Besides," he said, "don't forget Barcon's office was once my father's."

She had forgotten that. And how Barcon had gloated that he now occupied the office once held by the vaunted Torstan Davorin. No wonder Drake insisted on taking this chance to strike back. And he would know the inside of that building better than she, or probably anyone else would.

She didn't like the idea of the Raider risking himself for what was essentially symbolism. But he had not quibbled over her going, and he had more reason even than she to want to strike this blow, so she would return the favor.

"Us, then," she said.

"Yes. Us."

And in the glance they exchanged was much more than a simple mission plan.

Chapter 36

THEY WERE HUDDLED in the thick scentbrush beside the building that had once been the council hall of Zelos, a large structure that now housed the massive bureaucracy it took to oversee the looting of Ziem and the subjugation of its people. The smell of it, that fresh, head-clearing aroma it let off when touched would give them away to any Ziemite. Fortunately, a local plant that was of no use to them was beneath Coalition notice.

In the beginning, Drake's father had said that one day the Coalition would collapse under its own weight. That tyranny always defeated itself in the end. Drake had never been content with that—just waiting it out. At sixteen, he'd been hot-headed and eager to fight back.

If he had known then what he knew now . . .

But then, he had only wanted to fight. He had never wanted to lead. Somehow, perhaps from seeing the burden his father bore, the way the people's faith in him had worn him down, he knew it came with leading.

And yet here he was.

An explosion lit up the night sky in the same moment he felt a thump beneath his feet. Across the compound, a cloud of smoke rose, mingling with the night mist, now turning orange—and to them, bright, bubbling green— from the flames erupting below. In the distance, he could see the outline of the fusion cannon, hulking, massive, deadly, aimed at Zelos. He could even see faint outlines of glowmist where the troops manning it were gathering beneath the huge weapon to try and see what was happening.

Whatever Teal had used, it had been effective; the clamor and shouting had begun, with troopers and officers both streaming out of the various barracks and buildings toward the new, gaping breach in the compound wall.

"Now," Kye whispered, and started climbing. They were using, appropriately, the same tree the twins had used.

Kye, ever light on her feet, dropped down into the compound, making no sound at all as she landed. He followed, aware of both how dangerously close to breaking the alarm beam the branch came under his greater weight, and the more audible thump his landing made. But there appeared to be no one anywhere near them; all were involved in searching for the ones who had set off the bomb. They would not find Teal, he knew, because he knew Zelos like the native son he was, and because they would likely be looking for an attacking force, not a single man.

Still, they kept to the shadows and mist as they silently made their way toward the doors. When the Coalition had used the council building as one of their walls, and then knocked doors out on that side to connect the two, he'd wondered if that was standard procedure, or if they had expected more resistance than they encountered and wanted the secure place to fall back to if necessary.

They certainly hadn't gotten much resistance, he thought. Not then, anyway. Ziem might as well have hung out a welcome banner, for all the opposition they'd shown. Of course, in large part that was because the Coalition had come in knowing whom to target, thanks to that traitor Ordam. Who had handed them the keys and then sicced them onto the lodestar of what resistance there had been: Torstan Davorin.

Yes, Ordam had handed Zelos and nearly all of Ziem over to them not just without a fight, but eagerly. He'd betrayed them all, without a thought beyond turning it to his own advantage.

He has things he has no right to . . . would it not be worth taking whatever the pretentious blowpig does have for the sheer pleasure of it?

Oh, yes, it would be worth it. And he loved Kye all the more, if that was even possible, for seeing that. And having the courage and audaciousness to do it.

They reached the doors on the darkest side of the building. He had been hoping they hadn't changed the system, and that the individual sentry's pass card would still open the main doors also. But it turned out to be needless; the door was open, apparently unlatched in someone's haste to get to the scene of what they likely assumed was an attack. He'd figured they probably had twenty minutes at most before somebody realized there was no force coming, no real attack. It might take five more for someone to think—Coalition troopers posted here were not known for their cleverness or initiative—that it might have been a diversion.

Unless it was Paledan. Drake doubted that man would be so easily fooled. He was thankful the major hadn't been here long enough to whip into shape any of the smarter ones.

Once inside, Drake led the way. He hadn't been inside this part of the building—Paledan's office was in the other end, looking out over the compound—for a dozen years, since the Coalition arrival. But while it was now festooned with the trappings of Coalition dominance and power, the floor plan was the same, and he didn't need a light to find his way to the office that had once been his father's.

The card and password made short work of getting the door open. As a precaution, the first thing he did was cross to the far wall and open the window. It looked out toward Zelos, and he wondered how Barcon lived with looking out at the city he'd betrayed every day. Of course, he didn't think he'd betrayed them at all, he thought he'd done them a favor and that they were all too stupid to realize it.

A secondary escape route now open, one that also allowed them to hear the tumult going on a hundred or so yards away, he turned around just in time to see Kye pick something up from a case behind Barcon's pretentious desk. It was too dark to see what it was. Then she reached up and touched the large painting on the wall above the case. A painting, he realized with a mix of amusement and repulsion, of Barcon himself. Looking officious and imperious as he gazed down his long nose at the viewer.

"Surprised this isn't on the opposite wall so he can gaze upon it daily," Kye muttered.

He had to smother a laugh at that. And a renewed surge of emotion made it impossible for him not to lean over and drop a kiss on her ear. She turned her head, her lips brushing over his chin. Even that small connection awoke his body anew. He gripped her shoulders and took a step back. "As much as I want to pursue this, this is not the time, nor do we have time," he said.

"Too bad," Kye said with that crooked, impish grin he'd come to treasure. "Because the thought of doing it in his office has a certain appeal."

He nearly laughed aloud even as he fought down the urge to take her right here, on Barkhound's fancy desk. And realized suddenly that all his gloom, his doubts about if they would ever win this battle, if there was any point to keeping on, vanished when he was with her. She had such energy, such vitality, that it seemed to overflow into him and he felt renewed. He thought he could fight on forever, if he had her at his side.

But he knew they had no time to waste. He reached for the frame of the painting along one side. Pulled. The painting swung out, revealing the safe set into the wall—a large metal door with a set of three displays and a keypad that were apparently the lock.

"I should have known it couldn't be that easy," Kye muttered.

"How lazy is Barkhound?" he asked softly.

"Lazier than any real member of the species," she said. "Why?"

He didn't answer, but reached out and keyed in three sets of four numbers in rapid succession. Each display showed the numbers in glowing red, then flicked to green the moment the fourth number was pressed. There was a whoosh as the heavy, airtight door released.

He heard Kye draw in a tiny breath, and by the time he glanced at her she was grinning. "The lazy barkhound never changed it."

He grinned back. "He did not."

Her grin faded. "I'm sorry. Your father—"

He held up a hand. "That is an old pain. But it is also the reason he likely didn't bother. For as far as he knew, the only man who knew the original combination was long dead."

He turned back and pulled the heavy door wide. There was a large stash of money, from Coalition vouchers to Romerian withals, taking up half the space. The other half held various items, some of which he recognized—angrily—as having been confiscated from Ziemites now dead, slaughtered no doubt by Barcon's order.

"Clean it out, or just the things he has no right to?" she asked, reaching in to pick up a small, golden carving. He saw it was of a blazer, wings outstretched and long tail curled upward. It was intricately done, with each leathery scale showing in detail. It reminded him of the sculptures she'd given the twins.

He heard the sound of blasters from outside, but they were still distant so he steeled himself to ignore it. There was nothing he could do from here. Kye's head had snapped toward the window, but almost as quickly she turned her attention back. She was one of a kind, his Kye.

His Kye. He swallowed tightly before answering her.

"Let me look at these first," he said, reaching to the shelf that ran across the top of the vault. Several papers and books he set aside, although his jaw was tight as he recognized some valuable antiquities of Ziem, histories and drawings. He picked up what had been beneath them.

Kye was preparing to empty the contents into the empty pack they'd brought when he stopped her.

"What?" she asked.

He showed her what he'd found, in the very back of the safe, beneath and behind everything else, as if it had been tossed in, buried, and forgotten. The Coalition data device still showed the last thing read on the small screen.

"It's the key," he said.

"To what?"

"Everything." And once more, he had to make the decision to sacrifice the immediate gain for the better chance at more later. "We leave it all. Back as we found it."

He did not have to explain. Not to Kye, who immediately began replacing the few items she had removed, back into their original positions. He did the same, burying the small device once more with these treasures of his world, aligning them precisely as they had been before. He closed the heavy door. It took him a moment to remember the process from all those years ago, but he managed to reset the lock, erasing the record of this opening. Then he swung the painting back into place.

Kye led the way back, and they got out the door just as the clamor from the perimeter began to die down. Teal had given them exactly as long as he'd said he would. They scrambled up and over the wall and headed for the mountain.

Chapter 37

"THIS IS CRAZY," Brander said.

"Yes."

"You think a truce flag is going to stop a Coalition officer from taking out the Raider the instant you're close enough?" Kye demanded.

"I don't know," the Raider admitted. "I've never had a Coalition officer ask for a meeting before."

"So you're thinking this makes him different?" Brander asked incredulously.

"You said yourself he was."

Brander grimaced. "I didn't mean softer. Harder, colder if anything."

"Agreed."

"So doesn't that make him more likely to blast your head off? Especially if taking you out is why he's here?"

"Possibly."

"But you're going anyway," Kye said, her tone sour.

"Yes."

"And not so that you can kill him?" Brander asked again, as if he still couldn't believe what he'd said when he'd first told him he was going to go. "I could understand that, at least, we could take him out and—"

"No. I have good reason to want him to leave alive."

Brander let out a sound that was half growl, half snort of disgust. "And just what am I supposed to do after he kills you?"

He turned to look at the man pacing the room then. The man who had stood beside him since childhood, and whom he had more than once trusted with his life. "You must take my place."

Brander scoffed. "As if anyone could."

"No one man is irreplaceable."

"The Raider is," Kye insisted.

He shook his head. And began to pace himself, Brander stopping now, as he tried to find the words to explain to them. "I'm not sure when I realized," he said slowly. "In the beginning, I was blind with anger, and wanted only to strike out, fight back as no one seemed to be doing, until they killed me. And I expected that to happen quickly." He hesitated, glancing at Kye. "I think I wanted it to happen."

"Explains some of your insane moves back then," Brander said dryly.

Kye said nothing. But she looked away, as if she did not want him to see her face.

"But when it did not," he went on, "I began to think that maybe, just maybe we really could fight back. Not beat them—I never expected that—but perhaps get to a point where they decided it wasn't worth it."

"Our planium is worth a great deal to them."

"And," Kye added, "they don't consider it ours anyway."

He hated that she sounded so bitter, but he understood. He went on. "At some point, I realized the Raider wasn't just a man. He was an idea. He stands for everything they have taken from us, and everything they still wish to take."

"What is left to take?" Kye asked, that bitter note still there.

"The idea of Ziem itself. Our history, the truth of where we began, who we became, who we are. Why our world works, why we have avoided war for centuries. Why we have never resorted to war with each other. And now the Raider stands for those who have died by Coalition hands, and for those who yet will. He stands for those who fight, those who cannot, and even those who will not. He is a symbol, an idea. And as long as he exists, the soul of Ziem will survive."

For a moment, both Kalons were utterly silent. Then Brander said, his words teasing but his voice soft, "If I'd known you were going to give a speech that inspiring, I would have dragged you out to the gathering room so everyone could hear it."

Kye said nothing, but when she looked at him, the bitterness was gone from her face, and that alone was worth much to him. So much.

After a moment, Brander coughed pointedly, then grinned at them and spoke again. "Never mind. I'll just go and . . . do something."

"Do that," Kye said, never even glancing at her cousin.

He headed for the door, put his hand on the handle, then looked back over his shoulder at them. "I know everyone respects you too much to just walk in, but you might want to think about a lock on this thing anyway."

"Just walk out?" the Raider suggested, his eyes never leaving the woman before him.

He heard Brander laugh as he did so, pulling the door securely behind him.

"I am glad he doesn't mind. Us, I mean," she said.

"He was for us long before I admitted to myself it was . . . inevitable."

Kye smiled at him. "I am more than glad you finally did."

And then she was in his arms, and all thought of what this battle was about, of what the Raider stood for, vanished from his mind. In these moments, and in these moments alone, he was simply a man who had found something he had never dared hope for.

And who tried not to think, at least while she was in his arms, while they were wrapped around and in each other, about how easily it could be taken away.

Much later, when he lay temporarily sated—for with Kye, it was ever only temporary—she stirred against his chest and asked quietly, "You feel you must do this?"

"I cannot explain—"

He stopped as she laid a gently finger over his lips. "I did not ask for an explanation. I only need to hear that you are certain you must."

"I am."

"Despite the risk."

"I must know who this man is, if we are to fight him."

"Then so be it."

He tightened his arms around her at her simple acceptance. "I'm sorry, Kye."

"I knew it would be like this. I knew before you warned me." She shifted then, lifting up to look down at him steadily. It struck him anew that she had never asked him to remove the mask, the scars, in these times, touched him as if they did not matter. And he felt a sudden jolt as he realized she would be the same if the mask was real.

"But this," she said, stroking her hand over his body in a way that set his pulse pounding and had him surging to readiness all over again, "you and I, us . . . we are worth any price."

Her words echoed in his mind the following morning as he settled the silver helmet on his head, readying himself for the meeting ahead that could well result in them both paying the ultimate price. He knew how he would feel were she to die, and he supposed she would feel the same if he had guessed wrong and this was all an elaborate ruse to lure him out to take him down.

But the other part of their bargain took precedence now. Nothing, not even this glorious thing between them, could interfere with what had to be done. For all the love they had found, both physical and of the heart, would mean nothing if Ziem was in the end crushed.

And so, after checking the scars one last time, the Raider left his quarters and headed out to meet the man whose supreme mission was to end him.

Chapter 38

THE RAIDER SAW the flare arcing through the night mist. The single green swirl told him both that Paledan was approaching, and that so far all was according to the agreement. He'd been a little surprised that the Coalition commander had so easily agreed to his terms, that he come alone, wait at a given point partway up the mountain until a squad of Sentinels met him, and allow himself to be blindfolded with a heavy canvas bag over his head before they took him to the place set for the meeting. A place he'd chosen himself for the open lines of sight down toward Zelos, and multiple points of cover above, where Brander and a small contingent would be waiting, just in case.

He heard the faint hum of an air rover. Looked up, and saw one of the quick, small crafts slide into the thicker mist in the even deeper shadows of the mountain, turn, and then hover. Had he not been looking right at it he would never have seen the faint green shape. Or caught the narrow length of the long gun now brought to bear on the meeting sight.

Kye.

He had no doubt it was her. Watching over him with that deadly accurate aim of hers. He grimaced ruefully at himself. He'd told her she could not come with him, for many reasons. The risk, of course; Paledan might well decide to not forego this chance to take out the Raider once and for all. But also he didn't want her face in the Major's mind, irrevocably set as one of the Sentinels.

And finally because, despite his vows to the contrary, he knew if she was down here with him he would be distracted, determined to keep her safe, and he was going to need every bit of his wits to deal with this man.

He'd ordered her not to come with him.

But he'd neglected to order her not to come at all.

He heard the call of a trill, a bird that had been extinct on Ziem for over fifty years. That, and the fact that it was fairly easy for even the most vocally nonadept of them to emulate, was why he had chosen it as the signal. And he had no more time to worry about Kye. He just had to have faith she could take care of herself, and wouldn't endanger herself unnecessarily trying to take care of him.

He had more faith in the former than the latter.

He could hear them now, approaching on foot, slowly, as necessitated by the fact that the man they were bringing was blindfolded. He stayed in the dark shadows of the rock of the mountain, watching. Three figures walked together, the one in the middle being guided by the other two. The Harkin brothers, who had volunteered. It was already generally known that they were with him; they had no family to use as hostages, so it mattered little if Paledan saw their faces.

They stopped several feet from where he stood. Teal yanked the heavy bag from over Paledan's head. The Raider watched as the man first scrutinized his surroundings, in all directions including vertically, much as he himself had when choosing this spot. He also noted the man showed no sign of worry, but merely stood, quietly. And again, he reminded himself it would not do to underestimate this man.

Nor was Paledan surprised when he stepped out of the shadow of the rocks. In fact, even in the faint light, the Raider could see a hint of acknowledgment, as if this were where he would have hidden himself. He reminded himself that he must roughen his voice, as he'd always done with Kye, before. It had become habit whenever he put on the helmet, but he must make sure now, because he'd been in Paledan's presence as Drake too often to assume he would not recognize his normal voice.

"I compliment you on your choice of venue, Raider," Paledan said, speaking first. "I would have chosen the same."

"So I have risen to your level?" the Raider asked, amused. "I'm flattered."

Paledan laughed. It sounded utterly genuine.

"It is not something that happens often," the man said.

In another man, it would have sounded boastful. In this one, the Raider suspected it was rather an understatement.

"I believe you," he said.

Paledan studied him for a moment after that. Then, glancing around once more, he said, "I presume you have this place covered?"

"At a distance," the Raider agreed. "Far enough that we are in essence, as you requested, alone."

Paledan nodded, accepting the assurance.

"I am not sure I would be so quick to believe," the Raider said, curious.

Paledan smiled. "I am only so because I have heard the Raider is a man of his word."

"I have heard the same of you."

For a moment, the two men just studied each other, and the Raider thought what an odd thing war was. That two men on opposite sides in the battle for an entire planet could stand thus, and simply talk, even admiringly, to each other.

He felt the breeze that tended to sweep down the mountain at this time of the evening. It caught at the bottom of his longcoat and swirled it. He knew the effect, as if he were wearing a cloak, like the warriors and rulers of old. It had been one of the biggest ironies of this whole venture, that he who had rarely worried overmuch about his appearance was now conscious of every aspect of the Raider's, aware of the power of image and the force of reputation and image.

"I have come here," Paledan said abruptly, "to suggest a bargain."

"I'm listening."

"I offer you a pardon."

He hadn't expected this. But he didn't let his surprise show, merely said casually, "Pardon?"

"The hunt for you will be called off, the price on your head rescinded."

Interesting. . . . "And the Sentinels?"

"Your fighters will be given amnesty."

"Meaning?"

"They must confess, be listed, but no action will be taken against them."

"Speaking of pardons, you must pardon me if I say it is not likely any of them will trust the Coalition's word on that."

"It is not the Coalition's word I am giving. It is mine."

The Raider couldn't help lifting a brow at that, although he knew it was mostly hidden by the helmet. He found the fact that the man saw those as two different things very telling. "And what must I give in return?"

"Nothing."

He nearly laughed. "I see."

"Do you?"

He shrugged beneath the dark armor. "You want the Raider to do nothing. Cease to exist."

"Yes."

"And you will allow me to simply . . . stop? Let it end there?"

"Yes."

"Why?"

Paledan shrugged in turn. "Let us say to honor a valiant fighter."

"Terms often used in the description of a dead fighter."

Paledan laughed. "It is nothing less than the truth. I respect a man who has done so much with so little."

"And a bloodless victory would not hurt your standing, either."

"It would not," Paledan admitted with an unconcern that the Raider felt was real. "But that is not my interest."

"Nor, it would seem, is personal advancement." For an instant, surprise flickered across the man's face. "So, the rumor is true? You declined a promotion, because it would have taken you out of the field?"

"Your information is surprisingly extensive."

The Raider merely smiled.

"But it is true. I am ill-suited to be chained to a single position, even at Legion Command."

"Or . . . perhaps especially there?"

Once more, Paledan laughed. And the Raider once more thought that, were the galaxy different and had they met under other circumstances, he could well have liked this man. It was disturbing, for he had always been able to think of the Coalition as a monolithic entity, evil throughout. Yet this man, alone among all he had encountered, seemed different. Which meant, the Raider reminded himself, that he was also not to be taken lightly. He would not be as predictable, or as hidebound by Coalition rules and regulations.

"I will tell you, Raider, my predecessors may have underestimated you. I do not."

"One man and a handful of fighters against the might of the Coalition? What real damage could we possibly do?"

"I would take you and your Sentinels over most of the garrison stationed here," Paledan said.

"Is that a compliment to mine, or insult to yours?"

For a third time Paledan laughed. "Both."

"Do you not take some risk, saying such things?" the Raider asked. "I've heard the Coalition does not welcome such talk from within."

"That standing you mentioned," Paledan answered. "I gauge it well."

"I regret that I cannot enhance it for you."

"So your answer is no?"

"It is no. It was always no."

"Then why did you agree to this meeting?"

"Curiosity."

"And learning your adversary?"

"And that."

Paledan nodded, as if he'd expected no less. "And if I were to make the same offer to your fighters?"

"Do so. I want none who are not wholehearted."

Paledan studied him for a moment. Then he shook his head slowly. "You are an exceptional man."

"You need to widen your circle, then."

The Raider half-expected him to laugh again, but he only nodded. "Perhaps you are right." He glanced around, and up, toward where Kye was hovering. Clearly, he'd known all along someone was there. "I trust your Sentinels will not shoot me in the back as I leave?"

"They will not shoot first."

Paledan smiled slightly. "If you change your mind . . ."

"I will not."

"I am sorry to hear that." Paledan lifted a hand to his brow and snapped it into a full salute. "You would be a credit to the Coalition, Raider."

"Their price is far too high."

"I cannot argue that," Paledan said, startling him.

And then he startled him further by holding out a hand, angled upward in the traditional Ziem greeting, and stepping forward. Within reach. The man, unlike his predecessor, had done his homework. His instinctive reaction was to return the gesture, allowing the brief grip of hands that signalled benign intent. But the Raider's brain, honed by the years of fighting, warned him that allowing a Coalition officer, no matter his demeanor, get that close was unwise. He wasn't foolish enough to believe the man would need a weapon to kill him.

He had but a split second to make the decision.

He went with his gut and his assessment of the man and returned the hand grasp. And saw in the other man's eyes that he understood his thought process completely.

And then it was over, Paledan accepting the blindfolding and allowing the men who had brought him to take him back, via a different but just as circuitous route, as planned.

The Raider had barely gotten back into the shelter of the trees before Brander was there. "Didn't expect that," he said.

"Nor did I." He shook his head as they made their way back up the mountain toward the ruin. "I cannot get his measure. He has such rank he must be Coalition to the bone, and yet . . ."

"He seems . . ." He gave his second a sideways look when he halted. Brander shrugged. "He seems a straightforward man. Something I never thought to say about a Coalition officer."

"Exactly my problem."

They went on in silence, and they were almost at the ruin when he halted. "Tell the others of his offer. Any who wish to take it, must feel free to."

Brander blinked. "What? What if it's a trick?"

"They must judge that for themselves. It is not a decision I will make for them, either by withholding the offer, or saying I believe it is genuine."

"Do you?"

"I think he is a man of his word. But he is also an officer of the Coalition, and I have yet to meet one that doesn't put their goals above all else. I cannot reconcile the two, so I will say nothing."

"He seems—"

"—cannot believe you really did that!"

Kye's voice, in a pitch he knew too well, cut off Brander's words, and he finished hastily, "I'll just go do that right now."

"Coward," the Raider muttered.

"When it comes to my cousin? Absolutely."

That, he understood. And turned to face Kye, who had clearly had time to return her rover to its hiding place and make her way back—at a run, judging from her tossed hair and fierce expression.

"You let him get far too close! Eos, you let him grasp your weapon hand! There are so many ways that could have gone wrong," she exclaimed.

"It did not."

"But it could have. I can't believe you did that!"

"I had the Sentinels behind me, and you above. I was safe enough."

"He could have killed you before any of us could get to you."

"Have you so little faith in me that you think I could not hold him off long enough for help to arrive from a hundred feet away?"

She started to speak again, stopped, then again. And finally she let out an explosive breath. "I hate this."

"This is why," he said softly.

She looked at him then. "I know. But I find it makes little difference. Acknowledged or not, it lives within me."

"Kye—"

She held up a hand to stop him. "Never mind. I must do . . . something. Anything."

"Was not running from the falls to here enough?"

"That barely took the edge off," she snapped.

"Perhaps I can think of . . . something else, then."

She stared at him for a moment. "You might regret that, Raider. I am in a fierce mood, and it is aimed at you."

And back in the alcove, she truly was fierce, so fierce his body arched nearly double as she rode him, hard and hot, to a climax he thought surely would kill him, and he bit his lip bloody trying not to shout with the force of it.

And after, when he realized she was weeping, his strong, tough, fearless Kye was weeping, he didn't know what to say or do so he just held her, ruefully acknowledging that in this, the Raider was helpless.

Chapter 39

HE HAD BEEN holed up in his quarters for three days, poring over Kye's map, the information he'd gleaned from the crashed freighter and Barcon's safe at hand. At least he was able to do so, with Eirlys now aware and watching the twins. She'd even consented to running the taproom, which gave him pause, but Brander had offered to head down this evening to help, promised he would be with her to deal with any problems. And to help her keep the secret.

He'd honed and fine-tuned the plan, shifting Sentinels here, moving lookouts there, allotting what weapons they had—including Brander's acquisitions, what they now called the obliterator, and the rail gun—and deciding who was best suited for which tasks. He wasn't completely satisfied yet, but he was close. What he'd found in the safe meant the entire timetable had been moved up, and he had only a few days to finalize everything. That there would be changes on the fly he was sure, there always were, and flexibility was the key to the kind of warfare he waged. But the basics had to be there; everybody had to know what their goal was in order for them to reach it by whatever means possible, even if it meant diverging from the original plan. This was one of their biggest advantages, the ability of his fighters to think on their own, something the Coalition did their best to crush out of their own troops.

The door flew open. Scowling at the lack of warning, he spun around. His temper was on a blade's edge, honed by the increasing tension as the moment grew closer when he would have to send people to likely death.

He saw Brander standing there, holding a small, curled piece of paper. His normally insouciant second was white-faced, hollow-eyed.

He went cold.

"It's Jakel," Brander said harshly. "He's taken Eirlys."

"I'LL KILL HIM. I swear to Eos I'll kill him if he hurts her."

Brander was pacing as he spoke, because he had to move. He wanted to be away, to blast through any obstacle, mow down anyone in his path, to get Eirlys out of the hands of that slimy brute. The thought of that sweet, fierce girl at Jakel's mercy drove him to the edge of madness. And she would fight him, which would only anger him and make it worse.

"If he hurts her, he will die," the Raider agreed. By contrast, his voice was measured, low, but even deadlier for it. He had been deadly calm since Brander had explained the message the twins had sent via one of Eirlys's precious birds.

"Just let me go, right now, and I'll—"

"It has to be me, Brander. I am her brother. I'm who he'll expect." He was hastily removing the scars. Haste and that process did not mix well. "I will go out the back," the Raider said, referring to the narrow, tunnel entrance to his quarters.

"You mean *we*," Brander said sharply. "If you think—"

"I think you will go with me to Zelos, but you will stay back and not be seen."

He stopped mid-stride. Whipped around to glare at his commander. "In hades I will! I—"

"Brander. I know you would die to save her, but I need you alive, to get her to safety if I cannot. I need you to protect her."

His spurt of anger ebbed. "I . . . yes."

"Swear to me. You will see her safe," the Raider said, and he sounded haunted. Unease stirred along with the knot in Brander's gut.

"I will." He resumed his pacing. "I can't believe Ordam would do this. I never would have thought he'd have the nerve to take a Davorin."

"I do not believe it."

Brander stopped again mid-stride. The Raider had not said that in the tone of someone expressing skepticism, but someone who knew something else to be true. When he got there, his gut knotted even more fiercely.

"You think Jakel did this on his own?"

"I'm saying Ordam did not order this. He is ever and always a coward, and this is too open."

"I have always felt Ordam's hold on the brute tenuous, but—"

The door burst open, cutting him off. Kye rushed into his quarters, the slam of the door behind her echoing. "Is it true?" she demanded.

"The twins would not mistake something like this," Brander said.

She spun on her heel to look at the Raider, who had the scars off now and was finishing his transformation back into meek taproom keeper Drake Davorin. She frowned slightly.

"You are going as . . . yourself?"

"It is who Jakel will expect," he repeated.

Kye looked thoughtful, then nodded. "And it would give away too much for the Raider to sweep in to rescue her."

"That as well."

She studied him for a moment. "You're going to need to rough up your other cheek a bit."

His brows lowered. "What?"

She gestured at the mask now lying on the table. "You did that in a hurry. The skin is reddened. If the other side matches, it will look only as if you are flushed and nervous."

"An artist's eye," the Raider murmured. He glanced around, then quickly crossed to the table where the map lay. The sand Kye had used to dry the ink quickly, so one sector would not smear as she moved on to the next, was in a small bowl. He grabbed a handful and scrubbed his left cheek with it. Kye had followed, and when he stopped and turned to face her, she nodded.

"By Eos, can we go now?" Brander demanded, his panic growing in step with his anger. He knew the Raider would tell him that was a very bad combination, but he was in no mood to hear fighting philosophy now.

"I'll get the rover from the falls—it's closest," Kye said, turning to go.

"No."

She spun back at the Raider's short, flat command. "You can't think I'm staying here?"

"You must."

Kye stared at him. "I love her, too. She is my sister in all but blood."

"I know. But you must stay clear, Kye. You are my third, and if necessary, you must lead the Sentinels."

"But Brander—"

"I have my reasons, Kye. Because there is something even bigger than this," Drake said, his voice low and quiet. "Something that must survive any or all of us. And my little sister would be the first one to tell you that."

Brander felt that knot in his gut grow, for he knew Drake was right. Eirlys would die before she would see the rebellion fail because of her.

"In this, you must be Sentinel first," Drake said, reaching out to brush her face with the back of his fingers. "And there is something else. You must find the twins for me. They sent the message so they are free, but you know they will do something foolish if not stopped. They will listen to you. You must keep them away from Zelos, from Jakel. Bring them here if necessary. I think my time of hiding in plain sight may be over."

Brander knew his cousin well, and saw the moment when she decided. Her nod was short, almost curt, but definite. And once he saw it, his anxiety burst its banks and he snapped. "Now," he demanded.

"Yes," Drake agreed. "Now."

They were halfway down the mountain before the movement had settled Brander enough to ask, "You have a plan? Other than to blow them all to hades?"

"And Eirlys with them?"

"I know, I know. I just want my hands around Jakel's greasy neck."

"As do I."

He realized belatedly he had thought only of getting there, not of what they would do when they did. "How do we do this?"

"It depends on what we find when we arrive. Where Jakel is holding her. Whether he has taken her for strategic or personal reasons."

Brander stared at the man driving the rover; he'd insisted, saying Brander was wound so tightly he would pile them into a tree.

"How can you stay so calm? It's Eirlys!"

"Because I must. Because rage leads to mistakes. Because panic is the quickest road to death. Because they must think I am only a concerned brother." He drew in a deep breath. "Because I have had to learn it well these past three years."

Brander remembered leading his own first raid, and how he had hated the way he was always expected to have the answer, as Drake was. And then he had had to make a decision that sent a Sentinel to almost certain death while he stayed to complete the mission. That the man had survived was only due to luck, and he had never forgotten the weight of that decision. And Drake had carried it, alone and multiplied countless times, for years.

He struggled for a moment with what to say. Realized there were no words big enough. "I do not envy you, my brother. I'm sorry."

Drake glanced at him. Nodded. And that easily, as it had ever been, it was behind them. They were united once more, with a single, unyielding goal.

"We'll save her," Brander said. "If I have to burn Zelos to the ground."

"I would prefer not," Drake muttered. "But yes, we will save her."

In the end, they did not have to search at all. After hiding the rover in the trees on the west side of town, they headed through the alleys toward the main street. Some hundred feet short of that, they were flagged down by Enish Eck.

"Been looking high and low for you," the man panted.

Drake didn't bother with dissembling. "Do you know where he has her?"

Brander felt like thumping the man for the look that crossed his face, as if he were disappointed they already knew and he didn't get to be the news bearer.

"In the taproom," Enish answered.

"You're certain?" Brander demanded.

"That's what he said to tell you. And that he'd be waiting for you, Drake."

Drake went very still. "He told you to tell me this?"

"As soon as I saw you." Enish grimaced. "Well, he told everybody in the taproom, when he grabbed her. Before he threw us all out."

Brander's fury, simmering just under the surface ever since the twins' message had arrived, threatened to burst free at the image that formed in his mind. It echoed in his voice when he spoke.

"And none of you stopped him?"

Enish drew back at the sound of it. "He had a blaster, pointed at her head. Said he'd kill her if we didn't all clear out. What were we supposed to do?"

Brander swore, loud and harsh.

"She nearly cut his hand off, though," Enish said. "Broke a bottle and went right for him when he first grabbed her."

"Good for her," Drake said. He turned as if to go, then Enish spoke again.

"I could maybe round up some help," he offered. "I think I know some as would do it. For Eirlys," he added pointedly, as if he wanted to be clear no one would do it for the cowardly taproom keeper himself.

Brander wanted to punch him all over again, and only Drake's quick shake of his head forestalled him.

"No," Drake said, ignoring the slur. "We don't know what he wants yet. If it is a fight, you would all be unarmed and in danger."

Enish looked relieved, but also a little puzzled. As if he hadn't expected that answer. Drake had played his part so well, even the idea of him fighting was apparently bewildering.

They left Enish staring after them, and headed for the taproom.

"You must stay in the back," Drake said. Brander started to protest, but Drake kept going. "You must stay back, hidden so that you can get her out safely."

"And you?"

"Will do what I must."

As you always do, Brander thought. "You are the strongest man I've ever known, Drake Davorin," he said. "And I include your father in that number."

Drake looked startled. Perhaps it was the contrast of his words with Enish's insult.

They reached the back door of the taproom. Drake only glanced at the door to one side, that led to their home. The door was secure, as Eirlys kept it when she was there alone, and he keyed in the entrance code.

"You should take a weapon," Brander said for at least the third time since they'd left the ruin.

"The cowardly tapper has nothing to do with them. And I will need to play that part long enough to assess. So . . . a blade at most, I think."

Brander subsided into silence as the door swung open and they slipped into the storeroom. Once inside they stopped near the entrance to the taproom, listening.

"—will be sorry for this."

Eirlys. Brander felt a rush of relief. She was alive and talking, at least.

"And who will make me sorry, sweetling?"

The relief was quickly replaced by a resurgence of fury at the oily, ominous tone of Jakel's voice.

"My brother will—"

Jakel's laugh cut her off. "Your brother the coward?"

"You call him coward," Eirlys exclaimed, "when you come with two Coalition troopers just to talk to a girl?"

Two? They could take them, easily, but to do it without Eirlys getting hurt . . .

"And he's not a coward," Eirlys added fiercely. Brander sensed Drake stiffen. Felt the jolt of fear himself.

No, Eirlys. No, no, no, don't go there.

But she kept going. "If you only knew—"

She stopped abruptly. Had she realized what she'd been about to betray?

"If I only knew what?" Jakel's tone had turned coaxing, but at the same time the threatening note laced his words.

"What he used to be like," Eirlys said, sounding defeated. "Before."

She'd saved it, Brander thought, renewed admiration kicking through him.

"Oh, but I do know," Jakel said, almost crooning in a way that turned Brander's already roiling stomach. "Do you think I've forgotten the glorious Drake Davorin, rising up after his father's death to lead? I've always thought it suspect that he caved so completely. And you know what I think?"

"I know you don't," Eirlys said, disdain clear in her voice.

"Don't what?" Jakel sounded disconcerted.

"Think," she said flatly.

The sound of that meaty hand striking her nearly had Brander roaring into the room. Only Drake's hand on his arm stopped him. He looked at his best friend incredulously; how could he stop him after that? But the moment he saw Drake's icy eyes, he knew Jakel had just sealed his own fate.

"Foolhardy, aren't you? As I was saying, you know what I think? I think it's no coincidence that the nights the Raider strikes, your brother isn't here."

Brander froze. There was a moment of silence before Eirlys said, "What, you think he's helping the Raider? He's a coward, remember? You said so yourself."

"Even cowards have their uses. They are . . . easily manipulated. And there is no better place to hear things than a taproom where men's tongues are loosened by brew."

He had that part right.

"I must say, though," Jakel said, "I thought he would show up sooner once he knew you were in trouble. Perhaps he is even more craven than I thought."

"What makes you think he even knows what you've done, you blowpig?"

To Brander's surprise, the man seemed to ignore the insult. "You may be right. Perhaps no one cares enough to tell him. Perhaps I should make it more . . . urgent. Would the sound of your screams do the trick, do you think?"

In the instant he began to move, he again felt Drake holding him back.

"Stay," he whispered. "You must be her escape. No matter what happens, you must get her away."

It hit him in that moment why Drake had insisted he be the one to accompany him. It wasn't just that Brander would die to save Eirlys.

It was that if there were absolutely no other choice, he would let Drake die to save her.

While Kye would die herself before she'd let either of those things happen.

Drake stepped past him and into the taproom.

Chapter 40

"IF WE HAD A private party scheduled, I've forgotten," Drake said, his eyes scanning for others besides the two near the door. To keep people out? Or in?

"Oh, we're going to have a private party, Davorin," Jakel said, and his dark tone was made even more ominous by the note of delighted anticipation that underlay it. "And you'll be the guest of honor."

So it was him the beast wanted. Did he know? He could not, he was not that bright. But he might suspect . . . something.

"Drake, get out. He's evil, he'll—ahh!" Eirlys's words ended on a yelp of pain.

Every muscle in his body went tense. He wanted nothing more than to blast Jakel to bits right now. With lightning speed, he calculated distances, reaction times, probable responses. Anyway he figured, Eirlys got hurt at best, and the worst didn't bear thinking about.

Jakel nodded toward the two troopers. Drake pretended not to see them move toward him, and casually walked behind the bar. The two hesitated, looking to Jakel.

"Jakel, Jakel, let's be reasonable," Drake said, adding a well-practiced nervous laugh, while his inward laugh at the idea of this man being reasonable about anything was very real. "Let's talk about it. Over a brew? Or perhaps some of that lingberry you so like. On the house, of course."

He turned as if to take the bottle from the shelf behind him. Saw in the mirror the two troopers, still standing where they'd stopped. Drones, he assessed. No move made without exact orders.

Or they were uncertain of the task at hand, he thought as one of them gave Jakel a sideways look.

"Don't take me for a fool, Davorin."

"I don't." *You're not quite stupid enough.* "What is it you want, then?"

"I know you're working with that brigand, and you'll confess to it before I'm through."

He felt a spark of relief. Jakel suspected something, but not the truth. He widened his eyes as if fearful. "Brigand? There's some sort of thug on the loose?"

Jakel swore, an oath that was half slur, half ugly promise. "You know be-damned well who I mean. You're working with that Raider."

Drake let his expression change to one of sudden understanding. He laughed, carefully judging how to make it sound. "Well-done prank, Jakel. You had me worried."

"Take him!"

The two troopers began to move toward him again. He threw up his hands. "Hold, here," he said, letting every bit of the fear he had for his sister echo in his voice. The two men stopped. Apparently, they took orders from anyone. Or else their hearts really weren't in this, he thought, seeing the way they looked at the brute who had brought them here. "This is absurd, Jakel. You know I am . . . not of the temperament to get involved in such things. And everyone knows I think the Raider is mad, at the least, to even try to go up against the Coalition."

His words rang with veracity, because they were true. He'd known it was mad from the beginning.

For the first time, Jakel looked uncertain. But his determination, or innate obstinate inflexibility won out. "I know I am right, and I will soon have the proof. From you."

He calculated his next words carefully, for he had seen Jakel loosen his grip on Eirlys in his moment of doubt.

"Let us go to Barcon then, and talk of this. He is your administrator; let him decide."

"Do you think he will help you?" Jakel sneered. "He wishes this as much as I do. He only lacks the nerve to command it."

So he'd been right. However much Barcon Ordam might want this, he wouldn't give the order. But he wouldn't stop his wild slimehog, either.

"But I'm sure he never meant you to involve Eirlys," Drake said. "He has always been very fond of her."

That put another flash of doubt in Jakel's soulless eyes. Before the man could speak, he gestured to Eirlys. "But I must take him something. A gift." He laughed again, differently, as a man who wouldn't hesitate to try and bribe his way out of trouble. "Eirlys, there is a bottle of that particular brand he likes in back. Go."

He saw her register the slightest emphasis he'd put on the word "brand," as Jakel snapped, "She doesn't leave this room until I have you secured. Take him!"

The troopers rushed this time. Rounded the end of the bar. Drake slapped a hand down on the surface he'd polished so often. Leapt, clearing it easily, coming down on the other side within a few feet of Jakel. Saw the man jerk back. He pretended to stumble upon landing, careening into Jakel.

In an instant, his dagger was at the man's throat. But Jakel managed to keep a grip on Eirlys's arm, despite her struggle; the man was brutally strong. The only good thing was, he couldn't both hang onto her and fight off Drake at the same time.

Clearly uncertain, the troopers raised their blasters.

"Don't fire!" Jakel yelled. Apparently he did not trust their ability to miss him.

"Let go of her," Drake said.

"Then they will shoot you."

"And likely hit you. But if they do not, I will surely cut your throat."

"I will order them to shoot her!"

He would. Drake could see it in his small, shiny eyes. He could also see the dawning of understanding in the eerily red depths; Jakel was beginning to realize that no cowardly, beaten tapper would manage to get a blade to his throat, let alone with two troopers in the room. He would be more convinced than ever now that Drake was more than he seemed.

And more determined to extract that information.

He couldn't think about that now. Not while the beast still had Eirlys. "Let her go," he said, "and I will release you."

"I don't believe you," Jakel said. "They would kill you instantly."

"I don't think so. For that would spoil your fun, would it not?"

He saw it again, that feral, brutal maliciousness, in Jakel's expression. Knew the man had no intention of going to Barcon before he had that fun. He was thankful for the cool numbness that had overtaken him, for it kept at bay his dread of what was to come. Everyone in Zelos had heard the tales of Jakel's glee in torture. But he could see no other way. No way that was not too great a risk for Eirlys, and he could not see her hurt, or worse. He could not.

"Let her go," he repeated, "and I will go with you."

Jakel went still. "Without a fight?"

"Drake, no. You can't." Eirlys's voice was tight, strained. He could see her fear, see that she knew what awaited him. "I won't let you."

"You must. Go. As I told you," he added, reminding her of his allusion to what was in the storeroom.

He moved his dagger, away from Jakel's throat, yet kept it close.

"Drop it," Jakel ordered.

"When she is gone."

"Again you take me for a fool."

"Let her get to the back doorway. Then I will drop it."

Jakel thought, his brow furrowed with the effort. After an agonizing moment, he let go of her arm.

"Drake!"

"Go," he ordered, in the low, harsh voice of the Raider. "Now."

He could see the anguish in her face as she backed up, never taking her eyes from him. He held his breath. Once she got to the doorway, she would be safe; Brander would take over. He would see to her.

She reached the doorway. The troopers raised their weapons. Aimed at him. Jakel jerked away. Enough to give them a clear shot. No choice. He dropped the dagger.

The troopers closed in. Eirlys vanished from the doorway. Drake knew he'd seen a hand grab her from inside the storeroom. Brander. She would be all right.

He, on the other hand, was headed into hades.

Chapter 41

KYE FOUND THE twins in the bell tower. And nearly fell prey to their booby trap; the wire strung across the stairway was practically invisible.

"Clever," she said, loud enough for anyone hiding above to hear.

"Kye!"

Lux's cry echoed off the tower's stone walls. The twins bolted from where they'd been hiding behind the wreckage of the biggest bell, the one that had once sent deep, booming peals of vibrating sound across Zelos. This had been her third stop, after their home and, thinking it would be very like them to hide under the Coalition's nose, the tree next to the compound wall. She had been standing there, pondering her next move, vaguely aware of the absence of the cannon that had been moved back to the ridge above the mines yesterday, when the thought of the bell tower had occurred to her.

They nearly knocked her off her feet with fierce hugs.

"Eirlys," they began, sounding frightened in a way she had never heard from this near-fearless pair before.

"I know. Your brother and Brander have gone for her."

That quickly, the fear ebbed. For a moment, she envied them their youth, their faith that not even the force of the Coalition could stop the man who was the cornerstone of their life. She realized in that moment she did not know what the twins thought of the public Drake, how they felt about the façade, if it had fooled them as it had her and everyone else. She knew only that, to them, he was still the man who would protect them unto death, regardless of what the rest of Ziem thought.

Which was how this might well end. Not that she did not have faith in Drake, and near as much in her cousin, but she also knew the Coalition too well to assume anything.

"Come, we must go. Quickly."

"Where?"

She had been pondering this all during her search. It had helped to keep her mind off Eirlys, Drake, and Brander. If this was more than just Jakel unleashing his vileness on a girl alone, if there was a chance this wasn't just his personal evil but something to do with the Coalition . . . if they somehow suspected Drake wasn't who he appeared to be . . .

She suppressed a shudder. If the Coalition suspected anything at all, all the Davorins would have a price on their heads. And she knew their ruthlessness well enough to know the twins' youth would not save them.

"Bring them here if necessary . . ."

"We're going to the Sentinels," she said. Excitement flashed in the two identical sets of eyes that looked up at her. "But you must say nothing, and do exactly as I tell you."

They nodded, their lips pressed tightly together. It took her a second to realize they were implementing the first instruction right now. Despite her worry, she felt a spark of amusement.

"Stay close, then," she said, and led them down the stairs, dodging their trap once more.

She took her most indirect, convoluted route, even though it would take longer. The twins held up surprisingly well, and except for a couple of times when the sight of a beast or bird startled an exclamation out of them, they kept to the rules she'd set. They seemed to realize the importance of it, and every time she glanced at them in the glowmist, their expressions were solemn.

I should not be surprised. They are, after all, Davorins.

By the time they went down the ladder into the main room of the ruin, Eirlys was already there. The twins ran to her, exultant, crying out everything they had likely suppressed on the long trek.

But Kye only had one image burned into her mind. Eirlys had been crying before she ever saw the twins. She looked both stunned and devastated. Kye stopped in her tracks.

Brander, who had been with Eirlys, started toward her immediately.

"Where is he?" she demanded.

"Kye—"

"Where is he, Brander?"

He let out a breath. "Jakel has him."

She stared at him, so many things rocketing through her mind she couldn't pick one to say.

"He gave himself up to him, Kye. To save Eirlys."

Everything in her seemed to seize up, even her heartbeat faltered.

"He's . . . dead?"

"No." Brander said it through clenched teeth. "Not yet."

He grabbed her arm and pulled her into the Raider's quarters. She didn't even resist. She was thinking of the brutal enforcer, of what had been left of others who had fallen into his hands; there had too often been barely enough to bury.

Brander turned as soon as the door was closed.

"Jakel suspects something, but it seems only that Drake's been working with the Raider. Eirlys says he's been watching. Noticing that when the Raider struck, Drake wasn't at the taproom. That he is often on the mountain. And, of course, there's his obsession with his name."

"Little."

"Yes, it is little enough evidence. And if called upon there is . . . someone who will say he was elsewhere at those times. In Sanguine."

In her torment, it took her a moment to realize what he meant. The woman Drake had said had provided information.

"But that will not stop Jakel," Brander said, derailing thoughts she did not care for.

"No."

"He will try to torture the truth out of him."

"Yes."

"And Drake will never give in."

"No."

"And if he gains the slightest suspicion that Drake actually is the Raider, he is as good as dead."

She couldn't even summon up a single word answer for that. For, too clear in her mind's eye was the knowledge that Drake wouldn't just die, he would die hard and ugly.

"Kye—"

She shook her head sharply. She had never felt anything like the chill that had come over her now. It was a cold deeper than the ice atop The Sentinel, more barren than the rock above the Edge. She could hear the buzz going around the room outside; thought idly that a careful listen would likely tell them which, if any, of the Sentinels knew the Raider's true identity.

She found her voice at last. "Jakel has always hated Drake. In the way a weak creature hates a stronger, smarter one."

"I know. Even a brollet recognizes the danger of a clever wolf."

"He wants to prove Drake is . . . ordinary, by breaking him. Bring him down to his own level." She was pacing now as she spoke, her mind racing.

"And because he's a Davorin."

"Yes. He would do the same with or without suspicions of a connection to the Raider."

Brander nodded. "He needed only the excuse."

She stopped. Turned back. "We need to do a raid," she said abruptly.

Brander's gaze narrowed. "How can we do a raid when he is—"

She cut him off with a wave of her hand. "That's exactly why we need to do it."

Brander blinked. "Echo that?"

"We need to do a raid, now, tonight."

He stared at her.

"Jakel is stupid, but he is shrewd. We have to make sure he doesn't make that jump."

Her cousin looked suddenly thoughtful. "So a raid . . . while they have Drake locked up."

"Yes."

"Show them he's not the Raider."

"Exactly. It might keep him alive."

"Assuming he still is," Brander said, his tone grim.

Her heart slammed in her chest. She'd known it was possible he was not, but hearing it said aloud made it even more real.

"He is," she insisted, for her own sake as much as convincing her cousin. "I would feel it were he not."

He gave her a sideways look at that, but the mocking comment she half expected did not come.

"So this raid you want to do . . . ," was all he said, bringing them back to the subject.

She nodded. "It has to be something . . . outrageous. Right under their noses. Something the Raider would do." She took a breath, then added, "And you need to be the Raider."

His brows shot upward. "What?"

"Who better? You're his second, you know the way he works, plans."

"So do you."

She gave an inelegant snort. "I know you are my cousin and look at me as such, but if you really think I could fool anyone into thinking I'm the Raider—"

"That's not what I meant," Brander said. "No one sane—or at least no man—would ever mistake you for anything but a woman. I just meant you know how he thinks better than any of us. That," he ended with emphasis, "is without doubt."

Brander was probably the only one who knew the depth of her connection to his best friend. And the Raider himself had told her of his support, of how Brander had been for them together before he himself had dared to even think about it. So she met his gaze steadily. Gave him the honesty he deserved for that. "I love him."

Brander rolled his eyes. "I know that. I've known that for years."

"Even when I hated him, I loved him, too."

His expression softened. "You never hated him. It was merely that the Drake you loved was hidden. And as the Raider, he felt he could not ask you to risk the cost of . . . loving him."

"He did not have to ask. Love does not come—or go—to order."

Brander was quiet for a moment before saying softly, "I see where all the wisdom in the family went."

She was not used to such gentle understanding from her usually teasing cousin. And they had strayed from the subject at hand.

Nervous energy bubbling over, she began to pace. His quarters seemed hollow, and much larger without the Raider's immense presence.

"You're nearly his height and size, and his cloak will mask any difference. The helmet and the mask will do the rest."

He shook his head. "Not the mask. The Sentinels will know it's me, and that would give away to all of them that the mask is part of the disguise. It may come out in the end, but I won't make that decision for him by displaying it."

"But you'll do it?"

"I cannot match his skill. Or his planning. Most of all, his inspiring the troops. I'm a poor substitute."

"You, in fact, are not. You just haven't had to be."

His head snapped around. "Careful, my cousin, you strayed perilously close to a compliment there."

She stopped her pacing. Turned to look at him straight-on. "I have been a fool there, as well, if I have not told you how much I admire what you've done. The Raider would not have been able to accomplish as much as he has without you at his side."

For the first time in her life, Brander had no quick retort. He simply stared at her for a long, silent moment. "What has brought this on?" he asked softly.

"Perhaps the final, undeniable knowledge that the next second is not guaranteed, let alone tomorrow."

Something changed in his eyes then, something she recognized because she'd seen it in herself. "Some would say that is reason enough to avoid . . . entanglements."

"And some," she answered, as softly as he had spoken, and keeping her gaze on his face, "would say it is the best reason to seize what you can of happiness while you have the chance."

Brander was very perceptive, under the mask of insouciance, which in its way was as much a disguise as the Raider's scars. And she knew he'd taken her meaning by the way his gaze suddenly darted away.

"No one stays young for long in war," she said. "And Eirlys hasn't truly been a child since her mother threw herself from Halfhead."

He winced, and she guessed it was from more than just the memory of the loss of Iolana Davorin.

"Perhaps," Kye said, "Drake and all of Ziem should think more of how they lived, the love they shared, and not so much about how they died. Besides, I think that he has changed his mind about the place of love in war."

Before Brander could respond to that, there was a knock on the door to his quarters. It swung open before either of them could respond, a measure, she supposed, of the Raider's absence.

Pryl stood there, his expression grave. "Some of us are wondering if you've a plan yet."

Brander and Kye exchanged glances. "A plan?" he asked tentatively.

Pryl grimaced. "To get Drake—the Raider."

Brander and Kye exchanged a startled glance.

"Please," the old woodsman said. "I've known for an age. I watched that boy grow up, don't forget."

"I see," Kye said slowly.

Pryl shrugged. "He needed it secret, I kept it so. Although I think others have guessed as well."

"Does he know you know?" Brander asked.

Again the shrug. "Seemed best never to speak it aloud. Not everyone can keep things close. So, is there a plan?"

Brander glanced at Kye, then turned back to face Pryl. "We need to make sure the Coalition doesn't find out they really have the Raider."

Pryl blinked. "And how do we do that?"

He gave her a glance and a smile of salute. "Kye solved it. The Raider has to strike again. Tonight."

Chapter 42

CAZE PALEDAN HAD seen some horrific things in his Coalition career, but outside of the debris of battle, this might just be the worst. He looked at Jakel, noting the gleam in the man's eyes that told him he had enjoyed this. He looked like a man turned loose in a treasure room, only his avarice was for cruelty and inflicting pain. He was taking in deep breaths, as if savoring the smell of blood. Men like this, who took a perverse pleasure in simply hurting others, were useful tools. But if you let the leash run out too far, it was likely to snap, freeing them to turn on you. He wondered if Ordam had ever even considered that.

He looked again at the man chained to the wall. He wasn't standing— clearly he was far beyond that—he was hanging from the cuffs that dug into his wrists, fresh blood running down his arms. His face was so battered, his body so bruised and burned and bloody, he was barely recognizable as the taproom keeper. Paledan wondered idly who was looking out for those troublemaking twins. Likely the sister.

He turned back to the perpetrator of this torture.

"Does the administrator ever require subtlety or nuance from you?" he asked with a raised brow.

"What?" The man looked utterly puzzled, as if the words were from some alien language.

"I thought not," Paledan said. "Leave. And leave me the keys to those chains."

Jakel frowned. With his heavy brows and rather simian face, it was an expression that came closer to making him laugh than cower.

"Have you not incapacitated him? You've had him for hours; surely you've been able to render him no threat by now."

The frown deepened. Paledan didn't know if it was because he again didn't understand the words, or didn't wish to give up his fun. Either way, he did not care.

"He hasn't confessed yet," Jakel protested. "He hasn't said a single word." A look of blissful satisfaction flashed across brutal features. "He screamed, though. He'll break."

"Out," Paledan ordered sharply.

For a long moment, Jakel just stared at him. Paledan didn't move, merely stood, holding the man's beady gaze. He could read clearly in the man's expression that he was sizing him up, wondering. He didn't like having men like this around. Brutal men had their place, but not if they weren't controllable. But then, that was a reflection of Ordam as much as Jakel.

He almost wished the beast would try.

"I want him back," Jakel said finally, and there was clear warning in his tone. "I haven't finished yet."

Yes, you have. "I'm sure you do. Now go."

He did, reluctantly, handing over the keys with even greater reluctance. With a last glance cast over his shoulder at his victim, Jakel left the dank, dark room. Probably to run to Ordam.

"Think . . . you could take him."

He spun around to look at what was left of Drake Davorin. His face was bloody and swollen from Jakel's fists and cudgels. He could barely see one eye; the other was swollen shut. Blood from countless cuts and splits in his flesh streamed over his body here, had clotted in a darkening mass there. What skin he could see was either reddened from burns, or pale, too pale, and from the rasping breaths, he suspected the internal damage was substantial.

He hasn't said a single word. . . .

And yet he had spoken now.

Paledan walked to the wall and unlocked the chains from the wall. He eased the man down to the floor, aware there wasn't an undamaged spot on him to grab. He heard a breath rush out of him, the tiniest expression of relief, coupled with a barely audible groan at what had to be horrible pain from his shoulders.

"I think one day I will have to," he answered, crouching beside Davorin.

"Watch . . . his left."

He was almost amused. "I've noticed he is ambidextrous in his strength."

"With a brain . . . he might be dangerous."

He truly was amused then. And admiring. The man had to be in agony, his every breath harsh and wet, yet he joked. "As he is, he is merely hazardous, in the way of an angry slimehog."

"You insult slimehogs."

Paledan couldn't help himself, he laughed. But at the same time, he was assessing. "If you had come over to the Coalition, you would be a general by now."

The battered head came up then. Paledan couldn't imagine the strength of will that simple act had taken.

"I'd have nothing to fight for. And nothing in me to fight with."

What was he admitting, this broken, bloodied man, the taproom keeper he had always suspected was something more? It made no sense, that he would resist through Jakel's torture only to speak to him without any coercion at all.

"I am sorry to see the Raider end like this," he said on impulse, something he rarely succumbed to. "Had I been the one to capture you, you would have been treated with the respect he has earned."

Davorin laughed. Despite it all, he laughed. And when he spoke, his voice got stronger. "Even if I were . . . the one you seek, it would not end. The Raider is not one man. He is an idea. An idea you will never be able to kill."

Paledan saw the man's eyes close, and realized he had slipped out of consciousness after that effort. He straightened, and stood there studying the prisoner. The strength he'd exhibited here had proven what he'd always suspected—there were hidden depths to this man. But at most, he'd thought he might be aiding the notorious fighter. But now he was considering a bigger possibility.

That he was himself the Raider.

Was it possible for a man to lead such a double life? And yet, what a perfect disguise—a beaten, cowed taproom keeper. But that keeper had a family he was responsible for, and Paledan knew firsthand he took that responsibility seriously.

It seemed impossible, and implausible. And yet . . .

Davorin had already proven, with his resistance to Jakel's brutal methods, that there was amazing strength in him. And his words about the Raider had been those of a believer, despite the accepted certainty that the taproom keeper had long ago surrendered such thoughts, if he'd ever had them to begin with.

But if he was the Raider, how in hades had he let himself be captured by the likes of Jakel?

There was more to this. He was certain of it.

He stepped out into the hallway. The guard outside the door snapped to attention. Paledan pondered for a moment giving in to the odd urge he felt to order a medic to aid the prisoner, but he knew too well that would draw far too much attention of the wrong kind. And it was likely too late anyway. If Davorin lasted the night, he would be surprised.

But he could at least stop the damage here. "If Jakel returns, keep him out of there."

The man's eyes widened. "Parameters, sir?"

Paledan gave him a wry smile. "Necessary force."

The man gulped, but nodded. Paledan started down the hall toward the outer door, but then turned back. "And that does not mean you are required to bleed before taking action."

"Yes, sir. Thank you, sir."

He issued an order into his handheld comm link, and by the time he got back to his office, the trooper he'd summoned was already there. Standing at attention and saluting despite being only half in uniform.

"I caught you after your duty shift," Paledan said, noting his attire.

"Yes, sir." The trooper swallowed. "I thought a quick response was more important than a perfect turnout."

"Good decision," Paledan said mildly, noting the man's name; he was always glad to know who in his command had some sense of their own. That went against Coalition policy, but he had always believed not allowing their able people to think for themselves would cost them in the end.

Clearly relieved, Trooper Gratt took the seat indicated. Paledan took his own chair behind the desk. He did not waste time with formalities.

"You were there when Davorin was captured," he began.

"Yes, sir. Although . . ." His voice trailed off and he lowered his gaze.

"Honesty," Paledan said, "would also be a good decision."

Gratt drew in a deep breath. "Yes, sir. It wasn't exactly a capture, Major. He surrendered."

Paledan leaned back. "Did he?" he murmured.

"It was an exchange, sir."

Understanding began to dawn. "An exchange?"

"May we go off the record, sir?"

"As far as I'm concerned, we have been," Paledan said. "This is my own inquiry, not the Coalition's."

Gratt visibly relaxed. "Jakel," he said, his distaste clear in his tone, "had Davorin's sister."

And there it was, Paledan thought. The piece that made it all make sense. "Which one?" he asked.

Gratt blinked. "Sir?"

"Which sister? There are two."

"Oh. Uh . . . the pretty one? The blonde—I don't know her name," he added regretfully, like a man who wished he knew more than just the woman's name.

Not Lux, then, Paledan thought, since Gratt did not show any evidence of being the twisted type who would think so of a child. For a moment, the memory of one who had had such perverted tastes shot through his mind, but for only a moment. In his view, Ulic Mordred had gotten exactly what he deserved and was not worthy of even that much thought.

"So Jakel took the sister?"

"He grabbed her in the taproom. Ordered everyone out. I think he's been watching her for a long time."

"And Davorin traded himself for her?"

"Yes, sir. He was who Jakel really wanted."

"I see."

"I think he just wanted the chance to torture Davorin. I heard he's hated him since they were children. And I think he believes he's working with the Raider."

"And what do you think?" Paledan asked.

"I think that's unlikely. I've spent some time in that taproom, and the man's hardly the type."

Or he's very good at hiding.

Brakely's voice cracked through the comm link on the desk. "Major Paledan."

He leaned over and tapped the transmit key. "Go ahead."

"Sir, the river guard post has been hit. Three troopers down and a crate of hand bombs missing."

Paledan went very still. "And?"

"Sir . . . it was the Raider."

"They're certain of that?"

"He was seen. Helmet, coat, and all. And he left the calling card."

Paledan glanced at Gratt. The trooper said nothing, but his expression was that of a man who'd been proven right.

"Thank you, Brakely," he said into the comm link. "Send the senior officer on duty there to me."

"Yes, sir."

He leaned back in his chair once more. "It would appear," he said, "that you were right. That will be all, Gratt."

The question was, he thought after the man had gone, was whether appearances mattered at all when it came to the Raider.

Chapter 43

"WHAT ARE YOU doing?"

"What do you think?" Kye snapped at Brander.

Her cousin, usually so cool and unflappable, didn't sound either at the moment. She didn't care. The river raid had gone off perfectly, the point had been made, and she would wait no longer.

"Kye—"

She spun on him before he could finish whatever protest he was going to make.

"Jakel has had him for too long. I'm going after him. And not you nor anyone else can stop me."

"Kye, there's no way. You'll die."

She stared at him. "Don't you understand? If he dies in there, I'm dead anyway."

"Kye, he may already be—"

"He's not."

"Even if he's alive, you don't know what kind of shape he's in. And if they've figured out he's the Raider—"

"They haven't. Not from him."

"Kye—"

"Do you know him so little, truly? He would not break."

Brander sighed. "No. Jakel could torture him unto death and he would not break. But physical torture is not all that the Coalition has at their command. And when Jakel cannot break him, they will turn to that."

"Do you think I don't know that?"

"Then you know what he will do when Jakel has had his fun, when Drake realizes they will have what he knows whether he wills it or not."

She gave her cousin a bleak look, for she knew all too well. The three of them, who all knew too much, enough to destroy the rebellion, had agreed on this long ago. Faced with the end, with any sense that they might break and talk, or that the Coalition was about to use methods they could not fight, they would find a way and end it themselves. And she had no doubt Drake would do it; he truly would die by his own will before he would talk.

She heard a murmur of voices, and only then did she realize they had an audience; several of the Sentinels had arrived. Mara strode toward them.

"You're going to rescue the Raider?" she demanded.

"Or die in the attempt," Brander said sourly.

"Yes." Kye left it at that, since it answered both. She didn't bother to deny that Drake and the Raider were one and the same.

"I'm with you," Mara said instantly.

"And I!" That was Pryl.

"Us as well," said the Harkin brothers in unison.

"And me." Maxon this time.

Kye looked at them all. There was no mistaking the determination in their faces.

"I cannot ask any of you to go on this mission," she said. "For Brander is likely right, it's suicide."

"He is the Raider," Pryl pointed out. "And how many times has he risked himself for one of us?"

"Countless," Kye agreed, remembering vividly each time he had done so. "But he would not wish it."

"Nor would he wish you to risk yourself for him," Brander pointed out.

"Especially now," Mara said. Something in the other woman's voice drew Kye's gaze to her face. She saw the knowledge, the understanding there.

A commotion near the fire drew her attention. And then she heard two voices, in unison, as the twins ran toward her.

"Kye! You're going for him?"

How had they known, so quickly?

"You are, aren't you?" the twins chorused anxiously.

She looked back at them. "I am."

They looked so instantly relieved, she felt a qualm; she understood it with Drake, but how could she justify such faith?

By getting Drake the hades out of there.

And she would, she thought. Or die trying. For she'd meant what she'd said to her cousin. If he died in that hole, she'd be as good as dead anyway.

Eirlys broke away and came toward her. Kye read in her eyes the fear, the looming grief. It overshadowed even what had to be the shock of realizing that both Brander and she had been with the Raider all along.

My brother is the Raider, Brander his second . . . and you've known all along? Eos, Kye, you are his third and you did not tell me?

It had taken a while for her to come around. But Eirlys held this fight as important as they all did, and eventually she did. She was learning fast. And she would learn even faster now.

Before the younger woman could speak now, Kye put a gentle hand on her shoulder. "I will bring him back," she said, "or I won't come back."

"So then we will lose the both of you?" Eirlys said, sounding as bitter as Kye had ever heard anyone sound.

"Eirlys—"

"I'm sorry. I know you love him as much as I do. You are pledged in all but formality. But we've lost so much, I can't bear to lose him and you too."

Kye went still. She and Eirlys had never discussed her relationship—her changed relationship—with Drake, although she knew the girl knew. As if she'd read her thoughts, Eirlys met her gaze. "You are my sister, Kye. I have long thought of you that way."

Kye felt moisture pooling in her eyes, and she hugged the girl fiercely. "And I you, Eirlys Davorin."

"Promise me we will ever be so, no matter what."

Kye knew what she meant. If she could not rescue Drake, or if he was already dead. And she understood now more than ever what Drake had once told her, of how it pained him to see his young sister so versed in the painful reality of living in a conquered city on a conquered world.

"Always," Kye whispered.

Brander, who had, with unusual tact, hung back to give them this moment, now stepped up. Close behind Eirlys, Kye noted. "We're ready," he said. "Let's go."

Kye shook her head. "You cannot, Brander."

His brows shot up.

"You must not go with me. You have to survive, to take over if it goes bad and he is unable to."

"So I'm to let you go on your own?" he asked incredulously.

She drew herself up. "I will not be alone. I will have the finest of the Sentinels at my back."

"You will," he acknowledged. "But I'm supposed to sit here, safe and in hiding, and do nothing?"

"I was hoping," Kye said, "you might put that big, noisy new toy of yours to use."

He drew back slightly. "The rail gun?"

"If they thought we were blowing up the planium mines . . . ," she began.

Brander stared, and then grinned. Widely. "Cousin of mine, you are as brilliantly clever as the Raider always said you were."

Those words warmed her beyond measure, but she had no time now to relish it. "Speaking of the Raider, I think you should do it in his guise. And be sure the miners see you."

"One more layer of doubt that they have him," he said, clearly planning rapidly now. "The northernmost, I think, as far from here as possible. It will take care to make sure none of them are hurt, but I'll manage."

And you'll be getting used to being the Raider in the process. For Drake had been right; the extraordinary warrior of Ziem was an idea as much as a man.

"And in the meantime," she said, yanking her mind away from the possibility Brander might have to do just that, "I'll send some who have willing family in town to round them up to descend on Barcon's office. Corner the little skalworm, threaten him about some grievance. Make him afraid for his own worthless life."

Brander frowned. "To what end? You think he will just order Jakel to let Drake go? Or that Jakel would obey him if he did?"

"No. But he will summon every guard in the building to protect him."

Brander's expression cleared instantly. "That he will, the coward." He grinned at her. "You have learned well, cousin."

"I grew up with you, didn't I?"

He laughed. Then he reached into his pack and pulled out the bulky hand weapon she'd seen before, when he'd been testing it. She remembered her shock as it obliterated everything it hit, but only what it hit, in utter silence, not leaving anything larger than dust behind. Even if the target was only grazed, it worked.

He handed it to her. "It might help. You remember how it works?"

She nodded. Took it gratefully, but gingerly. Took her blaster out of its holster and tucked it into her belt, and put the new weapon in its place, safer from accidental firing, which would probably obliterate her.

Brander turned to go, but stopped to look at Eirlys, put a hand on her arm. "If it is possible to save him, she will."

"I know." Eirlys put a hand over his. Her jaw was tight, but her eyes were oddly alight as she looked at him. Kye realized suddenly that until now, the girl had not known of Brander's double life, almost as risky as her brother's. "You must take care. I cannot lose you, either."

An expression Kye had never seen before crossed Brander's face. There wasn't a trace of his usual insouciance or flippancy, and their absence changed him completely. "Promise me you will stay here?" he said, and the solemnity echoed in his voice. "You have no experience with this."

"Yet," Eirlys said with determination. "But yes, I will wait until I learn. And someone must rein in the twins just now. They are fierce."

When he had gone, Eirlys turned back to Kye.

"I must go now as well," Kye said.

"You have a plan?"

Somehow, she thought figuring it out as she went wouldn't be a comforting answer. "I will use whatever is to hand. Brander's toy may well solve the biggest problem. And I have good, solid help. You saw how many have volunteered. Some will provide diversions, some will be ready to fight, some to get him back if I can't."

Eirlys winced, but said evenly enough, "How will you get to him?"

She would do, Kye thought, with a feeling of pride that told her how completely she did consider this girl her sister. And Eirlys would learn, as she'd said. "That, I don't know yet. I'll need to get inside the compound, into the building, but—"

The twins yelped simultaneously. Both women shifted to look at them.

"We know how!"

Were they anyone but the Davorin twins, Kye would never have taken the suggestions of two thirteen-year-olds seriously. But they were who they were, and so she listened. And when they had finished, she laughed.

And set out to save the man she loved, and Ziem needed.

Chapter 44

KYE MISSED THE spot at first, before reminding herself that seven paces past the mistbreaker tree was a shorter distance for the twins than for her. She backed up a couple of steps slowly, peering intently through the mist. She still saw nothing. She knew there had to be a scentbrush close by; she could smell it. She took one more step back. Spotted a thick tangle of branches that looked utterly natural, and yet completely masked the ground behind them.

She slipped behind the screen of branches, realized that in the mist even she would likely be concealed from someone standing right where she had been. The twins had done a brilliant job of hiding their passageway to trouble.

A memory came to her, of Drake glumly speaking after one of their escapades.

"They always make me think of that old riddle about what's easy to get into but hard to get out of."

"What?"

"Trouble."

And now, with a bit of luck and a lot of help, their cleverness just might save their brother's life.

She brushed at the ground, at the layer of dirt, twigs, and leaves that looked like nothing more than normal ground debris. Felt the edge the twins had told her about, dug her fingers in, and lifted.

The opening to the small passage was both encouraging and defeating. She would fit through it, as they'd guessed, but there was no way to bring Drake out this way—his broad shoulders would never fit. But she had assumed as much; after all, the twins had been focused on getting themselves down here, not adults. And she was amazed they'd done it as well as they had, and wondered how long it had taken them to dig and how they'd kept it secret.

She turned to Maxon and Mara, the two Sentinels who had accompanied her, and signaled them to wait. They knew to divert anyone who got curious, and had flasks of brew to splash about if the Coalition found them, in the hope they'd be assumed just another pair of downtrodden Ziemites who'd wandered off the path in their stupor, perhaps in search of a hidden place for a drunken mating.

She took hold of the rope the twins had used to lower themselves down the tunnel's short vertical entrance. It was only a drop of about her own height, and the tunnel itself was small enough that she had to crouch to get through, but with some inventive twisting, she was soon on her way.

She moved on a few feet, where the passage widened and connected to a much more formally constructed tunnel. It was larger, but much of it was taken up by old, no longer used pipes and conduits, abandoned when the Coalition had brought in their own systems. The air was surprisingly fresh, and she guessed the twins' shaft served as ventilation for the forgotten tunnel.

She kept going, thinking all the way. She would just have to get him up to where the Harkins would be using skills that had once built many of the buildings of Zelos to cut an escape hole in this one. It was going to take them time, but she was likely to need every second of it.

She reached a spot where the tunnel narrowed slightly, guessed that she was passing under the wall. As she went, she pictured the layout the twins had given her. They weren't much on specific distances, using instead their own size for measuring, but she knew how far the compound wall was from the wall of the building, and kept that in her mind. Their rapid-fire directions played back in her head.

"It comes out—"
"In a storeroom where—"
"They keep cleaning stuff."
"There's a panel—"
"But it's loose and you only—"
"Have to nudge it."
"Then go left and—"
"Jakel's room—" Lux had made a face at this *"—is at—"*
"The end."
"Watch for the guard at—"
"The connection with the—"
"Big tunnel but—"
"He's usually asleep."
She'd hugged them both, and they'd hugged her back.
"Save him," they had said together. "We know you can."

This time, their faith had bolstered her. "With your help, there's a chance."

"He is ours."

"And we are Ziem," Lux had added, "As much as any Sentinel."

"Indeed you are."

The panel they had mentioned did indeed slide easily away. Almost too easily, and she had to grab it before it clattered to the floor and alerted anyone within earshot. She crept across the room, which was thick with the dust the items stored there were supposed to deal with. She could see tracks across the floor, small feet, likely the twins.

She listened at the door for as long as she could stand. She heard nothing, and edged the door open just far enough to steal a look. The low, dingy corridor outside was dimly lit, and utterly silent. But in the distance, there was a cross-tunnel, brighter and—

Feet. A pair of booted feet stuck out into the corridor. As if someone, probably the twins' mentioned guard, was sitting in the brighter passage and comfortably lolling back with his legs outstretched.

She backed up, thinking. She could take him out, but needed to figure out how to do it without giving him time to call for help. She didn't want to fire a weapon that might echo and be heard, so she'd need total silence, and—

She froze as she heard a loud crackle from that direction. Then shouting. It took her a heart-stopped split-second to realize she was hearing the shouting through a speaker. And then she recognized the shouting—almost hysterical—voice and grinned despite herself.

Barkhound.

The man sounded like he was under attack by a squadron of Coalition fighters. The Sentinels had obviously found a nice crowd to descend on his office.

The feet she'd seen scraped the floor. She heard an oath, and a description of Barcon she'd only heard from her own side. The guard stood, but seemed in no hurry to rush, as ordered, to the man's aid. Kye waited, barely daring to breathe, and at last, the man went to the lifter and hit the summoning button.

Her mind raced as she waited to hear the distinctive whoosh of the lifter doors sliding closed. He hadn't spoken to anyone else, and she hadn't heard another voice, but that wasn't proof positive there wasn't someone else here. For all she knew, Jakel was in his little playroom. Maybe with the two troopers he'd brought to the taproom as backup.

So be it.

She drew her blaster and nudged the door open slowly. When silence reigned, she crept forward, taking care with every step. She reached the junction. The guard's chair sat at an angle, alone in a small corner. There was no sign of anyone else.

For the first time, she took a long look at the door another ten feet down, at the end of the corridor. Was Drake in there? What horrors were housed there? Was he even alive?

She beat down the questions, knowing the only way to answer them was within reach. She took a last listen and glance around, then went forward as quickly as she could and still maintain the silence.

The door was locked. Hardly a surprise. A hit from her blaster would do for the knob, but it would also announce her to anyone inside. She listened yet again, and heard nothing from inside. But something about the walls and the door itself nagged at her, and she backed up a step.

Thicker. The walls protruded slightly into the corridor here, as if they were thicker than the rest. Why?

It hit her like a nauseating blow to the stomach.

Soundproofed.

All the reasons why Jakel's playroom would be soundproofed careened through her mind. It took every ounce of will she had to shove them out. That left her with nothing but cold, emotionless determination.

She switched her blaster to her left hand. The Raider said she was a better shot with her left than most were with their dominant hand. She hoped he was right. She drew out the weapon Brander had given her, the one he was still trying to duplicate. She armed it at the lowest setting. Aimed it at the door handle. Fired.

The handle and lock silently vanished. The door, loose now, swung a fraction open on its own. She moved swiftly. Shoved her way in. Weapons up. Ready to fire.

The room was empty.

Except for worse things than she had even imagined. Chains, prods, blades of all types. And metal and power devices whose purpose she could not even conceive of.

And blood. There was blood on the floor, on the table in the center, that heap of clothes piled against the wall was soaked with it, and the wall behind—

Her gaze snapped back to that bloody pile of rags.

Except it wasn't.

She darted around the gruesome table. Knelt. Nearly screamed.

Drake.

Barely recognizable. Battered, swollen, bruised, cut, burned . . . broken. Limp and unmoving. Cold.

She'd never felt anything like the chill that took her now.

Her brain hammered her heart with the obvious.

He was dead.

Drake, and the Raider, were dead. Dead and thrown on the floor like so much refuse.

And he had died hard and ugly, just as she'd feared. At the hands of that sub-human.

The chill became ice. Nothing mattered now, except her new life's goal. She would see Jakel dead. And it would be as painful and as long as she could make it last.

Chapter 45

KYE REACHED OUT, wanted to touch him, but there seemed no place that wasn't damaged. And telling herself that he could feel nothing now didn't help.

She would find Jakel. She would find the monster who had done this, and she would carve him into too many pieces to count with his own laser pistol. And if they killed her for it, so be it.

Her teeth almost chattered with the iciness that had overtaken her. She clenched her jaw. Made herself look, take in every detail. She wanted to etch into her mind the memory of what Jakel had done. She wanted it emblazoned there, for when she found him. But now . . .

She had to get Drake out of here. She could not leave him here, alone. She could not bear even the thought of it. She would get him out, and he would rest in that final peace on the mountain he loved. She had been too late to save him, but he would lie free, eternally. Somehow she would—

Her gaze snagged on his face, his cheek where the scars would have been, had he not shed the disguise. Blood there, as in so many places. It dripped slowly over his bruised face, bright, red, wet.

It finally got through the numbness.

Blood. Fresh blood.

He was actively bleeding.

Her fingers shot to his throat, heedless now of anything but the fierce hope that seized her.

Nothing. She pressed harder. Held her breath.

There. Faintly. Barely. But there.

A pulse.

He was alive.

Kye felt a shiver of joy ripple through her. He was alive.

With the greatest effort she had ever made, she tamped it down. All reason told her he was barely hanging on. If she could even rouse him, he might not be able to move. And she could not carry him.

She had to assess, she thought, forcing herself to logic. It hurt her beyond measure to inflict more pain on him, but she had to move him, had to see just how badly he was injured and where.

She eased him away from the wall with exquisite care. Only now noticed the lock dangling from the metal loop in the wall, where the chains that held his wrists had likely been fastened. Anger stirred anew, low and deep. She banked it. Time enough after he was safe.

That he would likely die in the process did not escape her.

"Live, Drake," she whispered. "Live. I will get you out of here."

She checked for broken bones first. His legs seemed intact, in fact almost undamaged, save the old scar, from his first encounter with Jakel's laser pistol. That seemed an eon ago now, and she didn't even waste a moment reproaching herself for not having guessed when she'd thought she'd seen Drake favoring that leg at the same time.

Jakel had apparently focused his evil tools elsewhere. When she got to his hands, those hands that had touched her, held her, stroked her, she found every finger on the left broken, and all but one on the right. She felt the wetness of tears hitting her own hands before she even realized she was crying.

Useless, she snapped at herself. *Tears are useless.*

She continued her inspection, guessing from the huge, dark bruises on his torso that Jakel had at some point resorted to a bat or club of some kind. He could have broken ribs, which would made even this much movement dangerous, puncturing internal organs. A row of raw, red burns across his chest, and the bloody X she found carved into his flesh over his heart, probably with that bedamned laser pistol, told her more than she would ever wish to know about the kind of torture Jakel had inflicted.

She could not carry him. But she would find a way.

That logic she'd forced told her there was no way he would survive being moved.

And yet he would certainly die if she left him. As if she could.

Yet in the end, it was never really a question. She knew as well as she knew her own heart that Drake Davorin would rather die free today than cling to another day of life in this dungeon. And that if she left him, he would find just enough strength to end it, dying on his own terms rather than Jakel's.

And suddenly, the chains binding him were too much. She pulled out the obliterator, still on low, and aimed it at the metal links, as far away from Drake as she could get them. She hesitated, but Brander had sworn that while it couldn't take out anything large, it made up for that by affecting only what it hit.

She fired.

The chains vanished without a sound. Drake did not even react. She quickly looked away from his bloody, ruined wrists.

"You will be free, my love," she whispered, touching his battered face with only a finger, all she dared.

She gasped as one Ziem blue eye fluttered open. Her breath jammed up in her throat and she couldn't speak.

His swollen lips moved. Barely. She heard a whisper of sound. Her name?

All the things she wanted to say hovered, and yet she couldn't find the words for any of them. She had a mission now, and unless she achieved it, nothing else mattered.

"Drake," she said, "We have to get you out of here."

He made a low, despairing sound. "Seem . . . so real."

"I'm here, Drake. Can you move at all?"

That eye—the other was swollen shut—seemed to narrow. Then closed. "Vision . . . again."

She could barely make out the mumbled words, couldn't imagine what it took for him to talk at all. Some part of her mind registered that he'd brought up her image here before, and she thought later she would be pleased by that, but now she bent over him, speaking urgently. "Drake, listen to me. I'm here, I'm real, and we have to get you out of here before Jakel comes back."

That eye opened again. Stared at her. She could almost see him fighting back waves of what had to be agony. "K . . . Kye?"

"Right here," she said, trying to smile.

"No. Can't. You . . . must go."

"We're getting you out of here."

"Kye . . . please . . . save you."

"I will not leave you here."

"Must."

"I must," she said, "get you to Mahko."

The eye closed again for a moment. "Too . . . late."

"No!" Her cry was ill-advised, but she could not stop it.

"Dying, Kye. Feel it."

"No." This time it was barely a whisper.

"Love you. Get out."

"Drake—"

"Give me . . . that much. Live."

His eye closed again, and his head lolled to one side. For a moment, she feared the worst, but that same weak pulse beat in his throat.

It was as well he was unconscious. She stood abruptly, looked around the foul room. In a corner, she saw what appeared to be a long, heavy coat or smock of some kind. So Jakel didn't get blood on himself? Her stomach curled, and she promised herself later contemplation of how the man would die, slower and longer than any of his victims.

She grabbed up the heavy cloth garment and brought it back. She laid it out next to him. It took longer than she had hoped, for she feared hurting him further, but eventually she had him lying on it. She swiftly tied a knot in the end of each sleeve, then grabbed them up. And pulled. Pulled harder. Leaned into it so far that had the stitching given way she would have careened across the room.

It took much of her strength and all of her weight, but he began to slide across the floor. She heard him groan, but kept on. It became easier as she gained momentum.

At the door she stopped, listening. Then opened it. Still silence. She peered outside. It looked the same as when she'd come in. She pulled the door wide, propped it open. She raced over to the lifter, hit the button. Once they were upstairs, she could call one of the Sentinels with the diversion group for help moving him.

The moment the lifter arrived and the doors slid open, her heart sank. She could hear, down the lifter shaft, the sound of shouts, and heavy thuds. And then blaster fire. Something had gone wrong up there, and this path was cut off.

A light lit up on the lifter panel. It was being called back up. The doors began to slide closed.

Instantly, she grabbed up the guard's chair and slid it in the door's path. It creaked as it tried to close, and for a moment she feared it wouldn't stand the pressure. The metal bent, but held. A warning light activated on the panel and all motion stopped.

She spun around and ran back to Drake. He lay frighteningly motionless, but thankfully unaware.

There was only one option she could see. Back the way she'd come. But while she thought she could get him through the old utility tunnel, and Maxon could help her lift him out, the size of the twins' hand-dug passage was something else. It was just too small for a man of Drake's stature. And even with help, digging it out would take too long, for Drake's sake if not for the risk of discovery. If things had gone badly wrong up top, the Coalition could be already searching the grounds for intruders.

But there was no other choice.

She began to move, thinking she would have a long, hard pull to think of what she would do at the end of it. And it was longer and harder than she'd imagined. She was more than fit, but her hands hurt, her back was tight with the strain, her legs wearying too soon.

It is nothing—nothing—compared to what he has been through.

She pulled on, and on. When she reached the narrow spot at the wall, it was a close thing, and she had to leverage him up over the small lip. It would be difficult, but she began, chanting inwardly that they were almost there. They were nearly through, and she stepped over him to pull from the other side, banging her hip on one side and the holster on the other.

The holster.

She froze as a thought slammed into her.

She turned it over in her mind, and then nearly laughed aloud as she realized she had the solution literally at hand.

She would blast the tunnel larger with the Coalition's own weapon.

The weapon Drake had stolen, in the guise of the meek, cowardly taproom keeper.

How fitting, that in the end, he would save them both.

She began with the lowest setting, not wanting the passage to cave in, but it was taking too long. She upped it and it was better. She carved it out carefully, marveling rather warily at how the material just vanished.

She had just judged it wide enough when she heard footsteps approaching. She darted back into the shadows, appealing to all the mountain gods she didn't really believe in, even to the Spirit, that it wasn't the Coalition, not now. Not when they were so close.

When Maxon's face appeared, she nearly went weak with relief. She said his name, keeping her voice to the lowest whisper she thought he could hear.

"Kye?"

"Yes. I need your help, and Mara's. I have him, but he's badly hurt. You'll have to pull him up."

She shuddered to think what tying that rope around his battered ribs would do to him, and tried to pad it as best she could with the coat. He did not stir at all, and she thought of checking to see if he had survived the long drag through the tunnel but it didn't matter now. Nothing did except getting him out and away from here.

Once it was done, they hauled him up easily enough, then threw the rope back down to her. She scrambled up, closed the hatch, and hastily covered it as best she could, given that the hole was larger now; she doubted they would ever use it again, but the Raider had taught her never to discard an asset that still worked—they had too little.

She fought down her dread; she could not afford that luxury. Could not afford any feelings right now.

They carried him with great care. Now that she was outside, she could hear shouting coming from all over the compound, heard the sound of rovers whooshing through the air and large transports in the distance, heading for the mountains where Brander had clearly created such a commotion with his rail gun that the Coalition was responding in force. And drawing all their attention, as planned. It was a dangerous game he was playing, but she had faith in her scapegrace cousin; he would manage.

She knelt on the deck of the air rover beside Drake's too-still form as they raced for the ruin, and safety.

Chapter 46

"YOU HAVE MADE a grave miscalculation, Jakel."

Paledan looked at the man, contemplating the quirk of nature that sometimes brutal creatures—for he thought of the man as little more than a beast—reflected their inner nature. He'd once heard Blakely joke that if a blowpig mated with a muckrat, the result would look like Jakel, but be kinder. He thought that fairly accurate.

"Blame your guard, who left his post," the man said stubbornly. "I nearly had Davorin talking."

"You tortured him nearly unto death and he told you nothing."

Yet he spoke to me.

Paledan pondered the words Davorin had spoken before passing out. The Coalition dealt in power and force, and had little use for ideas and less for ideals. They cared for nothing that couldn't be gained by force, and the concept of a belief that wouldn't die even when crushed, that people would hold unto death, was dismissed without thought.

And yet . . .

"It would appear Davorin's standing in Zelos is higher than I was led to believe," Paledan said thoughtfully, glancing once more at the symbols on the wall, the Ziem sabers. "Why else would so many risk their lives to divert our attention from his escape?"

Jakel snorted. He was pacing Paledan's office like the muckrat Blakely had mentioned, lumbering, heavy arms swinging. "You call surrounding that half-wit Ordam risking their lives? The man couldn't fight his way out of a crawler web. I doubt he even knows how to fire a blaster."

"On that, we can agree," Paledan said.

Jakel appeared to interpret that as encouragement. "I still don't understand how Davorin escaped. He was incapacitated, I swear."

"He appeared to be, yes."

"And the door lock was just . . . gone. How in hades did that happen?"

Paledan had an idea about that, but it was hardly something he would share with this man. "Mysterious."

Jakel flicked a glance at him. Apparently, he felt braver, because he said, "You unlocked his chains from the wall."

Paledan lifted his gaze then, locked it on Jakel's face. The man stopped in his tracks.

"You do not," Paledan said without inflection, "wish to open that subject."

Jakel backed up a step. Threw up his hands. "No, no, I. . . . Look, give me some men, I'll find Davorin and drag him back here."

"You will not."

"But—"

"You will, however, answer to me from now on."

Jakel blinked. "What?"

"We are agreed Barcon Ordam is unable to command a curlbug, let alone a man such as yourself, are we not?"

"Uh . . . yes?"

"And am I correct in thinking he has treated you with less than respect?"

Something hot, almost red, flashed in the monster's eyes. "Oh, yes."

"Then it should be a relief to answer to the Coalition, should it not? And have Coalition backing at your disposal?"

The man's expression lightened. "Yeah. Yeah, sure."

"And the chance to teach Ordam that respect?"

The avid expression that came over Jakel's face then warned Paledan that this man would have to be dealt with. But for now, he was a tool to be used. And Barcon Ordam had outlived—by a large margin—his usefulness.

"Then come with me."

He strode out of his office. He never looked back; he didn't have to, he could hear Jakel's heavy tread close behind him.

They found Ordam huddled in a chair in his office. He let out a yelp of terror when Paledan threw the door open without knocking.

Ordam let out an audible sigh of relief when he saw who it was.

"Commander! You must have them arrested, all of them. I ordered the troopers to take them when they were here, but they refused!"

"My troops," Paledan said, "do not take orders from you."

Ordam cringed. "Of course, of course, but you can order it now, surely? I can identify them all."

Paledan looked around. The office was remarkably tidy, given that some thirty citizens had been gathered, shouting and making demands, not two hours ago. They had taken care not to destroy or damage anything, Paledan thought. Under orders?

"On what charges?" he asked, his tone one of mild curiosity.

"Since when does the Coalition care about charges?" Ordam's tone was incredulous.

"Contention valid," Paledan agreed. "But explain how you justify tying up those troops 'protecting' you against an obviously orderly group, while a prisoner escaped and the mines were attacked? How did you not realize it was a ruse, a diversion?"

"How could I? They stormed this office! They accused me of being a traitor to Ziem, of handing them over to . . ."

His voice trailed away. Paledan smiled. "And did you not?"

"It was for their own good," Ordam protested. "You don't understand these people."

"But you, being the special creature that you are, do."

It hadn't been a question, but Ordam nodded rapidly. "Exactly. Most of them are stubbornly independent, and foolish; they don't know what's good for them. They need a guiding hand, to show them."

"I would, had I the time, spend a few minutes explaining reality to you, Ordam. But I have other demands on my time at present. And so, I will leave your education on the price of treason to someone else."

He glanced at Jakel, then back at Ordam. "One other thing. He works for the Coalition now."

Ordam looked merely puzzled. Until Paledan nodded at Jakel and said, "He's all yours."

Paledan heard the screams all the way down the hall.

BRANDER STARED down at the broken man in the narrow bed. Even if the truth hadn't gotten around, the disguise was hardly necessary now, he was so battered. He had stopped Mahko barely halfway through reciting Drake's massive injuries, because he couldn't bear it.

"I'm so sorry," the healer whispered, his expression devastated. "I have eased his pain slightly, but I can do no more for him. He does not have long."

Brander dropped more than sat in the chair beside the bed. He felt a touch, a gentle squeeze of his shoulder. Eirlys. She was about to lose the man who was both brother and father to her, and she was trying to comfort him? He couldn't even look at her.

"I will be just outside," she said, and he wondered that she was able to think at all, let alone think to give him some moments alone with Drake.

For a long time, he couldn't bring himself to look at the man he had grown up beside, planned beside, and fought beside. But when he finally did, he realized Drake's eyes were open, at least as much as they could be given the swollenness of his face where Jakel had beaten him.

He tried to speak.

"Bran—" The hard B sound was too much for bloody lips, and he stopped.

"Don't try to talk," Brander said, leaning in.

"Have to. Things . . . need said."

"Drake—"

"Twins. Look out for."

"Of course. You know I will, until you're able."

Drake's eyes closed. Brander heard the hiss of sound as he labored to breathe. Then he was back, looking at him steadily. "Not . . . this time."

He saw the knowledge in his best friend's eyes. Saw the resignation there, and could only imagine the pain he must be in for it to be there.

"You must—" again, his lips seemed to protest making the sound, but this time he forced himself to go on, stronger now "—take over. Raider can't die."

"You are the Raider."

Drake gave the barest shake of his head. "An idea . . . a symbol. They will fight for you."

"No."

"They will. Use the scars, the helmet. The legend . . . has to go on. If the Raider dies . . . Ziem dies."

He couldn't do it. He wasn't Drake. Oh, he'd fought beside him, he'd carried out missions on the edge of crazy, but he was no leader. Not in the way Drake was, inspiring all, bringing out the best in them, and single-hand-edly keeping the Coalition endlessly on guard.

"Swear to me."

The words were barely audible, and Brander knew talking was weakening him.

"You are . . . the only one . . . I trust to do it. Swear it."

Brander met Drake's gaze and did the only thing he could.

"I swear."

Drake let out a long, weary breath of obvious relief. Brander understood. Knew that Drake knew it would have been easy for him to promise just to ease his passing, but that he would never say it unless he meant it. For all his sins, and they were many, Brander Kalon was a man of his word.

He thought Drake had drifted off, and caught himself checking to make sure he still breathed. And then, softly, he heard, "Eirlys."

Brander's own breath caught in his throat. "I will see to her. Always."

Drake's eyes opened then, and he saw the understanding there. His brother in all but blood knew. He drew in a breath, let it out slowly, and then admitted it out loud for the first time. "Yes," he said, answering what had not been asked.

Drake's nod was barely perceptible. "My . . . blessing." Something shifted, and for an instant, the old Drake, the Raider, was looking back at him. "As if you'd require it."

"No," Brander admitted. "But I will treasure it."

And, that simply, the bond between them was renewed, brothers by their own choosing. That it was likely the last time they would acknowledge it made it a bittersweet thing, both unwanted and necessary.

Drake's eyes closed again, and this time he did not stir again. The sound of his breathing was like a rasp over raw nerves, painful, hated. The only thing Brander dreaded hearing more would be the moment when it stopped.

He couldn't just sit here and wait for that damned, eternal silence. Nor did he want to watch Eirlys and Kye sit here, waiting helplessly for the death of the man they loved. Or watch Mahko hover, regretting that his healing skills were not enough. The fact that no healer's skills were enough wouldn't matter to the gentle man.

No healer's skills were enough.

For a long moment Brander didn't move. He barely breathed. And then he leapt to his feet.

"Hang on, Drake." He said it as if he'd already assumed the mantle of command. "You just hang on."

Then he turned and headed for the door.

Chapter 47

EIRLYS STARED AS Brander slipped on his coat and slung the long gun over his shoulder.

"You can't leave. Brander, he's dying."

He picked up his pack as if she'd said nothing, but she saw his jaw go rigid.

"He's your best friend, and he's dying," she whispered.

He whirled then. "Do you think I don't know that? Do you think I can't see the darkness in his eyes, and the knowledge in his face. I know he's dying. *He* knows he's dying."

"Then how can you leave him?"

He looked at her for a long, silent moment. In his face, she could see some kind of battle was raging inside him. Brander, the ever nonchalant, ever joking, Brander looked dark, haunted . . . and deadly. Whatever his reasons for this choice that dumbfounded her, the decision had not been easy.

Twice he began to speak, then stopped. As if he wanted to tell her something and had to remind himself why he could not. And then, before she could do more than cry out his name in a final protest, he was gone. Leaving her to deal with the debris of the end.

And the imminent death of her beloved brother.

HE'D DONE THE right thing.

He couldn't tell her. She had accepted Drake's approaching death, with a bitter submission that was unspeakable in one so young. He could not bear to be the one to raise hope in her when even he knew it was most likely futile. Yet he had to try. While there was the slightest, faintest possibility, he had to try. For Drake was not only the heart and soul of their fight, as Kye had said, he was his brother in all but blood.

And the brother in blood of the girl whose distraught gaze seared him to his soul.

He'd done the right thing.

He repeated the words with every step for the first hour after he left the rover at the highest point he could take it without becoming a target. After that, the climb had grown difficult enough that he dared not spare the attention to any thought save staying upright.

But he'd reached the Edge. From here on, there was no cover, nothing to mask him from any eyes turned this way, including the Coalition. He wasn't even sure where to go from here; he knew only that the stories said that she dwelt beyond the Edge.

And that she knew if anyone dared trespass there.

He barely made it a blaster's shot past the last tree when he was stopped cold by a voice that seemed to come from both above and behind him.

"No further, son of Kalon."

It wasn't the Spirit, unless she had a booming bass voice.

But whoever it was apparently knew who he was. Coalition? Were they guarding even the Edge? But whoever it was hadn't killed him on sight. Not that he would mind overmuch at this point.

He held his hands out from his sides, to show they were empty of weapons. Then, slowly, he turned around. "I seek the Spirit."

"As do most who dare venture into her realm. Most die."

He still couldn't see the speaker, but by turning, he could now guess about where he was, and how the rocks ahead were echoing that booming voice all around him.

"That is what I wish to prevent. A death. A death that could doom all of Ziem forever."

There was a moment of silence. Then, "And what death could be so important?"

Decision time, Brander thought. If this was a Coalition trap, his answer would spring it. His mission would fail and Drake would die. That he would as well was merely an afterthought.

The Raider was dying anyway, Brander told himself. *And if he dies, the rebellion dies with him.* For no matter how much Drake might think the mask mattered more than the man behind it, Brander knew he was wrong.

"How do you face it? Knowing they want you dead more than anything else? Knowing they hunt you every day, all of them?"

"Simple, my friend. I think of myself as already dead."

That conversation had been months ago, when the latest Coalition effort at a "wanted" placard—with a drawing as inaccurate as the rest had been and a staggering reward amount—had gone up on every wall left standing in Zelos. And the flat, unemotional tone of the words told Brander that they were in fact truth. And he saw the sense of it; you could not be mortally afraid if you thought yourself already dead and were waiting only for your body to receive the message.

And now it had.

Brander thought of what Drake had suffered—the broken body, the agony, and the mental torture of knowing his death was imminent. Of knowing he would be leaving his family alone in a hellish world. Of knowing now that the woman he loved had risked her life to save him, only to learn he was going to die anyway. Compared to all that, a quick death by blaster if this was indeed a trap, would be Eos-sent. And his death would mean little.

But Drake's . . .

What death could be so important?

"The Raider," he finally answered.

The only sound was the wind whistling through the barren rocks. For a moment, Brander thought he was alone again.

"Please," he said, not above begging for this. Surely she would help, if she could? Had she not been helping the Raider all along? "It already hovers too close; it will soon be too late. If it is not already."

There was another long moment of silence. Bleak despair began to settle into his soul. This had been folly, useless folly. He would not be there for his best friend's last moments, and for nothing. He—

"Follow."

Before the command had faded away, a huge shadow loomed up, followed by the man who cast it. Tall, lean, but broad-shouldered, the man's powerful build belied the slight limp Brander noticed. He said nothing more, but turned and headed up the mountain.

Whatever impairment the man had, it did nothing to limit his speed as they climbed. He clearly needed no guidance on the path Brander could not even see, and so he trusted the man's obvious knowledge and simply followed as best he could in his wake.

It seemed an age before the man slowed. He had never looked back to see if he was followed; either he assumed Brander would keep up, or did not care if he did not.

A few paces later, the man stopped before an exposed section of the mountain's stone, weathered and clear of any growth because of its vertical face.

"I suggest you close your eyes," the man said, not even looking over his shoulder.

In his puzzlement over the words, Brander could think of nothing to say. And in the next instant he had no one to say it to; the big man stepped forward . . . and vanished.

For a moment, he just stood there, gaping. Logic argued with the illogic of coming here in the first place, looking for some sort of magic. If he could believe in the Spirit and her powers, why should he not believe this?

Follow.

He closed his eyes. And stepped forward.

He felt nothing. The ground seemed solid, stable under his feet. He realized with an inward grimace he was wary of opening his eyes. That prodded him into doing just that.

It was a cave, tall and narrow. And oddly warm, a comfort after the cold damp of the mountain. A bare arm's reach away stood the man who had led him here.

"You took less time than most," he observed, his voice tempered now, as if he reined it in here in this place. Before Brander could decide if that had been a compliment, the big man pointed to a large, flat rock to his left. "Your weapons."

Every instinct he had rebelled, but Brander realized the long gun at least would be useless in these close quarters. He laid it down on the rock. He disliked giving up his blaster, but accepted it as necessary for the moment. He placed it beside the long gun and straightened.

The big man didn't move. Brander frowned. Then realized. His fingers danced over the hilt of his dagger. He rarely took it off, and even when sleeping, it was close at hand, his last line of personal defense. But that thought only reminded him of all the sparring bouts he and Drake had had, practicing with the lethally sharp blades. In fact, one of those, many months ago, had been the last time he'd seen Drake laugh. And now he would probably never see that again.

He'd gambled by coming here, and now he must play by the house rules. He pulled the dagger out of the sheath, the one Eirlys had made for him, and put it on the rock beside the blaster.

The big man turned and headed deeper into the cave. He was walking toward what looked like another blank wall, and Brander wondered if he would again vanish in that impossible way. But this time he veered right, and Brander realized the wall stopped a few feet short of the side wall of the cave. The man stopped there, looked back and commanded, "Wait."

It chafed, when time was so crucial, but Brander didn't see that he had any choice. He looked around, but in the dim light it looked like nothing but an ordinary cave. An oddly warm cave, yes, but just a cave.

"Come forward."

He hadn't expected the command so quickly, but was grateful. He walked to where the man stood, then walked past him as the man gestured him onward.

He stepped into what appeared to be a living area, with weavings hanging on the walls and thick cushions for seating. It was even warmer in here, warm enough he knew he would be comfortable without his coat. It was also well lit, although he wasn't sure of the source. The walls glowed faintly, from what he couldn't tell.

Then one of the weavings he had thought against a stone wall moved. A feminine hand gripped the edge of it, pushing it back. A woman emerged from behind it. Dressed in a simple gown of pale blue, she was tall, slender, and had long, vividly red hair.

Brander's breath caught. And then the woman stepped into the full light of the room and he knew. He stared, beyond gaping. Utterly astounded.

For, before him, some years older and marked with scars, yet still beautiful, stood the long-dead Iolana Davorin.

Chapter 48

DRAKE HAD NEVER realized how long it could take to die. His life lately had been full of instantaneous death—comrades blown to pieces, or less than pieces as his father had been. He'd always feared a long, lingering death, had wished to go as his father had, in an instant with perhaps not even enough time to realize what was happening.

But now, the fate he'd feared was here. And as he drifted in and out of awareness, he realized he'd never accepted that he might have no control in the matter. He couldn't even lift a hand to his blade, to end this agony himself. He doubted he would anyway, not now. If he was still in Jakel's hands, he would not hesitate, but Kye, his precious Kye had risked her life to free him.

And thanks to her, he would die a free man. He would thank her for that, if he could hang on long enough.

"Hang on, Drake. You just hang on."

He remembered hearing the words, but he had not responded, not only because it was beyond him at that moment, but because he thought Brander had understood the inevitability, and he had not the strength to convince his stubborn friend if he did not.

The aware times were both heaven and hades. Being awake meant the pain was close, searing, digging, until he felt as if his flesh was peeling off his bones and his organs turning to scalding liquid inside him. But it also meant seeing Eirlys one more time.

Seeing Kye one more time.

A different kind of agony stabbed through him. Their moments together had been far too few, and he wondered if it might not have been better for both of them now had they never given in to the fierce need. But the thought of never having had that brief time, of never knowing what a true connection of mind and body was like, of dying without knowing, was a thousandfold worse. It was too much, and he tried to focus on his sister instead. She understood. He could see it in her face.

He knew that for sure in the next minute, when she brought in the twins. The pair were pale, and quiet as he had never seen them before. He wasn't sure they should see him, like this, but Eirlys stared him down even now. "They have the right," she said. "And they'll not believe it otherwise."

It took all of what little strength he still had to hold out a hand to them. They each grasped it, the jolt from the broken bones Jakel had left him with barely registering above the constant thrum of pain. He didn't, couldn't react.

He just looked at the pair that had been the bane—and the bemused joy—of his life for more than a dozen years.

"Watch out . . . for your sister," he said to Nyx. The boy nodded, but his jaw was set. This was going to be hard on him. But they had each other; he had to believe they would get through.

Drake looked at Lux, whose cheeks were streaked with tears. "Don't get him into . . . too much trouble doing that."

"Don't," she whispered. "Please don't."

He was filled with an ache that somehow arced above the physical pain of his body. An ache that he would not see them grow up, would not see the adults they would become, not see where Lux's clever mind would take her, and what things Nyx's ingenious methods would produce.

"Love you . . . both."

The fog, deeper and darker than anything Ziem had ever produced, began to swirl around him. He wandered, lost, the tiny part of his mind still prodded by the pain, thinking for the first time of what he would leave behind, of the hole he would leave. Better now than when he'd begun this, when his sister had been yet a child and the twins even younger.

He felt the fog descend, and wondered if it was for the last time. And almost hoped not to wake up this time.

"FOR ALL THEIR clashes, they will be lost without him," Eirlys whispered as she looked at the twins, huddled by the fire. Kye could barely look at them herself; seeing the irrepressible pair brought low at last was too much.

"He is their anchor, their base, the safe place they always knew they had," Kye said. "He is the reason they are as brave—and reckless—as they are."

Eirlys shifted her gaze to Kye. "He has ever been that to all of us, hasn't he?"

Kye met her gaze. She who always hid her emotions did not even try to hide the tears. The pain was so great it was pointless to even try.

"It is so wrong that he, of us all, should have to pay this ultimate price."

"I never wanted him to—"

Kye hushed her before she could even get the words out, pulling her into a fierce hug. "You think I do not know that? You must not blame yourself, or what he did will be for nothing. You would never have asked him to give himself up for you. But he is the man he is."

"I would rather have died myself," Eirlys said, and Kye hugged her tighter.

"As I would die in his place now, were it possible." And she meant it with everything in her.

"I know."

"It is he we cannot do without. Despite what he says, he is the soul of Ziem, and . . . and . . ." She simply could not go on.

Eirlys said softly, "I so wanted you and Drake to be pledged, so that you would really be my sister."

Kye's breath caught in her throat. "For so long, we've not thought of anything beyond the next fight, or the next chance to strike at the Coalition. But I wish we had said to hades with our fears and all the reasons not to."

"But he would not set aside his duty to take anything for himself."

"Bedamned noble idiot," Kye muttered.

Eirlys let out an agonized, sharp laugh. "My brother in three words."

Kye did not know how long they stood there before Mahko emerged from his quarters. One glance at his face told her nothing had changed.

"I must go back to him," Kye said. "I cannot bear that he might be alone when . . ."

"Nor can I." Anger flashed across Eirlys face. "Although the thought clearly causes Brander no pain."

"I do not understand his reasons," Kye said gently. "But I do not doubt that he has them."

Eirlys shook her head. And then went still as the action brought the hearth into view. The pair who had been huddled before the fire were gone.

"Where did they get off to?" Kye asked, noticing now as well.

"I don't know," Eirlys said. "I'm—" She broke off suddenly. And Kye knew she'd been about to say as she had so often, that she was glad they were Drake's problem, and not hers. "I guess they are my problem from now on, aren't they?"

Kye thought her heart had been utterly shattered the moment she'd seen the truth in Drake's sky-blue eyes, but there had apparently been one last piece clinging together, for it fractured now. She was crying before she even got to the door of his quarters.

HE FELT THE PAIN sharpen now, knew he was headed for the surface again. Mahko was there, trying to tend him. He wondered if the healer could, or would, ease his way, but asking him to go against his nature and training and end a life instead of trying to save it seemed very wrong. As wrong as it had seemed to ask Kye or Brander and give them that to carry.

But he didn't know how long he could go on. And he apparently couldn't will his stubborn body to simply surrender.

"Hang on, Drake. You just hang on."

He groaned, helplessly, as a wave of fresh agony swept through him. *I can't. I can't.*

And yet he did.

Much later, deep in the swirling darkness of that fog, he became aware the pain had lessened. And then it lessened even more. He heard voices, or perhaps just one, gentle, soothing, assuring. This touch did not hurt, it eased. And when he was able to open his eyes slightly, he saw only a blurry figure in a flowing robe, gleaming unlike anything he'd ever seen.

At last, his pain-battered brain thought. At last it was here. The end. Of the pain, the regrets, everything. He'd done all he could to see to his family, and must trust Brander to see to the future of Ziem. He knew it was not what his friend would have wished, but he also knew his word once given was sacrosanct; he had promised and so would he do.

Drake had never expected to welcome death when it came, had doubted stories of those who did, but he understood now. The simple fact of the end of the torture of his injuries, of the cessation of the fierce, consuming pain, was enough to make him grateful it was finally going to be over.

And, in the moments before, his mind cleared enough for him to think of that odd, swirling figure and wonder if perhaps the old tales about the guardians that came for everyone at the end were true after all.

He opened his eyes, surprised that he still could. But more surprised by what he saw.

Another kind of guardian had come for him. Or perhaps his weary brain had simply conjured up this familiar form in its last, dying moments. It did not matter, not now. He was grateful, if a little puzzled by how real his now painless body still felt. Perhaps the actual process of dying took longer than they knew.

He looked at his mother. "It's over now?" he asked.

She smiled. It warmed him, and brought back to him the days before his father had died, when she had looked like this all the time. She appeared weary, but herself, beautiful as she had always been. And yet, she was different. Which of course she would be, in whatever otherworldly place she existed, even if it was just his mind.

"Yes, it is over," she assured him, her voice gentle.

Her voice was the same. "Thank you," he said, even as he wondered why they were still in his quarters, why everything looked as it had.

"I am so very proud of you, my son. You have done what we could not."

"I didn't do enough. Father would have driven them out by now."

"Your father was an orator, an inspirer, not a fighter. You have become both."

He didn't question that she knew of the Raider. Or of his double life. Whether she was ethereal guardian of an afterlife he hadn't really believed in, or a fragment of his mind still functioning, she would of course know.

"I understand, now," he said. "Why you could not go on without him."

A memory of Kye's face, twisted with an inner pain of her own, stabbed at him, startling him with the fact that he was still able to feel that kind of ache. *I hope she is strong enough to go on. Were it reversed, I am not sure I would be.*

"She is a good, strong, courageous woman, Drake," his mother said, somehow knowing of his thoughts. "I could not have chosen one better to stand by you. And to stand for Ziem."

"I wish we had had more time."

Still pondering how she'd known his thoughts, he wondered if perhaps it was some power that came after death. Or again, perhaps she knew because she was merely a projection of his dying mind.

But if that were the case, why was she alone? Wouldn't he have projected his father as well, since he never thought of one without the other? Odd, how much easier it was to think without the pain. And as nonsensical as it seemed, he asked the question. "He did not come with you?"

She frowned then, clearly puzzled.

"Father," he said.

Understanding dawned across her face like the sun rising on those rare days free of mist.

"Oh, my sweet boy, I am so sorry. I did not realize where your mind had gone." She reached out, took his hand, squeezed it. He felt a faint echo of the pain from the fingers Jakel had broken, one by one, joint by joint. But more, he felt her touch, felt the grip of her fingers, as real as if it were . . . real.

He stared at her. "Mother?"

"I am here, Drake. Alive, breathing. As are you."

"But—"

"And you must believe how incredibly proud I am of you, and of what you have done, my brave, brave boy."

He grimaced. "I'm not brave. You don't know how many times I was afraid. How many times I wanted to quit."

"And yet you did not. My dear, beloved son, what else do you think bravery is?"

He did not understand any of this. It seemed real, and yet that was impossible. It had to be some trick of the mind, perhaps to ease his passing. Didn't it?

She laid a gentle hand on his cheek. It did not hurt. "Do not doubt, Drake. You are alive. And soon you will be yourself again."

"And you?"

"I am here. I have ever been with you."

He scowled at that.

"Yes," she said, with a sad expression that seemed to say she knew she deserved his anger. "That is a lengthy tale best saved for another time. For now, I will only say that I am sorry it had to be this way. But the vision was so strong, so clear and specific, I knew there was no other road."

He stared at her. Silently tested her words by drawing in a deep breath, and flexing the parts of him that had been damaged the worst. She saw, and understood.

"You are alive, my son," she repeated. "Although you came as close as it is possible to come and not cross over," she said. "Had Brander not come for me when he did . . ."

"Hang on, Drake. You just hang on."

Astonishment flooded him. "Brander . . . knew? He knew you were alive, and where to find you?"

"Yes and no."

At the expression that apparently crossed his face, she laughed. It was a sound he'd not heard since well before his father's death.

"He came for the Spirit," she said. "He did not know it was me."

Shock rippled through him, so many things coming clear at once it took his breath in a way hovering on the brink of death had not. "You. You're the Spirit."

She merely nodded. A lock of that red hair fell forward, and he was blasted with a memory of playing with it as a child, tugging on the thick strands and winding them around his tiny fingers.

"You . . . the notes . . ."

"I could not resist," she admitted with a smile. "You did not truly need my advice, but it is the curse of motherhood to need to offer it anyway."

"No. I did need it." His innate sense of fairness made him add, "You were right. You were always right."

"I not only saw things, I sometimes learned things. People bring the strangest offerings to the altar of the Spirit."

Another realization hit. "That's how you knew about the fuel cells, the food, the air rovers, and the rest."

"Yes."

And yet another. "The feather. In the notes."

"A tribute. Do you remember what he called me?"

"His little hawk, as your name means."

"Yes."

It was all coming at him so fast it made him feel sluggish. But it was better, so very much better than the pain. . . .

"It really was you, here. You . . . healed me?"

Her expression changed, went solemn, and sad. "I could not save your father. They left me nothing to save. But since then, I have learned much, absorbed much from the magic of our mountain, in preparation for the battle to come. You were alive, and I was determined they would not steal my son from me."

A spark of the old anger flickered. "They did not steal me. You left."

She laid a gentle hand on his brow. "I know, my son. And I know how it must have felt to you, that I chose death over you and your brother and sisters. And I will not lie; in that moment, I did make that choice. It was too much to ask; I could not stand what I saw you would have to do, not on top of your father. The pain was already so great, and you know my connection to the pain of our people. I feel what they feel. On the death of your father, I felt their fear, their pain, their grief. All of them. On top of my own, it was unbearable."

She stood suddenly. He raised himself up on one elbow, still surprised he could do it. It did not hurt, but it wearied him as if he'd run from his quarters to the flats and back again.

"You must rest. It will take some time for you to regain your strength. But Ziem must see the Raider again, soon. So do as you're told," she added, much as she had when he'd been a child.

He dropped back down onto the bed, both because he needed to, and because she was, after all, his mother. Only then did he notice the odd way she was holding her left arm, twisted to the outside so that the palm of her hand faced forward. Seeing the direction of his gaze, she spoke.

"Later. There will be time for stories. And I must rest as well. A healing of this magnitude is a costly task." She smiled at him. "In the morning, when you are stronger, your sister and the twins. But now, there is a young woman who needs desperately to see you. I do not think she had much hope that I could restore you."

"She has little. She has seen too much."

"And that is what you are to all of us, Drake. Hope. And hope can take us a great distance, when it is coupled with courage and skill, as it is in you, my son."

He did not know what else to say, so he repeated what he'd first said to her, only this time with full understanding, even if he did not know the whole of her story. He'd never really thought about what it must have been like for her, seeing the future and being unable to change it, only to prepare.

"Thank you." He decided that was too sweeping—he did not want her to think all was forgiven. So he added, "The pain was . . . immense."

And echoing pain flashed in her eyes. But when she spoke, it was not of her abandonment, his pain, or even the Raider. "You wish to thank me? Continue the fight. Make Ziem once more a place of peace and wonder and mystery, that children are free and safe to explore. And then," she added with a smile he could only describe as mischievous, "give me a grandchild to explore it with."

She was gone with a flourish of that flowing robe.

And a moment later, there was Kye. Their gazes locked, as if neither of them dared to believe that they had truly been given another chance. His mother's words echoed in his head.

A grandchild.

Perhaps with Kye's incredible turquoise eyes.

Or his mother's flame-touched hair.

She ran to him. Strength flooded into him at her first touch, as if she was willing her own to him. And he realized what his father had meant, one long-ago day when he had said that he and his mate were stronger together than the sum of their strength apart.

Neither of them spoke. They did not need to. Tacitly they agreed to steal this time, to take it for themselves, they who had taken so little and given so much, nearly including their lives.

Eventually they would rise, and fight again.

But for now, they simply held each other.

Chapter 49

DRAKE WAS A LITTLE surprised they were taking it so calmly. The flexibility of children, he guessed. Although there had been that moment when Lux had reached out, as if she feared he was but a specter and her fingers would go right through him. He'd even felt a twinge of pity for his mother when they'd shrugged off her amazing reappearance with little apparent interest; they'd been so little when she'd taken that climb up Halfhead, and barely remembered her at all.

"It is only to be expected," she'd said composedly.

But they had not clung to him like this since they were those four-year-olds, and he could not deny it warmed him. As did their easy acceptance of the fact that he was indeed the Raider.

"We thought so," Lux said quietly.

"All along," Nyx agreed.

Kye's presence did more to give him strength than anything else. She would have no more of hiding what they were to each other, and that was quite clear to one and all.

And he could hardly rebuke her for it, no matter that the thought of the risk she'd taken, even knowing he was likely already doomed, gave him chills. Not when he was feeling stronger with every minute spent back among the living. In a moment, he was even going to try standing up and see how it went. And once he was on his feet, he was going to take care of something he should have before; he wanted Kye pledged to him as soon as possible. He wanted her to have the Davorin name, and the official standing that carried, not to mention the inseparable bond with his family, should he not be so lucky next time.

He glanced at Eirlys, who was standing next to Brander. She had, it seemed, forgiven his friend, both for leaving while he lay in his quarters more dead than alive, and for hiding his own standing with the Sentinels.

"When you are up to it," Kye said softly, "it would do The Sentinels a world of good to see you."

"I think some of them don't quite believe it yet," Eirlys said.

"Took me a while myself," Drake said dryly. He glanced at the people in his quarters. The people who meant the most to him. Even the mother he'd thought he would never forgive, and yet who had given him life. Twice.

"I gather they all know the truth now?" he asked.

Brander shrugged. "More of them already knew than we thought, so there didn't seem to be much point in hiding it from the rest of them any longer. And I can't say finding out the Raider is you hasn't been energizing."

Drake grimaced. Kye laughed. "They always wanted a Davorin to rally to. Now that they know you are the Raider, they will be unstoppable."

Drake hoped she was right. The people of Ziem had rallied already, risking themselves to divert attention and allow his escape. Although escape was hardly the word for it; Kye and Kye alone had done it. Right under the Coalition's nose.

"Paledan," he murmured.

"Now there's a riddle," Brander said.

"Yes. He stopped Jakel from killing me."

The other three winced. He himself felt a ripple of repulsion just saying the name of his torturer.

"Why?" Brander asked.

"I don't know. I only know that another session with the man would have . . ."

He gave a shake of his head; remembering those agonizing hours was not productive at the moment. Nor did he want to speak of it now. Perhaps ever.

"Tell me how you found a way to get past Paledan," Drake said. "He's no fool."

"I used the rail gun," Brander said. "Near the main mine. Told the miners to get out because I was going to blow it. The guards believed me."

And that would surely draw the new commander, given the mine was the only reason the Coalition was here. Ziem had little else of interest to them.

He shifted his gaze to Kye. "How did you find a way into the cellar?"

He saw Brander and Kye and Eirlys exchange glances. He lifted a brow at them. Realized with a little shock how odd it felt not to be wearing the scars here.

"We didn't," Kye finally said.

"They did," Eirlys said, nodding toward the twins.

He drew back, shifted his gaze to the duo who were still sitting on the bed beside him. They looked up at him, Nyx's gaze a bit mutinous, and Lux looking thoughtful, always a danger sign with her.

"When it was nearly over," he said softly to them, "when I could feel I was on the edge of dying, it was you two I thought of. Of how I would miss you, would never see you grow up, never know the people you would become. I think it was only that that kept me here long enough for our mother to work her . . . magic."

He saw their eyes widen, saw moisture glisten there, saw their lips part as if in awe.

"So how did you do this?" he asked.

"We didn't break the rules," Nyx said.

"You only said no more climbing—"

"The walls. And no more—"

"Skulking around outside—"

"The Coalition compound."

The familiar—beloved—patter gave him a new burst of energy. "So?"

"We didn't climb the wall, we—"

"Dug under. And we didn't skulk outside—"

"We went inside."

Drake closed his eyes for a moment. Shook his head. But he was smiling, and he made sure they saw it. Once they realized he wasn't angry, the words came so rapid-fire he gave up trying to remember who said what and just listened to the flow. How their small tunnel had unexpectedly connected with an old, bigger one, which in turn connected with a newer one running the length of the compound, how they found other tunnels leading off from the main one, how they had gone back several times, exploring the underground labyrinth and finding many things. Including Jakel's private torture chamber.

He suppressed another shudder at the name.

"Kye planned out the rest," Brander said.

"Better stay on her good side, big brother," Eirlys said with a smile at Kye. "I think she could do just about anything she had to."

"Oh," he said softly, his gaze fastened on Kye, "I intend to."

And it was Kye, then, who suddenly turned to face his mother. And he recognized her stance, the set of her delicate jaw, and knew what was coming before she spoke.

"While I am beyond grateful to you for saving him, and owe you my allegiance, my life, and anything else you wish for that reason, I would still like an explanation."

Drake held his breath, flicked a glance at his sister who appeared to be doing the same. His mother turned, faced Kye straight on. "Interesting," she said, "that it is you who asks."

"They would not," Kye said. "They would tell themselves they should just be glad to have you back, and not to question it. But that does not mean they do not deserve an explanation."

"Kye—" Drake began.

"Don't," she said, never taking her eyes off of his mother. "She left you. She left you with a sister barely nine and twins barely more than babies to raise. She let you all think she was dead, for nearly ten years. Let you believe that she had not loved any of you enough to stay through her own pain. She had plenty of time during the climb to Halfhead to change her mind, but she did not."

Iolana Davorin took it all without a flicker of emotion, not the barest change of expression. Kye crossed her arms, and recognizing the stubborn body language too well, Drake tried again to intervene. "Kye—"

She cut him off, her tone becoming almost militant. "I know she is your mother, and you don't feel you have a right to be furious. That's fine, because I'm furious enough for all of you." She turned back to his mother. "I have watched Eirlys struggle to accept her mother's loss, have heard her wrestling with the realization that it would have been easier on all of them had you actually died with their father. And I have watched the twins, too clever not to know they were pitied, called those poor, abandoned orphans behind their backs."

His mother winced slightly at that, but Kye was on the attack now, and there was no stopping her. "But most of all, I have watched Drake. I watched him scramble to hold what was left of his family together. I watched him subjugate his nature to keep the rest of the Davorins off the Coalition agenda. And then I watched the rise of the Raider, fighting the fight we'd thought impossible, risking his life time and again. And while I was too long blind to it, it was then Drake began to appear ever and always exhausted, because he was carrying two impossible loads, either one of which would have been too much for most men. And you left him to do it alone. If there is a reason worth doing that to your son, I bedamned well would like to hear it."

To his surprise, his mother turned to look at him. "You have chosen well," she said. "She is worthy of you, and of Ziem."

Drake's gaze flicked to Kye. "I know," he said softly.

For an instant, that softness she so rarely let show warmed her eyes. But she didn't let up. "Never mind the flattery. I would prefer a straight answer."

Iolana faced her accuser. "What reason would be worth what I did? Ziem. I had seen her future, without him. And her destruction."

Kye frowned. "You did this to him because of your vision?"

His mother shifted her gaze to him, and Drake saw moisture making her vivid eyes even brighter. "You think I did not fight it? Of course I did. I did not want any of this. But the future was unambiguous, unequivocal."

"You always said your visions were . . . open to interpretation," he said.

"Before, they always were. Arbitrary, coming for this but not for that. Full of symbols that could be taken one way or another. But this one was unmistakable. Without her leader, Ziem died. The Coalition using her up, and then destroying her as they have so many other worlds." Her eyes were haunted, in that way he remembered from childhood meant she was seeing things no one else could see. "Nothing left but rubble, floating in the void," she whispered. "Her people, all of them, incinerated in one mighty blast."

There was such horror and anguish in her voice, in her face, that Drake felt an unwanted pang for this woman who had abandoned them. He heard the stir in the room; Iolana Davorin's visions had been as legendary as the Spirit had become. He saw her draw in a deep breath, as if to steady herself, and then she went on, focused on him now. "When I first began to see, I thought that leader was your father. After they murdered him, the vision became clearer, sharper." An odd, sad sort of smile curved her mouth for a moment. "And I saw it was to be you, as you are now. Grown tall and strong, brilliant and brave. The only one able to do what must be done. I fought what I saw, for I had lost so much already. I did not want you to be the one. But the vision of Ziem without you to lead cared nothing for my heart, and would not change. It never changes."

Again he felt a pang; what use was seeing the future if you could do nothing about it? He imagined himself foreseeing Kye's death and being helpless to change it. It would be a very special kind of hades.

"I was beaten. I went up Halfhead with full intent," she said. "I meant to put an end to my agony. My people were shattered, and I felt their suffering. The Coalition had taken the man I loved. And now fate was demanding my beloved son. It was the only way to end my pain."

"We saw you fall," Drake said, his voice hoarse. "Half of Zelos saw you take the plunge. No one has ever survived Halfhead."

"And yet I woke up days later, alive but badly injured, and being tended by Grim."

Drake still found the silence of the towering, formidable figure that hovered ever close disconcerting. Kye and Eirlys had told him they had at first wondered if there was more to the relationship than loyal servant, but they had seen no sign.

She held up the arm that did not bend properly. "I nearly lost all use of this. Far too many bones were broken, and it felt as if my lungs had taken in half of the Racelock. The pain made me wish I had died. But Grim, my loyal friend, and the magic he'd found in the mountain and learned to use, kept me going."

The big man shifted uncomfortably under their scrutiny, and his mother was quick to continue. "I began to realize that I had survived for a reason. Some higher purpose. And I spent much of these past years learning what that was." She smiled, and for a moment he saw the woman he remembered—beautiful, ethereal, and of impossible grace. "It was Grim who began the Spirit legend, not I. But it took hold. And I have ever watched over you, and the children. Never doubt, Drake, that I love you more than you will ever know. For more reasons than I can explain."

"Then why did you stay away?" Kye asked.

"So the Raider could be born." She focused on Kye now, and something new had come into her voice. "In order for him to become who he had to be, the man Ziem needed, he had to fight to build the strength he would need. And the vision said he had to do it alone. He had to learn to carry a great load, so that one day he could carry an even heavier one." She glanced at Drake, and the pride he saw there warmed him despite his ambivalent feelings. "And you have," she said softly.

She turned back to Kye. "You know him well, and you knew him then, how reckless he could be. Had he not responsibility to hold him back, he would have died as his father did, in a blaze of Coalition fire. But I knew how much he loved them—" she gestured at the twins and Eirlys "—and needing to be there for them would slow him down until he was ready to be the leader Ziem needed. They would do what I feared I couldn't—keep him alive."

He couldn't deny his mother's words; after that day, he had been reckless, crazed with anger and grief, and ready to march into the mouth of hades to avenge his father's death.

"I watched," his mother said, turning now to look at both him and Kye, "and waited. I learned, both how to fight—again thanks to Grim—and how to harness the power of the mountain for my healing. I knew you would rise to fight, and when you did, I would be ready to help."

"What if I had not?" he asked.

"I knew you would," she repeated. "I had foreseen it. And you are your father's son. And, although you don't wish to hear it just yet, mine."

She was right about that, Drake thought, but held the words back.

"And now," Brander observed, "we really do have a meeting of legends. The Spirit and the Raider. The potential is . . . staggering."

Kye's gaze shot to Brander, then back to his mother, then to him. "Indeed," she said softly. "We must use this. The Spirit and the Raider, two Davorins, standing together for Ziem. Posters, like the ones of the Raider, stenciled everywhere. Every Ziemite with a scrap of courage will rally."

"So I have some worth?" Iolana asked Kye directly.

Drake watched as she faced his mother once more. "Yes," Kye said coolly. "I have not forgiven you as they have, not yet, but I will use you."

His mother smiled, and it was clearly in approval.

"You have chosen well. She is worthy of you, and of Ziem."

No, he thought. She is worthy of much more.

Chapter 50

IT WAS A QUIET—for the moment—assembly in the gathering room. For a place usually the sight of planning for battles, or for fight-weary Sentinels to rest and recharge, the room looked almost festive. Garlands of mistflowers draped the walls, candles cast a golden glow, and the fire on the hearth warmed the room. Even the Sentinels looked different; all had cleaned up as best they could, donned their most presentable clothes, and stood now eagerly awaiting something they had not seen in too long—a genuine, honest day of celebration.

Kye took Brander's offered arm, touched despite herself at how much care he'd taken, his jaw clean-shaven, his usually somewhat wild hair neatly combed, and his black coat looked both formal and new, as if he'd had it stored away.

Her own dress was something she had never expected. She had thought she would become pledged to Drake wearing the plain ceremonial robe that was the best she had, which was not saying much. But last night, his mother had knocked on the door to his quarters, which Drake had turned over to her for this night. While, she suspected, the Sentinels did their best to get him drunk on this, his last night of being unattached.

Iolana Davorin had brought an offering, and one Kye found hard to refuse, one of her own gleaming white robes.

"I would offer it merely because you are pledging to my son," she had said. "But please know it is out of respect as well. I have learned of the woman you have become. You are not only that artist of no small talent I remember, but a brave, bold woman and fighter, and a perfect match for him. You hold his heart, and I know you will see to it well. And I will wait as long as it takes for you to, not forgive me, but accept me as one who loves him, too."

Kye had bitten back the comment that rose to her lips, that abandoning him and her other children was hardly an act of love, because she was beginning to see it had been just that. But an act of love for this place, this mist-shrouded planet they all cherished. She had seen with clarity that her son was the only one who could save it, and so she had offered him up, and done what was necessary for him to learn what he had to learn. Kye understood, but she still couldn't quite give it her blessing.

But she could accept this offering. As a first step.

And then Eirlys had joined them to fuss with the robe, and, to her surprise, said Mara Clawson and Tuari and others were all bustling about in the gathering room, preparing. When Eirlys was done, Kye found herself looking in the polished metal that served as a mirror at a woman in a gleaming white dress, tucked in at the waist and flowing out gracefully behind, and with a garland of white mistflowers around a loose knot of long, dark hair that looked as if one good tug would send it cascading down.

She would not shame him, she thought as they stepped into the gathering room.

Eirlys left to stand with her brother while Iolana had made her way to the front of the room to stand before the mantel of the hearth, the most imposing structure in the room. She would, as the wife of an elder of Ziem, perform the pledging.

"Of all the things I regretted as I slipped so close to death, the biggest was that we had not pledged. I would have you own my name and my soul formally, before everyone, as you already do between us."

She had not hesitated for an instant at Drake's heartfelt proposal. She had realized, with a pang, that he was also assuring she would not be alone should he truly die, that she would have his family as her own. But she remembered her own wish, as he lay dying, that they had not let the war stop them, and she understood.

To her surprise, she heard music, a quiet, gentle tune from past days, played with some skill on a lap harp. When she saw it was gruff old Pryl at the strings, she felt her eyes sting with unshed tears. She smiled at the man, and saw his own eyes look suspiciously moist as he smiled back. The music changed, his fingers picked up the pace, and a joyous fanfare blossomed from the strings.

And then she saw Drake and her breath left her in a rush. He was dressed in full black—his father's pledging clothes, Iolana had said, her eyes moistening when she'd recognized them and realized he'd kept them all this time—but for a slash of white mistflower on his shoulder. Tall, strong, his eyes bright and clear, his dark hair brushed back from that face so beloved with or without scars.

A face no longer masked. It bore scars in actuality now, but thanks to the skill of his mother, they were already fading. But it was the first time he had ever appeared before them all without the Raider's disguise, confirming what Brander had told them. She also knew that this meant his life in Zelos as he'd known it was over. As did he. But he had told her he did not mourn this, not with her beside him.

"Where I will ever be," she had whispered back, vowing to treasure him even more after nearly losing him forever.

Brander bowed as they reached him, handing her off to his brother in all but blood. And Kye's sister also in all but blood, but soon also by law, did the same for Drake by lifting his hand and placing it over Kye's in the traditional way.

Iolana began, reciting the pledging ceremony that had been banned on Ziem since the arrival of the Coalition. This simple act, once so common, so affirming, was now an act of defiance, and everyone there knew it. It added another layer to the already joyous occasion, and when the final words were spoken, when she and Drake were bound together for eternity, she felt nothing short of triumph. And in his eyes she read the same emotion; they had not just pledged to each other today, they had pledged to their world.

"You have sealed what was a given, you were made for each other," Iolana whispered to them. "Ziem has their first family once more."

And that night, there was no sneaking back to the alcove, no hiding, no worrying who might overhear. For instead, they had another gift from his mother, one glorious night alone, with no one to interrupt, in a surprising cave warmed by the mountain itself, and planned for their every comfort.

"Revel," she had said with a wink. "Time enough to worry about what's coming. For tonight, just be with each other." And then, after a moment, she looked at her son pointedly and added, "And work on that wish of mine."

It was much later, when they had sated the first driving need, made even more powerful by how close they had come to losing it, when she finally asked. "What wish of hers?"

Drake, to her amazement, flushed. Lowered his eyes. "Something she wants, when Ziem is free and safe to explore once again."

Kye didn't dwell on what that was going to take, she wanting nothing to mar this night. "What is it she wants?"

His mouth quirked as he at last met her gaze. "A grandchild to explore it with."

A sudden burst of emotions flooded Kye, things she had never felt, had never dared let run. A child. Her child. Drake's child. It was insane to even think of and yet . . . *when Ziem is free and safe to explore once again.*

"We should work on that," she said, knowing he would see her acceptance of his mother's wish for what it was, acceptance of everything. They would be a family, that first family of free Ziem.

"With pleasure, my mate," he whispered. And set about the task.

Chapter 51

A HUSH FELL over the room as Brander finished fastening the map to the wall. Up high, so it was visible to all. Drake had asked her to keep this quiet so that he could unveil the entire plan at once. She had, though excitement was fairly humming through her.

Brander returned to the floor and took a place next to Kye as the low murmuring, the wondering, began again.

"Nice work," he said to her quietly.

She gave him a brief smile of thanks; she had worked hard on it, but right now, her mind was focused on what was to come.

The door to his quarters opened and heads swiveled. The murmuring got louder when a tall, slender woman with flaming red hair rippling down her back stepped into the room. The woman known to them for a decade, sight unseen, simply as the Spirit was in her flowing robe, but beneath it, she wore the rugged outfit and dark planium armor of a Sentinel, complete with a blaster at her hip. Over her shoulder was the pack marked with the symbol of the healer. She could not have made it more clear that she was prepared to both fight and heal alongside them.

The scars that marked her—forehead, cheek, throat, and the twist of her arm—only added to the impact. She came with a steady, youthful stride, and Kye was reminded yet again she was but eighteen years older than she herself. It was unsettling to think this woman had had a son nearly ten and a daughter on the way when she was Kye's age now.

She paused beside them as she passed. Kye looked at the woman who was the mother of her mate. "Tell me," she whispered, "does your vision happen to show if we win?"

Their gazes locked. Iolana seemed to find what she sought in Kye's expression. "Nothing so useful as that," she said wryly. "There never is."

"Annoying."

"Very."

They exchanged the briefest of smiles, and Kye thought they just might, someday, have a relationship of sorts.

Iolana came to a halt in front of the map. Turned, and the gathering fell silent. Most stared at her with a sort of awe, still not quite used to the presence of this woman who had been a mystical creature, almost of myth. Kye supposed for some of them, that she was the Davorin matriarch come back to life was just as mystical.

For a moment, Iolana simply looked at them all. When she spoke, her voice was quiet, yet somehow seemed to carry to the farthest reaches of the room. As it had when she had pledged Kye to her son. "For many years now, I have been apart. It took time to mend my wounds, my heart, and to accept that the future I had seen was inevitable. But now, it is time for me to stand, and stand I will. No longer as the Spirit, but again as a Davorin, I will stand. With the people of Ziem." The door to his quarters opened again. She smiled. "With my son."

The quiet was absolute as he came into the room. Kye's pulse always picked up when she saw him, even after just minutes apart. But now it kicked into a race as he passed, his fingers briefly brushing over her hand as he walked, upright and strong once again. He crossed over to stand beside his mother. There was little resemblance, he took so after his father, but it did not matter; they were together, the Spirit down from her mountain and the Raider out from behind the mask he had been forced to wear for so long.

Iolana's voice rang out this time. "I give you, not the Raider, but Drake Davorin."

The cheer that went up echoed off the walls of the ruin until it was a physical thing, a vibration Kye could feel in the room. It continued, never ebbing, only growing. She understood, for just three weeks ago, they'd been gathered in this very room, waiting for word that he had finally died. And she had been huddled helplessly at his bedside, torn between hanging on with every last ounce of her being, and letting him go because his pain was so great.

Yet now he stood before them, strong, tall, whole. And her pledged mate.

Their ranks had swelled since word had gotten around that the Raider was indeed Drake Davorin. Including the man who now stood in the front row, looking at Drake steadily, determinedly. He had arrived offering his service as an experienced mechanician, something they were in sore need of; Brander couldn't do it all. He owed them, he had said, or rather, Drake. It was only then that she learned of the incident in the alley behind the taproom, when Drake, with only a stained bar apron as a weapon, had saved a little girl from the ugly predation of a Coalition monster. The mechanician's daughter.

She was not surprised. She suspected there were others here now for similar reasons; for all his blatantly displayed cowardice, Drake had still managed to help more than one resident of Zelos during his exhausting double life. The masquerade, the awful double life that was over at last. Jakel had seen to that, and in a way, even his mother. By bringing him back from the very edge of death, she'd made it impossible for him to go back; it would draw far too much attention and curiosity. But even if he dared risk it, the Coalition had taken the decision out of his hands by destroying the life he had worked so hard to build for his family; the taproom was now only two standing walls and a pile of rubble, payback for the impudence of escaping Coalition custody.

Not to mention the death sentence now on his head.

"You've got a price on both your heads now."

Brander's words, half joke, half serious, echoed in her mind. Along with her own response.

"They'll regret this. They've unleashed you now."

And they had. Unleashed him to be fully, not the Raider but something even more dangerous to them. The son of now two legends, one of whom stood beside him now, and one who was forever enshrined in the memories and hearts of all Ziemites.

And after tonight, all of Ziem would know.

"I am honored," he said, his voice tight with emotion. "But we must begin, for time is crucial now."

The atmosphere changed in an instant. They became the Sentinels once more.

"Time," he said, "and timing. For on this day, two things have conjoined. The Coalition post commander is traveling to Legion Command to give a status report."

"He left on schedule," called out a lanky man in the front rank. "Saw him board and the transport take off myself."

And the moment the transport was gone, the images Kye had done, somewhat hurriedly, had gone up. Despite the rush, the image of the Raider and the Spirit side by side, this one to be stenciled in color to show the fire of Iolana Davorin's hair, and the gleaming silver of the Raider's helm, was powerful. She knew he'd thought the words Brander had come up with, *Back from the dead and down from the Edge, to fight for Ziem,* a bit too dramatic, but he was outvoted. And even he had had to admit he'd been wrong when he saw how it had caught on in Zelos already.

Drake nodded and continued. "Second, today is the day they will move the fusion cannon from the ridge back to the valley."

A ripple of excited sound went through the gathering. They all knew the fusion cannon was the ultimate weapon the Coalition held over Zelos. And Kye knew Drake had ever walked that hair-thin line, always trying to judge how far he could push without driving them to use it.

"The crash," Brander whispered beside her in sudden understanding. "That's what he found in that freighter, the schedule for the airlift."

Kye nodded.

"I figured out this is why he wouldn't kill Paledan when he could have, but how did he know when he would be gone?"

She whispered back. "I'll tell you later about a little midnight visit we made to the barkhound's office."

Drake went on. "We all know what it means if they get that weapon back in position in the valley. So today . . . we stop them. Today, together, we destroy it."

A roar went up this time. He let it go for a moment, but quickly brought them back under control.

"Each team will have an assignment. A position. A job. And each one is crucial, whether it seems so or not." He looked over at Brander. "Brander Kalon has the first, and possibly most critical task. To take out their communications."

A murmur went around this time, speculation on just how he was going to manage that. He'd been reluctant, did not want to be away from the main fight so long, but he was the only one of them who knew that particular terrain well.

"All of their communications," Drake added. "So they not only will not be able to talk to each other, but they will not be able to call for aid."

A stir among the Sentinels. "You mean block them even from Legion Command?" The voice that called out sounded incredulous.

"I do. We now know where they've hidden the main communications array."

Kye remembered the moment in his quarters when the subject had come up as Drake, still testing his strength, had paused to look at her map once more. The room, as was often the case lately, held five, she and Drake, his mother, Brander, and back in a corner the ever-present—and silent—Grimbald.

Drake and Brander had been speculating on the likely places for that array to be hidden when Grim had spoken without prompting. One of the few times he ever had; he would answer if spoken to, but rarely initiated any conversation except with Iolana.

"Maybe Halfhead?" Brander had just suggested. It was a mark of progress that neither Drake nor his mother winced at the mention of the place where she had tried to leave this world.

"It is above Halfhead," Grim said.

Drake had spun around—no wobble with the quick move, as there had been the first couple of days he'd regained his feet—to stare at the big man.

"On the peak of the Brother," Grim said, referring to the taller mountain that had matched Halfhead before the crack that had created the sheer face that was now a dominant landmark above Zelos.

It made sense. It was the tallest mountain in the east range, and a signal sent from there would encounter no obstacles to dilute its strength. The Coalition had had their system in place before Zelos—and all of Ziem—had even realized what was happening, when they were still under attack and in shock at the invasion of their peaceful world. And once the Coalition had confiscated all vehicles and weapons, there would have been no way to get up there anyway. But now, they had the air rovers. . . .

"You know this for certain?" Drake asked sharply.

"Now, yes." Grim's expression never changed. "I did not realize at the time what it was I had seen them building."

Drake had peppered him with questions, and then Brander, the only one of them who had been to the top of the Brother. And the last, vital piece was theirs.

"Mara," Drake called out now, snapping her back to the present.

"Here!" the woman called out.

"Your people are here."

He took up a marker and put an X on each side of the landing zone, sparing a split second for a glance at Kye, as if to apologize for marking up her work. She grinned at him; this was what she had been waiting for from the moment she'd discovered his secret, to see both men she loved as one, no longer hiding.

"You will send a bird when the airlifter arrives." The woman nodded.

"Dek," he said to the young man, who stood beside Tuari, who was his aunt and only surviving relative. "You will be at the bell tower, and when the bird arrives with the message, you will climb the tower and turn your scope on the landing zone. And when the ship lifts off for the move, send up the flare."

They had decided to use Brander's push flares, that dragged the glowmist along with them, making it visible for miles to those with the vision. They had few of them, but there would never be a more important mission than this.

"You remember the code?" Drake asked.

The boy nodded. "One for go, two if there's a problem."

Drake smiled at him, and the boy practically bloomed before Kye's eyes.

"Harkins," he called out then.

"Here!" rang out again from Galeth.

"You will place your lookouts here."

He called out and marked a half-dozen places on the map, all with clear views of the high valley leading from the mountains to Zelos. Galeth turned to the group clustered around him and snapped out a name for each position as quickly as Drake had named the spots.

"Teal, the lowland lookouts will be here."

He repeated the marking of another half-dozen ground spots, this time placed near the only paths for ground troops to move toward the Brother, the Ruin, and the mines. Kye saw nods of understanding in the room as they realized now why Brander, at Drake's order, had been going among them testing for who had the best mist vision; it was those Sentinels who had been given this mission, since they would be in the thickest mist.

The briefing went on, a small group armed with every explosive they had left assigned to damage the emplacement in the low valley near Zelos, so that at the very least they would delay the Coalition's ability to use the thing against the city. Squads of fighters were assigned to each possible path to reach the mines, their only task to stop Coalition passage however they could.

"Destroy what you must to cut them off, but with care," Drake said. "We can rebuild, but only if we are left something to do it with."

He went on, each remaining Sentinel given a task. And each task was accepted without question. Even though some would likely die in the effort.

She noticed that none of them asked who would actually be trying to take out the cannon when it was at its most vulnerable, in that hour when it would be unfastened from the base on the mountain and rigged to be lifted off. That hour when there would be only as many guards as could fit in the airlifter, but they would all be fully armed and on alert.

Because they all knew that this, the most dangerous of tasks, would be the Raider's. And she wondered how many of them still thought of him that way, how many were still wrestling with the fact that the man who had risen to fight and the man they had expected it of had turned out to be one and the same. She had the feeling the combination had resulted in a bigger, more fierce loyalty and urge to fight than either one alone would have.

"If they do get it airborne," Galeth asked, "how will we destroy it?"

For the first time, Drake hesitated. He looked at her, and she saw in his eyes the echo of the pain of his decision. Since she was the best shot of them all, it was the only logical, the only possible one to make, but that had made it no easier on him. Neither had her own insistence that she be allowed to play the part only she could play.

And in the end, he had made the decision a leader must make.

When he had taken her in his arms last night, it had been with a sort of desperation she understood. And she had clung to him in turn, each of them knowing without saying that this could well be the last time.

She spoke to them all for the first time. "I will shoot it out of the sky," she declared. "Over the high valley."

She could almost see the progression of their thoughts, from now understanding yesterday's orders to evacuate any remaining people from the area to the relative safety of the mines, to the final realization, the one that had nearly torn Drake apart. That if it came to that, if she had to destroy the cannon from her air rover, even with a long gun, she would have to be close enough that the resultant explosion would destroy her along with it.

The room had gone utterly silent. Many looked from Drake to her, then back. They drew in a deep breath almost as one. Straightened spines in the same way. As if the last bit of strength they needed had just been given to them by this further demonstration that their leader, who had already nearly died in this cause, and his pledged mate, were still willing to sacrifice as much as they.

Finding his voice once more, and seizing the moment, Drake spoke one last time.

"We don't have their weapons, or their numbers, but we have our mountains, our mist, and our knowledge and love of this place. Use them."

And with that, the Sentinels—and the Raider—went out to fight.

Chapter 52

EIRLYS TRIED TO not start pacing again. It chafed at her beyond belief to stay here, in the safety of the ruin. With the exception of a small detachment Drake had left to guard this stronghold—and her and the twins, no doubt— they were alone. But the more she paced, the more restless the twins got, and that was never a good sign. Drake had extracted a blood oath from them that, for just this fight, they would stay put. She supposed it was in part because they realized how close they had all come to losing him that they had complied readily.

Well, readily for them, she thought ruefully. It had only taken ten minutes of bargaining, and the promise of a ride in an air rover when it was done, to get it.

At the moment, they were trying to lure Slake into a game of chaser to pass the time while Mahko prepared a meal.

"Us—"

"Against you because—"

"We're only children—"

"After all. And—"

"Not for money—"

"But for fun. And maybe—"

"That shiny pouch."

The man responded with a doubtful glance at her as he fingered the silver pouch he wore on a strand around his neck.

Eirlys laughed in spite of her nerves. "If you're as bothered by being stuck here as I am, it might help," she said. "But I warn you, they were taught by Brander."

The man's eyes widened. He looked at the two, who had put on their most innocent faces, warily. As well he should. He wouldn't be the first the twins had surprised. They had even surprised Brander once or twice. The last time, he'd laughed aloud at how they'd fleeced him, and said proudly there was no more he could teach them.

That moment played through her mind, as it so often did, bringing back the odd, swelling feeling that tightened her chest as he took his unexpected defeat at the hands of two then ten-year-olds so delightedly. Which in turn brought back all the emotions she'd been swamped with when she'd realized Brander had been fighting side by side with the Raider—her brother—all along. Not the least of which was self-recrimination for not realizing it before now.

And now they were out there, risking their lives. She should have insisted on going, underage or not. But it had been impossible to refuse Drake, not when such a very short time ago she had sat shivering in his quarters, waiting to hear the dreaded silence when his harsh, pained breathing finally stopped.

"I have to know you and the twins are safe, or I will not be able to do what I must."

And so now, the people who mattered most to her in this world were out there, fighting a desperate battle to save something of the world her father had warned they were losing.

That thought sent her mind scurrying to the astonishing reappearance of their mother. The revelation that she was alive was incredible enough, but that she was the mythical, powerful Spirit who lived above the Edge almost put the tale into the realm of impossible. And yet it was true. Eirlys could not doubt that. Had she not pulled Drake back from the very doorway of death? Had she not healed him so completely that barely two weeks later he was back to himself and strong enough to lead this battle?

And even she is out there, fighting with him. While I am trapped here, uselessly.

Only then did she realize she was pacing again. She glanced to the big hearth, where the twins were absorbed in their game. They were in the early stages, gauging their opponent's strengths and searching out his weaknesses. Brander had indeed taught them well.

And as she thought of him again, up on that mountain, alone, she could no longer stay in this room. Spacious though it was, the cellar walls seemed to be closing in on her. She headed for the ladder. She thought of warning the twins to stay put, but decided it was best not to plant the idea that they might not, and made her way up.

Once above, she walked toward the lookout. It was Tuari at the moment, who, despite the calm at the moment, was alert and ready, and heard her coming long before she got to her.

"All quiet," she said.

She nodded. "Mahko is fixing a meal. Slake will relieve you when he's eaten."

"Brollet stew again?"

"Yes. But he scrounged a bit of flour, so there's a loaf as well."

The woman's expression brightened.

She looked toward the distinctive shape of Halfhead, then to the heights of the Brother beside it. Somewhere, up there, in the sunlight above the mist, Brander was awaiting the signal that the Coalition ship had lifted off. And up above the high valley, on Highridge, the Raider awaited that signal, plus the signal that Brander had succeeded, and the lookout signals as it passed.

Waiting.

It seemed as if all of Ziem was waiting.

There were those who said they had deserved what had happened, for failing to be aware and ready. They had trusted their isolation too much, had shrugged off the rumors that the infamous Coalition was expanding into this sector, thinking themselves safe enough. And so they had been caught unprepared when reality had descended upon them.

And there were those who had said fighting back was impossible; their population was small, mostly unarmed, and untrained for anything like the might of the Coalition. They were the first to surrender, to voluntarily put on the yoke of Coalition servitude, and they had sickened her.

And she had thought Drake one of them. The things she'd said, the names she'd called him, and the worse ones she'd thought, still ate at her. Especially now. When she had wished he would do something, fight back, she hadn't taken into account what it would mean if he did. Hadn't realized how it would feel, to face the very real possibility of his death.

But she had faced it now, it had been all too real in those last moments before the arrival of the Spirit . . . her mother.

And that brought her back to Brander, who had pulled off this miracle by fetching her. She wished she could have talked to him more about that, and why he, the most practical, logical man she knew, ever given to reality, had taken such a chance. The one time she'd asked, he'd simply laughed and reminded her he was a gambler, was he not?

Yes, he was that. And so much more, no matter that he tried to hide it. He—

A fluttering sound of wings drew her attention. The darkest of her birds, by coincidence—or perhaps not—one of the few adept at night flying, flew past her and landed on the feeding platform Brander had built. She hurried over, and gave the bird a handful of feed as she hastily pulled the tiny curled message out of the capsule.

Airlifter here, it said, and the time had arrived. She blinked, and double-checked her timer. The bird had made the trip in just over ten minutes, shaving nearly two minutes off the expected time.

"Well done, little one," she said, laying out another handful for the swift creature.

She turned back to Tuari. "It's begun," she said. "The ship is here."

The woman looked at her own wrist, and Eirlys knew she was marking the time before the expected lift-off of the airlift, to make the short flight up to Highridge and the cannon emplacement. Drake had been timing this for months, until he had a decent average for the weekly operation. They knew that, after the ship's arrival, the crew was allowed a short break for food and drink and to prepare the rigging for deployment. This ran anywhere from thirty minutes to an hour; she knew that since the commander was off world, Drake was guessing this would run closer to the longer limit.

"Hope the kid doesn't mess up," the woman finally muttered.

"He won't. Did you see his face when Drake gave him the assignment?"

Tuari smiled. "Yes. You're right." She gave her a rather long look. "Your brother is . . . well, it's unbelievable, what he's done."

"Yes."

"He took such abuse, for so long."

She winced. "Yes."

She took the spotters again, trained them on the mist above the low valley. If Brander's special flare worked as expected—and she had full faith it would, for she knew his skill well—they wouldn't even need the glasses to see it. But it was something to do, and she was desperate for that just now.

Chapter 53

DRAKE SHIFTED course just slightly, slipping the air rover behind the screen of the trees. He knew his path well; he had traversed it many times in the planning stages of this, the final battle. He had tried not to think of it that way, but he knew in his heart and his gut that it was. They had this one chance, and there would never be another like it. If they won, the fight would go on. If they failed, Ziem would be lost.

And many, if not most, of them would be dead. He suppressed a shudder as he tried to shore up the mental walls against the enormity of what he'd done.

He'd used them all, even the young ones who should still be in school, in this last raid that depended on precise timing among so many that they had slim chance of succeeding. But there was no future for Ziem if they didn't take this chance.

He'd sent countless of his people out to fight, against horrendous odds.

He'd sent the woman he loved out to certain death if she had to carry out her mission.

He felt a soft touch. His mother, placing her hand over his. He glanced, still not accustomed to her presence. And yet her touch calmed him, more than it had even as a child. Was the change in her? In him? In the insanity that had become his world, how could she have this effect? Was there more to this Spirit legend than she had yet told him?

It didn't matter, not right now. What mattered was that she had insisted on standing beside him for this.

"I can never make up for how I left you, Drake, but I will be there. Whether you wish it or not."

He understood, at least in theory, why she'd done it. Even agreed that he would not be who he was, had she not left him to do what had to be done alone, to fight his way through it all. But he was not yet convinced it had all been worth it, not when he feared this final battle would be futile.

"It is right, Drake," she said softly. "You have done everything that could possibly be done."

He glanced at her. She was, unexpectedly, smiling.

"I know your doubts," she said, so quietly he knew the men behind them could not hear her. "They are needless."

"You have . . . seen this?"

"I do not need to. I know you."

He turned back to the controls; he knew the course well, but well enough to know attention was required.

"We will do this," she said. "For your father. For Ziem."

He glanced at the woman beside him once more. And he saw a strange emotion in her face, her eyes. And for the first time, he felt a hint of what she'd been through, of how much it had cost her to stay away for so long. This had not been easy for her, either. But she, as had his father, had always seen the bigger picture, the far-reaching consequences. He had thought that the fact that she had survived her leap hadn't changed anything, since she hadn't intended to survive; she'd intended to die and leave them forever. But she was here, at his side, and he wasn't sure how he felt. And figuring it out was a luxury he couldn't afford right now.

She had fallen silent, and in truth, there was nothing more to say. But she did not remove her hand. And, as if he drew the final bit of strength he needed from it, he finished that wall, the one that kept his emotions at bay. He felt the icy calm descend, felt the sense of command, of destiny overtake him. He thought now only of what must be done.

He had worn the coat, the helmet, all the trappings of the Raider except for the scars. He had his own now, although she had assured him they would fade, in time. He did not want to risk the change now, not on this mission. The silver helmet and the dramatic silhouette Kye had turned into a symbol of all they stood for must be there still, reminding them he was still the man they'd followed into battle.

And now they would follow him into hades, if that was where this led them.

Drake would have pondered that. The Raider allowed it no time or energy.

They settled into the position he'd chosen on Highridge.

And waited.

BRANDER HAD LOST track of the various scrapes and bruises he'd acquired. He'd known he would have to park the rover and scale the last, steepest five hundred feet on foot, but hadn't worried overmuch about it. He'd done it before, after all, just months before the Coalition invaded.

In sun-season.

When he'd been fourteen.

He scoffed inwardly at the thought that at twenty-six he might be less nimble. Even if he were, he was a lot stronger than his rather skinny fourteen-year-old self had been. Which, considering he was carrying three hand weapons plus the flare gun and his long gun, was a bedamned good thing.

He kept going, pushing himself for more speed. He wasn't behind schedule, but it was irritating him that it was such slow going. He had to be there and ready to move the moment the airlifter took off to head for the cannon. It was a mere three-minute flight for the big ship, so there was no time to spare. Everything hinged on this; nothing else would happen until he got this done.

Maybe that was it. It just seemed like this was taking longer because of what it meant. When he'd climbed this peak at fourteen, the fate of his entire world hadn't depended on it.

Leaving his dark armor in the rover, trading it for the gray clothing Eirlys had found for him, clothing that would blend into the gray of the bare rock of the peak, hadn't helped; several of the spots that were stinging would have been protected, but the tradeoff for the camouflage was worth a scratch here and there.

And then he was above the mist, and sunlight poured down on him. It took a half-second for his eyes to adjust, and then the square shape of the installation leapt into focus. It was even bigger up close than he'd thought it would be. Four large, curved antennae on top faced each direction, along with a massive metal structure he knew was the transmitter that could send burst transmissions all the way to Legion Command.

It was too big for the stolen obliterator he'd lugged along to take out, but they'd expected that. The rail gun would have been perfect, but they'd run out of ammunition for it and it was too big to handcarry up here anyway. He'd just have to get inside and find the most crucial part of the array and take that out. He'd studied what they had, the schematic from three years ago. Provided, he'd recalled with a start, by the Spirit. If they lived, he'd have to ask her how she'd managed that one. It was outdated, obviously, but it had at least given him an idea of what to look for.

He found the door, set almost seamlessly in the side of the enclosure which was, he thought with an ironic grimace, made of planium.

"Of course," he muttered under his breath as he studied the closure.

It was an intricate lock, like the ones they'd installed at the compound gates. But unlike those, this one required no eye or palm scan; they must have assumed no one would ever get up here except themselves, after they'd confiscated all small airships.

Drake will hang you with your own assumptions, you skalworms.

He thought for an instant of using the obliterator on the lock; it would be instant, but it had been taking a bit longer to recharge after Kye had used it to rescue Drake, and he feared it might only have one good, full-strength hit left in it, so he didn't dare. Instead, he pulled out the laser pistol.

He knew he would have to move fast, had to assume what he was about to do would send some kind of alarm to the Coalition in their compound. Speed would then be of the essence; he had to get inside and take down the communications so quickly that they would think it was all part of the same malfunction. They were gambling that once en route, the transport would not turn back, that moving the cannon took priority over everything, even a communications breakdown.

But then Brander had always been a gambler.

He flipped the lever on the pistol. Focused on the charging light as if it were the sun visible for the first time after a winter of Ziem mist. Again, time seemed to crawl before, at last, the light went green.

He waited. Stared down toward the low valley. If that special flare he'd built didn't work the way he'd planned, dragging the mist up with it so he could see it from up here, even in the sunlight, this was all going to fall apart. But it would. He knew it would. It had to. He'd wondered about giving Dek the responsibility, but Drake had seen something in him, and Brander had to trust that. Besides, the Coalition would pay less attention to a boy merely appearing to play in the bell tower.

If this worked, the rest would go like clockwork. Drake had seen to that. There wasn't a damned detail the man had missed—he'd thought of things that never would have occurred to Brander, and dealt with them. And then he'd planned for the unexpected, which made Brander respond that that was a contradiction, for Drake had expected them. He had a plan, a back-up plan, a back-up to the back-up, and another after that.

He suppressed a shudder at the thought of what they had nearly lost. For all his talk of Brander taking over if he died, he knew with absolute certainty that he would never, ever be able to do what Drake did. He—

A fountain of green boiled up out of the mist over Zelos. A single flare. The transport was lifting off.

Now.

He sucked in a breath as he lifted the laser pistol. "May the Spirit help—"

He cut off the automatic, ingrained words with a laugh. He had neither the nature nor the desire to dwell on mystical things, but the truth of the Spirit had even him pondering the strange turns that story had taken.

Get it done, Kalon.

He pressed the trigger. The red beam shot out. He had to go slower to carve through the planium. Counted down in his head. Five seconds. Ten. Fifteen. Twenty. The cuts met. Swiftly, he reversed the weapon and hit the lock a sharp blow. It fell to the inside. He noted the connection that had no doubt already sent the alarm, but only as he slammed the door open.

Dark.

He shoved the laser pistol into his belt and grabbed the cellight in the same motion. Thumbed it on. With his left hand, he flipped the lever on the obliterator, scanned, that countdown still ticking in his head. Thirty seconds. Bare wall. Thirty-five. There, console. Faint lights blinking. Get to it. Set the light down. Grab the obliterator. Forty. Find it, find it, the core. Yank the panel. Forty-five. Nexus of connections, or anything that looked like it. Nothing. Forty-five. Wait, there. There! Fire . . .

The tangle of fiber, cables, and crystals vanished without a sound. Every light on what was left of the console went out. He darted outside. The antennae were motionless, dead atop their perch.

Fifty-three seconds.

Seven to spare.

Brander grinned. He yanked out the flare gun, aimed it in an arc down into the fog, and fired. It went, stirring the mist into a roiling stream of glowmist that flowed down the mountain.

"Over to you, my brother," he said.

Chapter 54

FROM HIGHRIDGE where they were waiting, silently, tensely since the moment the flare had gone up from the landing zone, Drake saw the stream of eerie green light tumbling down the Brother like a river through the Ziem mist.

Brander had done it.

He reached for the comm link in the control board of the rover, and turned it on for the first time since they'd stolen them. An empty, vacant hum came out of the system. He counted down the agreed-upon minute, when Brander would turn his on as well and test that it was down for certain.

The silence held. Not only were they without the concise, effective orders he had no doubt Major Paledan would have given were he here, they were without communications altogether. They couldn't even call for help. A force would likely start for the Brother, to check on the communications, but the Sentinels would hold them back. And the miners, who had been greatly inspired by Samac Rahan's sacrifice, would about now be circling the guards there, forcing them into the mine, preventing them from coming to the airlifter's aid when it arrived.

Never would the Sentinels have a better chance to strike a crippling blow.

His mother was staring down the high valley. "One and two," she said softly, counting down the signals from the lookouts all along the valley. He headed the rover along the ridge, toward the cannon emplacement.

"Three," she said. He upped the speed, dodging the last of the thick forest. Then they were in the sparsely treed boundary.

"Four."

He brought the rover to a sharp halt just inside the last line of trees. He could see the huge barrel of the fusion cannon looming above, over the mines. At his hand signal, the small force leapt out of the rover, readying weapons. He looked at his mother.

"You do not have to do this," he said, although they'd been through this before.

"I know."

"You are a healer. And we will have to kill."

"Then I will remember what they did to you. Five," she added.

He had no time for more, he could only accept, and believe. Compared with what he'd had to accept over the past weeks, this was little enough. He jumped out of the rover. She was on the ground beside him before he could offer her help.

"Six," she said softly.

Thirty seconds. He signaled the men. Swung the long gun around, checked the load one last time. Realized he was barely breathing. Forced himself to breathe deeply, preparing to sprint. He heard the sound of the ship five seconds before it loomed out of the mist. The men tensed, but he held them with an upright fist. The craft adjusted course, upward. In less than a minute, it was hovering over the huge cannon mount.

The bottom hatch opened. The cannon sling unrolled. Four Coalition troopers rode it down. The temptation to strike now, while they were vulnerable, was great. Drake held. It was the cannon they had to destroy, and the only way to do that was to wait until it was free of the mount and vulnerable. He hoped to use the big airlifter itself; if they could take it down after it had lifted off, both it and the cannon would crash down the mountainside, destroying both.

He inched closer under cover of a low line of rock that jutted up in a line along the cliff edge. The other Sentinels spread out as planned under that same cover. One of them disturbed the nest of a muckrat, and the creature squalled and darted over the rocks. One of the guards spun around, firing before he could possibly have seen a target. On edge, Drake thought as the blast, low and wild, dug into the rock a bare yard past his feet.

He heard a laugh in the distance. The other troopers, mocking their companion for his jitters. He listened to the metallic sounds of them unfastening the cannon's base from the mount, then fastening the lift cables. He inched upward to risk a glance.

The ground under his feet shifted. He realized the ledge had been undercut by that wild missed shot. It was crumbling. He grabbed for a small outcropping of rock. Got his hands on it a split-second before the ledge went. Heard the sliding, clattering as the crumbled rocks slid into the chasm. He was dangling from the side of the ridge, held only by fingers that were already feeling the strain.

He could hear the guards approaching, making no effort at stealth, in fact running. Closer. Closer still. They'd reach the spot where he'd been standing in seconds. And he was hanging here, helpless, an unmissable target. And even if they did miss, one shot would likely send the rest of this entire side of the ridge sliding down to the canyon floor, him with it.

He could only hope it took them, too. And then the others could finish the job he'd so ignominiously failed at—

A voice rang out, echoing off the rocks. "Pillagers of Ziem, you will hold!"

Drake's breath caught. His mother. Or rather, the Spirit, for there was no doubt it was she who spoke. The running footsteps halted. He heard the scrabbling sound, as if they had skidded a little in their abrupt stop. Heard another, as if they had spun around. He had a sudden image of her, robes glistening white in the sun, fiery hair flowing in the breeze, and that voice. . . . Even Coalition troopers were not immune to the power of myth and legend and image, it seemed.

The outcropping he clung to began to shift. And there was nowhere to go. Nothing to grab. He was going down. He scrambled, as if he could overcome the pull of the entire planet by sheer will. He slipped farther. His brain was racing, gauging, calculating, looking for any way out. There was none. His mother's risk had been for nothing. It was going to end like this, after everything. He—

Something hard, solid, and strong latched onto his wrist. His downward slip halted. He couldn't even look up—his face was jammed against the rock. And then, slowly but steadily, he was pulled upward. And then he had the other arm back on solid ground. It was all he needed.

He regained his feet. For an instant, he stared at the man who had rescued him. Grimbald, probably the only man with arms long and strong enough to have done it.

"Thanks, Grim," he whispered hastily.

"You are my lady's."

It was said in a voice more suited to the greeter at some elegant gathering. Someday, he was going to get the answers about their connection. But not now.

He spun and risked a look over the small ridge of stone they were behind. What he saw was so close to what he'd imagined that it startled him for the instant he could spare for such thoughts. The five Coalition guards were staring at her, practically gaping. To them, it must have seemed she had loomed up out of nowhere, magically.

Their backs were to the ship. And to the single guard they'd left behind.

He saw Pryl and the others, creeping up behind the five. They were sticking to the plan. Although the sudden appearance of the Spirit of the Edge had hardly been part of it. But it was working. Beyond his hopes. The armed men were frozen, as if she had indeed cast some sort of spell over them. It was three to the five, but he knew his Sentinels had never cared about the odds.

"I will take the last guard while you do what you must."

Drake's gaze flicked to Grimbald as he spoke. The man's face was impassive, unreadable, but his tone had been final. Drake didn't hesitate. He nodded. They edged their way right, to where the ridge dropped off, the last of the cover between them and the airlifter. The single guard appeared nervous, uncertain. Drake saw him shout something to the pilot of the ship. He appeared to listen to the answer, then shook his head no vehemently. The pilot must have called out something more, for the man turned to look up into the open hatchway.

"Now," he ordered under his breath.

Drake barely had time to notice Grim's limp didn't slow him at all before the man did exactly what he'd said. The last guard was down. The sound of blasters came from behind them. The Sentinels' battle with the five guards was on. He ignored it. He had to. The airlifter was already lifting off. The pilot's orders were clearly to protect the cannon at all costs. Even if it meant leaving the guards behind.

He had one chance. One chance to end this now. If he failed, it was a near certainty that Kye would die doing what he hadn't.

He launched himself. Caught one of the cables securing the cannon in the instant before it was out of reach. He could hear the fastenings straining as the airlifter rose above him. Slowly, but steadily. Once it cleared the ridge, it would swing around, head for the low valley, and Zelos. He had to get it done before then. He didn't try to hide, had to hope the pilot was focused on getting out of the rocky terrain.

He blasted one of the cables. It parted. One corner of the cannon base sagged. The ship wobbled slightly as the weight shifted. He needed the other cable on the same side. But he couldn't hit it from here. The cannon's huge barrel blocked any shot. He was running out of time. He shoved the blaster back into the holster. Made a desperate leap and grab. Caught the rim of the barrel's opening. For a moment, he hung there in space from the mouth of the weapon. The ground was falling away ever more quickly. He swung himself, driving with his feet. Nearly lost his grip. Second try, he caught the edge of the platform with his heel but slipped. Third the same.

It was no use.

But he could hit the cable from here.

The platform would drop, probably violently. The cannon itself might break free under its own massive weight. Either way, he'd likely go down with it. Looked like he was going to make that fall after all. He just had to hope he'd gauge it right and hit the rock outcropping, not go tumbling down the side of the mountain. Hitting the rocks would hurt, but he wouldn't survive plummeting to the valley floor.

He let go with his right hand. Drew the blaster. Fired. In the same instant, the platform twisted as they cleared the rocks and the wind hit. Missed. His left hand was straining. The rim of the barrel opening dug painfully into his fingers. He ignored it. He only had to hang on long enough to make this shot. He aimed again.

A hit. The cable split down to one slender strand. It would give, he knew. But when? Over Zelos? Couldn't risk it.

He fired again. The cable severed. The platform gave. In that instant, he doubled himself up, got one heel on something solid, he wasn't sure what, and shoved off. Let himself fall. He caught one glimpse of the airlifter careening sideways, the cannon swinging wildly.

Then he hit the rocks and everything vanished.

KYE REGISTERED the lurch of the airlifter. She thought she'd seen some-one jump, but she couldn't be sure from here. Nor could she spend the time wondering, fearing it might have been Drake. She had a job to do. It was up to her to make sure the thing crashed. She saw the payload—that bedamned cannon—hit the side of the ridge. The airlifter struggled, tried to regain sta-bility.

She had to see that it didn't. No matter the cost.

Air rovers weren't designed to be at this altitude; they were low-level fly-ers, but Brander had worked on them all and bought them enough altitude to fly at the Edge. And she'd spent the last two weeks, when she wasn't honing in her range and accuracy with the long gun, pushing the little craft's limits. She knew exactly how high she could take it and not lose maneuverability. It would be high enough. And her weapon was loaded with Brander's special round. There was only one, so she didn't dare miss.

She marked the airlifter's position. Guessing at its course when it was ca-reening around, its speed erratic, was difficult, but there was no choice.

"We have our mountains, our mist, and our knowledge and love of this place. Use them . . ."

She dove the little craft down into the mist, and under its cover, sped toward her best guess.

She popped up out of the mist a bare hundred yards behind the ship. Felt a spurt of satisfaction as she swiftly took in the situation. The airlifter was fighting its own cargo, side-slipping as much as it went forward. More im-portantly, the cannon had shifted, in fact looked as if it were about to break free. Her mind raced.

She calculated how much time she had before the ship got over the low valley. Was it enough? Could she get off a shot at one of the remaining cables, sending the cannon plummeting, and still have time to get clear? She desper-ately wanted to think so. She did not want to die now, especially now . . .

She quashed the thought. She couldn't risk it. She had to take the weapon itself. She refused to think about it, slammed the door on the knowledge that the sight of it exploding would be the last thing she'd ever see.

The airlifter careened sideways once more. The cannon swung again. Slipped, held only by one of the surviving cables. The pilot was good, and managed to keep from slamming into the ridge. Barely. But he was wildly off course, dangerously close to the mountains.

"We have our mountains . . ."

An idea flashed in her mind and her breath caught.

She had to make a decision. Now. Swiftly, she checked the readouts on the terrain display. Calculated distance, trajectory, time. She need both hands to shoot, so keyed in her course. The autopilot politely advised her her choices were unsafe in the current terrain. She overrode it.

"Hold it," she breathed to the unlucky airlifter. "Just ten more seconds."

The airlifter steadied. Lurched again. Steadied again.

Now.

Her little craft shot forward. Straight at the ridge. She snapped the long gun to her shoulder. Sighted in with the ease of long practice. Let out her breath to still her body to the utmost. Nothing must throw off her aim, not even breathing. She waited.

Five.

Four.

Three.

Two.

One.

She fired.

And slammed the rover into max speed with her foot.

The rover shot forward. Her round hit the cannon. The world erupted into fire and sound and blast wave.

In the tiny fraction of a second before she was enveloped, that blast wave shoved her forward. And into the shelter of the ridge.

She saw the glow of the explosion, heard the crashing, tumbling rock. The air rover shuddered, but behind the massive wall of mountain, it stayed airborne.

She was alive.

It was done.

Chapter 55

THE CELEBRATION was ongoing out in the gathering room. Watchers had told them it was happening in Zelos as well, where the news that the cannon had been destroyed had spread like the mist rolling down the Sentinel. The news that the Coalition troops were in chaos without communications, that Ordam had vanished, and even Sorkost was in hiding came close behind.

Soon enough, Drake would have to think of what the Coalition would do in retaliation when they regrouped, what Paledan would do when he returned. Likely immediately order another cannon, but installing and calibrating the things was no small task, and they had destroyed both the mounts along with the cannon, buying them some time to plan and prepare. So, for now, he let the ebullience of success cheer them all. He would go out and speak to them soon, congratulate them all on a job well done with few losses on their side, while allowing them all, himself especially, to grieve for the three Sentinels who had died and the several who had been injured in this effort.

But for now, he lingered here in his quarters with the five who had planned it, plus the three who made his inner circle complete.

His mother had offered to ease his new bruises and the headache, but they were so minor compared to Jakel's damage, he told her to save her strength in case someone else should need it. And then he had given her a sideways look. "What happened up there, what you did, holding them at bay," he began.

"That's the value of complete surprise," she had said lightly.

He wasn't sure he believed that that was all it was. But that was also for a later time. Now that he would have that time.

"Nice little weapon, that obliterator," Brander said to him now. "But you'd better take it."

"Why?" Drake asked. "You're the one who discovered its capabilities."

"But you're the one wise enough to have such a thing. I'd be out vanishing anybody who annoyed me."

Drake laughed, although he questioned Brander's assessment. Of both of them.

"Too bad we don't have a charger for it," Kye said.

"Or the power to supply a charger," Drake said.

"I've been thinking about that," Brander said. "I might have a way to steal a bit from our overlords. I drew something up a couple of weeks ago, so when things settle I'll fire up the holoprojector and show you."

"The holochip!" Nyx's exclamation was sharp with sudden memory, and, at his words, his twin instantly leapt to her feet and began to dig into her tunic pocket. She came out with a small holochip and handed it to Drake.

"We forgot," she said.

"Because of—" Nyx began.

"Everything," Lux finished.

Kye put a gentle hand on both their shoulders in understanding. They looked up at her and smiled. She was theirs now, they had solemnly told her after the pledging. And she had laughingly asked if that was welcome or warning. Their grins told her it was both.

"Explain?" Drake suggested.

"We found this—"

"In one of the rooms—"

"Underground. Well, really it—"

"Sort of fell out—"

"Of a man's pocket—"

"And we grabbed it. He never—"

"Even noticed us—"

"And we left right away."

Drake's gaze narrowed. "You were in an underground room with a Coalition trooper?"

"No!" Lux said quickly.

"He was—"

"More of a . . ."

Drake lifted a brow at his little sister. "More of a what?"

"Officer," she said reluctantly.

"On his way—"

"To the commander's office."

"Dear Eos," their mother whispered. Drake looked up at her. "And I thought becoming the Raider was the biggest challenge you faced."

"Not," Drake said dryly, "by a long shot."

Eirlys looked from the twins to Drake, and then Kye. She gave an exaggerated "Whew," and wiped her brow dramatically to emphasize her relief at not being saddled with the responsibility for these two.

"Don't get comfortable," Drake said warningly. "We might be too busy to deal with these two for a while yet. Maybe a long while."

"Are you ever going to look at it?" Nyx, back to his ever-practical self, asked.

Brander shoved off from the wall he'd been leaning against and grinning at the exchange. He picked up the single piece of equipment they dared use, a small holo device that ran off batteries and sent no signal beyond a few feet. The projection was iffy, cutting in and out, but the reader was functional. Brander turned it on, and by habit checked the battery level.

"Full enough for a while yet," he said.

Drake nodded, glad no one would have to risk taking it into Zelos and recharging it for a while. Especially since it was usually he who did it, with the hidden, highly illegal charging dock behind the portrait of his mother which appeared from the outside to be fastened firmly to the wall above the bar. The wall that was one of two still standing, Dek had told him. It didn't matter. That part of his life was over, and he wouldn't miss it except for the relative safety it had provided his family.

The reader screen came to life and showed the contents of the chip: one holographic recording and a single file that appeared to be text-based. It bore the title *Tactical Stratagems for Dealing With Overwhelming Force.* That could be of interest, but it would be wisest to run the holograph first, while the battery was at its strongest. Even as he thought it, Brander hit the button to do just that.

An image appeared above the device. It was slightly misshapen, and given to the slight skips the worse-for-wear device was prone to, but it was clear enough to see and hear.

The man in the Coalition uniform of a general looked a bit stiff, as if he were not used to having to make such recordings. Then he spoke, the skips breaking his words into staccato bursts. But the meaning was clear, and Drake thought they all must have gasped.

The device spat out a burst of static and the image vanished. Stunned, Drake still stared at the spot where it had been. His heart was hammering in his chest.

"Holy Eos," Brander whispered.

Drake looked up then. His head still ached slightly, but it was nothing compared to this. There was an even fiercer fire in his eyes, a new determination surging through him. Possibilities were exploding through his mind, and he knew this was the key they'd needed.

He surged to his feet, ignoring the slight wobble. Kye was beside him in an instant, her steady arm supporting him.

"Can you manage something to provide a bigger image?" he asked Brander.

As usual, his second did not ask why, just immediately went to the logistics. "How big?"

"Enough for all to see it in the gathering room."

Brander drew back slightly, and he could see him thinking of the effects seeing this holograph would have. "I . . . think I can rig something, but—"

"It only has to last once through that holograph. If it blows up after that, it does not matter."

Brander nodded and grabbed up the projector. He left his quarters, clearly headed for his workbench in the main room.

"It's real," Eirlys whispered.

Drake looked at his sister. He remembered Kye telling him of the day when she had brought up the tales of Trios, the stories he had always dismissed as myth. He felt Kye's gaze, turned to meet it, and saw she was thinking of the same.

"I wish," said a quiet voice behind him, "that your father had lived to see this day."

He turned to look at his mother. "I wish it as well," he said softly.

She nodded. "But now . . . you must become the Raider once more. And I," she added with a glance at the twins that was so close to wary he almost laughed, "must convince those two to consider the possibility that we are related."

"Good luck," he said. And found he meant it.

She crossed to the twins, who eyed her nearly as warily as she was looking at them. Kye, who had given them space, now came and took his arm. "She will have a difficult time, persuading them to accept her."

"Yes."

"But you have?"

"Accepted, yes. Forgiven? Still working on that."

"As am I."

He gave her a sideways look. "I should tell you what she did up on the ridge."

She lifted a brow at him. He wasn't sure how to even describe what had happened, and before he could find the place to start, Brander reappeared.

"Got it," he said.

"You'd best think of what you will say, then," Kye said. And then kissed him, a kiss so full of promise it scrambled his thoughts and made him wonder if he could come up with a coherent sentence ever again.

Chapter 56

IN THE END, HE gave up the effort and decided to let his heart choose his words.

"I am not a speech giver," he said as he stood before the crowd amassed in the gathering room. "I am a fighter."

He had to pause for the raucous round of cheers to ebb before going on.

"But you have the right to know this. It is not over. We have not won. We have lost compatriots. Some of you have been hurt. But we have also hurt them. And they will wish to hurt us in return. Before long they will begin taking it out on those who do not fight, because they cannot get to us."

He heard the murmur go through the crowd, the unease.

"We will protect them as best we can, but if you cannot face this, if it is too much to ask, leave now. No one will hold it against you, for you have all already given more than should be asked of anyone. If you wish to escape Zelos, we will help you and those you love as best we can, to get over Highridge to the badlands. It will not be easy, nor a swift journey on foot, but you will be safer there."

For now.

No one moved.

"How will we protect them that stay?"

He looked out at them, and let a grin loose. "It will take the . . . least notorious among us."

Laughter.

"There will be a dozen of us in and around Zelos at all times. And we have communications now."

"Thanks to the brilliant Eirlys Davorin's brilliant birds," Brander put in from where he stood a few feet away. "Far beneath Coalition notice."

Drake saw his sister smile, looking quite pleased.

"And you all know who is with us now," he added, gesturing to where his mother stood off to one side. The slight figure in the white robes with the flaming hair spilling down her back stood out even in the flickering light of the flame-lit room. "And if the presence of the Spirit is not enough to inspire you to fight on—"

"And the return from death of the Raider!" someone shouted.

"Drake Davorin, you mean!" called out Pryl, who had been one of those who, he'd learned, had guessed some time ago.

A cheer rose from the assemblage. Drake felt Kye's gaze on him, glanced at her, and saw her smile. He had to admit this was balm to his soul, a soul battered by the disgust and antipathy of his own people when he had been but the lowly, beaten, cowardly taproom keeper. Many, in fact most, had apologized to him, said they should have known Drake Davorin would never buckle to the Coalition. Brander had turned that into praise for how well he had played the unwanted role.

Some had approached him with wary looks, as if they weren't quite sure what to think of his miraculous recovery; others were simply grateful he'd survived.

As am I, he'd thought, relinquishing once and for all the wishes he'd once had for it all to end, even if the only way was death.

When the cheering at length died down, he began again. "There is something you must know," he said. "For it makes all the difference."

He nodded at Brander, who reached out and twice tapped something on the imager he'd managed to rig together. For a moment, nothing happened, but then the image of the Coalition general leapt to light in the air above the machine. A gasp at the sight of a Coalition officer larger than life swept the room. Drake had expected this, and as requested, Brander had set it so that the message would freeze at first.

"Please," Drake said. "I want you all to see this, hear this."

The room went quiet. Brander tapped the same button, only once this time. And the holographic recording began to play.

Not one person in the jammed room made a sound as they watched the man in the Coalition uniform speak. Now, in this larger version, Drake could see the man's expression more clearly. He was worried, and it was obvious.

"Major Paledan," he began, and everyone in the room leaned in. "This message . . . confidential and of highest urgency . . . a warning . . . could be headed your way soon . . . circulating among the rebels in this quadrant . . . Claxton's Treatise—" a gasp went up around the room at the familiar name "—adapted for small forces ... already been found . . among Clarion rebels, and . . . Zenox . . . it is spreading . . . rebel groups . . . suspects the traitor Claxton . . . masterminded . . . used Dax's skypirate contacts . . . Triotian—" another gasp, even louder this time, at the mention of the infamous Dax and the world they'd half-believed was a myth, Drake most of all "—communications and ships . . . command of the king . . . and prince . . . disseminating it. Legion Command has ordered . . . copies destroyed. Possession is grounds . . . immediate . . . execution. The file . . . this chip . . . facsimile of the primitive version . . . paper. Keep . . . eyes open, Major. Don't need . . . tell you . . . chaos their knowing . . . tactics could cause . . . after losing . . . Triotian sector. Rebellion is spreading . . ."

At the end, the image again snapped out of existence, but the last words seemed to echo in the cavernous room.

"Rebellion is spreading . . ."

"And so this is what you must know," Drake said, putting every bit of power he had into his voice. "Trios, her king and his son, the skypirate, Claxton—it's all real. They beat them. And it's spreading. There are rebels on Clarion, on Zenox."

He scanned the room, looked out over all the Sentinels who had fought so hard even when the odds had been so stacked against them, even when there was no hope of success, when they knew they were already beaten. And he spoke the words that would change everything.

"We are not alone."

There was no explosion of cheers. No round of applause. Not even a whistle of approval. What he saw, looking out over the fighters of Ziem was a sense of awe at what they had just seen.

And more importantly, hope.

And for once, he did not quash it with the reminder that they were to think of themselves as already dead. For he looked at Kye, and accepted what he had finally realized. That a willingness to die for freedom was only the beginning.

It was much better to have something to live for.

The End

About the Author

"Some people call me a writer, some an author, some a novelist. I just say I'm a storyteller."

—Justine Dare Davis

Author of more than 60 books (she sold her first ten in less than two years), Justine Dare Davis is a four-time winner of the coveted Romance Writers of America RITA Award, and has been inducted into the RWA Hall of Fame. Her books have appeared on national bestseller lists, including *USA Today*. She has been featured on CNN, as well as taught at several national and international conferences and at the UCLA writer's program.

After years of working in law enforcement, and more years doing both, Justine now writes full-time. She lives near beautiful Puget Sound in Washington State, peacefully coexisting with deer, bears, a tailless raccoon, a pair of bald eagles, and her beloved '67 Corvette roadster. When she's not writing, taking photographs, looking for music to blast in said roadster, or driving said roadster, she tends to her knitting. Literally.

Find out more at:

justinedavis.com

facebook.com/JustineDareDavis

Twitter: @Justine_D_Davis

Pinterest: pinterest.com/justineddavis/

Made in the USA
San Bernardino, CA
27 April 2020

68853029R00183